CW01079777

OUSTED

James M Hopkins

To Julie-Anne
Great to work with
you!

Best wishes

ISBN: 978-1-5272-1482-8

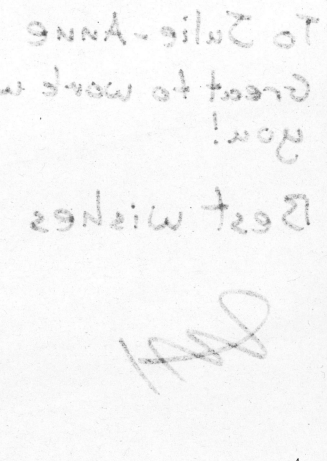

Connive

Prologue

As the war's impact crossed the country's own shore, the people suddenly had a lot more to say. With most of the population largely ignoring the ongoing conflict, it was only since it affected individuals directly that interest was sparked. A decisive downturn in the economy occurred since Britain made moves away from Europe with multinational corporations strongly tied to the European Union making it clear with job cuts that they were losing faith in the United Kingdom. If it hadn't been for thousands affected by joblessness, the war could have continued unwatched and uncared for by the majority.

Leighton sat forward, hunched over a laptop on the coffee table and wishing he could have joined the protest like he did regularly in his early-twenties. The news he followed was on a series of concurrent marches that were being described as containing the largest crowds that had congregated on London since the Stop the War coalition marches against Tony Blair's actions over a decade ago. Again, it was turning out to be a war in a foreign land that had the power to unite people across class and geography within the country.

Shannon sat alongside her husband, listening to music on the television that simply whiled away time in the background. She rested her head on his shoulder so she could casually read each update to The Vigilante news website as they came through. It was late into the summer evening and the room was dim with only the screen glow from the electronic devices and a nearby street light that shone in through the window. Neither had torn themselves away from their intense focus to shut the windows or pull the blinds down and were barely aware of the ease that someone could see in to the small rented house's living room. However, the lack of privacy was worth the cool breeze that finally came to take the edge of the enduring heat that the rest of the day had provided.

Alive

Chapter 1

They had it all planned out, as ready as anyone could be. In the cupboard under the stairs, Leighton had arranged two rucksacks, carefully prepared and packed with his most cunning and finesse. He referred to them as the 'Thrive-All-Kit' because in his own words, 'survival is for pussies; if it's hitting the fan, I want to *own* this shit!' Shannon regularly rolled her eyes whilst they were being prepared and she would often say, 'Leighton, we don't have the money for this,' or 'I am most *certainly* not carrying that in a hurry' to which he would more often say 'money won't mean that much if we actually *need* this' and 'you won't have to, I'm carrying that'. She did give her input over the months that the preparation went on, with the bags being packed and repacked. The fishing rod was her idea. The tomahawk and stiletto dagger were certainly not.

"We've got a three-month old baby!" Shannon was near screaming.

"I know that. That's the reason I've packed muslin squares and Terry nappies. We also have string so we can wash them in a river and make a washing line drawn out between some trees."

"Wow! You've really thought in depth about your bullshit idea, haven't you?"

"Yes, I've just become a father, I don't want to be a not-a-father again and I definitely don't want to be dead, especially when we have been blessed with the foresight such as this," Leighton replied zealously. "Viruses have hit Europe and tensions are stretched around the planet. With countries like Germany looking further east, Britain is going to be left grasping onto the tattered dreams of a lame, hungover superpower that hasn't realised it has fallen in a spiral of disgrace. We want to be at least one step ahead of the rest. That's what the Thrive-All-Kit gives us. Security. We can walk from here in the event of an attack on Britain, live off grid in the woods and hills and start building our own civilisation. We can be away from town lights and falling bombs at the drop of a hat."

"We could just walk out with a quickly packed bag and get the same, don't need to buy all this crap!" Shannon gestures her arms over a small living room, scattered with neatly organised piles of items Leighton was wrapping together and placing into each rucksack.

"That's survival, Shannon. With this, we live, we thrive and give Zeke a chance. This gives Zeke a life!"

Shannon slumped down on the couch, narrowly avoiding catching her posterior on the sharp edge of an army-grade hand axe. She sighed. "You're right in some your ideas," she said with shut eyes. "It's best to be safe and even just popping to the shops with Zeke requires hours of preparation."

"That's the spirit, honey. With my preparedness and your African survival instincts, we'll be like the Adam and Eve of the Bear Grylls generation!"

Shannon laughed and Leighton sat down alongside her, picking up the axe in one hand and putting his fingers around the back of Shannon's neck with the other.

"Shannon," he said.

"What?"

"I love you. I just want you to be safe." Leighton gestured the axe towards the play mat on the floor, "And him of course. Perhaps with a little brother or sister, eh?"

Shannon pushed him away. "Get your hands off me, I want a cup of tea. At least while we have an electric kettle to hand."

Leighton obliged.

The night settled in. The sound of electronic nursery rhymes and static jingled through the air via the baby monitor, and the television news reader spoke on the verge of being drowned out.

"-And in today's headlines, Muharid have taken majority control of three separate cities during coordinated attacks last night, Mosul and Erbil in the north of Iraq and Tabriz on the border of Iran. The Russian president immediately made an official statement, purporting that this could only have been made possible by the American armament of the rebel group in the region and that sources he has with the Iranian government have verified this. This is yet to be confirmed nor denied by our own sources in the area.

"The newly appointed president of the United States opened an emergency press conference where he vowed to end the war in the Middle East by any means necessary. He specifically delivered a message to the Iranian supreme leader to stand down and allow the people a true democratic choice. The conservative Republican president has not been shy to speak openly to other leaders in his short time in office.

"The prime minister has announced support for the end of conflict, stating that the U.N. needs to enforce an immediate ceasefire in the region. This display of backing comes at a time when the U.K. is close to securing a ten-year trade deal with the U.S. that will also provide a strengthened military alliance between the two countries.

"Later in the show, Desmond Hodgson will be giving us an in-depth opinion on how this could affect the United Kingdom's relationship with the rest of Europe, a relationship now strained by the leftist swing in ideals across the E.U. and the differences in opinion on how to best deal with the Middle East crisis. A deal being worked out by the prime minister directly is looking ever more tenuous."

The news continued to drone on, Leighton and Shannon sat back, taking in what they had just heard. "Why are Britain hanging on to America? We should be at the door of Europe, hat in our hands. Instead our government continues to be scared and overwhelmed by these warmongering assholes. We're just as bad, this government need to be ousted. Shall we start a revolution? You can be the Angela Davis to my Che Guevara."

Shannon stared blankly at the screen, breaking her gaze with a small laugh that came a little too late. "You can't let it affect you, you know? You must keep your head down and focus on keeping little Zeke clothed and fed. We can't really change the whole world; we can only make our little world, Zeke's little world, as good as that can be."

"I know," Leighton resided.

Chapter 2

The venetian blinds were folded aside and light flooded into the bedroom, dissipating the thin lines that were previously decorating the back wall. The sun had only just reached the position above the surrounding valley edge to light the room enough to wake Mina in the usual subtle way that she enjoyed so much about living far outside the city. The fresh air blew in as she opened the single glazed windows wide and hooked the latch on the window sill. It carried with it an almost overpowering aroma, mixed with lavender, compost and dewy grass all at once. Mina breathed deeply and noticed that the memories of London mornings, with the smell of exhausts, pollution and human sweat that clung to the humid air, were fading rapidly. The memories replaced with the fragrances of her new life.

The thin dressing robe that Mina wore was open at the front and she revelled in her station, leaning out of the first-floor window with the cool pungent breeze leaving prickles on her chest. She turned reluctantly and hung her dressing gown carefully on the hook on the back of her bedroom door, pulling out the creases before turning to her wardrobe. She pulled out a heavy pair of jeans and a chequered shirt that she tucked in neatly. Sitting down at her dressing table, she put on a necklace with a large, red-stoned pendant set in gold.

She looked at her angular features in the mirror, contemplating the make-up she would wear. After those few moments had passed she picked up just her eye-liner, mascara and a red lipstick that was worn down almost to the plastic. As she drew along the bottom lids of her eyes, she thought about how futile this part of her morning routine was. She lived alone, around three miles from the nearest village, but was still stuck in the routine she once had. She had had to look good at all times then. What good would it do her ex-husband's reputation if she turned up at the school gates in dirty clothes or unmade-up face? She had always dressed well though, that was just how she had been, even as a young girl. Her ex-husband's needs had taken the fun out of it in the last few years. It was better now the actions returned to being for herself.

As she finished delicately applying lipstick to her slender lips, she smiled to herself. This was for her alone. She stood and turned to the full-length mirror and admired herself for a moment before leaning in closer and noting that she still needed more bleach for her hair when she found the right product.

Mina sat down on a wooden bench that faced out on to her garden turned allotment. The bench had two seats either side of a small square table that joined them together. She placed down her coffee that emitted swirling tendrils of steam into the morning air and righted the overturned ashtray that ran condensation off the underside as she did. The garden stretched on a gentle slope below her. It had been a meadow when she had purchased the house nine months ago, but now it was home to several pristine earthen rows that ran away from the house.

She smoked half of her cigarette, slowly enough that most burnt away of its own accord and she sipped her coffee leaving just a touch of her lipstick on the edge of the mug. She wondered how she had ever managed to smoke as much as she did before the divorce. She also wondered if it was a sign of that inevitable end to her relationship that she managed to cut down to the two-a-day habit that remained, so quickly after it happened. She had tried to go cold turkey, but something about her morning and bedtime routine meant that she could never quite shift those last two from her daily pattern.

Her bare toes curled around the grass as she stepped off the patio. A thin grass path led between each of the rows of bare earth and she followed the path across the top to a small tool shed. The door rocked on the hinges a little as she had yet to prioritise fixing it high enough up her list. She picked up a small gardening fork and trowel and carefully walked down to the bottom end of the garden.

She worked her way up each of the planting beds and took out individual weeds that had used her hard-worked earth as a new place to grow. She wanted growth, but she wanted lettuces and carrots rather than dandelions and more grass. Kneeling on the neat, soft grass, she dug around the weeds and placed them into a bucket nearby for composting later.

The sun had risen to full height and had started to fall again before Mina had finished her work, but the earth was completely bare by the time she was done. Tomorrow was the day she could start planting her first crops. She left the cleared garden for the shade of the kitchen, took off her rings and washed her hands in the large ceramic basin of her kitchen. Splashing her face, she could tell she would likely have caught the sun. The skin on her forehead felt tight already. She thought to herself that she was used to seeing better heat in spring than in summer, she had gotten more sunburns in April than in August. Perhaps she was just more careful with her pale skin in August while the April sun just caught her unaware.

Chapter 3

Tariq turned a corner and the small, cramped alley that he departed opened into a wide street. A steady flow of people swept him into their midst and he immediately took to keeping a brisk step with those others. The feeling was calm as stretched out groups of people trudged along each pavement. Some jogged in the road to get ahead or catch up with groups of friends further on. Others carried banners and placards above their heads, with messages of anger and peace alike bobbing gently with the throb of the crowd. For the number of people on the street, it was quiet, only a light hum, barely drowning the sound of idle engines in the jammed road separating the pedestrians that all moved in the same direction past the multi-story buildings that lined the road.

Tariq walked alone amongst the masses, the crowd thickened and slowed as it got closer and closer to the London Eye. Police cars to his left slowly followed the last of the traffic and stationed a road block on the other side of the road to stop any more coming into the area. The void between the double red lines quickly filled up with protesters and reporters with heavy cameras, picking up their pace in the additional space. They all desperately wanted to get forward to get the best views of the speakers. The sound of megaphones and rhythmical shouting flared up ahead, still just out of range to be heard clearly. A police riot van moved its way slowly forward bumping and being bumped by people as it carved its slow path through them. This was met with angry shouts of anti-establishment rhetoric. Tariq lifted his phone sporadically to his mouth to repeat some of the words that were said and fill in the feeling and atmosphere of the crowds and the event onto record.

The black gates of Downing Street finally came into view as Tariq weaved his way in and out of the tightly packed crowd. Tariq himself was below average height and a lean build. The elbows and bodies throwing themselves against him tried to put him off balance and came close to succeeding several times. He kept his recorder on the whole time and noted some of the banners he saw criticising the government's latest decisions. He wasn't even sure if his voice would be determinable when he returned to listen to the recording later, but he certainly wanted to get as much as he could. One note for himself was to perfect his shorthand and bring an old-fashioned notepad and pen. A path opened its way to his right and he caught sight of a building's steps. He broke through the gap at a fast walk. He climbed up the busy steps and lifted himself onto a low wall to one side that gave him a sight out over most of the streets around the famous black gates, lined with a plentiful police presence.

A man roughly Tariq's own age joined him on his vantage point, wielding a large black camera towards the noisy crowd ahead. Tariq ignored the man at first, continuing to dictate onto his recorder the chants that were coming from the front of the crowd. Cries of "no more war", "drop the sanctions" and "give us back our democracy" came ringing out, shouted out first by a megaphone and followed by the angry group of people that had forced their way to the front of the gates.

Tariq's unintended partner atop the wall shouted over the hubbub, "Hey, I suppose you are a blogger too?"

It took a moment for Tariq to realise it was aimed at him and stopped the recorder before answering, "Yea, I suppose so. I am at a placement at The Vigilante newspaper. I am studying journalism. Who are you with?"

He was a rounded man and wore a long and straggling black beard and unkempt hair. "I'm with myself. I write a blog that has a few thousand readers. I am trying to give an honest view from the people."

"Great!" replied Tariq. "Have you seen anything going on yet worth blogging about?"

"Not so much more than the general feel of the event. I have tried to stick near to the police lines so far. Those areas can get more aggressive and tends to be where we can catch the motherfuckers out when they think they can't be seen in all the ruckus. I want to make sure they don't get away with brutality without it being shared with the world," the man said. "So, what's your name?"

"I'm Tariq Al-Noor. The world we are now in allows us to make sure that everything is seen. The leaders shouldn't be allowed the same privacy that they are trying to remove from their people. What's your name, then? And what's your blog called?"

The man tried to answer, purposefully quietly and was drowned out by the calls of "police brutality" and "shame on you."

"Don't worry, something is kicking off right there." Tariq had to yell to be heard above the commotion and rising noise, pointing towards the far end of the gates. "If you want to join me for a closer look, come on!" Tariq gently tugged at the man's shoulder in the direction of the steps and jumped down into a gap between a large single group of people sitting on them.

The two pushed themselves forward, slowly winding and ducking between shoulders and bodies blocking their route. By the time they could see the front of the crowds again, the line of police had returned to a calm alertness. Tense muscles and darting eyes peered back at them from beneath the body armour and slightly tinted visors. A younger officer on the second line smirked along with some of the funnier shouts from the crowd that opposed him. The crowd itself seemed much more animated with people jostling for a better position. They seemingly fought each other for a chance to shout something as they looked straight into the eyes of one of the men or women in black and blue uniforms. Over to Tariq's right, a man shook each section of the metal barrier as he shadowed two policemen roughly ushering a young woman onwards. The man shouted, "police brutality" and "shame on you" over and over, occasionally joined by a few of those around him. Tariq pushed to catch up with the man, but the force of the crowd surging against the barrier stemmed his path and he quickly gave up.

The angry man along the barrier fell forward as three police officers took two of the barriers apart in front of him. They used the man's momentum to take him to the ground and they quickly snapped plastic cuffs on his arms behind his back. The man screamed and kicked as he was pulled up and shouted for help from his fellow protestors. Before the man was out of sight around a corner, Tariq heard a few additional cries of "shame on you", joined in with by a good collective of the nearby crowd.

Tariq turned back towards the gate to see his new companion rapidly taking as many photos of the disappearing man as possible. He let the camera drop around his neck and fumbled in his pocket to produce a card which he placed roughly into Tariq's hand. The man's explanation was lost – as was Tariq's "thanks" – to the rumble of chants and noise, but he placed the card deep into his trouser pocket. He then tried to lip read an additional response from the man, but fell short of deciphering. He simply pointed to himself and then in the direction away from the gates. The man responded by pointing at himself and down at the ground. Tariq nodded and shook the man's hand before starting to push his way against the tide of human traffic.

Tariq realised after a short time that the resistance was lessening and more and more people were starting to disperse down the various streets around him. He turned away from the steps opposite as it became apparent that the main show was over and those in the fringe had had enough for the time being.

Chapter 4

After Mina had loaded the panniers and basket to her mountain bike she sat back on the saddle and let it coast easily down the gentle slope leading her to town. If she had thought about it earlier, and had been more flexible after seeing the cottage, she would have decided on living downhill from the village. She was fine now, but pedalling back up the long incline with all her groceries would certainly leave her with burning muscles as always.

The wind buffeted her ears as she cruised down towards town. Following the path of the stream that ran almost straight alongside the left edge of the rocky, dirt path, she made quick progress. To Mina's right, the northern wall of her valley rose high above her, grew trees that bent from the ground at an impossible angle to gain their height. It was steep enough to seem a wall and made her house feel protected from intrusion and any cold north winds. The other side of the valley was a steep, but far more manageable rise, covered in a deep, yellowing grass and holding sporadic thorny bushes that mottled its surface. This was her valley. She was the only one that lived in it and its sense of security stayed with her on her regular journey into the nearby village

As she came into town, a rough stone bridge that crossed a few feet of rushing water marked the end of her dirt track and placed her on the concrete of a more civilised walkway alongside the road. Behind her, the walls of her valley seemed low, blending in with the rest of the rolling hills that covered the area. She knew it was waiting for her, like the dog that she could see outside the grocers, its head in its paws, patiently awaiting its owner. She pulled her bike up alongside the grocer's window and kicked the bike stand down. She picked her purse out of the basket and turned around to see the dog's owner leave the shop.

"Hey, Mina," said the aging man. He had thinning wiry hair that seemed to cling desperately to his scalp and chin and a hoarse voice that had problems of its own. "It's been a while since I have seen you. How are you? Is the old cottage still on one piece?"

Mina answered shyly, "The house is holding itself together, Bruce. And I suppose I am too. At least all the problems with the house seemed to be cosmetic."

"I can't believe it stayed standing with no-one to tend for it all those years. I would love to come up and see the grounds up there sometime. I doubt I would fare that long old walk, though. How come you still haven't cleared the driveway going up there yet?" He asked.

"I don't see too much point in all that, seeing as I haven't got myself a car again yet. I've got crops growing up there now to be ready for summer. I may have made the plot a little big as I spend nearly all my days tending to it."

"You still in that city lifestyle, aren't you? Shooting big. A phrase I will tell you is 'eyes bigger than your mouth'. Living in the country, here, you'll learn that a single wheelbarrow of good crops will far outweigh a field of spindly leaves," Bruce said adamantly. "You'll eventually want that road clear anyhow, ready for when your daughter visits, right?"

"Yeah, I fear I may be a fair while away from that now. Something to keep working towards." Mina sounded a little sullen and petted Bruce's dog on the head tentatively. She couldn't remember its name, if she had ever known it. She noted to herself not to share any of her more personal information with anyone. That news about her daughter shouldn't have spread as far as Bruce.

"You keep working on it, love, I am sure you'll do right by her. From what I've heard that arsehole you got back in the city is not worth owt at all."

Mina shuddered slightly. "I haven't *got* him anymore, thank the lord. I had better get moving, my mother will expect to me to answer her call in an hour. Keep well, Bruce," she said a little more dryly than she had meant to. She was annoyed that telling one person about her divorce and ongoing custody battle had spread so far around the village. She had hoped to escape people asking her about that saga so regularly.

She stepped into the cool, dark interior of the grocers. "Hello, Mina!" a warm, female voice called from behind the little cash register at the back of shop. "I have your order out the back, all ready for you." Mina thanked her as the slender lady darted swiftly into the back room. "I kept it on a pallet for you this time," she called, her voice now muffled by the intervening walls. "I couldn't remember how you would load it onto your bike. Is it better this way?"

"Thank you, Grace. I will just load it straight from there," Mina replied. A broad smile opened up her face. Grace's arms were stretched out wide carrying the green pallet in front of her. It made her look small. Mina reached and took the heavy load. She sidled uneasily through the door and Grace made a motion to try and help in a way that would have been futile anyway.

"When should I expect not to see you any more then?" Grace asked with a smile.

Mina thought for a moment. "Oh," she said. "Well that depends on whether farming is my bag, I suppose. I will be coming for some things anyway. I haven't the plans to grow all the fruit I need yet."

"It will be less though, right?" Grace asked concernedly.

"Yes, likely," Mina replied. "We shall see, Grace, if I manage to make any surplus good enough to sell, then perhaps we can come to some cheap arrangement for you to buy from me instead."

"That London attitude still hasn't worn off you completely. Give it *another* nine months and perhaps you will have slowed down that little bit more. I am being rude prying, I'm sorry. How is the divorce going?"

Mina wondered how that was less rude or prying, though Grace always meant well enough and had been there for her since she moved. "Gone and done. Signed, sealed and delivered, Friday past. Custody continues, I suppose. Though once I have worked on my place here and can show that I am stable then I can appeal how things are now. I am in a better secondary school catchment than him in this area and that will certainly work in my favour when she's a little older."

"I would have expected to see you at the pub then," Grace said. "You should have come down; I'm sure plenty of the bachelors would have brought you a glass of wine or two! You know, Mina, I often worry about you up there in that house all alone. It's been a long while since anyone took that place on and it's so far out from anyone else."

"I appreciate it, Grace. For me, it's perfect. The opposite of everything that lead to– well, you know. I feel freer. I feel like I will live a lot longer too. It's also a piece of the world that's mine, to tend to as I wish. He gradually took everything from me, I gave up so much to be with him, thinking I was making the right choices. This is more the real me and that valley looks after me."

"That valley makes for a lovely walk, I must say."

"Well you need come up there more often. You will always be welcome for tea. If I don't see you from the field first, my door will always be open."

"And you remember that you need to get out more too. There are plenty of us down here that won't turn you away. Especially on a Friday night, at the pub, at eight o'clock. If you come down to the village only once a week, then should be it. You don't have to be all alone." Grace looked each way down the empty street. "I am making a cup of tea now, I'll put one on for you. It'll give you a bit of energy for your ride back."

"I'm okay, thanks," Mina said. "My mother is calling shortly. I sometimes wish I hadn't given up my mobile phone. Not all that often though. I had better get back now. Thank you, Grace. It is good to know that you guys down here have my back."

"Always. Ride safe," Grace said, lingering in the doorway of her shop to see Mina ride back down the pavement.

Mina unbuttoned her blouse as she climbed the steps from the basement pantry that held two chest freezers and a full-size fridge. She didn't want to have to repeat her trips to the village too often and so she overpopulated all three as much as possible to save her from that uphill ride becoming so frequent. The evaporation of her sweat from her torso felt good, but she soon felt clammy as it dried. She contemplated a quick bath, though the ringing phone foiled any action towards that plan before it started.

She took a deep breath as she removed the handset from the kitchen phone dock. "Mother," she said assertively.

"Mina," came the reply. A short pause stretched out over static filled line. "How are you getting on?" Her mother sounded dry and worried even in her first words.

"I am alright, I just got back from the village." Mina waited a moment. "Yourself?"

"Not bad, Mina. I spoke with your sister today."

Mina let the statement hang. "-And?"

"She is getting her divorce too," her mother said finally.

"She got caught, huh?" Mina pulled her blouse closed with one arm across her middle.

"She didn't go into much detail. She said that she has got a good lawyer, so she will probably get custody of her two little ones. That's good."

"Everything goes her way. I wouldn't be surprised."

"I know you two have your problems, Mina. I think it would be good for you to meet up, you know. You have a lot that you can help each other with. Words that would benefit the both of you." The static built up in both their ears. "Come on, Mina, it has been so long since you spoke. You were so close when you were kids. When you were young adults, you were always there for each other. *Always* had each other's backs. She put herself out so many times to help you with Rebecca, while you supported Drew with his job." Her mother sighed and Mina drew a tight line with her lips. "You both shared so many precious moments together. Please just-"

"It's funny how you use the word 'share', Mum," Mina interrupted.

"Mina, don't be like that. She is your sister, your blood. It was a mistake that she made and is sorry for. She has tried to contact you so many times in the last year."

"Are you really surprised that I don't answer her calls, block her emails and never want to see her again? Would you go befriend that woman that tore you and Dad apart?"

The static filled the silence. "Mina." Disappointment filled her tone.

Mina's, "Yes," was all that she replied with.

Again, the static floated across the line. "How is your house?" her mother asked, her voice audibly trembling.

"It's great. I love it!" Mina spoke over-ecstatically with a fake smile that she tried to force down the line.

"Do you want me to call you later?" her mother asked, sensing Mina's mood.

"When you do, mum, I don't want this. This thing that you do. I need you as simply *my* mother, not just my sister's." Mina hung up before her mother's response could come.

She was infuriated. She spent ten minutes trying to meditate on the front porch before she stomped back into the kitchen, rolled a cigarette and resumed her position on the porch, even angrier that her mother had made her light another for that day. Her blouse and hair whipped wildly in the breeze that blew suddenly and forcefully around her.

Chapter 5

Tariq rented a bedsit above a corner shop on a side street in London, south of the river. He shared a bathroom, but the room that Tariq resided in was a bedroom, living room and kitchen all within the same four small walls. He was sat on the edge of the bed with his knees resting under a desk just big enough for his laptop, notepad and a bottle of water. The increase in protests in the last weeks had meant his usual evening pastime of reading news articles and forums online had been disrupted, but tonight it was quiet and he was due to catch up on the latest news from a more distant perspective.

The time whittled away as Tariq trawled through websites, clicking straight from his favourites at first, but quickly being distracted by other articles, links and other – both necessary and unnecessary – research. For some pieces, he read deeply into conflicting reports on the same event, jotting down discrepancies to consider further as he read on. As the evening wore away he became more interested in the user comments under each article than the journalist's words themselves.

Tariq rummaged through his bag to find a new notepad when he came across a crumpled piece of card at the bottom. He straightened it against the wobbling desk. It bore only a code in the top left corner, 'AH6015' and a website printed in the lower right, TruthSeeksVoice.com. The rest of the card was plain white with no embellishments of any kind. It was the first time Tariq had properly looked at the card – crowded as the situation was when it was received – but it was enough of a random chance meeting that it piqued his curiosity.

He eventually followed a trail of links, through articles the man had allegedly written and social media outlets until he came to a site he had never come across before. It was simply laid out, mostly white with black text. He signed up to the site with the handle he typically put down on unfamiliar sites, T3LM. After only a few minutes of waiting he had a message from a user 'AH6015'.

AH6015: Hello, Tariq.

T3LM: Hi AH, nice trail to find you through. Great blogs. Are you well?

AH6015: I am indeed and I hope you are the same. You seemed conscious and aware, I am glad you found me here. So, Tariq Al-Noor is not a very English name. Where are you from?

T3LM: I grew up in Port Said, Egypt. Though my mum's dad was British. I think one of my dad's grandparents was British too, but not sure. My mum taught me to read English from a very early age and hence why I wanted to study over here. It is always good to find new like-minded people. Are you allowed to tell me your name, or is that secret?

AH6015: Ah, it is a secret here. Maybe in real life, we shall see. What was it about journalism that caught your attention?

T3LM: When I was growing up I saw the effects of corruption and learnt that it was rife across the world, people are enslaved and downtrodden. These people need a voice of truth, perhaps that which your website seeks.

AH6015: A valiant and concise answer. Do you practice those words in the mirror?

Tariq looked at his computer screen with chagrin.

AH6015: Never mind. I am sure you don't. What about the paper you work for, though? Do you think they share your same principles for candour?

T3LM: I needed a placement for my degree and this one came up. It is a hard industry to get into, we were advised at university to take what we could get.

AH6015: -And what an industry it is. Would it to surprise you to know that The Vigilante is owned by the same man that holds over a quarter of UK readership across various guises of the same message? Are you religious, Tariq?

T3LM: I am and am not. I fell out of love with the institution of religion, but it is a good way to live. To be good to the world that bears us and kind to those that share it.

AH6015: Have you thought that in the same way that all the papers - more generally mainstream media in its entirety - are controlled by a handful of people, religious 'institutes' are too? Every single one preaches the same message. Each of the most popular religions build on the last, Islam a furtherance of Christianity, Christianity of Judaism. Just by using a new prophet they can tailor the ideals to best control the population of that time. Certain people read certain papers or watch certain news channels, where all the content is tailored for those specific people by a single person or corporation so that they all accept the same message.

T3LM: I have thought of that. The problem of not going through the system first is that no one takes you seriously. You end up being some mad blogger sitting in some disregarded corner of the internet that no body tunes into because they lack citation and credibility. No offence to you of course. The people that share the truth and are genuinely a force to be reckoned with have gone through the relevant 'institution' first and come out with hard facts that can't be ignored. No one would have listened to Manning or Snowdon otherwise. I intend to get my degree, work for a few years and build my circle of influence before I can delve deeper into the cracks in the system that people need to know.

    AH6015: I can help to open the cracks.

Tariq watched many links to other websites with videos and new articles coming through the messenger. Tariq opened each in order and skim read each page. As more and more came through, in various languages that were automatically translated, Tariq started to realise that they were all relating to the same series of events.

At first there were several links directly alleging to prove the American and British involvement in the set up and arming of the Muharid group. A few links went over to Arabic language transmissions, supposedly from Muharid deserters, that detailed the support they had received from American provisions. One man went into detail as to the reasons for originally joining the group and that it was the shift in ideal from freedom against the corrupt governments to being a conquest for resources that came just after a significant rise in the quality of arms that were being 'found'. Another article showed satellite images of the U.S. army base that was supposedly taken by Muharid that inferred that no attack truly took place and that the base and equipment was abandoned two days prior to being publicised in western media as 'a massive loss to the U.S. army', supposedly after 'a shock inception left the base open to a rapid attack'.

The next few links that had come through were focussed on Russia. Contrary to the image that had been built up in Tariq's familiar news sources, Russia had purposefully avoided any bombings of U.S. flagged bases. The Russian president in the most recent articles had said 'that policy would stop immediately after intel had shown that most American flag bases in the region were directly being used to either supply the terrorist organisation or were being run entirely by Muharid', knowing that they wouldn't be attacked by their true enemies. The Russian led peace-coalition had agreed in principle to a ceasefire and prospective truce deal with the governments of Iran, Iraq and Syria, that could lead to a new state being born across the north of the three existing countries and allowing the group to self-govern to the freedom ideals that first drew the group to action. One Iranian website even went as far to say that a proposal for an oil trade agreement had already been drawn up in draft that would give a significant source of riches for the new country to recover the infrastructure that had been lost in the fighting.

The last set of links were introduced by AH6015 as the most troublesome. The North Atlantic Trade Organisation was on the verge of dissolution, with the leading countries within the European Union already supposedly having the beginnings of deals in place to create a new trade union alongside Russia and China. France and Germany had watch status granted to the Shanghai Cooperation Organisation, which if NATO fully dissolved would be granted a full seat at the table and a renaming of the organisation. All that was spoken was preceded by uncertainty and speculation, but the sheer number of links that related the same pieces of information caused Tariq to be distinctly perturbed by what he read.

He jumped on to the mainstream media sites he was familiar with, hunting through any articles he could find that could be related to what he had read. He desperately tried to find some semblance of repetition of those that he had seen. Tariq went through to certify that the articles were written by genuine sources and found that in the countries that they printed in, they were well respected and well-read journalists and news companies. Hours passed and by the time he brought himself back to message the distributor of the news, all that remained on his screen was:

    AH6015: Worrisome, right?

    AH6015: [offline]

Chapter 6

Flowers bloomed either side of the entrance as Leighton pulled the car from the narrow country road. In as many times as they had visited his parents' farm he had always found it difficult to pick out the right turning. At least in the early summer, he had his mother's flowers as a marker.

A large farmhouse lay at the end of a long driveway, hemmed in by thick hedgerows. Branches grazed against the edges of the car. Leighton reassured Shannon that they wouldn't scratch the paintwork. Rearing up behind the farmhouse, lay a silo and as the road started to drop downwards they could see the barns off to each side.

Shannon loved coming to the farm, part of its existence reminded her of growing up, though she could only have wished that the farmhouse she had been brought up in would have been as grand. She was excited to see how Zeke would take to the farm and the outdoors, however it was likely to be at least half a year or more until he would be at an age to get the most out of it. At less than five months old, he would probably show no more interest to the grandeur than he would have their rented magnolia walls at home.

The main door came open with some effort behind it and Leighton's father stepped out onto the gravel. Leighton pulled the car to a stop close to the door and his dad made a motion for him to wind down the window on the passenger side. "We are about to get out anyway, Dad," Leighton said to him, stopping Shannon's reach for the controls.

He could just about hear his dad cooing through the back window, tapping on the glass. "Expect a lot of this sort of thing," he said to Shannon, quietly.

"I forget they haven't seen him since his first-time home," she replied. "At least I can leave them to it, should mean I can have a drink, right?"

Leighton switched off the ignition and removed his keys. "I'm pretty sure wine will be mandatory. You packed the breast pump anyway. You'll probably end up missing Zeke, the amount they will want to be cuddling him."

Shannon got out and walked straight over to Leighton's mum, who was just coming out through the door. Leighton had to usher his dad out to one side so he could get to Zeke. "Let me get him out and then you can say 'hi' properly." His dad lingered close to the car trying to catch eye contact with the freshly awoken little boy. Leighton struggled with the seatbelts that were carefully and intricately wrapped around the car seat. "Dad, do you want to grab some of the gear out of the boot while I do this?"

"Yea. Sure thing," he replied excitedly.

"I can take something," Leighton's mum said, walking towards the car. "Is it just the two days you're staying for?"

"Yes. Is that still alright?" Shannon answered for him, covering for his frustration with the car seat.

Leighton's dad opened the boot of the car, "Are you sure you've just brought what you need for two days?" The boot was a carefully tessellating assortment of baby equipment and bags. Flat packed travel cot, changing bag and two small suitcases were visible. "What on earth are you planning with this?" Leighton's dad peered around the open boot with an axe in his hand.

"Phil, your son likes to feel prepared. I have already given up trying to quash it," Shannon answered.

"Ah, good to see he picked up something useful from all that time I felt I was fruitlessly preaching at him about organisation. I was hoping it would just help him in getting a good job rather than him preparing for some kind of apocalypse."

"Well, he had to get some of that Michaels madness eventually," said Leighton's mum.

"Kerry, you wait until they see my new energy supplies I've had built in. Our son is going to be jealous"

"Oh yes! You got the geothermal generator working finally?" Leighton asked, now stood with the car seat and baby carrier by his leg. He offered his free hand to take a bag from his dad to take in.

"Yes, I did, it works a treat. We are officially in energy profit, selling back to the grid now in three quarters of the year," Phil said proudly. Kerry rolled her eyes and got handed parts of a baby changing table. "I'm going to start work on the battery cell next month. With the numerous turbines we've got, it won't need it to be too big. If there's one thing I can rely on around here it is the wind blowing. I just want it enough so that if I need to repair any of the systems, we have enough power in the interim."

Shannon spoke, "Now I see where Leighton gets it from. I'm sure when we've got enough money together to buy our own house, it will be laden with all sorts of energy saving gadgets. Yes, I did see the green grant website thing you were looking at!" she directed at Leighton. "And talking of the wind blowing, let's get this stuff inside. I know the sun's out, but this wind is still chilling."

A few trips by Leighton and Phil later, Shannon had turned the largest spare bedroom into a nursery. Kerry told them again that they could have used two of the rooms, but Shannon happily ignored the lack of floor space that remained and suggested that they couldn't sleep in separate rooms yet. Leighton quipped that he might be the one to use it, though he could never sleep properly when away from Shannon.

Zeke slept in the temporary cot and Leighton lay back on the bed while Shannon arranged their clothes into some of the empty drawers around the room. "You okay?" he asked.

"Yea, I'm fine. I like coming here, though you know it always reminds me of my dad."

"Shall I get you a drink?"

"It's not that bad, I need to get some milk prepared for this one first. You should go and have one though. Make a rum and orange and I might be tempted for a sip."

"I'm not that fussed. Mum's making a roast and it'll be ready soon. I'll have a beer then."

"I hate your breath when you drink beer. Have something else."

Leighton laughed. "I guess a rum and orange then. For you."

The table was laid out in the kitchen as though a restaurant, with attention taken to arrange each mat and utensil. A large roast chicken, bowl of mash potato and plates of boiled vegetables lay down the middle.

"I hadn't thought about Zeke," Kerry considered.

"Don't worry, Mum. We'll just put him down in his play chair. He can't eat any of this anyway," Leighton replied.

They sat to eat, arms crossing and bodies leaning across each other as they filled their plates exuberantly. Shannon piled up hers as much as Phil and Leighton did, making a remark about nutrients for breast feeding when given a shocked expression by her husband. They laughed. Shannon noticed that Kerry did not give herself as large a portion as the rest, but in the enjoyment of the food it was forgotten.

When the meal was finally devoured, all four of them sat in a lethargy, filled bellies restricting movement in all but Kerry. She efficiently worked to clean away the serving plates, confident that everyone was well fed.

Phil said, "Kerry. Leave all that, let this food go down and I'll load the dishwasher. Please, sit down."

Kerry defiantly took one more set of glasses into the kitchen before slumping down in the chair. She sighed.

"Did I tell you that I started stockpiling last week?" Leighton asked.

Kerry darted a glance at Phil, who answered, "Why bother? You know you can just come here if anything happens, right?"

"Well, what if we can't get out of town? We need to at least have some stuff for an emergency. We have enough tinned and dried food to last us a month or two on top of our normal supplies, and that's eating as well as we would normally with no rationing. In the case that we are stuck at home," Leighton said.

Shannon rolled her eyes towards Kerry, who let out a snigger. Shannon lent over to pick up Zeke. Kerry said, "I guess he gets it from his father."

Phil ignored the remark. "I think it's great. It's your duty as a man to provide for your family. I think that should most certainly include emergency situations, don't you think, Shannon? You must feel safer, knowing that if the 'shit hits the fan', as it were, you are going to be able to eat and stay inside. Much better than fighting the hoards and riots that will hit every corner shop and supermarket."

Shannon hummed. "I suppose you're right, though I think that there are more important things to focus on than collecting knives and axes in the cupboard under the stairs," she said drily.

"Is that what my son is putting you through?" Kerry asked.

"Yes, indeed. We have toys spilling out of our ears and a cupboard full of junk we may never need. Our house isn't exactly big enough to warrant the ill use of space like this," Shannon replied.

"Hey," said Leighton. "You said the other day that you were cool with it. That I was being a good dad by looking out for my family this way."

Shannon said, "I would say anything to shut you up about it. There is near enough nothing I could do to stop you. Even if I wanted to. It is *cute* though." She grinned at him.

Leighton looked sullen. Kerry spoke, "Aw, look at him. He means well, bless him."

"Come on, Mum, you could at least try and sound a little less patronising. You reckon it's a good plan, Dad, don't you?" Leighton said.

"I do. Of course," Phil said convincingly. "Come, Shannon, bring Zeke and I'll show you a stockpile that'll put whatever my son has to shame!" He gave a jovial glare to Leighton as he pushed his seat back. "-And just because you are a parent yourself, it doesn't mean you get out of taking the rest of the dishes to the kitchen."

The heat of the sun could be felt overhead, but cool air still whipped around them as Phil and Shannon walked from the house to the barn. It brought a shiver to both Shannon and Zeke, who she pulled a little closer to her chest. The few trees on the grounds did little to stop the momentum of air speeding across the acres of flat farmland that surrounded the complex. The barn was the largest building on the farm, Shannon supposed it would be big enough for a full-length swimming pool.

Phil pulled a large bunch of keys from his pocket and muscled open the ageing padlock across the doors. Inside the barn it seemed smaller than the outside portrayed it to be, but soon Shannon realised it was due to the amount of hay and straw against each wall. As they stepped inside, the smell hit her. The mixture of meat, smoke and stale grass made her feel ill from the intensity. Above the mass of straw bales was a jutting shelf a few metres wide with a ladder near the door and another at the far end.

"I want you to feel safe, Shannon," Phil started. "Above there we have at least a year's supply of grain, mostly wheat. That's a year for Kerry, myself and you three. We want you to be sure that if anything happens, even if you lose your jobs and need some food, you all come here. Okay?"

Shannon remained silent, taking in everything within the barn.

"We've got meat too, should you prefer. I've been smoking a lot of it to keep it good. Now we're getting a bit older we had to cut down on the number of animals we keep. It helps us stay self-sustained. Don't really want to hire any help, seeing as we have everything else down ourselves.

What I'm trying to say is, we can put all of you up indefinitely. I want the best for my grandson. And you, of course.

"I almost hope something does happen to have you guys here more. Kerry would have loved more kids, but, well we had our problems after Leighton. She would be over the moon to have Zeke around. We know you should get on with your life though. Any time you need babysitting, a weekend off, bring him round." Phil paused briefly. "Ah look, I'm rambling. Anyway, you got free energy, free food, two spare rooms, any time. I guess that is all I am trying to say."

Shannon said, "Thank you. Leighton has got some supportive parents, doesn't he? Hopefully it won't come to the end of the world or whatever he thinks is going to happen. The weekend off here and there won't hurt though, I am sure." She smiled sincerely and gave him half a hug with the arm free of Zeke.

Chapter 7

Mina arrived at the pub early and there wasn't anyone around that she knew well enough to talk to. She sat in the corner with a gin and tonic and waited for Grace, who was supposed to arrive at any moment. The pub was dark and full of the typical smells that fought to overcome the pungency of the pub's dog. The walls were well decorated with remnants of the village's past. Black and white photos of its famed brass band, rustic weapons and tools, and taxidermies of small game animals that made Mina cringe to look at.

Mina picked up her half-finished drink and her bag and took a place outside in the front smoking area which consisted of a row of large barrels with heated canopies above. Given the early summer heat they were not switched on. After just a few drags of her rolled cigarette she saw Grace walking cheerfully across the green. The bells from the nearby church rang out for eight o'clock.

Grace came straight up to Mina and gave her a tight hug. "Perfect timing, Grace," Mina said while pointing towards the church tower.

"Ah, you know me, I like to make an entrance." Grace rummaged around in her clutch bag for a slim cigarette and lit it appropriately gracefully. Her nails looked freshly done, long and filed to a delicate red point in stark contrast to Mina's nails cut down as short as they could be, but at least clean and coated for her night out.

While they smoked and talked, Mina finished her drink and after stubbing out their cigarettes simultaneously, Grace slipped her arm through Mina's and trotted her towards the bar. They took a bottle of wine and a jug of iced water and by Grace's decision, took a table that was in direct line to the door and with no tables blocking their route to the bar.

Over the next hour, the pub gradually filled up with people, nearly all of those entering offering a polite 'good evening' to the two women. Grace was much more the social animal than Mina was and so the evening generally consisted of Mina being pulled into all sorts of conversations with people that Grace knew well and that knew her well. Everyone had kind words for her, but Mina was much more attuned to the jealously shown by other women and the lecherousness of the men that vied for her attention. She tried to tell Grace this only to be told that she was looking too deeply into it all. Mina could see why her friend got the attention she did. She was certainly a beautiful woman and spoke articulately, the time spent cycling paid dividends to her figure and men and women alike pontificated wildly as to why she had not married. Though, as much as Mina tried to raise Grace's awareness of what people were saying, it was embraced more than it was ignored.

A group walked into the pub. They were ordinarily dressed, smart if anything compared to the rest of the patrons, but something about them made Mina take note. They gave her a bad feeling and she didn't recognise them from those in the village that she had met or seen before. Grace told her that they were from the 'estate' as it was known in the village, but they certainly weren't as dodgy as some of them from that area. She knew them by sight, but not by name.

A little later, the pub became very cramped and Mina and Grace, losing their table, had resorted to standing outside under one of the heated canopies with a few other friends of Grace's. Grace was telling them about her investments in a few businesses around the area, explaining how she managed to have such a nice house working as a grocer. Each of the barrels at the front of the pub were surrounded by people and a few other groups were stood across on the green itself, pint glasses in hand being swung around in extravagant story-telling. The group that Mina had seen earlier on fell over each over, laughing as they came out of the pub's side door and overhearing Grace's talk of investments, came to stand with them.

They probed Grace for information. Grace answered their questions eloquently and vaguely, trying at every pause to move the conversation onto a different subject. Mina nudged her friend a couple of times and suggested getting another drink. Mina could sense a devilish ambition in the oldest of the group, but didn't want to make a clear scene over it in case they tried something too aggressive. It was clear to Mina what their intentions could be with someone clearly well off and open to talk, but she didn't think that Grace could see through it as easily. Grace's two friends even concernedly asked her if she was fine, and she replied that she was, and they eventually wondered off towards home, citing an early morning trip to see family.

After they left, a silence dropped over those that remained in the circle. Mina decided it would be an opportunity to pull Grace away, but the next few moments seemed to pass in front of Mina so quickly that she felt as though she was moving through mud while everyone else was on fast forward. In reaction to Mina picking up their bags and putting her arm through Grace's to guide her to the bar, one of the men in the group facing them made some comment to Grace about her 'anxious little girlfriend' which had the effect of rooting Mina to the spot with a sudden wave of anxiety and anger thrown together. Grace immediately held onto Mina tightly and defended them from the accusatory words that continuously spouted from the mouths of the group. Mina, in her immobile state, had a surprising thought that to an outsider walking past, they probably did look like a couple. Stuck in that thought, Mina missed completely whatever words came from Grace next and so was caught even more by surprise at what resulted from it.

One of the women, taller than both Mina and Grace, threw herself towards the pair. She managed to push Grace to the ground while missing Mina completely, whose arm simply detached like a lizard's tail from being clasped around

Grace's. Before Mina could even turn to see what was happening, four farmers describable as 'burly' ran in and pulled the unknown woman from her friend, pushed the others back and started to close in on the group until they knew that they stood little chance, two averagely built against four farmers that looked strong in arm albeit a little rounded of stomach.

Mina broke from her dismayed trance to give Grace a hand up from the floor and preceded to wipe her down of the gravel that had gotten into her hair and clung to the back of her dress and jacket. While she did this, the farmers walked back over to tell them that the group had been officially barred for the evening. Grace insisted against the farmers' will that she would buy them all a drink, the act of which seemed to whisk Mina along in all the commotion and downing of shots. Grace seemed – as she did with everyone in the pub – to know the farmers well and spent a few minutes talking and laughing about what had just happened, brushing off being knocked down with ease.

It was, after a few minutes, Grace that suggested they go back to her place to relax in case the barred patrons decided to come back in time for closing. As much as she didn't show it right away, Mina could tell Grace was at least a little shaken up.

Grace's house was well kempt, every single item had its own place that seemed to make it stand out from the rest. In her living room, she had a baby grand piano, polished to a vibrant shine, a few of her sporting awards from her youth still had a pride of place on top. She had no TV which meant that two cream leather sofas lay opposite each other. Mina and Grace lay on one together, Grace's legs lying over Mina's. They each held a large glass of red wine.

"I should have stood up for you better," Mina said angrily.

"You shouldn't worry yourself, darling. It's just the local chavs – even if they don't dress as such – they just go around bullying for no reason. There is nothing you could have done to change the situation. -And anyway, it was just a little pushing and shoving," Grace replied.

"I knew that they would start something with you as soon as they walked in. I could have protected you. You mean a lot to me, Grace, and I know that that sort of thing does affect you, no matter how hard you think you are."

Grace pushed her foot firmly against the side of Mina's face. "You know I'm as hard as nails," she said playfully.

Mina pushed the leg away, spilling a few drops of wine on her blouse. "Damn, look what you made me do. Anyway, I am being serious, I need to stand up taller. Especially for you. Being as you are one of a very elevated and exclusive group of people I actually like."

"Aw, you always get so soppy when you're drunk, my love." Grace nudged her again in the side. Mina caught her leg under her arm and held her calf tightly.

"I thought I was always soppy and protective around you. Did you not notice?"

"Perhaps I didn't," Grace answered.

They shared a few seconds of silence before Mina shook her head and let out a sound of disgust. "I am done with wine," she said reaching to place the glass onto the shelf behind the sofa.

"You!? I never thought I would see the day you give up before me. Do you want to have a cup of tea, a cigarette and then pass out upstairs?" Grace asked.

Mina thought for a moment, her head lolling about dramatically as she did so. "Yes," she finally answered.

Chapter 8

Tariq woke in the early afternoon. After staring blankly at his phone screen for a moment, he reached over to open his laptop. The browser was still open from the night before and after it refreshed itself, he noticed a message icon on one of the pages.

AH6015: Are you going to join the marches tonight? It's due to be a riot. Perhaps literally. Thousands will attend and it's well planned across the board.

The text was followed with a plethora of links to various awareness groups and events on social media. Tariq opened them up to see huge numbers of people pledging attendance.

AH6015: Where are you going to be starting from? You're south of the river, right?

T3LM: South of London Bridge is the closest rally point for me. I need to phone my mentor at The Vigilante to find out for sure where he'll want me. I am on the live-feed team for it tonight.

AH6015: Well, I hope only truth will you be spreading.

T3LM: Of course. The truth is key. Someone at the office will be proof-reading and editing where appropriate, so I can't be held fully accountable for the end output to my name.

AH6015: Do your best, brother. Let me know on here where you will be, it would be good to catch up if we can in all the commotion.

Tariq lay back on his bed, he wanted to make sure that he had as much energy as possible before he set out for the night. It wasn't due to start until eight o'clock and the final meeting of the different groups outside the Houses of Parliament wasn't predicted to occur until close to midnight.

Tariq walked, carrying his small rucksack, usually reserved for his bike rides, filled with a few snacks, a water bottle, spare pen, notepad and two external phone chargers. It was a couple of miles from his flat to London Bridge, but he covered ground quickly with a purposeful stride. He had arranged before leaving that he was going to meet 'AH6015' on the corner of Montague Close, just south of the river.

He waited on that corner for twenty minutes. The number of people grew rapidly and he noticed the proportion of those wearing earthy or bright colours – the typical garb at most of the protests and marches that Tariq had attended – to those wearing black hoodies or dark tracksuits was declining. A few of the eyes peering over bandanas and scarves gave him glaring looks and Tariq felt himself withdrawing towards the walls of a nearby building. It wasn't much longer until 'AH' came through the crowd towards him. He had shaved his moustache, but left the beard intact and he was bigger across the middle than Tariq had remembered of him. He was dressed in a dark blue hoodie and black jeans, looking well integrated into much of the crowd that surged and pressed around him.

"Tariq," he said as he approached. "Good to meet you, my man." He stretched his hand out and Tariq took it. They exchanged small talk for a few minutes before it became apparent that the crowd was starting to move. As they walked along, the sun lit the underside of the clouds – only covering half the sky – a vibrant rust colour.

Tariq and 'AH' carried light conversation as they went onwards, both pausing from time to time to record or write down some notes for reference later. As the sunlight failed and the orange street light took over, the noise of the crowd picked up. The pair walking together noticed some graffiti tags starting to appear on some of the walls they passed. Random words and names appeared first, but eventually they took a more stable form from one to the next. The word 'KoYΔ' started to appear frequently. Neither of them knew the meaning, but both took note due to its regularity in repetition.

The river continued to push its darkened waters in the opposite direction to the flow of people walking alongside it. The buildings lining the other bank glowed passionately, a distorted reflection of their amber glow floating above the water. Tariq had expected to have seen a police presence appear alongside the throng of people that they were a part of, but even the better part of an hour after he had met up with 'AH', he had not seen a single uniformed officer. The realisation of this was not just limited to himself, he could see up ahead that more black-hooded men were geeing themselves up. A racket of noise – shouting and chanting – came back from towards the front. Gloved hands waved into the air, some grasping hold of heavy bats or sticks. The crowd near the pair grew in unease and some of those more vulnerable were starting to fall behind or move away from the main crowd down more lightly travelled paths.

'AH' and Tariq kept a steady pace and soon realised that they were separated from both the main groups that had started as one. Behind them, those carrying banners and ahead, those carrying weapons. Tariq supposed that it was where journalists best operated, separating the reasonable man from danger whilst close enough to it themselves to retell the story later.

An instant after turning and passing under a wide overpass, the gradually rising tension snapped like a cord in front of Tariq's eyes. From watching the growing group of black clad people in front of him, walking almost in unison, to an instant explosion of energy around them. It stopped the two journalists in their tracks. Before 'AH' had even had the wherewithal returned to him to pick up his camera and start taking pictures of the events unfolding in real time, smashed glass was thrown up into the air with some falling near enough to skitter across the ground between them and the group causing the carnage. The sound was replicated multiple times giving the effect of being near a fireworks display that was out of sight.

Their senses returned and with it an overwhelming urgency. They both had a fight in their minds to stay with the group, the desire to find safety chewing through their sense of duty to document the story. Tariq started hastily typing into his phone, eyes still locked on the group ahead of the them, to keep note of progress while 'AH' got his camera rolling and started taking hard footage.

The first targets were a line of shops on the left-hand side of the street that were undercut from the high rise flat block above them. Nearly all the windows were smashed in, leaving a jagged, glistening outline around each frame. The shouts were deafening with only a few clear words making their way above the rest. Screams of, "get weapons" and "missile up, lads" were among similar sentiments. Civilians and shop owners streamed down the street away from the carnage, some helped on their way by forceful pushes or throws from hooded and masked men. Some cars tried to turn around to get away, but after quickly finding themselves blocked in, most were abandoned in the haste of their owners' escape.

A small group of men with rucksacks took to ascending the steps up to a footbridge that joined the second floor of the building with the other side of the road. Several flares and fireworks were set off from there, aimed high over another building between them and the Jubilee Gardens. A pair of them broke off and started to unfurl a banner that stretched across the footbridge. Either end was branded with a stylised word, 'KoYΔ' and 'Revolution is NOW – Rise Up!' written in between. A few fireworks went off target and careened through the windows of the opposite building, bringing with it a heavy shower of glass shards to the pavement below. Tariq kept his distance, edging backwards with slow steps until the underpass that they first passed under protected him from above. Behind him an equal and opposite force of commotion occurred, people were running past the other entrance, a few of the bold coming to within a few paces to see what was happening, but none staying long.

Tariq and 'AH' slowly followed the black-clad group as their path of destruction stretched onwards towards the London Eye. Left in their wake were hollow shops disregarded as though by a powerful storm and smashed and burning cars abandoned in the streets. A few of those that owned the shops or cars were in tears, making phone calls to the police or insurance companies even as the storm that created their loss continued unabated. The pair felt unseen as they passed under the bannered footbridge. They carved a path through the ruin that avoided coming too close to the burning cars. Ahead, most of the group, which was probably a few hundred people to start with, converged with another coming from the east at a crossroads. A small portion carried on straight ahead, hunting down untouched cars and windows and ensuring that anyone that might try and stop them was forced to flee instead. The rest turned right, towards the river. Tariq and his accomplice vaulted the centre of the road and another fence that surrounded a pedestrian zone. Some single floor buildings ran on the right of it in a line towards Jubilee Gardens. They both kept low, now parallel to the main group of revolutionaries – probably now referred to as terrorists on most media outlets – so they could remain unseen.

At the end of the line, 'AH' pulled up. Tariq hadn't noticed how out of breath the man was. "I need a rest, dude. My heart is pounding," the man said, reaching into a pocket for an inhaler.

"That's absolutely fine, my man. I need to pull myself together too. I am shaking too much to even type right now," Tariq replied. He hunkered down with his back to the wall and took some deep breaths. Once he felt back in control, he hastily typed in a few more paragraphs into the phone and sent them off to the editing team at the paper. He did it as much to announce the danger he was walking into as for the benefit of the reader, although he knew that there was no way to get an evacuation procedure put in place for him. The risks he took now were his alone.

After a look at 'AH' that told him the man was still not ready to get moving, Tariq crawled to the edge of the building to try and spot the group. The main congregation of people was starting to gather at the end of the street on the other side of the pedestrian zone, coming together patiently as stragglers still in the process of destruction spread along the rest of the street like the tail of a comet. Back at the first crossroads, Tariq could just make out a group of around fifty hooded men that seemed to be guarding the ways that they had come from. Tariq looked back to the main group that looked as though it was squaring up to the London Eye itself. He was shocked at how organised and regimented they were. It was as if each man made up only a small part of a greater being. In effect, they were. The supposed revolution was a cause worth coming together for and they certainly didn't have the appearance of a self-serving group of individuals. They were purposeful and it felt like each of them knew their ends and how to get there. The last piece of information that scared Tariq more than anything else was the continued lack of police.

Chapter 9

Leighton sat back, feet resting on the coffee table wishing he could have joined the protest himself. Shannon sat alongside while music videos whiled away time in the background. The interest from both, however, was on the live updates from the latest protest in the capital. Most of the commentary was based from within the largest group that formed north west of the city centre and seemed to be comprised of several journalists from the same paper. There were brief intermissions as updates came in from other areas. One that seemed to be picking up a little bit of momentum was following a group south of the river that seemed to be dividing into two separate groups. The only reports of any trouble were coming from the south bank, with 'isolated incidents' of vandalism and petty theft.

The couple casually read the updates as they came through, diverting their eyes from the television as each did so. One came up that caught the eye more than the rest. Opening with a picture of a burning shop front, an orange banner hung above the flames, before the resolution could fully render, it resolved to a grey rectangle on the screen instead. They didn't read the text that came up below the space that should have provided the image, before they refreshed the page. When it had finished loading, neither the text nor the image reappeared. Shannon and Leighton both stared at the screen patiently waiting to read what had happened, but after five minutes, it still hadn't been shown and more posts on the north London marches had been entered.

A few more posts referencing violence, burning vehicles and missiles being launched over the heads of civilians, all tagged as by the journalist Al-Noor, came up in quick succession. They were all short excerpts that were a maximum of three sentences in length.

"Seems like it's finally getting exciting," Leighton said.

Shannon was on another chair reading on her tablet. "What's happening?"

"Probably just a bit of petty vandalism getting the journalistic treatment, let me scroll back down and read it for you." Leighton scanned down the page, but before he could start reading, the page automatically refreshed and returned a page without those entries included. "They seem to be gone. The page just refreshed."

"Those three just disappeared too?" Shannon asked.

"I think so," Leighton replied. "I think it is just something wrong with their servers, it must be overloaded and struggling to keep up." The baby monitor started beeping and Leighton stood straight up to go visit Zeke's room and check on him. "See if there is anything on the twenty-four-hour news channel while I am gone, that looked like it could be fun."

Tariq watched on as the organised group spread out across the junction. They set fireworks off in low arcs over the park, towards the London eye and down the street that passed to Tariq's right. Those people who had stuck around to watch the progression of the group started to flee rapidly, keeping heads low and backs bent in fear of receiving a strike. As the area vacated, the group of black-clad people spread out, letting the smoke from the fireworks fill the area. The light, grey smoke started to dissipate quickly, but in its place a thicker and darker smoke billowed up and blocked Tariq's view of the group.

"Hey dude, do you have a spare black jacket?" Tariq asked 'AH'.

"Yea, it's just a light rain jacket though. How come?" 'AH' said.

"Well," Tariq started. "That group has just blocked our view of what's happening, check it out." 'AH' poked a head around the corner as Tariq indicated with one hand and a made a grunting affirmation. "If we are going to continue to live up to our title of 'journalist', we are going to need a better view." Tariq waited for a nod, to ensure that he was being heard over the noise. "I propose we leave here, cut back across to the road there and join the back of that group."

'AH' took a few seconds to process the information, a tentative and almost fearful look plastered on his face. He went to speak and hesitated again. "Oh, okay. For the truth." He then proceeded to pull the jacket out of his bag and hand it to Tariq, replacing it with his expensive camera and lifting a much cheaper digital camera from one of the side pockets. Tariq gave the man a reassuring smile and tap on the shoulder before donning the jacket and pulling the hood over his head. Tariq swung his arms out wide to show off his disguise. A shrug was the only response to the gesture. "I'll follow you," 'AH' said finally.

Tariq replied with a grin, "I thought that would be the case."

Tariq led them back the way they came until a break in the buildings and, keeping low, strained to see through the smoke that was now filling a large area around the intersection. After a moment, he reached his hand back and gave 'AH' a short tug on the jumper to ensure he followed. They kept their heads down as they passed across the empty pedestrian zone. The smoke continued to get thicker as they got closer to the intersection and over to their right, the flicker of orange light dancing on the underside of some fresh billows of smoke indicated the cause of it. They reached the outer fence that separated them from the road and Tariq adjusted his cycling bandana over his mouth and nose to help breath. He noticed that 'AH' had also pulled the front of his hoodie over his own face.

The other side of the fence was enough upwind of the fires that they could now see a number of cars, an ice cream truck and large van razed and they could finally make out the group of black clothed rioters moving directly up the road to the

London Eye. Tariq and 'AH' both walked quickly and purposefully to meet the back of the group, constantly adjusting scarves and hoods to match the people that they were going to assimilate with.

The pair went unnoticed as they fell in just behind the back ranks. The group moved slowly and it was a few minutes of shuffling before they reached the Eye itself. Tariq grew comfortable enough to send out a message explaining what he had just done to the editing team with a note that further details will follow. 'AH' was still visibly nervous, the hands on his camera shook and his eyes darted trying to focus on the back of every one of the heads in front of him. Tariq noticed that the group looked significantly bigger from up close and wondered if another group had joined under the cover of the smoke. It certainly appeared to be the case, but the darkness and confusion that had veiled the last half an hour could have easily thrown his judgement off.

Passing under the two large supports of the London Eye triggered a flurry of movement and commotion. The familiar sound of smashing glass rung out as if all around them. The main group split apart rapidly, some moving off north to create a blockade against anyone coming in, another set brushed past the two journalists to do the same on the street they had just come down. Tariq stepped on to the river bank path itself. Ahead, a group started smashing their way into the control rooms and docking station of the London Eye's pods, to his left a large group were already through the doors into the London Dungeon buildings via the ticket office and lights were being turned on in windows up to the third floor. It all seemed to happen so fast, Tariq felt as though his head was swinging back and forth rhythmically attempting to keep up with it all.

Tariq started climbing up onto the awning overhanging the path to get a better view. It was almost instinctual for him to want to see the whole picture and try and fathom the unfolding events. His accomplice looked nervously up from below and after placing his hands on the scaffolding that

Tariq had climbed, clearly decided the best place for him was on the ground. From his vantage point, he could see people running in all directions away from where he was. Black-clad men at the near end of the dock were smashing into the pods before they left and were using gasoline to set fire to each one before it left on its path up to the top. The first pod was left rocking violently as acrid smoke poured into the night sky above the Thames. More lights fired up on the building opposite and drew Tariq's eye to the windows at the top. People were leaning out of them and some were stepping out carefully onto the high roof. A huge, bright orange tarpaulin banner was unfurled, again reading 'KoY∆ – THE REVOLUTION IS NOW! – KoY∆' in the now familiar stylised writing and thick matt black letters. Tariq took the best photo he could of it and, while his camera was on, took shots of the burning pod, the crowd below him and the burning cars further back up the street. He put his phone away quickly and checked to see if anyone around him had noticed, but every person seemed to be moving pointedly and with great haste to fulfil the plans they had clearly made.

A strong piercing light caught Tariq's attention from the south, in line with the Westminster bridge. Tariq looked away and clenched his eyelids tightly to shift the purple spots in his vision and learned forward to get the attention of 'AH'. The man was looking straight up at him. "Sorry, mate. Did you just say something?" Tariq asked.

"No. I was about to ask you what was going on though. How's it looking?"

"About what you can see, huge banner, burning pods, well organised destruction. There are some bright lights shining from down by the bridge. They are new, I know it's a long shot, but do you have any binoculars?"

'AH' laughed. "You don't know me well enough yet. Of course, I do." He rummaged into his bag for a moment before pulling out a small pair of binoculars in camouflage paint. He threw them up and Tariq caught them easily with one hand.

Tariq found it hard to see through the lights, but could see that they were currently situated at the top of stairs at the level of the bridge. Once he dipped the lenses enough down the steps to block them out, he saw uniformed men for the first time in about an hour. They weren't regular police uniforms, though. He looked down to 'AH', startled and shouted, "I think the army are pulling in!"

"What?" 'AH' replied, obviously starting to become even paler, visible even in the orange light that filled the area.

"Uniforms, but not police. Looks like grey urban camouflage, I can't quite make it out. Their lights are dazzling."

A few men overheard that were passing underneath. "Hey, you. You say uniforms." The man spoke with an unfamiliar accent. Possible eastern European to Tariq's ear.

Tariq pointed in the direction of the lights. "By the bridge, coming this way. Can you see the lights there?"

"Yes, I see. One of you get a megaphone, tell everyone that you pass that the resistance is here," the man said to the others with him. They split off quickly, just breaking stride as they passed each of the other people in their path. The one that had spoken ran into the docking station and Tariq watched. The sight of three pods burning caught his eye until the man returned wielding a megaphone.

The man pulled down the scarf across his face and from the docking station shouted over and over, "The resistance is here! The resistance has come! Everyone together!"

From every corner, men came running onto the path and filed in behind a line that had somehow managed to pick up riot shields as they marched in step towards the oncoming soldiers. Tariq lifted the binoculars, the soldiers ahead were much clearer now. They were about a third of the distance to the bridge and were clearly armed with side arms and shields of their own. Looking at the men from the group that they had joined, he noticed that there were also hand guns among some near the front.

Tariq yelled incoherently and dropped the binoculars down into 'AH's startled hands. He slid himself onto his stomach and slowly let himself over the edge. It was a good distance to drop and Tariq took a deep breath before letting go. Tariq landed heavily and fell backwards onto his small rucksack which painfully pushed some of his items into his spine. He let out a gasp, but 'AH' quickly came to pull him to his feet.

Still recovering from the loss of air in his lungs, Tariq said, "Both sides are armed," closely to 'AH's ear.

Before he could be answered, pops struck loudly through the air and instinctively the two of them dropped to the ground. Tariq pointed up the path they had come down and they both took to a stooping run to the cover of the building's corner.

"We are leaving now. This was too much half an hour ago," 'AH' said breathlessly as they pulled up.

"I'm with you," Tariq replied.

After running for some time and stealing a pair of bicycles that had been left unchained, Tariq was returning to his neighbourhood. It was a neighbourhood that seemed too much the same and yet so different. Tariq was sweating insatiably even in the cold night air and he left the stolen bike down a shop ally about half a mile from his house. His legs felt as though they could barely support his weight, in part from the fast and panicked cycle from central London to home and partly from the scene he had left behind. He knew in his heart that people were dying there and didn't fully know the cause that was worth a large group of people to most likely be throwing their lives away for. The revolution sponsored by whatever or whomever this KoYΔ was.

Tariq's street felt as if four thousand miles away from the fighting rather than the four that it was in reality. It had the same old bustle. The kebab shops spilling a light into the road that was disrupted by the throngs of drunk people harassing the staff for faster service. Bars were left with a few lingering

61

patrons smoking cigarettes and taxis passed through, cutting each other up to claim fares. It was too normal. -And Tariq was too different.

Chapter 10

The unchanging road lay out ahead as far as the two beams of light broke through the darkness. Zeke was fast asleep in the back seat and Shannon struggled to keep herself awake too. She had gotten used to taking naps whenever Zeke did, but in company she felt obliged to stay awake in respect for the driver.

"It seems you won over my uncles and aunts this evening," Shannon said.

Leighton replied, "Really? I didn't do anything special.

"You did, you were protective of me when everyone started fighting and got me and Zeke out of the situation. To my aunts they will see that as a really good thing."

"You have to do that in the situation, I don't want drunks falling over on Zeke or bumping into you. All I heard about was how much weight I had put on since they first saw me. They were asking if you could cook at the next party, because it is obviously good food. Do you know what caused everyone to get rough, anyway?"

"I have no idea. I heard that there was a guy who was trying to steal beer that everyone had brought, but wasn't one of us. He tried to chat up one of my cousins, I think. So, he must have been someone's friend because otherwise they wouldn't have kicked off on each other. Best to stay out of those, just everyone being drunk. You can see why I hate going to family parties, now."

"Well, they are certainly livelier than mine," Leighton said. A two-hour drive still lay ahead and he flicked open the coffee flask. "You sleep, Shannon. Make the most of the opportunity." He had barely finished speaking when the rhythm of Shannon's breathing slowed. He turned the radio up a touch to match the noise of the road and engine.

Once home, Shannon and Zeke had enjoyed a lengthy sleep and Leighton was positively caffeinated. They spent an hour or so trying to put Zeke down into his cot. As much as they attempted to be fast between car and bed, before he reached it, he was wide awake and refused to go down quietly. Leighton lay with him, sat up in bed, while Shannon, newly re-energised, put a few of their clothes back in the drawers and washing basket as appropriate. Leighton shushed her, but as she slinked into bed alongside them it was clear that Zeke's eyes were open.

Each time it appeared he had fallen asleep in Leighton's arms, Zeke's sleep was broken as he was placed into the crib. Leighton resided himself to staying upright to cradle his son. Neither of them were too ready for sleep after Leighton's coffee and Shannon's nap in the car.

"It still feels like only yesterday that we brought him back from the hospital, doesn't it?" Shannon asked.

"It feels like only yesterday that I found out you were pregnant. I think that the feelings of that day will always be as clear as glass. Child birth, though. I don't think I have ever gone through anything as scary," Leighton replied.

"You big baby, it was nowhere near that bad. Hurt like hell, but not that scary." Shannon touched her abdomen at the scar that was now hard and barely noticeable except by touch.

"Well, let's be honest it was not that bad for you, because you were high as a kite the whole time. I was sober watching it all unfold."

"So, let me get this right," Shannon said incredulously. "You think the birth of our child was worse for you than it was for me?"

"Yea, well, while you were gasping on the gas and air I was being jostled by a room full of doctors and midwives, watching the heart rate monitor for Zeke bouncing up and down. Every time you had a contraction his heart rate went from a hundred and fifty down to sixty or at some points, forty beats per minute. I was seriously weighing up the fact that he was going to die. Then they start faffing around with a monitor on his skull, but instead of making it clearer it kept coming unstuck and the heart rate was flat lining on the machine. I was thinking to myself, this is eight months' hard graft and no prize. I was shitting myself, trying not to let it show so that you wouldn't freak out."

"I didn't even know that at the time. I was in agony from the induced contractions. I couldn't have cared less for any other machine than the one providing relief. Though that was seeming to get less and less effective by the breath. I suppose that's why there were so many doctors."

"I bet you don't even remember them preparing you for theatre. They put the spinal injection in before the local anaesthetic had taken effect and you puked all over the floor and on one of the nurses who seemed to try to catch it. You were near enough passing out by then."

"All I remember of that, was after the anaesthetic had started and I was laid down with the sheet in front. I didn't even realise they had started doing their thing until I heard the first cry," Shannon said.

"They didn't say anything about starting. I was just sat there in the way looking like a tourist in scrubs with a camera around my neck. The worst bit after that was they pulled him out and then said I could see him, but they put him on a table at the tail end. I had to block my eyes as I walked straight past the surgeons stitching you up, fighting the urge to have a look at the goriest sight of my wife I would ever hope to have."

"Well apart from for that one photograph, I didn't get to see him again for three hours, while I was waiting to regain feeling in my legs. I was wiggling my toes with all my mental strength so I could get out into a wheel chair and see him. It was unbearable. There was just one nurse in this entire huge open room and just me lying there, paralysed. At least I knew you were with him." Shannon cooed and stroked Zeke's head. "I'm so happy to have him. It was all worth it."

"He looks well asleep, I'm going to put him down properly," Leighton said. He did so and that time, Zeke barely stirred.

Chapter 11

The day that Mina looked forward to all week came around. Thursday evenings, Rebecca stayed at her Nan's house and Mina knew that she could call and get a real chance to speak with her daughter. Mina refused to call Drew, regardless of the reason to do so. The chances were too high that she would also have her sister answer the phone and she wasn't ready for that. She spoke to Rebecca regularly enough when she was called directly by her, but Thursday evening was her chance to take charge and reach out to her only daughter herself.

The phone rung, Mina loved the anticipation, knowing who was to answer the phone.

"Hello, Nan's house, Rebecca here," came the innocent voice.

"Hi, lovely. It's me, as always at this time," Mina replied.

"Hello, Mum. You always call when I am here."

"It's because I know that it will always be you who picks up the phone and I like talking with you. How is school going, honey?"

"It's fun, today we had dancing class. I got paired with Jennifer and we got to go in the big hall. We had loads of space to spin around. Then we had a maths lesson and after that, English. Maths was boring, but we read poems out in English and that was really fun. Nan picked me up after school and made fish fingers and chips with ketchup. What was your favourite thing you did today, Mum?"

"My favourite thing today, before calling you of course, was picking some flowers from the meadow. Would you like it if I sent some to you, Rebecca? I will find some in your favourite colour and send those. What's your favourite colour today?"

"My favourite colour is…" Rebecca paused. "Nan, what is my favourite colour today?" she called away from the phone.

Mina heard her own mum in the background. "You should know, darling. What was it yesterday?"

"I think it was purple," Rebecca replied.

"You think? Do you still like that colour now, like the curtains in your room?"

"I'm not sure." A long pause came. Mina waited patiently.

"Well, tell your mum that you aren't sure then," Mina's mum said eventually.

"Mum, are you still there?" came Rebecca's voice, clearer again.

"Of course, I am, Lovely. Did you decide on your favourite colour?"

"I think I will say I'm not sure. Is that okay, Mum?"

"Absolutely, that's probably the best colour to choose really. Do you know why?" Mina asked.

Rebecca made a few loud fillers and tapped on the phone handset. "I don't know. Why is that the best colour?"

"It's the best colour to choose because it means I can send you all the flowers I have picked and then whichever colour you pick to be your favourite will be there!"

"You're going to send me all the flowers? Yes!" Rebecca turned away from the phone again. "Nan, Mum is going to send me all the flowers."

"All of them? That's great," was her nan's simple response.

"When can I come and visit you, Mum?"

Mina's heart jumped a little. "Ah, my lovely. I wish it was as easy as saying yes."

"Why isn't it?"

"Oh, darling." Mina paused, not knowing how to continue. "I will tell you what, though. I am making a lovely house here. It has a beautiful garden with a meadow. The meadow has flowers of all different colours and smells wonderful. The bees really love it. One day you will be able to come and play with me here. I built a swing for you in a tree that you can have a go on and it goes really high!"

"I want to see the meadow and play on the swing, Mum! That sounds better-than-dancing fun."

"You will. The problem now is that it isn't finished. It isn't ready for you yet. It may take a little while, so I need you to be patient. Can you do that for me? That's why I will send you flowers. Then you will have a little piece of that meadow with you. Can you wait until it's ready to come and visit, though?" Mina felt a lump in her throat.

"I am not sure, Mum. Must I wait? Don't I get to choose?"

"I wish you could choose. I wish *I* could choose. We don't always get our choices, Rebecca. Sometimes we must do things a certain way. I do promise you that by the time we can choose for you to come, it will be ready for you. You will have your own room and we will decorate it together."

"Can we paint it purple?"

"You can paint it whatever colour you wish. It is empty right now, waiting for you."

"Thanks, Mum."

"I love you, Rebecca. You had better go and do your homework before bed. What have you got to do today?"

"I have to do spelling," Rebecca said, making a noise with her tongue out just after.

"Spelling is good, Rebecca. It means you can write and learn words that make you sound intellectual and articulate."

"What does that mean?"

"It means you can sound smart. Now, be good for Nan. Tell her I love her."

"Do you want to say it to her?"

"No, you tell her."

"What about Daddy?"

"Perhaps you should go do your spelling. Next time we speak you should tell me a new word you've learnt. Can you do that for me? Can you remember your favourite word?"

"OK, Mum. I love you, bye." The phone clicked before Mina could respond.

Mina felt instantly both drained and elated. She couldn't spend much longer without her daughter here. Every week, these calls would reinvigorate her sense of purpose when on other days it could feel totally destroyed. She had all her dreams to fight for. Dreams of Rebecca playing in the meadows. Mina knew she had those memories yet to create. She couldn't give up.

The phone rang with Mina still stood next to the handset.

"Hi, it's Mina," she answered.

"I know it's Mina. I called her!" came the woman's voice.

"Ah, Grace, very good timing."

"Pub?" They both said in unison.

"Yes," Mina responded.

Chapter 12

Tariq had read through the live-text feed from the night of the riots to see if there had been similar incidents across the city at the same time. He had difficulty even finding any of the posts associated with his story. Either some of his messages had not been sent or received correctly or his posts had been deemed not worthy of entry into the list. The latter didn't seem to ring true to him though. There were a number of other reporters listed, most of whom were following a tame series of events led by peaceful activists. Some of his earlier posts from the night were up, but none containing any reference to KoYΔ or the violence he had witnessed. He shuddered as he replayed the last images of the night in his head of the two groups stepping slowly towards each other and the echoes of gunshots that followed him as he fled.

He angrily called his mentor at the paper, but was fobbed off without any serious reasoning as to why he had been blackballed from the article. The man rambled on about nothing, stuttering over his words. All Tariq got was the task of writing up what he had witnessed and if it was good enough it could get published in the submissions portion of the website. Tariq was peeved. The insomnia of the last few nights, unable to truly sleep nor truly wake still left its mark on his mind. Since the night of the KoYΔ riots – as he named them in his head – the anger towards The Vigilante and his mentor's disregard was the first thing he could recall actually feeling. At least for the time being he could use the energy to do something productive. He sat down and started typing. At first, an overview of what he could recall, then occasionally referring to his sent messages and recordings to fill in the gaps and complete his picture of events.

He worked solidly for hours until only the light of his computer screen lit the room. Nearing the end of the story he became overwhelmed by emotion. He realised that he hadn't yet found out what had happened to them. The people that for a short time took him in, even while they were destroying everything around them and striking fear into civilians and no doubt the police at the same time. He felt like the time among them gave him an understanding of why they were doing it. With everything the government was apparently doing cloak-and-dagger, it felt justified. He felt that if he was there again now he would have helped them, assimilated with them, taken up their fight for the people. A people unknowing of the situation they were being forced into.

The zeal grew up inside of Tariq as his exhausted mind ran over the same details repeatedly, each time developing feedback and growing in intensity. He succumbed to tears before realising what needed to be done. His article could save those that had offered him sanctuary. He needed to share the message on the largest platform he had so that everyone could know what was happening. He started a new article there and then. This one was to detail everything that he had learned about the British government in the last few weeks since meeting 'AH6015', a man he felt was more truly his mentor than his coach at The Vigilante.

Halfway through a sentence he noticed a flashing icon on his screen. It was 'AH' messaging him. Tariq told him about the article he was writing and 'AH' agreed that regardless of what happened with the paper, he would share his article on his own site. 'AH' then shared the real reason he had come on to talk with him. He gave Tariq an address and the note that should he need to vacate the city he could head there. This came before a flurry of links into foreign news articles from across the web. Muharid involvement in the north of Iraq had brought together U.S. and Russian troops into a supposedly accidental firefight that was responsible for deaths on both sides. Russia and Germany had now contracted a military alliance and were preparing action on

Britain for the war crimes committed in the Middle East. Supposedly, a deadline for the prime minister to step down and face the international criminal court had been set for in four days' time. This revelation brought with it much research that lasted until the orange glow created by Tariq's curtains flooded the room. There was nothing about this anywhere in the UK's mainstream media. He reacted simply by texting and sending messages to every news broadcaster he could think of. This needed to break. The population of Britain deserved to know. It should know already.

Feeling accomplished yet debilitated, Tariq finally found sleep.

Tariq awoke again, well into the late afternoon. The only thing that stopped him from rolling over and going back to sleep was the urgency he felt to get his article published. He splashed cold water over his face to help wake up faster and almost immediately after reached for his phone.

"Greg," his mentor answered.

"Hey, man. I sent you that article you wanted."

"Great stuff, I will check it tomorrow."

"There's also another article alongside it. I think it is tremendously important. I have been able to find out some information from overseas sources that isn't being broadcast in any way in this country. You can be the first paper to leak the news. It's massive."

"How massive?" Greg asked, audibly irked.

"We need to tell the British people about a large-scale attack on their homes and work spaces if we don't immediately bring our government and leaders to justice for war crimes."

"Oh," Greg said, nonplussed "That. Well, I will let you know now that there is no chance, regardless of what you think you know, that we will run a fear article based on rumour." Greg sighed loudly on the phone. "Journalism isn't all that, here. We aren't revolutionaries, we have a duty to the people to also maintain peace. If we run articles like that it could lead to more riots, looting, violence and that is *not* good for anyone."

Tariq started to speak his retort, but was quickly cut off.

Greg said loudly and assertively, "I will see you tomorrow, right? Great. Bye for now," before preceding to hang up the phone. The tone lingered in Tariq's frustrated mind.

Tariq took himself down to The Vigilante's offices early the next day, printed article manuscripts in his hands as he walked determinedly through the rotating doors. At this point he hadn't slept straight or at night in a week. At that moment, it was only his pure stubbornness and persistence that kept him moving on and helping him avoid a collapse into a long and overdue sleep. He knew Greg would be in the canteen at this time so he went straight there.

Greg looked up from his phone with a start as Tariq pulled out the chair opposite him. He took a seat and leant forward with the printed articles pressed to the table in front of him. Greg took a slow sip of his coffee, unfazed as if he had known ahead of time that he would be accosted by his very tired and tenacious protégé at this very moment.

"Morning, Tariq," he spoke first.

"Morning, Greg. I wanted to speak to you about the article in person. I know you can be reasonable on this. The people of the country need to do what they can to stop them falling into a war that it will never win. More importantly, a war they are thrust into because of the aristocratic greed of the political class. We, as human beings, need to give them a chance to do what's right, even if we don't tell them what to do. In this case, we must only present the facts – and quickly – and then leave any decisions to the people of the country." Tariq sighed deeply, having run out of his planned words so soon. "Would you not want that opportunity if your life was to be taken out of your hands?"

"Tariq, I must say that I love your tenacity, but we have two problems. One," Greg extended his index into the air.

"One, is that I have no documented proof of what you are saying. Two, is that even if – and that's one massive 'if' for you – if you could prove it, we have a duty to keep people safe. If we release the article saying that the country is liable to be declared war upon in – what is it? – three days, then that will certainly create chaos to anyone who reads and more importantly, believes it." Greg calmly took another long sip of coffee. "Two. Even those that believe, and if they were in large enough numbers, would they be able to enact the necessary powers to bring the prime minister to 'justice'?" Greg put quote marks in the air around the last word.

"That would be the whole point and whole necessity of it. All it really needs is enough people to demonstrate the desire to weed out the bad apples from our government and for the major powers around the world to realise that it is only the leadership and the people should be spared of the grief which I am pretty sure they are lining up to inflict, given all that Britain has done in colonisation and building of empire in the recent history of the world," Tariq said.

"That is all well and good, but if these other powers have already made a decision about us then we have already lost. For every one percent of the population that are ready to take up arms and fight for whatever is right – or wrong – there is only probably another nine percent that agree or disagree in any visible way. Ninety percent of the population will either not understand at all, will assume that somebody-else-will-get-the-phone, or just bury it out of site with a rhetoric of lies-and-propaganda," Greg said. Tariq felt like he was losing the battle convincingly and hung his head. "Tariq, it means a lot to me that you have gone to all this effort, but I would strongly urge that you drop this."

Not meeting Greg's gaze, Tariq said, "I can't."

"You're a smart guy, Tariq. Possibly smarter than me. I can see a great career in journalism ahead of you. This fire and passion you have right now will take you far, but it needs to be a long-lasting flame and right now you are going to burn everything around you and then wink out. This idea you have can burn a lot of bridges, so show that you can listen to advice and let it go."

Tariq let the words sink in for a few moments. "Should I let people die, when I know I could save them?"

"You won't save anyone with this. As with a lot of bad things that are set to happen, the Mayan prediction for the end of the world along with countless horror stories that never come to life, this may never happen. If it doesn't, you could be the *cause* of many deaths amongst rioting and violence that could spread from these words like the root of a weed. Just think about that, Tariq. You need sleep. Go home and get some and we will talk tomorrow morning. There are a few things around here that I need your help with, but I need the you that came in on that first day, not the exhausted you that is sat before me now." Almost as an afterthought he said, "The article from the London Eye is fantastic, by the way. Brilliant writing." Greg then stood up and took the last gulp of coffee, leaving Tariq drained and alone with the clattering of cutlery and the rustling of reports that filled the canteen.

Tariq's flat was situated above a corner shop that his landlord ran. Over the last year that Tariq had rented from him they had developed a friendship. He existed as almost a father figure to him. At this time, Tariq had still not seen anything that had dissuaded him from his belief that Britain would be attacked tomorrow and neither had he seen any whisper or rumour of it in the main stream media.

He spoke with his landlord and friend about what had happened while they shared a cigarette in the ally next to the shop. He told him that he was going to be leaving in the early morning, because he didn't feel safe in the city and urged him to go too. The response he received was that he couldn't leave his livelihood, even for a day. He mentioned that it would be deemed a selfish act, though only referring to himself. Tariq was set in his mind and bought the supplies he would need to take on tomorrow's journey. At the very least, the likely outcome was that he was to spend a day cycling out in the countryside north of the city and get the exercise and fresh air that he desperately needed.

The last thing Tariq did before he returned upstairs was to pay off half his rent that was due in two weeks' time. He realised that it made no sense to do so, but he felt as though the gesture would indicate his seriousness on the matter.

Chapter 13

Mina looked out over her small homestead. Some of the crops had already been harvested and her basement was well stocked with those early yields, the gaps in the field now replaced by mid-summer plants to keep it going and reduce her need for journeys to the village grocers. The last time she had gone was merely for some niceties that she loved, but hadn't yet grown herself; tomatoes, asparagus and courgettes. She had grown her own courgettes, but they tasted disgusting for some reason she couldn't work out and so had left them to freeze until she was desperate.

As Mina walked barefooted in between the split rows of her garden, she noticed movement from the corner of her eye. She paused and stared into the treeline that covered the steep north side of her little valley. She caught another movement at the edge of her vision, closer to the house. Crouching down slowly, she moved behind a strawberry bush at the lowest part of her growing plots. She waited a moment and then breathed a sigh of relief as she noticed that it was just two young children of an age – by Mina's eye – that couldn't have been too far into double figures, if at all.

The boy and girl jostled each other as they walked, the girl was almost knocked over by one of the boy's more emphatic shoves and looked miffed. They didn't act as if they had seen Mina, who remained low at the other end of the garden. After a few moments the boy halted, staring straight towards where Mina thought she was hidden. He yelled indecipherably towards her and quickly shuffled behind the girl when Mina stood up, smiling. She called back, "You found me."

The two children stood coyly as Mina slowly treaded towards them. As she neared them she opened her arms and knelt a few feet away to meet their eye-line. The girl, who from up close looked the older of the two, spoke first. Her name was Chloe. Mina asked who the boy was, who turned out to be her smaller brother called Joseph. She told the girl she had a pretty name and when asked her own name, Mina said that they should just call her 'The Garden Lady', because it was easier to remember. The boy said abruptly that he was just being looked after by Chloe and had to follow her here and asked not to be told off. Mina said that she wouldn't and found out from the girl that she liked her flowers and that was why she came.

The boy dragged his feet as Mina whisked the girl off to find out which were her favourite flowers. Next to the flower beds, Mina told the girl to wait where she was and decide which ones she wanted to keep. She left her while she grabbed a plastic pot and a hand fork. Chloe asked her why she hadn't got scissors instead. Mina explained that she liked the flowers too and so didn't want to cut them and let them die a week later. She told Chloe that if she dug the flowers out and kept them in a bigger pot, then they would live a lot longer and even flower again next year if the girl was to take them home and plant them in her garden.

Mina turned around to find Joseph with his arms out in front of him, an earthworm winding through his fingers as it writhed its way from his muddy palms. To Chloe's disgust Mina placed the worm carefully into the flower filled pot that the girl held. Chloe stuck her tongue out and went to put the pot down on the raised flower bed. Mina placed a hand gently on the pot to stop her and explained that the worm will help the flowers grow and it also meant that they could both take a living thing that they liked back home with them.

The girl carried the pot at arms-length as the two children walked off down the path towards the village. While Mina watched with a warm heart, Joseph kept trying to reach his hand into the soil which eventually led to the girl holding the plant close under one arm to keep him away. Once out of sight, Mina sat herself down on her back porch and cried with longing for her own child.

Shannon asked, "So what are we doing with your day off tomorrow then?" The kitchen was lit only by the other room's light through the doorway as the kettle hissed away in the corner.

Leighton walked through, temporarily dimming the room. "I don't know, normal stuff. I want to get out the house, that's for sure. Why don't we take a walk up to the barrows? I'll carry Zeke."

"Oh, can we take a picnic? I bought some olives and things yesterday." Shannon showed some genuine excitement.

"Yes, we can take whatever you want."

"I know, we will take speakers, blanket and a picnic and we can have our own little day out, listen to some summer tunes and eat until we roll back down the hill! How does that sound?"

"That sounds perfect," Leighton replied. "I am hoping that the weather will stay good for tomorrow, it is meant to." Leighton realised the kettle had finished and poured the water onto the tea.

"Oh really?" Shannon asked, noticing that Leighton had put the milk in first. "That's savage."

"No way, I make your tea this way every time and you have never complained. Not a single time!"

"Really? No wonder your tea tastes terrible."

"Terrible? You are lying. You would have complained ages ago if you thought it was that bad," Leighton said, grabbing his arms around Shannon's waist playfully.

"I lie because I don't want you to be offended!" Shannon retorted as she was nearly pulled over by her husband.

"You're lazy, then! You finish the tea." Leighton gently pushed her towards the kettle and the steaming mugs.

"Careful!" She said mockingly. "There's boiling water here." She ran and pushed through Leighton, ducking underneath the arm in front of the doorway. Having escaped into the living room, she quickly lay down on the couch with

81

her feet up on the armrest. "While you are up, you can grab the tea!" She exclaimed, laughing.

Leighton resided and stirred the tea, fishing out the teabag from one of the cups. As he sat down next to Shannon, he handed her the mug with the teabag still floating in it. "That's your punishment for being lazy," he said with a grin. Shannon pretended to sob and Leighton shushed her, pointing at the ceiling that became the floor of Zeke's room. "Oh yea, I nearly forgot to tell you, tomorrow after our walk, I need to stop by at the army surplus store. They mentioned a couple of weeks ago that they were getting new stock in yesterday or today, can't remember which."

"Alright, I am surprised that you haven't just signed up to the army already just to get the equipment," Shannon said. "-And anyway, ha, you have the controller so find us something to watch. Not the news, it's all I've had on today."

Chapter 14

The alarm came on and with it a light in the far corner of the room. Tariq focussed his eyes on the light to help him wake, but was groggy. The thought of a long bike ride this morning was not seeming as good an idea as he had figured a few days prior. He fought those feelings off, he knew it would be good for him regardless of the other reasons that he picked that day as the one to do it. The ride would take his mind off other elements of his life which weren't moving in quite the direction that he would have hoped. He needed to clear his mind of its own distraction.

By the time he stood at the kitchen counter eating his scrambled eggs, he really felt like he might be considered stupid for taking those blogs and internet forums into account. Part of him agreed that his boss was right to not publish anything that he had written, but another part of him wanted to maintain his conviction. He wanted to the point of need to have that self-belief, maybe it was by will of God that he found that information and if he had been more assertive, then he could save lives. Or he could have ended up with no job to go back to at all. Perhaps just these few days off would give him the breather he needed to refocus or reconfirm his beliefs. It all depended now on whether he was right or wrong. Either way he was already prepared for the worst, he just needed to hope for the best.

Tariq pulled open his waterproof bag, mostly already packed from the day before and added a bottle of water from the freezer. He changed into his cycling shorts and jersey and picked up his trainers on the way out the door. Taking one last look at his small bedsit before locking it up, he pondered the messages of warning that he had read. It is possible that this was the last time he would be here.

As he walked out into the cold air, the buzz of the city reached his ears. He pushed his bike around onto the street and the pavements were still fuller than he expected with life. People shouted drunkenly from taxis and the lights from kebab shops and burger trucks spilled out into the hazy dark air. In contrast, he saw some airport shuttles likely to be running their first jobs of the new day for people which were considering this hour the beginning of a day rather than the ending of the last. For Tariq, it felt like it could be both. His sleep had been broken with vivid dreams that woke him, some that had recurred sporadically since his childhood. He had slept some hours and that would have to be enough for now.

It was the middle of the dark hours, not one that Tariq saw often away from his computer screen and the forgiving warmth of his flat. It was very cold, especially as he was dressed ready for plenty more miles of cycling. He felt safer in the dead hours than he did being on the roads during the day. More space on the roads in general meant he was given a wider berth than usual. As much as the additional space, he felt as though it was equally his sense of purpose that pushed back against those encroaching on him.

He cycled north, taking the straightest roads he could and was met with the sunrise to his right as he skirted around the edges of Hyde Park. By the time he reached Barnet the rush hour had really started to kick in. He had to cut his way in and out of traffic and the usual feeling of invisibility that being a cyclist in the city offered returned. It was much slower going than Tariq had hoped, but every mile – however slow – was a mile further away, a mile safer.

Leighton took his fresh coffee out into the garden, leaving two eggs to poach in the microwave. Even a day off from work deserved to start early, especially when the June air was this refreshing. By ten o'clock it was already warm enough that even shirtless, he didn't get goose-bumps. Looking up, he saw a contrail that had turned on itself and he spent time working out if it was two crossing each other, but on closer inspection it could only have been the one plane. Shannon was dressing and feeding Zeke for the day and playing him his favourite album, so they believed, over the portable speakers in the bedroom. Zeke rolled around on the bed and Shannon had to lift him occasionally during getting dressed, to put him nearer the centre.

Leighton's eyes remained on the sky, concerned at the fading contrail's unnatural change of direction. His coffee had long grown cold. He opened the side gate to get a better look to see if the plane was still flying against its original path, but it was no longer visible. He turned back to the south-east and followed the man-made cloud's abrupt end down towards the horizon with his eyes.

He shouted for Shannon to grab Zeke and come and see what was happening. Shannon's music interfered in the conversation and Leighton had to sprint up the stairs to get her attention. He told Shannon that he thought something big, something bad was happening and she replied with angst that he wanted her to carry Zeke outside – prospectively into this danger – to have a look.

"I need you to judge it, come on! Pass me Zeke, look straight past the church tower. If I am wrong in what I think I have seen, then I am wrong. If I am right, we get our bags and leave right now," Leighton said with urgency.

By the time Shannon got outside, other houses had been vacated with their occupants staring in confusion at the horizon. She looked out, covering the sun from the edge of her vision with her hand. Small black specks suddenly became noticeable to her. Once she saw one, a lot more became obvious. She squinted and made out the movement of many slow flying planes.

As she returned Leighton spoke, "You think?"

"For all the days to have as holiday, huh? That's what I think." Shannon shrugged "Is there anything on the news, it could be a big air show."

"No news coverage. Total misdirection. Come and see," Leighton said, flicking the television through the twenty-four-hour news channels. "Sky News, nothing. BBC, nothing. Even RT has nothing, no breaking news, nor scrollbar. What the fuck? That, outside. That is not normal. There's far too many to be an air show that hasn't made the news." Outside, cars were being fired up and panicked phone calls were occurring between those at work and those shielding young children on the couple's street.

"Ok, Leighton." Shannon paused. "Maybe you're right."

"I'm right?"

"Get the air rifle and tomahawk, I will feed Zeke before we leave. If we are wrong at least it will be a nice adventure for our day off. This is what we were going to do anyway."

"If this is the first time I am right about anything, I very much wish I wasn't," Leighton said, taking the stairs two at a time.

"Hold on, don't get ahead of yourself. I am not saying you are *definitely* right. Perhaps just right enough," Shannon yelled up the stairs to her hurrying husband. His laugh responded.

The morning started with anxiety sitting deep in Mina's stomach. A bad feeling that she couldn't shift even while she pushed herself through her normal routine of getting ready. She was up earlier than she was used to and attributed the tensing knot in her stomach to a bad dream that had already slipped through the early morning memory like an oiled creature that couldn't be caught, but left a coloured stain that indicated its prior presence.

The sun had only just broken the lip of the valley by the time she had got outside to the porch to enjoy her morning coffee. She could feel the warmth of the sun on her, but the air was cold and still and her out-breaths of smoke billowed out impressively and hung stagnant in the air for some time. The knot remained and a sense of impending doom settled over her thoughts. She sat for some time after her coffee was finished, but was unable to reach into her memory for any hints at to what she dreamt about so terribly that this malignant feeling was still hanging around her.

She busied herself in the garden, weeding out the rows of vegetables. She was well on top of her patch and she was quickly done picking out the fragile little shoots of unwanted plants from among the sprouts of her potatoes, onions and lettuces that had rooted strongly. They had flourished throughout the warm spring and were now nearing a harvest. By the time she had finished, the sun was covered by cloud and the stillness of the morning was well past with gusting winds coming in from the south-west flipping her hair over her face as she walked back up to the house.

While Mina prepared herself some eggs for her breakfast the nagging feeling in her stomach continued. She watched the boiling pan with eggs rattling around violently as she thought on it. Perhaps she had missed something, a phone call or an appointment. She mentally pictured her routines through the day and the week to see if anything was obviously missing, but she came up short and switched on her radio to distract her. It was still early as her work had not taken long and a breakfast news programme started, full of static and only just audible behind the noise of the eggs battering against the pan's sides.

Mina faintly heard a man talking about an emergency conference that was taking place between the British Prime Minister and the German Chancellor among other European heads of state. The meeting was supposedly called for late last night and was taking place in Paris this morning. She heard words like 'war-crimes' and 'horizons' mentioned, but with the radio so low it was only the significance of those words that brought them to her ear. She turned the volume up and took the pan off the heat. The man on the radio had an interview with someone else who was in Paris at that moment reporting. "Thousands of reporters are with me, taking up almost the entirety of this plaza. It's an unprecedented meeting in the modern era and it comes after so much speculation and accusatory sentiment as to the involvement that the United States and Britain have with the rebel Muharid group in the Middle East. Here in France, previously such a strong ally of Britain, the feeling of the people is that they have been let down, that it is even harder when a country so close to their own is involved with what is seen as a terrorist organisation. In terms of who is in attendance – aside from the British Prime Minister – is the German Chancellor who is generally considered to be leading the proceedings although the French Prime Minister has the official position for that role, ambassadors from both Russia and America will be there along with members of the European Council and the wider United Nations. The situation is allegedly focusing on a single event, of which the news broke in the early hours of the morning – local time – when an explosive was detonated above Samara, Russia. It is currently alleged that the bomb was nuclear in design, although I have personally heard separate reports that it may have been a chemical explosion."

Mina mulled over the words, deep in thought as the reporter continued to talk on in depth about certain suppositions and speculations. She ate her breakfast at the kitchen counter, standing and gazing out into the garden, the radio drowned out only by thoughts of her daughter. She wondered if she was safe. Then she wondered if she was safe herself. Her life had run away from her, or she had run from it. maybe there wasn't anything she could have kept hold of from her old life that could have benefited her or her daughter. She willed safety to her little girl. She told herself she must send more flowers.

Mina gradually zoned back in to the conversation happening on the radio. "Well we are looking at a miniaturised warhead and that takes much more scientific engineering that could just be cobbled together by a rabble of extremist fighters working out of partly destroyed buildings and tents in the desert. The chances that they could stumble across the technology to create a weapon of this type are just so small that the vastly more likely option is that it was stolen ready-built or provided to them by a country – such as the United States or Britain as is being alleged – simply a much more believable story, as much as the population of Britain and the majority of America wishes to believe that the former is true.

"Our and your sources have documented the blast as something that would be hard to propose came from anything but a uranium-enriched warhead and as much as I would hate to be-"

The speaker cut out before a few moments of silence. Mina waited patiently for it to return, assuming that her radio signal was to blame for a dip in reception. Eventually a woman's voice returned. "Hi, this is Irene Blanche. I apologise for the loss of signal. Our technical team are doing everything they can to rectify the issues we are experiencing and we hope to return to that interview very soon. Meanwhile, a recap of today's shocking headlines."

Mina listened again through the headlines while she washed her dishes. She hadn't followed enough of the current affairs to understand how it could escalate the way it had done. She lingered on her thoughts with the voice of the interviewee running through her head. It was impossible to comprehend that the British army could be responsible for a nuclear explosion over Russia, an incident that whether an accident or not could be directly responsible for a new type of war. The feeling in the pit of her stomach became even stronger as she pined for her daughter. A tear ran down her cheek. She scrubbed it away hastily and reached for her tobacco.

Leighton and Shannon were changed and ready to walk out. The idea to drive had quickly been struck off when the cul-de-sac became jammed in almost an instant. Leighton had changed into heavy jeans, falling awkwardly over his army surplus black boots. He wore his grandfather's old RAF shirt 'because of the extra pockets' and over the top, a brown with red trimmed Russian conscript jacket he had picked up cheaply at a music festival in his youth. On his back, he wore the largest of the rucksacks and on his front Zeke looked out over the top of the red and black baby carrier, blissfully unaware of what might have been happening and still maintaining a wide-mouthed smile whenever his mother came into view. Shannon was dressed similarly with her matching boots, but wore a t-shirt and a puffed, hooded jacket. She wore a smaller rucksack, Zeke's changing bag over one shoulder and the air rifle on its strap over the other.

Shannon reached over and pulled the axe from Leighton's hand. "I'm not having you carry weapons with Zeke on you like that. What if you fall?" Her other hand pushed Zeke's messy, curly hair out of his eyes. He reacted with a single syllable babble and an adorable smile.

"He's such a happy baby. I hope he stays that way."

On that, they locked up the house and walked, as prearranged, along the road towards the edge of the forest park.

They had talked jokingly and seriously about what they were going to do and they had always agreed that the first priority was to get as far away from the town as possible, as quickly as possible, by foot. The forest park entrance was the closest way out of town and it led, after a way, into an evergreen forest and eventually into rolling hills. They would be safely away from town lights, dense population and uncovered land within half an hour and shortly after, they would also have the benefit of elevation from which they could make the best decision, but that was as far as their plan went.

That was exactly what they did. They passed cars with drivers offering cursory glances towards the trio, led by a man carrying a baby and followed by a woman seemingly armed to the teeth. Those that didn't notice them, continued to thump their palms at the steering wheels and dashboards and eagerly closed the gaps as each car inched forward. The only effect being that the cars became slowly more condensed. As they reached the main road, the expansiveness of the traffic jam – created in panic – became apparent. Both lanes on both sides of the dual carriageway were gridlocked.

As Leighton and Shannon moved sideways between bonnet and bumper a driver jumped in her seat, startled to see the sharp blade in Shannon's hand reflecting the sunlight. Shannon laughed and continued to follow her husband and baby winding through the stationary traffic towards the fenced edge of the forest park. Some people that were already out of their cars were trying desperately to see what was causing the blockage, steering their bodies away from the couple, the effect apparent gun ownership would usually cause.

"Time to create a shortcut," Leighton announced, deftly pulling out a multi-tool and opening its wire cutters.

While Leighton got to work on making a new opening in the fence, Shannon looked out in awe of the cars lined up on both sides of the road. The swarm of black specks in the distant sky continued to leave a tremor in the air, not a physical one, but palpable all the same. Some people towards the front of the queue had abandoned their cars already and were walking alongside the central barrier whilst others more hurriedly jogged in the direction of town, assumedly to try and get close to friends or family. Everyone was too focused to notice Leighton cutting through the fence and no-one looked anywhere near as prepared as the couple and their baby did.

The fence was cut in a clean line and pulled apart from the top as pages in an open book. Leighton put his hand out to help Shannon climb through. Just after they had set down onto the other side, they both ducked as two jet planes raced from the horizon seemingly touching distance above their heads. Leighton shielded Zeke as the disturbed air pulled violently at his clothes and the leaves and branches around them and Shannon hunkered close to the ground to not lose footing in the shock wave. Zeke started to cry and Leighton belatedly covered his son's ears during the roar of engines

91

that followed on. Screams from the road followed them as they walked with good pace perpendicular to the road. A path separated two lines of tree shade and they kept to it, carefully treading around bared roots close to the cover's edge. Once the sound of the jet engines subsided the sound of the incoming mass of planes crossed the threshold of audibility.

They crossed into the full tree cover and kept up their pace as much as they could over the rougher ground, laden down as they were. More jet engines roared in the sky, but they kept their eyes down and forward. Silenced and dumbstruck, left foot led right foot led left foot. The hair prickled the backs of their necks, expecting explosion or fire to overwhelm them at any moment. Ten minutes passed, and another ten after. They each made vain attempts to see the oncoming planes, but could not easily do so through the thickening tree cover.

"We are nearly at the barrows, from there we can see over the town and get an idea of what is happening," Shannon began. "If you want to see, of course."

"One of us must, knowledge is power and sometimes you have to see to be sure."

"Smartarse. He can't see though, turn him around to face you." Shannon urged.

Chapter 15

She tentatively picked up the phone. "Hello, Mina."

A deep, wavering, male voice came from the other end. "I am glad you are in." The man took a couple of breaths, Mina could hear them stopping high in his lungs. "How are you?"

"I'm fine. Sorry, who is this?"

"Oh right, yea. I forgot that you don't have caller ID. It's pretty cool you know. You can see who's calling before you answer. Do you remember that? I am a little upset you don't recognise my voice."

"Andrew," she replied.

"You are correct," Drew said. His voice gaining a touch of strength.

"What's that noise? Are you walking past building work?"

"No, ah- Well. I guess that's why I called. You can see it right?"

"See what?" Mina replied curtly.

"No? No planes?"

"No, you remember I moved away from you by over a hundred miles, right? That whole thing. Why are you even calling?" She asked with exasperation.

"I made a mistake." He stopped and breathed heavily for a moment.

"Are you crying?" Mina asked.

He hesitated, "Uh, no. I wanted to say that I have made mistakes. You are my biggest. No that came out wrong. I mean, *losing* you was a huge mistake. I still miss you every day, Mina. I think of you every day. I suppose it sometimes takes something a little out of the ordinary – a big event – to make you realise. Damn, Mina, those fierce wolf-like eyes of yours still visit my dreams so often."

Mina interrupted. "What's happening there? What fucking planes? Are you high again, Drew?"

"Not high. I can't believe you can't see them. All over the skyline to the south and the east. So many damn planes, Mina. Everyone is panicking and running out on to the street to look up at them. It's not an air show. It's real."

"Real, what?" She was getting infuriated. "What sort of planes? Fuck." Her mind reeled around his riddles. "Where's Rebecca? Is she with you?" Her voice rose to a shout, partly from frustration and partly the rising volume on the other end of the line.

"She's not with me right now. I think that is probably for the best."

"Well," Mina said, "Where the fuck is she, if she isn't with you?"

"She's up north with your- with her cousins."

"Well, don't you fucking sugar coat it? Just say 'she is with your sister'. Why the hell is she with her? What are they doing?" She paused a moment, but started again before he could answer. "You're still banging her, aren't you? That's why *she* got divorced. You dog. You're still fucking my sister. You get high and start hallucinating all these planes and call me up to say you made a mistake and that you miss me and all this bull-shit!"

"Wait. We aren't sleeping together anymore."

"Anymore!" Mina blew out her cheeks. Her face was flushed with rage.

"She still helps out with Rebecca. Life has not been the same since you left. Not since that whole saga started."

"Um, the whole saga *you* started." A large rumble distorted Mina's phone line. "Drew?" she asked. For a moment, intermittent snippets of something loud threatened to blow out the speaker in the phone and she quickly pulled it away from her ear. It subsided. "Drew," she said again.

"Mina, I thought this was going to happen." Mina thought that she could hear him sob.

"What is that?" she asked.

"They are bombing the city. The next wave is stretching right overhead now. There was no way I could have avoided this. I can see south of the river from here and most of it is flat or on fire already."

"What are you bull-shitting about now? Do you need me to call a doctor? I think you are overdosing, you sound insane."

"Mina, please don't leave the line. Don't call a doctor, it will do no good. I need you here with me. In spirit, at least. I still love you. I love you, Mina," he said sincerely.

Mina was stunned. She never thought she would hear him say it again. Her heart gave a reminiscent pang of reciprocation. It was, however, quickly replaced with images of her own sister covering her shame. "Are you about to die, Andrew? You sound panicked. Are you about to kill yourself? Overdose? Is that why you sent Rebecca away?"

"I am, Mina, but I am not high, I am not overdosing, nor do I plan to. I am serious. -And sober. Look out your window and watch the world burn, Mina. Know that I burn for you. I love you."

Mina placed the phone on the kitchen counter and stomped out onto the porch in her bare feet. She looked to a sky that looked overcast above the walls of the valley. The only direction she could see in for any significant distance was west and it was clear all the way to the horizon. She returned to the kitchen, the last words that Drew had said only just sinking in with a wave of anger washing over her. *'Burn for you...'* she mouthed.

"There's nothing, Drew. The skies are clear. I am calling a doctor to come visit you now," she said after she had picked up the handset again. "Andrew, stay where you are, please." An unnerving silence responded. "Drew. Drew." The line was dead, she hadn't noticed. Her cheeks flushed and she hung the phone up, waited for a moment and picked it up again from the wall. She dialled his home number from memory.

An electronic voice told her, "The number you have dialled has not been recognised." She fought her growing shudders as she tried his mobile number. They were shakes of anger. The same message greeted her and she put the phone down. Her heart was pounding. Shakes of anger turned to fear. She wondered why he wasn't there when she returned. Only serious thoughts crossed her mind. She picked up the phone again ready to retype in the number in case her quivering hands had pressed the wrong keys, but after seven numbers she realised that her phone had not even given her a dial tone. She returned the receiver and tried again. No tone. She wiggled all the cables and connections on the phone and tried one last time. No tone. Her legs gave way and she met the floor heavily.

The trees were cut back leaving the barrow open to the sky and on enough elevation to see down to the church and sprawling town around. They looked out with Leighton holding Zeke's head close to his chest.

They saw the original clump of planes, now much larger in the sky and nearing the town. In tandem, other groupings were spaced across a sky that was crossed with contrails that merged at points behind where the planes were now. At the furthest to their left they could see a more massive group inching forward, clearly with the capital in its sights.

"I thought it would be long range missiles," Leighton said mostly to himself.

"Same," Shannon replied.

"Subsonic bombers seem a little old school. Don't you think?"

"Yes, perhaps it's not an attack after all. Could be some other reason behind it."

"Like what? There are better ways to scare people than waste loads of air fuel flying across Europe. In my opinion, they must be Russian. There's tension there, it makes sense."

"Does it?" Shannon said, "What about Germans, it could be their show of allegiance to the east."

"No. The Germans wouldn't be that easily convinced. It's a serious thing. If they are German, they are pointlessly vindictive. I think it stems from something our government has done. Induced physical retribution for sure."

Shannon had no answer, continuing to watch the darkness of the planes grow nearer.

The pair were rooted to the spot atop the highest barrow. The town spread out below them, the church tower near the closest edge and a few of the high-rise blocks sprouted out of the estates that made up most of the town. They could see the cinema clearly, the supportive red beams that would catch the eye on any day when all eyes weren't already captivated by the sky.

"How far are we from town?" Shannon asked.

"Around two miles, more or less."

"I hope more."

"Same."

"Wait."

The rumbling became almost unnoticeable in its consistency and rhythm.

The black swarm grew rapidly, stretching itself downwards towards the city like heavy rain clouds viewed from a distance. The dimension of time stretched itself such that the harrowing sight majestically seared their memory in a more distinct way than could be thought possible. Fires razed up in the centre of town, a high rise toppled slowly to the ground, the church tower seemed to be pulled down from within itself. A town decimated in an instant, they were glad they were not close enough to see people within the mess. They were blessed with that. And blessed with their lives intact.

Across the sky, the sight of bomb fall repeated itself over and over.

A flash caught their eye and they both turned their heads to the left. Shannon pulled Zeke in to her chest even closer. They were fixated on the horizon where the light had come from. Slowly a cloud of dark smoke rose from the horizon line. They watched as a massive grey dome rose up, refracting the sun's light around its edges, giving it definition and accentuating its unnatural looming pattern in the sky.

Tariq's muscles raged with lactic acid as he reached the top of the incline. The land had started rising about four miles behind him and was getting even steeper towards the top. It was made worse by the fact that his road bike was certainly not designed for riding on roads filled with potholes and expanses of gravel. He was grateful so far that he had not gained a flat tyre and instantly damned himself for thinking of it.

He passed a few people walking as he made his ascent. He didn't pay much notice, for if he had, he would have realised that they were all stood stock still, all facing in a single direction the way he had come from. He had spent the entire journey looking forward, in hope that he would continue cycling through to lunch with nothing to note. Then he would eat and cycle until dark with nothing to note. Then he could spend a night under the stars, get cold and cycle back home the next day, wrong, but tired. He thought this over in his head as he slowly crept his bike forward and higher.

He felt a pang of cramp in his calf and finally had to give in against the hill and dismount from his bike. He stretched his leg out, the curve of the top of the hill still in sight. No animal or person occupied the intervening space. Those he had passed would be small specks in the distance if he was to turn around. Trees lined the edges of his vision and the grass grew long and unkempt. It was as a serene a sight as he had seen since living in London. It seemed very foreign to him. The wildness of it seemed so out of normality. The expansiveness so unnatural.

In front of him, the ground lit up in a split-second flash. For that moment, he could see every blade of grass, every groove of bark on the trees as if in higher definition than his normal vision could provide. Time stretched out as he tried to process the image in his mind. His thoughts seemed scrambled as though he was trying to flick too fast through an unbound book and, instead of finding his page, he was simply splaying paper all over the floor.

It finally clicked a few seconds later, a bright light must have gone off behind him. He instinctively turned, and as he caught the light still waiting for him near the horizon, he slammed his forearm over his eyes and hunched forward. His skin prickled on his forearms and lower legs, extending as they were, bare from his cycling shirt and shorts. Tariq moved his arm from his face slowly, first looking down at the ground, which now looked dull and drained of colour, but for a purple tint of flash blindness. He ignored the burning sensation on his skin and lifted his eyes towards the source of the light. Where he expected to see the crooked skyline of inner London, he saw just dust. A tall, slender cloud rose up, expanding into an elevated dome of thick dark cloud. The sight forced Tariq to lose his balance and half lean, half fall back against the grass. The sensation on his bare skin grew but he was too dumbstruck to be concerned in that moment. He just sat in stillness, mouth hanging open. No fight or flight reflex, no panic, just serenity. And stillness.

He couldn't tell how long it had been that he had been still. The world seemed paused. All sounds seemed to blur into one. His brain couldn't engage with any of his senses.

He snapped back to reality as a warm rush of air pressed against him. It heated his skin like the rare equatorial south wind he remembered from his childhood home. It was this familiarity that eventually snapped him back to reality.

Chapter 16

Mina awoke in panic, blinking wildly at her blurred surroundings until the edges finally became a crisp resemblance of her kitchen as viewed from the floor. Her blinking slowed, each time she did her vision blurred over, taking time to return to normality. She lifted herself up, clutching the side of her head against a headache that seemed to be on both the inside and outside of her skull. As she righted herself, her stomach rolled and churned. She slowly let herself back down onto her back and stared up at the ceiling. She kept her eyes open, not letting her eyelids touch more than fleetingly when she had to blink. She suspected that she may have hit her head and had heard that it was not advisable to fall asleep with a concussion. Maybe that was just an urban myth, but being on her own made her cautious.

The telephone call she had just had flooded back in her memory, but in a dull haze. She spoke softly to herself. "He must have been high," she pronounced to the empty room. She shivered against the cold floor and gently lifted her head up again. "But why did my phone cut out? Or did I imagine that part in shock?" She rolled onto her front and pushed herself up slowly as to avoid a sudden rush of blood to the head. When she got to her knees she picked up the phone to hear no dial tones. "Was he right about the planes, the bombers? Would bombs in London cut the phone lines across the country? I suppose they could." She suddenly wished that she had either the internet or a mobile phone to see what had happened. She felt isolated, helpless in the moment. Her heart picked up its volume in her chest, enough to make her ears feel like they were ringing with the sound. "Fuck," she said calmly as her body exhibited all the signs of a panic attack. She battled with the thoughts about having passed out on her own. The realisation that she could have hit her head even harder instilled a heavy fear.

The battle flowed through her. She remained kneeling on the kitchen floor trying to focus on the inanimate objects that surrounded her and made up her home. The sanctuary that she created alone, for herself. She reminded herself that it was her valley. She tried to comfort herself with stillness.

Shannon broke down crying and sat herself down on the grass with the steep slope of the barrow gathering up the weight of her rucksack. Leighton eventually sat next to her after scanning the rest of the sky. The dark grey cloud lingered in the east. The top of it pushed northward, giving it the look of an inkblot smeared by a listless thumb. Leighton pulled Shannon close, her head falling onto his shoulder. Zeke reached a hand up and bashed it playfully against his mother's cheek. Failing to receive a reaction he started to sob along. Leighton rocked him, but his focus was all on Shannon.

"There's nothing we can do for them, Shannon." He pushed her hair back a touch. "Remember, all we can do is make a life for our little gentleman to live. Have a sip of water, I'm going to head back to the top and make a decision on where we head from here."

"Pass him to me, he's hungry." Shannon wanted his warmth against her in a vain hope that responsibility would provide her control and that his innocence could mend her soul. She stared as his puffy cheeks worked for her milk. His wide eyes looked up into hers. The sight of him made her feel a slight sense of security and reassurance or else at least the feeling that she needed to portray those emotions for his sake.

Leighton's mind worked as he made use of their vantage point. He had shed his bag and made use of a retractable telescope from his inner jacket pocket. With the planes coming from the south-east, heading north-west was going to be best, but that would take them straight towards more built up towns. North would take them too close to the motorway by the time it was dark and lay too flat to get a good snapshot of surroundings that they would benefit from. A wooded set of rolling hills lay around ten miles to the west, but they would have to avoid villages and towns on the way, just in case more attacks were to come. That would make closer to a fifteen mile walk in all. He caught sight of the town that had provided their home and shuddered at the destruction, before sitting alongside Shannon breastfeeding further down the barrows.

"There's a spot on the nearside of a hill, covered by woods and at least three or four miles from the nearest settlement. We can get there before dark and set up the tent for the night there. It's the safest we can be for now, I reckon, though the walk will talk a good few hours."

Shannon merely mumbled an acknowledging syllable.

"I wish I could work out what has happened. No news coverage and phone signal is lost." Leighton said, flinging the phone on to the ground away from where they sat. I just hope the people that made the decisions on this suffer too. I hope they can't return home either. I wonder if other countries have their news reports on what has just happened. The reality of it. Do you think whichever country that sold or built those planes is going to send us an aid package? Do you think this might just be it? Great Britain, a crippled and broken empire finally put down in bad health."

Shannon remained silent. She focused all her attention on Zeke. He looked peacefully up into her glistening eyes, drinking his fill of her milk. Leighton wondered if he could possibly know what was happening. Shannon was already in acknowledgement of the difference the world he would develop in was from theirs. The difference between most generations was rarely as stark as theirs would be to his. Usually it wouldn't be realised until the child was older, but at least she felt like sooner was better in this instance. If this thing was to happen at least in his early months he would not know any different. They had to deal with knowing what the previous way of life had been like. They would have something to miss and Zeke wouldn't. The thought gave some condolence to Shannon.

Tariq looked around him. He was completely alone. Ahead he could see the mushroom cloud being pushed to the left and leaning over imposingly in his direction. The city itself was obscured through a thick brown fog that looked stationary.

His skin felt hardened as if sunburnt, which was not a familiar feeling to him, but he recognised it. He put a hand onto the back of his forearm and released it quickly as it sent a stab of uncomfortable pain through him. Closing his eyes, he took a deep breath and thought about his situation. His only knowledge of nuclear attacks came from movies and books and of that information, which was only a little, there was not much he could rely on. Tariq recalled those weather-like maps from the films that showed fallout spreading out and causing more death in the surrounding areas. It must travel on the wind. A wind that was currently blowing somewhere near his direction from the blast.

"I need to move," he said aloud to no-one. He stood, plucking some grass as he did so and dropped it out in front of him. It flew easily off past his left hip. "I need to go that way," he said, pointing west. "And hope the wind doesn't follow me".

He felt flustered, returning to his bike which looked exactly as it had a few minutes before. He didn't know why he thought it wouldn't and he straddled the top tube. His throat was bone dry and he took a few gulps from the bottle attached to the frame. He pulled up his shorts so that the bottom hem wouldn't rub against the burnt parts of his legs and pushed on, over the short grass. He prayed as he went. He gave thanks for the foresight to leave the city, he hoped that he would get away quick enough and he hoped over and over that he would avoid a puncture.

He occasionally followed along narrow concrete paths that wound along the flatter slopes of the hill, but as they turned too far north or south he broke away and kept his direction true. After a short time, the ground fell away and he caught sight of the motorway up ahead. The junction just within view was jammed with cars in all four directions and along all the connecting slip roads, but in the direction he was headed, it looked clear. He supposed that any cars free of the block would have turned around given the situation. Unnatural fires cropped up among the still traffic. Tariq decided to stay clear and headed slightly further north to ensure he didn't come into sight of what may be happening there.

He met with the motorway at a dip in the road, clear of traffic on both sides and both directions. He dismounted and carried his bike over the barrier. His instinct still led him to jog over all six lanes. Although empty, it felt that lingering was not a safe option. Once on the other side he was on the edge of a farmed field. The dirt was churned up and the rows of planted wheat made sure he had to carry his bike to take it further.

He crossed two more similar fields before a sudden sickness arose. He was hungry. Very hungry. He had only had a few oat bars since breakfast and even that had been before he set out and before the sun had broken the darkness of the early hours of the morning. He almost threw his bike down on its side and rummaged hastily through his bag for his pasta salad with tuna that he had prepared the night before.

Mina eventually rose slowly and opened the top corner cupboard and pulled out some left-over Tramadol from it. She pushed one out on to the counter and it skittered and bounced erratically. She analysed the pain in her head for a moment then pushed out a second. She flicked on the kettle and waited patiently. Her body was still, but her mind raced on, flicking rapidly through imaginings of Drew, of bombings, of destruction and of Rebecca. Her heart continued to race, each beat reverberating around her chest cavity. She took her shirt off, carefully placing it on the back of one of the wooden breakfast stools and allowed the fresh breeze from the open window cool the sweat on her skin. She breathed deeply and focused on the rumbling of the kettle. She felt sudden urgency and turned back to the corner cupboard. She pulled everything out and spread it on the counter, turning each foiled packet over in turn. She found the one marked with Meprobamate 200 and popped out two tablets that bounced skittishly, coming to rest somewhere near the Tramadol on the counter.

Mina poured out a white instant coffee, and not waiting for it to cool further, took small sips to help her swallow the tablets. She shuddered as the hot liquid burnt her throat and blew desperately across the surface of her drink as she walked outside. She placed her feet carefully with each step, her legs still shaking and her shoulders hunching over as she walked. Mina picked up a blanket and her tobacco tin from the bench out on her porch and continued to walk towards the tree-line on the steep, north side of the valley.

Out this way she found her swing. A neglected front tractor tyre was tied by four ropes into the thick, lower branches of the tree growing out of the valley side. Mina place her mug and tobacco tin on a flat stump and reached to pull the hanging tyre up the incline with her. It eventually met with the ground and she managed to hook it on a thick, broken root that stopped it from swinging away. She rolled herself two cigarettes and downed her now-cool coffee before she took a perch on the swing. As her bum settled into the hole of the tyre and her body relaxed, she felt a warm wave pass over her and the pain in her head dulled appropriately. She lit her cigarette and once confident it would stay that way, she kicked her legs out and shifted the tyre on its long swing out. The ground descended rapidly as she went out over the decline and she held on tightly for the first swing. At the height of the swing she felt the unnerving additional motion of the heavy branch above her head bowing with her momentum. She reached around twenty feet above the ground before gravity took her back the other way. Looking over her shoulder, the ground seemed to rise too fast and a bump at the opposite zenith seemed inevitable, but the trailing blanket she wore over her was the only part to touch the ground and only brushed it gently. As it slowed, she took another smoke on her cigarette and settled into the pendula motion. The Tramadol and Meprobamate coursed into her blood stream and relaxed her into a fine rhythm, with her mind now solely focused on the child-like joy that the long swings through the air offered her.

An hour must have passed them by in silence near the top the barrow. The sky returned to emptiness and no people crossed their path. Intermittent sirens echoed in the distance. Leighton reminded Shannon that they must get to their safe point in time to set up the tent for the night. He offered her the choice to try the house again, that there would be no point destroying the same town twice. It could be the safest place to be, he thought. She replied that she did not want to linger in an opaque memory. They moved on. Leighton's first instinct seemed to be the safest in theory.

They moved north-west until they met the edge of the river, too wide for them to cross, but merely a tributary. It wound a path through the woods and then edged farmland. It was open to the sky, but existed without nearing any settlements for some way. They started to get close to a large town that encapsulated the river and they turned further west to get around it. They feared to enter the town for what they would find. Safety came in solitude right now, even if the skies were currently clear. They kept walking, even while Zeke breastfed at times and was carried temporarily by Shannon. The tent needed to be set up by sunset. That was the goal. It kept them walking with their tiring muscles under the strain of so much extra weight.

Eventually they reached the area that Leighton had picked out from atop the barrows. He looked up to the east and could just see the top of the barrow in the distance. It was the only sign of human intervention in the otherwise covered landscape. To the rest of the horizon they could see, any other signs of human life were covered by trees and wooded growth and hedgerows obscured any nearby roads. They set up the tent half a mile from the stream that turned into the tributary they had followed further down-stream. The silence and the lack of other human interference became shocking, their heavy breathing mixed with the sound of the wind carrying the occasional bird call. The lack of the sound of cars at what should have been rush hour was a daunting realisation. They felt it was best right now to keep a distance from any signs of human life.

Chapter 17

The tyre had stopped its deep swings long before Mina woke up again. When she did so, it was merely rocking gently against the breeze. She looked out to her right, towards the opening of the valley. The clouds were starting to break under the midday sun that beat down above the other side of the valley. The light that hit her was broken up by the fluttering leaves of the tree in which she hung. Her body hung limply, faint pins and needles pinched at her toes and finger tips. She tried to reconnect with her limbs and pull herself up, but the exertion required was too much. Her body felt like it was in the process of re-growing her nervous system before she would be able to control it from her position deep inside her own mind. She could still feel the tramadol in her system, her vision distorting slightly as if viewing the world through a film of slowly undulating oil.

Once she had enough control of her hands, she smoked her other cigarette, which complemented nicely the waning effects of her medication. It burnt out quickly and she eventually lowered herself through the centre of the tyre until she was holding on by just the lower, inner rim. She swung her legs forward and back gently until her feet touched the bank of the valley at which point she let go and flumped into the dirt.

She gripped her hands tightly into fists and stretched out her fingers repeatedly to fight the tingling that remained in the tips. Before she entered her house, she looked out down the valley in the direction of town. It was obscured from her sight, but her look lingered. She debated journeying down there to see if anyone might know more about what had happened, but the thought of the walk or the cycle conflicted with her brain that refused to balance her or focus her vision properly and felt as though it had been stuffed full of cotton wool.

Inside, she got as far as the small couch that lined the back wall of the kitchen diner and she sat heavily then lay down on her side. She curled her knees tightly into her chest, bare feet hanging off the edge in front of her were kept from slipping by hands gripped to her shins. Images of Drew flooded her mind's eye as she remembered him at his worst, high and dishevelled and at his best, caring for Rebecca in her early months of life. These images were replaced by those of Rebecca, her sweet and loving daughter. Her immediate feelings of pride quickly turned to fear for her safety. Mina urged her body to move, but it refused. Immobile, she sobbed into the crook of her arm.

Mina lay hours later in the same position, her tears long dried up and her body drained. She craved sleep again already, to escape the rotation of images and fear that passed through her mind. She needed to escape it. Slowly, she let go of her legs and stretched them out. Twinges of cramp started to flare in her calves, but she couldn't move any faster and let the pain take hold until she could lift herself up on weak, tingling arms. She took down a glass and poured water, taking a sip to sooth her parched throat. Popping out a new cocktail of medication onto the counter top took effort against her shaking hands. She realised that she hadn't eaten since this morning, but the mere thought of eating was too much and her stomach rolled sickeningly. The last packet read 'Flurazepam'. With that she would surely be able to sleep through a dreamless night, even from this early. She took the eight tablets in quick succession. She felt as though she could feel them run down into her stomach, her dry and contracted throat held the memory of them for long after she took a cigarette whilst sat on the kitchen floor.

Her body shut down before her mind could. She leant herself against the corner of two kitchen cupboards listening to the dripping of the tap above her head. Grey edges closed around her vision, feeling like they were pressing dully against the insides of her head. It hurt, but she took solace in the haze as it overwhelmed her completely.

Tariq's sickness lingered after he ate and continued his walk across the fields. At the next rise in the land, he saw a narrow road heading west and cut through the centre of an unplanted field to reach it. He felt happier being back on his bike. Throughout the hour that he ate and walked with his bike on his shoulder, he couldn't stop himself from turning to look back over his shoulder as if he would be able to see the fallout tearing through the air to hunt him down. In reality, he had no idea whether he would know if he was safe or not. He could see on his reddened skin that he was certainly not far enough away from the blast at the time to escape all the ill effects. Maybe he wouldn't know for years to come exactly how badly affected he would be.

He shook those thoughts away, focusing on the rhythm of his legs. He pushed hard until his legs were again burning, which didn't take long. He focused on that dull pain and kept to his pace forcing himself to look only forward. He listened attentively for any sound of vehicles behind him, but all was quiet except for the wind rushing past his ears. He realised he was pushing into the wind as he rode over the top of a shallow rise and it occurred to him that it should be reassuring, but it didn't settle the persistent nervousness that followed him as surely as he felt the fallout would be.

Gradually slowing, in part due to tiredness and in part due to feeling more self-assured, the dark settled around him equally as gradually. Tariq realised that he would need to find somewhere to stop soon. He fancied getting some shelter now that he had ridden so far. Being out in the open was not as appealing as it had been this morning when he was still full of the adrenaline that beginning an adventure brought. He was still well out into the countryside which is exactly where he wanted to be. He didn't like the idea of being caught in a large crowd surrounded by riots and other humans reacting in inhuman ways, trying to cram in as much life as possible before the end came. He hoped that he was wrong, that instead he would see human compassion, but too many years living in a capital city such as London as a journalist had tainted his outlook. The previous protests that inevitably turned violent, the riots and looting that seemed to be growing in regularity, confirmed the way he should feel. It was entirely a nurtured feeling and deep down he wanted to trust humanity.

Ahead he saw a small strip of land separated from a larger field by a low hedgerow. Tariq slowed and saw that it looked like an allotment of sorts, though why it should be out here made no sense to him. The shed looked poorly built and no doubt easy enough to break into so he dismounted and walked over to the iron gate that blocked the larger field from the road. A smaller wooden gate, tucked into the corner allowed him access to the smaller. The shed was padlocked, but it was not heavy. Tariq pulled out one of his bike tools and simply unscrewed the rusting staple from the shed wall. The walls were mostly lined with old, rusty tools, those that were new amongst them were shorter or smaller than the older counterparts and Tariq supposed a farmer must have given this patch to a child or their children to tend. The idea warmed Tariq as he dusted out the floor of the shelter just enough to slump down and take a drink. His legs were tired beyond anything he had felt before, his mind was too tired to reprocess any of what had happened today and those thoughts lingered out of reach like the fading memories of a dream in the minutes after waking.

He laid out his light sleeping bag and a thought dawned on him. At first it came with feelings of pride. He was right. At the very least there were some people out there that were right and he put his faith in those people to guide the last few weeks of his actions. After a small time, however, the pride waned and anger and disappointment rose. He could have saved others. He had no idea what the death toll would be for sure, but maybe, just maybe, if he had got that article out there, some would have escaped the country or spread out into the countryside and lowered the death toll. The last thing that stayed with him in the moments before sleep was a dash of concern at the sickness that he felt in his stomach.

Darkness set in and the couple and their son took refuge in the tent. Shannon and Leighton ate a little of their army supply food, protein and vitamins compressed into something like a toothpaste tube. It gave more sustenance than satisfaction, but it would keep them going till they could set up and start catching fish or game as was the plan. After an hour of darkness, the noise began. Rumbling started en masse, seemingly from all directions, turning into distant explosions.

Most of the precise noises must have been at least two miles away, but still shook the trees and startled them away from the edges of sleep. They lay in the tent with Zeke in between them to keep him away from any of the cool condensation that was formed on the inside of the tent wall. They had a four-person tent that split into two rooms and separated from a central area leading to the opening flap. The opposite room held their jackets bags and tools. The room they set up as the sleep room was simply laid with a thick roll up sleeping bag atop a blanket. Leighton slept the side nearest the edge so that Shannon and Zeke were nearer the centre of the tent.

Zeke always loved coming into bed with his parents and in the tent, it was no different. He felt the warmth of his parents' bodies next to him and was comforted, falling asleep quickly. It was said that white noise was reminiscent of the sounds of the womb. In this case it was the sound of jet engines that provided an audio backdrop for his ease into sleep.

Shannon was more than adept at sleeping still with Zeke able to hug onto her in the night. Leighton, however was a restless sleeper at the best of times and struggled with knowing that if he rolled over the wrong way he could crush his own tiny son. He lay rigidly on his back staring at the dark roof of the tent. He tried to calm his thoughts, focusing on the sounds around them. With open ears, he tried to determine every scratch and scrape of the creatures, desperately listening for anything to indicate danger heading towards them. Even though the most obvious dangers were from the skies, it was the possibility of the footsteps of men that worried him most. That's what he listened for with fear.

Before he was fully asleep, Zeke awoke, throwing his legs and arms against the ground. Shannon seamlessly awoke and rolled him towards her to allow him to take hold, instantly receiving a soothed response. Shannon fell asleep again almost instantly, the sound of Zeke's cheeks sucking in milk was soothing and finally led Leighton to his own sleep.

Strive

Chapter 18 - Day 1

Tariq awoke to the sight of dust motes dancing through thin beams of light entering the shed from the gaps in its construction. The air was thick with them and perhaps it was the sight alone that caused Tariq to cough and hack wildly for a few moments before pushing the door wide open and stepping – squinting – into the light.

It was bright, but he could only see a dull yellow circle blurred behind the clouds low to the horizon. "Well, at least I know which direction not to travel," he said to no-one. As he took in his surroundings of flat fields lined by hedgerows and his eyes adjusted to the light of day, he realised that whichever direction he faced, the same haze resided. It was like fog, but had a certain dirty quality to it that distorted the image of the horizon. It was thicker to the south and that concerned him.

He packed away his things quickly and was wearing his bag and supplies ready to go as he walked back out, eating a dense granola bar that he had saved for this very occasion. There was something about the landscape and the fog that urged him to get away from it as quickly as he could, but as far as he knew he had been sleeping in it all night and a few minutes to get his bearings was probably much more valuable to him in the moment. He pulled from his jacket's pocket - that also contained his recorder - a small scrap of paper. It had on it a list of towns in the order that he should follow them to attempt to meet up with AH. Unfortunately, it had been written with starting from home in mind and the first few names on the list would be too far south and west for him go searching for by them by road signs. He placed the paper back in the pocket and pulled out the recorder. "Day one," he said. He thought for a moment for what to say next. For once in his life, he had no further words.

He looked down at the last bite of the snack bar and imagined the brown dust settling on it and wrapped it up, returning it to a pocket along with the paper of directions. Hopefully when he came back to it later he would forget the image and eat it anyway. He had to dust off the handlebars and seat before he pushed his bike across the long grass to the road. Tariq took another glance toward the ill-looking, dust stricken sun before he started away in the opposite direction.

The sun shone through the leaves and cast mottled shadows on the side of the tent. Leighton and Shannon felt unslept, but at least in having a young baby they weren't unused to the feeling. Leighton crawled out of the tent and stretched deeply in the cool low sun. The axe in his hand cleanly reflected the light back along the arc of its blade and a thick plastic canteen draped its tubing around his forearm. Shannon joined him, placing her hand against his bare back to let him know she was there. The night wasn't too cool and they were easily warm enough with the body heat of all three of them in a double sleeping bag.

Shannon was wearing one of Leighton's thick shirts that she had borrowed to sleep in and the hem hung halfway down her thigh as she shook the blood into her legs. She watched Leighton trudge onwards through the brown earth under the broad-leaved trees that covered their tent and eventually out into the field that met it at its edge. Once the drop of the land took him out of sight she crawled back into the tent to see to Zeke.

The walk to the stream was around half a kilometre and trying to get used to the new environment, Leighton stopped regularly to get his bearings, making sure to keep the route back to the tent obvious. That was clear from a half-broken branch that bobbed listlessly with the wind. At the top of a low rise between the camp and the water, he stopped to take his small telescope from one of his deep pockets. He caught sight of the edge of a town in the distance, he could tell even at that distance that it would be as decimated as his home town now was. He folded the telescope away quickly and thrust it back into his pocket before the macabre urge to keep looking overwhelmed him. A chill wind pricked his skin and he shuddered before continuing.

Shannon and Zeke both drank well upon Leighton's return. He realised that he should have taken a rucksack and all the bottles the first time as he saw that half of what he had collected had already been off. A lesson for his imminent second journey. Shannon oversaw rationing and did so carefully for their breakfast meal.

The rations they had would last a week, so long as the temptation of overeating was kept at bay, they would certainly have to get used to the feeling of hunger. Trips to a nearby stream were to become a regular excursion for Leighton. It was very close to a spring that he took it from and it was as clear and clean, perhaps more so, than their tap water at home. Both adults were numb, barely speaking to each other and certainly not about anything that may conjure up any more harrowing imagery than they were already battling. They both knew each other felt the same and both fought it themselves. Energy was conserved whenever and wherever possible, the only excursions were that of Leighton for water and a short walk to the edge of the treeline by Shannon and Zeke. It was too soon to have a plan when they couldn't speak more than a few words to each other without welling up or shedding tears.

Mina awoke with a terrible migraine firing off in the side of her head. She pushed herself away from the kitchen cabinet and an equally sudden pain in her neck joined it as the weight of her head pulled down suddenly. She had slept with her chin on her chest as the back of her head was held aloft by the cupboard doors. Rolling on to her side she clasped the side of her head and tried to stretch her neck against the crick which caused her to gasp for a breath. She stretched her legs straight, her ankle rubbing against the wooden floor, and managed to fight off a cramp in her calf before it managed to manifest fully. "Bastard," she called out into the air.

A few moments of rolling around trying to get the various pains through her body under control, she realised that she was going to have to get up. The order of the day was to be coffee, painkillers and cigarettes. The electric kettle stood out against the thick hardwood counter tops that fitted the style of the building, but she counted herself lucky to see that it still held enough water and she turned it on. She fumbled around the kitchen wildly, catching herself from falling several times and having to offer up a blind flurry of hands to stop a cascade of mugs from reaching the hard-tiled floor. Eventually, the kitchen gave up its bounty and she left a fragmented trail of coffee on her way to the porch outside.

Leaving the porch with the dark ringed coffee mug and fresh cigarette butts in the ashtray, she felt clearer and the smells of her garden drew her down to check on progress. The sun kept the heat of the coffee inside her and she walked slowly down the middle of the garden, occasionally brushing her hands against plants and smelling their effect on her finger tips. She bent down to check the leaves of one of the potato plants and decided before she fully rose again, that lying down in the long grass would be much more beneficial than the rising headache that would have afflicted her had she done so.

When she did eventually stand up, the sun had moved significantly across the sky. She felt the need to get herself moving again and spent time slowly weeding through the patches of earth, pulling the broad vegetable leaves aside as she recreated space between each of the plants that she wanted. By the mid-afternoon, she took to going over the grass with her hand-push lawn mower. Twenty minutes into it a whisper of a thought came to her mind. Drew.

She brushed it off as she turned herself and the mower around, but only made it halfway across the strip before the whisper returned. This time it carried more force and the images and memory of the day before came flooding through every part of her conscious mind. She let herself down to the ground, her head coming to rest in a deep covering of cut grass. Her inner voice screamed and the vision of the inside of her eyelids was peppered with bright pinpricks of light.

She lay still for the best part of an hour before she returned to the house, barely having even a curtesy brush down of her clothes that were clung to by dry clumps of grass. Her clothes were left in the hallway before she ventured – with tablets and a glass of water in hand – up to her carpeted bedroom. As tired as her mind was, it was still proving to be unbearably full of noise and she needed her escape. She needed sleep and she wasn't going to make the same mistake as last night for the benefit of just a few moments between her and her bed. The darkness enveloped her again and a reprieving silence overwhelmed her thoughts.

Chapter 19

After riding west for an hour - quickly at first, but slowing as he realised his stomach couldn't stand up to his usual pace – he came across a sign towards one of the place names on the list. This meant that he must have drifted south a fair way, but at least he had joined on the right path a third of the way down the list. Coming from the other direction meant that he was diverted off towards the next town before he reached the town itself. This pleased Tariq as it made it feel like he was ahead and able to mentally cross the names off quicker and quicker as he wound along tight roads into deeper countryside.

Tariq rarely looked far beyond the stretch of road just ahead and the direction signs at any interchanges. He kept a steady pace, fighting down the feeling of sickness that surged whenever his pace did and as time went on he had to slow more and more to do so. At each point, he stopped and had his breath back, he filled in the gaps in his recorder's timeline piece by piece. By the time he had just two names on his list above the street address, he felt decidedly light headed. He knew he was close and moving slowly was far better than stopping, especially as only a small percentage of what had been a three-hour journey so far remained ahead.

He was lucky that the street address read 72, Main Road, a continuation of the road he was already travelling. He slowed gradually, peering over fences and around trees to catch sight of any numbers on the doors he passed. Eventually the number came into sight. white paint plastered roughly onto the green bin outside. A short and mostly overgrown path led up to a burnt orange coloured door, chipped of paint in several places.

Tariq pushed his bike over to the pavement and had to heave slightly to pull it up with him. His knock at the door immediately caused a stirring within and he could hear the sliding of curtains on rails above him before it finally opened. Tariq almost sagged with relief to see AH stood there, whose face lit up with a broad and welcoming smile.

"Well, I guess seeing as though privacy has now been granted to us in an excessive amount, I may as well introduce us properly. I am Anton and this is my girlfriend Jennifer's house."

"Nice to meet you, Anton. You know I'm Tariq." He reached out his hand and Anton took it. Tariq looked away for a moment. "Did-," he stuttered, coughing. "Is Jennifer here?"

Anton gave him a look as though he understood the tentativeness with which he had asked the question, then smiled. "Yes, she is upstairs. She isn't ready to meet anyone new yet. Being here has- let's say it has been hard on us all."

"Agreed, Anton. There will be no pressure from me, if she needs time," Tariq said timidly. "What do you have left by way of amenities? Any power, water?"

"We have pretty much nothing except for cold running water. The electricity ran until yesterday morning, but unfortunately that has gone. If you want a wash and a drink, you can use the downstairs bathroom to freshen up. I will get you a glass of water. You look beaten up, mate."

"I feel it. I haven't been so well since I left the city." Tariq hacked a thick mucus filled cough into his hand and grimaced as he swallowed its output out of politeness.

"As bad as you look, I am happy to see you. We honestly didn't think you would join us. I thought you would be too cynical to take heed and actually choose as difficult a path as you did. Well done, Tariq." Tariq could feel his legs quivering and nearly lost his balance. "Take a seat, dude. One water coming up."

Tariq followed Anton's proffered direction into the sitting room, dropping his bag in the hall as he went, and quickly sunk into the deep leather sofa. The room spun in his vision in a way reminding him of the extreme drunkenness during his first year in London. His stomach raged in a similarly reminiscent way. Anton returned with a glass of water and Tariq reached out a shaking hand to collect it. He sipped the water slowly, Anton standing over him with a concerned look contorting his face.

"So, tell me," Anton started with an almost childlike excitement touching his voice. "What did you see? Did you see *the* bomb?" It was obvious which bomb he meant.

It took Tariq a moment to collect together the separating scraps of his memory. "I saw *the* bomb. I was close enough that I am sure I would have been blinded if I had not been facing the other way when it went off. How did you know that had happened?"

Anton took a seat opposite. "We saw. The whole country could have seen that flash and with that looming cloud it was immediately distinguishable to anyone who has ever watched a disaster movie," Anton said, grinning.

Tariq felt his stomach clench hard and he fought back the urge to vomit. He went to ask where that bathroom was, but as he opened his mouth, sick the colour of pond water ejected itself onto the wooden floor. Anton darted up. "Let's get you to a bathroom, come on," Anton said. He put his arms under Tariq's shoulders and lifted him easily to his feet.

The perfume smell in the washroom was overpowering and even before Anton could let Tariq drop to his knees in front of the bowl, he vomited again, this time carefully enough to avoid getting any more on the floor.

Tariq was slowly sliding his back down the sofa. He had become more stable over the last few hours, but it only lasted for as long as his stillness did. From upstairs he could hear conversation that rose and fell in volume. After some time of it, the rhythmical thump of feet descending stairs reached his ears.

Anton sat on the opposite sofa again, purposefully close to the armrest furthest from Tariq. He looked concernedly at him, though Tariq only moved his eyes to meet his glance. "Tariq, how are you doing?"

Tariq grunted and managed a weak thumbs-up. "It will pass. This is just the worst bit."

"I hope that is the case," Anton replied. "Relax there, I've put some water for you on the side table."

"How is the town- the people in it, I mean?" Tariq murmured.

"Ah, yes. I should probably fill you in. Well, most people that live here commute into London, or up to Cambridge, so probably about half the town was out when *it* hit yesterday. So far, the only person to enter the town is you, and by what Jennifer was telling me, I think it has given people some hope that you are here. -But anyway, before you arrived there was a mass exodus, other than the one at eight A.M. of course. Yesterday, I suppose. I think half to two-thirds of those remaining filled their cars and left. The garage down the road had prices as high as two pounds a litre. Talk about capitalising on fear, though I have no idea what he thought that money would achieve in the long run. We heard more planes during the night and I think it is a matter of time until this town is hit.

"I am digressing. The people left throughout the course of the day, a surge at about twelve. By my calculations, that left most people with an hour of crying, an hour of panic, and an hour to pack all the bags they had and load the cars. Most of the people drove north, some east and a handful of men that drove south-west towards the smoke. They must have had wives in the city, or else had no will to survive any longer here, because anyone who has not been living in a cave – which might have been the case for those few – knows that radiation can kill in horrific ways. I reckon the sensible ones are those heading north." Anton nodded his head fervently as he spoke. "I think if you could get as far as Sheffield, you might just be out of range of anything coming in the future.

"Ah, we shall see, won't we?" Anton said to himself. "We are still looking to move north. We are holding out for one more night. I hope only one more." Anton glanced at the stairs through the open living room door frame and lowered his voice. "Jennifer still hasn't gathered herself enough to achieve anything." He took another glance. "Her parents both worked near Canary Wharf. I can't give her any hope. I saw the mushroom cloud. I've read up on Hiroshima. I just need to give her a bit of time before I clamp down on what we *need* to do."

Tariq sat almost motionless, nodding slowly and as infrequently as possible while Anton rambled on.

"You asked about the people here to start with. I would say there is about ten percent of our population remaining. It is mostly families with young children or individuals that work from home most days. From when I took a walk through, I spoke to about five people and everyone is fear stricken. There is a lot of praying and crying that can be heard if you step outside at night. I am just working on Jennifer's wellbeing so we can follow up on our plan. I am trying to remain as pragmatic as possible so we can both be safe."

Jennifer called from upstairs and Anton slowly got up to leave. "Rest well, my friend and let us see what tomorrow brings us."

All Tariq's weak voice could do was murmur appreciatively. As Anton left, Tariq pulled his legs onto the sofa and closed his eyes.

Chapter 20 - Day 2

Mina still felt sluggish as she dragged her feet down the stairs and into the kitchen. She flicked the kettle on as she pulled down a mug from the cupboard just above and filled it with instant coffee and milk. She stood there, leaning against the counter and barely able to focus on the world around her.

After a few minutes, she looked at the kettle which had clicked itself off while she wasn't paying attention. She poured the water into the mug and started to stir, but she noticed that it wasn't mixing well and looked pale. It was then that she realised that the water was not steaming. It hadn't boiled. She clicked the kettle on again and realised this time that the light didn't switch on. She checked the plug, which looked fine, and then walked over to try the light switch. She rocked it back and forth to no effect. She thought to herself that it must be a fuse and so went over to the basement door.

Opening the door and instinctively pulling the light cord, reminded her again that the electricity was off and she would need something to see down there. The first thing in the kitchen she could find to use was a lighter and a scented candle, so she made do with carrying it carefully to the far corner of the basement where the fuse box was mounted on the wall. None of the tiny levers were in the down position and so nothing had blown in the night. She turned them all off and then on again expecting the basement light to fire up when she did so. Nothing happened. She went back upstairs to check the kitchen light and the kettle, but neither worked so she blew the candle out and tried the gas hobs on her oven. Luckily, the match lit it on her first attempt and she was relieved to find at least one form of power remaining. She tipped the remnants of water from the kettle into the pot and sat down at one of her kitchen chairs while she waited for it to boil.

Once Mina had a hot coffee in her hands she looked over at the radio. It was potentially her only connection with the world from here and the last two days had been such a write-off that the thought of turning it on had never crossed her mind. She reached for the volume switch to turn it on and a pang of anxiety washed over her. She didn't know if she was yet ready to hear about what – if anything – had happened. She closed her eyes and took a breath before rotating the dial clockwise.

She was met with nothing. She reminded herself about the electricity again and fished through one of the kitchen drawers for a fresh pack of batteries. Once two of them were loaded into the back of the radio, she took it and sat outside on the porch, extending the aerial as far as it would go and placing it on the edge of the table. She needed to gear herself up again so rolled and took the first drag of a cigarette before turning the volume dial on again.

She listened to the expected static for a few moments, taking another drag of her cigarette and sip of her coffee. Slowly and methodically she went through the frequency range of the FM radio. She rolled the scanner back and forth a couple of times when a deeper static roared out, thinking she might be in range. It was only some interference. She went through the range again and then again in medium wave and found nothing. Mina noticed that she was relieved and resided to finishing her routine as if nothing else was happening in the world. The same way she did every other morning.

Tariq had had a broken night of sleep, but at a total of twelve hours of it, he had done the best he could. The time he had slept had been full of stress dreams leaving him feeling emotionally drained. The view of *the* bomb replayed many times, some with him looking out from its base and almost every waking was induced by the wash of heat from the blast. His stomach was already feeling more stable than it had been over the last twenty-four hours. A thought that he was over the worst of whatever he was suffering from – he assumed it was exhaustion – came to him and he clung to it. The remnant of the illness was a headache, which he mentally accounted for as dehydration from throwing up for the better part of the previous day's afternoon and evening. He was helped with that quickly as Anton came to deliver a caffeinated sports drink and pain killers. He told Tariq that he looked a little bit less shit, before he carried a tray of supplies out the room and up the stairs.

Tariq finally felt clear enough to take stock of the room he was in. The two deep leather sofas lined up to a television in the corner by the window. A blocked-up fireplace to the right still held a mantle displaying a few photographs and cheap statuettes, but very little else decorated the room. The pastel green had a recollection of a hospital hallway and added to the sparse and clinical set up of the room. Anton returned to find Tariq pressing the sides of his head with his palms. Tariq quickly set his hands down and turned to face him. Anton seemed to be running on habit as he sat down, picking the remote from the groove in the seat most central to the television screen and aiming it futilely at the screen. At the lack of response from the machine, he threw the remote hard, leaving the screen wobbling from the hit. Tariq watched him silently from the corner of his eye while he waited for his friend to cool down from his moment of rage.

Tariq tried to break the coldness emanating from the man opposite him. "So, what does 6015 stand for, Anton?" he asked.

"It means nothing. It's important for it to mean nothing. The things I talk about on my blog are dangerous to the 'system' and if the men of the system found out who I was then I would be silenced. I am sure of it." Anton replied.

"What about the 'A.H.' then, not your initials?"

"Not mine. I haven't been exactly honest about my name, even now. The initials are based on Anton Haus, a fleet admiral for the Austro-Hungarian empire during World War One. He was a hero and a shrewd strategist. Above all that, though, I kind of liked the name Anton and picked him as my handle pretty much arbitrarily."

Tariq coughed into his hand and an intense feeling of compression in his skull occurred concurrently, causing him to wince. "What's your real name then?" he asked.

"Now is not the right time for that. When you are either taking your last breath – which I hope isn't coming too soon – or when you fully have my trust – which isn't yet – I will tell you." Tariq involuntarily drew his eyebrows at Anton and released the look as soon as he noticed himself do it. Tariq heard gentle footsteps down the stairs and Anton responded visibly. "Right, me and Jennifer need to see someone down the street, so we will be back later. Continue to rest and you'll soon be at your best." Tariq thought he saw an anguished look on Anton's face, but couldn't be sure. He had resumed his horizontal position on the couch by the time the front door closed and slept again soon after.

The water eventually came somewhere near boiling, still only a few bubbles at the bottom of the pan and fewer still that took the journey to the surface. Shannon bounced Zeke on her lap while she watched the calm water hovering in a pan held by Leighton over a small fire.

"I don't think that it's going to get any hotter. It's been like this for ages. I reckon we just stick the tea bags in it now. It'll brew," Leighton said after a while.

"You are just overthinking tea. Just stick it in a cup," Shannon urged.

"You're forgetting that we only have 10 teabags, we have to enjoy them before they run out. There will be nothing worse after all this effort than to have a crap tea."

"-But at your rate we must add more cold water before that all evaporates. Long before it actually boils."

"All right, all right. Let's do it!" Leighton lift a hand up in concession. He threw in two teabags and watched while the sinuous dark tendrils reached out and faded into the darkening colour of the water. Shannon also watched, mesmerised at something so simple as tea brewing.

Leighton poured it out into a flask that Shannon held out. They sat facing each other, Shannon sitting with Zeke perched on one of her legs and Leighton holding the flask in front of his crossed legs. The tea tasted good to Shannon as she drunk it while Leighton still found it burning hot on his tongue. The wind picked up and blew the fire's flames past Shannon's arm that lay closest to the fire and furthest from Zeke. Leighton calmly watched it, feeling the coolness of the sheltered air around him.

They all felt the calmness of it all. The stresses of their old life seemed to lift from both of their shoulders as they passed the tea back and forth. A relaxing feeling washed over them. For now, it was just one fight that lay out in front of them. None of the possibilities for the future and none of the anxieties seemed to exist in that moment. Their foresight now existed at the point their bag of supplies would run out. Complex lives lived plugged into computers, following the stresses of eight billion lives through world-wide news and world-wide wars were all resolved into a single problem. Their lives had gone from being a game of almost endless permutations to that of betting on a flip of a coin. Live or die.

Chapter 21

The house still sounded empty when Tariq awoke. The pains in his body had shifted further from his stomach and further into his head. He felt stronger, but tremendously thirsty and was able to pick himself up in search of a drink. The kitchen was small and battered with wear on the cheap counters and floor. Tariq ran the tap to find that the last amenity had failed, but the fridge still hosted bottled water, cool from its containment, but not as cold as it should have been on his parched throat. He found a local newspaper on one side and he flicked though it quickly, finding no headlines that warranted reading further and as he flipped it shut, he realised that it was written just over a week ago. He thought to himself that this was probably now an archaic publication. The last run of a print that's name would be forever forgotten.

The sound of rattling keys caught Tariq's attention and he looked up from his seat at the kitchen table, through the hallway to the front door. The orange of the door seemed darker, compared to the yellow light that came through the small rectangle of frosted glass. It opened to a group of unfamiliar faces and bodies, wrapped up with bandanas, hoods and gloves covering most of the bare skin with the eyes of some covered by workman's goggles. Tariq's heart dropped as he raised his hands slowly from the table. He couldn't make out Anton's body in the crowd of people around the door.

An unfamiliar voice came from the front of the crowd. It held a monotonous tone, simply stating facts. "You are stricken with an unknown illness. We have decided that it would be best if you left the town right away. Those of us that are left here are forced to be cautious and aggressive in order to ensure the continuing lives of ourselves and our families. I'm sure you understand, given recent events. You have five minutes. You can take what you brought with you."

By the time the man was finished, Tariq had lowered both his hands and his jaw and remained dumbstruck for at least a minute while his brain struggled to comprehend what was coming at him.

"I can see that you are in shock," the man said. "As I said, we are very concerned for our own welfare – there are still kids here – and we won't hesitate to drag you out of town if you don't start moving RIGHT NOW!" The man yelled the last words abruptly and it was enough to shake Tariq to action. He stood up and headed straight for his bag in the living room. He carried the litre bottle of water with him as he went. The living room window showed even more goggled eyes and covered faces – some even in swimming goggles – watching his every move intently. Tariq's thoughts whirled around unceasingly as he hurriedly loaded his bag onto his back.

He walked into the hallway to see a path had been cleared for him to pass through, his bike was clear in the middle of the road. No-one wanted to get too close unless as a last resort. He stepped out to see the voice of the group standing closest to the door.

"Where are Anton and Jennifer?" Tariq asked curiously.

The reply came, "Who?"

Tariq sighed with frustration. "The people who were in this house this morning."

"Oh. They are being quarantined for the next forty-eight hours as a precaution."

"I can assure you now that they and I will be fine," Tariq started. "My sickness has already passed. I was clearly only suffering with exhaustion – and now – simply dehydration. Why don't we just sit this through?"

"It's 'Tariq' isn't it?" Tariq nodded to the man's question. "Tariq, most of us saw the cloud and debris left by the bomb and some of us even saw the flash that it gave off. It was clearly set off to kill as many as possible. We know you were closer to the blast than us and none of us know whether the blast held chemical or biological contaminants to spread and infect across the country. We see it as a perfect opportunity to carry the death further than a typical nuclear explosion would be able to. Those close enough to be infected, but far enough not to die, would flee away from ground zero." The man held Tariq's gaze so that it felt as if it was boring into him.

"You are all being unreasonable." Tariq averted his eyes and shook his head.

"Right now, we are being reasonable. Don't test our reason's resilience." The man pointed towards Tariq's bike. "You get to choose how you leave. Make a good choice."

The seriousness of the man's eyes finally wore Tariq down and he turned and walked past the other men lining his leaving parade. He brushed off the saddle of his bike and looked around. There were probably fifty or so people in the street around him. Seeing a clear path to safety brazened him and he tried to regard the eyes of each person. "I have studied much literature and science in my time and when you do that you start to forget. You start to forget that the majority of the population of this country and many others is not anywhere near those standards. You start to feel like humans are more than just animals clamouring for survival. It is only in moments like this, that you realise that that isn't true. Enjoy your survival. I wish I could see how long each one of you will last with all the eyes of your neighbours bearing down on you. Fuck you all and fuck your town. In fact, I think this country might just deserve what is happening to it." Tariq, lips pursed, held his middle finger up and scanned the crowd with it. Nothing left to lose. He pushed off and cycled straight out, trying to look relaxed, but pulled forward by a knot of urgency in his chest.

Chapter 22 - Day 3

In the kitchen of Leighton's family farm, the old couple sat fixated as they were perched at the breakfast bar watching the news on a small television. A kettle boiled water ready for a morning cup of tea. Life hadn't changed much for them since the attacks, and neither much had the news. They had just a few channels that were broadcast from outside the UK, they had tried to call their provider, but all they got was an automated message about the high volumes of calls. The only other thing they had as an indication that something may have been awry was the lack of communication from their son. They would usually get at least a text message every few days along with a phone call from Shannon to make sure there was nothing that they would need.

World news channels had yet to catch up with what had happened elsewhere across their country and without internet connection, they only saw and heard that which was broadcast. It mostly focused on the peace deals that were swinging back and forth in the Middle East. A de facto truce being declared and by all accounts soon to be finalised into a long-lasting peace deal put the mind of the restless at ease, to all those that could receive its message, at least.

Leighton's father, Phil, took the controller and start to flick through the few news channels available, looking for a story that had yet to be heard at least a few times already. The parliament channel had been down for nearly three whole days and instead broadcast the same as the world news channel next to it. One of the foreign news channels showed a crowd, German and Russian flags intermingled, waved both ferociously and joyously above the people's heads.

The narrator spoke in English. "...the large-scale aerial attacks are now nearly half-way though the seven-day campaign with military and economic centres now silenced completely. Members of the Russio-Germanic alliance have fled onto the streets already in celebration at the subduction of one of the greatest enemies to world pea-"

The channel suddenly came up static, shortly after being replaced with a simple screen stating *[The channel is no longer in service, you may have to reconfigure your set top box.]* Kerry, looked at her husband, concerned, urging him to quickly change the channel over to see if any more was being said elsewhere. The national news was displaying the same message. The only channel left was still replaying the same messages and interviews from earlier proceedings in the Middle East.

They talked together as the rotation on screen continued all throughout the day, an eye always on the screen expecting a breaking news story to flash up at any moment. Nothing obvious was coming to mind as to what the story they caught a glimpse of pertained to. The assumption they came to was that it was related to the main story.

The television continued persistently on its loop. Many hours later, Phil and Kerry fell asleep on the sofa waiting for the breaking news that they believed would eventually come.

With the Sun at its zenith, Mina sat smoking the last of her tobacco. She was already mulling over the thought of heading into town, though she had pushed it to the back of her mind every time it had tried to bubble up. She still didn't know what to do about Drew and she knew her phone line was still down from picking up the handset a few times a day. Most important to her was whether his mad babblings were true. It was only now, three days on, that she could even entertain the idea that it was a hoax. With him, anything was possible, but with him and the phone lines cutting out at the same time it was just enough coincidence to cause worry and not quite enough to lead to certainty.

Mina thought about Grace down in the town and the corners of her mouth raised a little at it. It was going to be worth going down there, because otherwise the whole town may as well have been Schrodinger's cat. The thought continued that perhaps she was the cat and everyone else was just purposely not observing her. No one ever bothered to wander up into her little valley – a fact she enjoyed thoroughly – which meant to her as an observer of the world, the town was the one with multiple possible permutations.

The scenario that most frequently replayed across her mind was that of a town that remained standing, and within it all its inhabitants. She would open the gate on the other side of the bridge and be confused that everyone greeted her in the normal way, with large grins and friendly nods of the head. She would confide only in Grace what she had been going through inside her own head since the phone call. She would be embarrassed and she would have to try hard to make sure no-one else found out about what she would from then on call her 'episode'. Her phone line would be fixed along with all the problems that she currently expected.

Mina tried to keep a containment on how often she thought about the other option. It regularly horrified her that the scenario described by Drew and the possible causal rather than coincidental death of her telephone line could be the reality. She might have got lucky to survive, out away from the town and city lights that would have attracted bombs in the night. She hadn't had a chance to see any dark hour since the call due to her coping methods. The image she held of a town – flattened – was sometimes met with the image of survivors alongside her, ready to work together to get to safety. Other times she only saw ghosts of the people she knew. She would talk to them as if real and consult with them about why they hadn't passed on. The final manifestation was the grimmest. She would be met with just death, empty bodies lining the streets and hidden under rubble. She would always push this thought away. She tried to focus her mind on a favourable outcome, though always with difficulty. She knew she had to find out.

Mina's feet dragged as she started on her way down the gravel path. She managed fifteen minutes of the walk before she deviated onto the grass and eventually into the trees. After another twenty minutes, she stepped back out of the tree line onto the path running back towards her house. She wasn't ready to solidify the condition of the town in her mind and instead sat back down on her porch running over the multitude of possibilities in her mind once more.

Tariq had holed himself up in an abandoned petrol station a few miles west of the town from which he had been so rudely ousted. At about a mile from the town's boundary, he had to work harder and harder to push forward. The fears he had had after watching the looming cloud three days ago finally caught up with him. He hit a puncture. It was slow enough that he couldn't recall where it may have happened once he had noticed the lag in the front wheel. He had spent the best part of an hour trying to work out where it was on the inner tube, but drenched in sweat on the bend of a country road he eventually came up at a loss. There was no mark on the outer tyre to indicate the damage and frustration and dehydration caused him to move on by foot.

The garage had clearly been abandoned in a rush and Tariq had found a rear entrance unlocked and ajar when he arrived. He was in a bad mood after leaving his bike on the side of the road about two miles away and he had to drag himself about trying to secure the place as much as possible. He had quickly found another set of keys for all the doors and had managed to lock down all the outer shutters quite easily. He felt fortunate that they were pulled down by hand rather than electric motor.

As the darkness had set in, he found that a generator had kicked in to power some dim emergency lighting around the building and under the forecourt and so he had then had to spend a long time walking around using a cast-off piece of two by four to smash all the bulbs in. He certainly didn't want to make himself too obvious a target to anyone, be they on the ground or in the sky. He was perfectly happy with a light source that he could turn off at will and the garage was well stocked with half-priced, ten pounds forty-nine, faux-metal torches and the appropriate 'D' sized batteries to last him some time.

He slept on a tattered couch in a staff room with no windows. It gave him enough of a feeling of security to sleep well, even throughout the headache that still burned at his temples.

The pitch darkness panicked him when he first awoke, but once he managed to find the torch that he held fallen asleep clutching and in the middle of the night allowed to roll just out of arms reach across the floor, he had regained his bearings. He spent the rest of the day taking stock of the garage's shop, restocking the powered down freezers for the food that he felt would be able to last longer in the slightly cool environment it offered. He was able to eat well and recorded his notes and read the last papers that were issued up to this part of the country, all now at least three days out of date.

As the evening drew in, Tariq built himself a cot by turning the sofa around so that it was almost closed in by the wall and its own back. He did leave a small gap so that in the event of hearing someone or something, he could slide into the gap with his sleeping bag over him and hopefully in the darkness he would be overlooked. He didn't think it would work, but in a room without windows, it subdued his paranoia just enough.

Tariq heard whistles and explosions gradually reach a crescendo nearby and a sick fascination overtook him. He stepped outside the fire escape and wedged it open with a fire extinguisher, constantly checking the set of keys in his pocket as he moved around. Scanning the sky, he started to see movement that blocked his sight of stars. The cloud-like mass appeared almost overhead as the horizon in all directions lit up with temporary flashes that popped like fireworks in brightness and frequency. His heart sank and a morbid feeling overtook him that that night may be his last.

He picked out the most expensive liqueur he could find, and collected a pack of cigarillos, a lighter and some cheap, giveaway binoculars and went out around the side of the building until he found a ladder that would take him up onto the flat roof. If the bombs were to land where he was, he may as well enjoy the final moments and embrace them head on rather than have them find him curled up, hiding in a small gap between a sofa and a wall.

Feet planted just below him on the top of the forecourt, he sat on the edge of the building's roof. He lit his cigar after taking a swig from the bottle that left a warm trace down his throat and into this stomach. It settled his nerves and he started to feel ready to witness his last sights of the world. Facing east he saw flashes amongst the orange glow of fire over the horizon. As his cigarillo burnt down, those sights got closer and closer until he realised that they must be now close enough that the fire and destruction must be over the town he had been forced to leave the day before.

Even though he couldn't see the town itself, he could make out a lot of the intervening distance through the binoculars which handily blocked out the direct lights of the fires and allowed him to feel confirmed that the town was in fact burning. He lifted his bottle in the air and muttered a few words to himself about karma. He laughed, said, "Fuck you," out loud towards the flames and laughed again, still holding his bottle high.

Tariq, still sniggering to himself, carefully stubbed out the last embers of his first cigarillo and lit another. The sniggering turned to a hysterical laugh and eventually to tears before returning to a hysterical laugh. '*I'm going to fly,*' he thought as he wondered how much flammable liquid was in the ground and pipes below him. Even flicking open the flame on the lighter might be enough, but it hadn't been so far. He knew that if anything was going to fall through a few thousand meters of air before hitting the garage, pure luck or divine intervention would be the only things that could save him. As his laughing died down he couldn't even work out if he cared or not. The faint tingling of drunkenness could be felt in his lips and fingertips and he lay back against the roof.

Tariq stared up at the sky and waited, perpetually tensing his muscles in reaction to the loud bangs and pops that came from all directions, bracing himself for whatever darkness was to come over him after an inferno was triggered around him. Ten minutes passed and Tariq looked out to his left, where the flashing lights and amber glows continued to raze. All the sparks of light were now in that direction. Nothing remained to the east or west, but for the orange ebbing glow of fire. As he watched out he saw the same thing replicating, moving its way meticulously further north. A relief washed over him. He might just have had that luck. He might just see another dawn.

Chapter 23 - Day 4

Tariq opened his eyes slowly into the darkness. Disorientated, he grasped around where he lay for his torch and eventually found it. As he stood up he felt his sense of balance struggle to keep him upright and he kept himself so with one hand on the back of his sofa turned cot bed. He reached the door which lead into the main shop front. It was day time, judging from the ambient glow that came through the window shutters and around the edges of the main door.

He felt horribly dehydrated and reached for a sugary drink from one of the warm open fridges. It tasted foul, but he needed the sugar. As he gulped down the drink, he felt the insides of his head press in. He hacked. "I am shit-noosed hungover. Damn it," he told the room.

He picked up a few papers from last week and headed through the pitch-black room that was his home to the fire escape and pushed it open to let in the bright morning sunlight. He winced and spent the next few minutes slowly peeling his eyes apart as they grew accustomed to the intensity. Eventually, he felt comfortable enough to take up a seat on a low curb with his back against the building, still within a couple of steps of the emergency door, *'well, in case of emergency,'* he thought.

The papers were only ever going to be a distraction. Full of last week's headlines from a past world and articles he had already read, they provided little stimulation. Perhaps too much stimulation would not have been what he really wanted in his slightly fragile state. He read through three different publications and most of the time he was reading the same headlines by different journalists. He always found that interesting though, how two different people could carve the same truth into different stories and wrestle the events around to match either their own set prejudices or the agenda that the paper was trying to align with.

With the papers thrown down to one side and his head leant back against the wall, the memories of last night started to creep back into the forefront of Tariq's thoughts. At first, he remembered the spectacle of it all. The lights flashing across the sky, the amber glow illuminating the trees and the thin tendrils rising out of the mass of flames dancing up, appearing to lick at the low, overcast clouds above. His thoughts roamed further back to his impression at the time of the town just over the trees. He visualised the flames encapsulating buildings that stood alone with rubble from nearby explosions leaning up against their foundations. Flames flicking through smashed windows. He visualised the house that he had resided in during his short time there. With the bay windows smashed out into the front garden, Tariq's image positioned him from the sick-bed sofa that he spent almost twenty-fours restricted to. In his mind's eye, he watched his false memory play over and over, progressing little by little as he imagined himself amid it all. He saw the flames flowing outwards from that living room catching fervour as they reached the new source of oxygen outside the building.

Memory and imagination continued to entwine themselves as the masked faces he saw looking in at him – while he was still sick and in shock – and the flames blew out into their faces. The faces never reeled from the heat, though he imagined their fabric masks burning and melting away, carried away by the heat rushing over the jagged shards of glass that remained. He carried the wild imaginings along until he was on the outside looking back in. He imagined the town's ring leader staring back at him from the doorway of Anton's house and he imagined the satisfaction of kicking the man back into the burning building. As he imagined this, his real memory of arriving at the house overlapped and as the man fell backwards, engulfed in flames, Anton stood behind with his broad welcoming smile splitting his face, his skin peeling from the heat that surrounded him.

Tariq shook himself free of the thoughts and focussed on the bends of a tree branch in front of him. He concentrated all his attention on the ridges and valleys that the bark created along its aged growth. He needed to be free of his mind. He needed distraction before the true realisation that Anton, who had put him up when he most needed it, was dead. Tariq's heart sank with his head. He wrapped his arms around it to try and fight off the emotion. "It's too much. It's too much," Tariq mumbled into his knees. He tried to fight off welling tears, not through fear of showing weakness – with no-one around for miles – but to fight off the reality. If he cried, then he knew it was real. "It's too much. Too fucking much," he bellowed out.

Chapter 24

Mina almost turned home again at the mere sight of the village as it now stood. It stood nowhere near as high as it had done just a few days ago. Mina fought her instincts in order to stay rooted to the spot. She was as eager to run as she was unable to move. Her head spun as she tried to take in the new view, as alien as it was. She felt as though she had walked the wrong way and ended up at a new village at the end of a valley that wasn't hers. To her left, the sight was still familiar down the winding road away from village and it grounded her. The road was pitted and potholed more than it used to be, but the lights didn't line it and it avoided the fall of bombs by that alone. She did not truly believe she would have this sight before her when she left, a sceptical part of her mind wouldn't allow the images to truly form in her mind's eye and even looking at it now, she lacked the ability to accept the image as real.

She edged forward, she could feel her ears trying to turn to every sound. Someone must still be here. The people she knew must still be alive, whether they had holed up in basements or fled in the night. She realised the knowledge that they were safe was merely hope. The hope welled up in her and urged her forward, step by reluctant step.

She trod delicately to allow her to listen out in all directions, but only the wind rushing past her ears came back so she had to carefully angle her head to avoid it. It was loud in comparison to the silence that filled the air, although it could barely be considered a breeze. The buildings were sprawled out over their footsteps as if pressed down by a giant foot that crushed the spine of the building as it came down. Further on, more and more rubble had been flung into the road. Her vision played tricks on her, blurring lines together and creating a faint haze in front of her eyes. In the distance, she found it difficult to determine where the square had once stood clear.

A noise rode the rubble and reached Mina's ears on the wind. As soon as it was noticed, Mina wondered how she hadn't heard it already. It was the distinct noise of pain and it rooted her to the spot suddenly. She almost lost the sound to that of her blood rushing and pounding through her ears, but when she refocused on it again she could tell it was close ahead. She turned her head slowly to pinpoint its origin as she took deliberate steps forward, the sound filled her with anguish and made her muscles tighten along with its oscillating volume. Shards of a red plastic door lay sprawled out from the skeleton of a doorway like blood spotted sick from an open mouth and she honed in. Once she was sure of the direction, she walked with more conviction, though still tentatively roaming her eyes around for any signs of life or danger.

Facing the doorway, Mina stopped again. The pain-filled sound ebbed and flowed. Mina, scared, scoured her mind for a sound that matched it in her memory, but nothing came. Images swept her mind's eye of animals slowly facing death, rummaging through decimated cupboards for food or finding a new home in the remains that humans had once again left free for habitation. The view inside was so different from what she could imagine that it took her almost a minute for it to compute. Her brain felt as though shaken and rearranged like a dog's beloved rope toy.

A croak, indeterminable, then, "Mina". With that single recognisable word, the haze of dark colours resolved itself into the image of what she was seeing. Grace.

She knew that under the mountains of rubble lining the streets were countless bodies bearing faces that she would have once recognised – and maybe still would have – but she had been drawn down and found herself a solitary living person. A solitary living person in need of help, but a person who had just had that help stumble through the archway with broken hinges.

"Mina, please help," Grace croaked and coughed, attempting to lift herself onto her elbows, but unable to twist the right way to manage it.

Mina snapped back to life. She was the help. She was possibly the only person that could get her friend what she needed. "Grace," Mina said dryly through her contracted throat. She intended to say so much more, but nothing audible would form on her lips.

"I need to get free, you have to help."

Mina, now adjusted to the darkness from the rough covering of rubble that covered the area, could now see that Grace had one leg covered by the remnants of a heavy oak book case that poked out from under the parts of ceiling, wood and brick that must have come down at the same time. "I'm here, Grace, don't worry," she said, swallowing the lump in her throat. Mina rushed to one knee to see if she could lift it up herself, but her fingers and back were the only thing to succumb to the motion and she let go quickly to straighten her spine. "It's not moving like this, let me think. You need water. Let me see what I can find that will help." Mina stroked Grace's hair to soothe herself as much as her friend.

Grace's voice burned her with intensity, "Don't leave now, Mina. Wait."

"I will not be able to free you if I don't go. I promise above anything else left in this forsaken world that I will return. I just need something to lever this off you and you can slide back. I will be quick, just a few moments."

"Mina, I am so glad you found me, I thought I was going to die here." Tears started to roll down the sides of her face, "I was so sure I would die, Mina." Mina's cheek also felt a tear streak down it.

"Well you are not now. Just stay here a moment." Mina stepped over some of the debris towards the doorway, then turned back to Grace. "Sorry." She made sure not to touch anything on the way out through a fear that a small knock would bring down the remnants of the building.

Mina stood tall and scanned the buildings on the other side of the road. She just needed anything long and strong enough to lift the weight that lay atop Grace. She noticed the glint of some metal and jogged straight across to it. The handle of some gardening tool lay out into the path, predominantly covered in a mortared brick wall that had come down on top of it and the rest covered in the brown dust that seemed to cover everything else in view. She grabbed it with both hands and the shovel slid out easily enough to surprise her and almost send her falling backwards.

Behind her, the sounds of her friend's pain and crying took another rise. "It hurts so much, Mina, please still be there." The words followed by an agonised scream. Clearly the shock of seeing another person, giving her hope was already wearing off now that she was out of sight.

Mina called out words of reassurance as she lugged the heavy shovel back to Grace's home. She continued shushing and murmuring soft words while she moved some debris from the back of the bookcase, before wedging the pointed end of the shovel as far underneath the edge of the book case as she could and pushing forward with all her weight. Mina's heart jumped when she saw it move. Grace let out a blood curdling scream. Mina tried to ignore the same noise that seemed to be coming from inside her own skull as she adjusted her grip to move the case further.

"Go NOW, Grace!"

"I can't, my leg is broken, I can't move it at all."

"No games, Grace, it will hurt a hell of a lot more if I drop this, I can't hold it up while you decide. Use your arms and shuffle backwards. It is now or it gets worse!"

"Don't shout, please, Mina. Give me a moment."

"Grace," Mina said, now red faced with the strain. "Move NOW. GO. GO. GO. Come on!" Mina only looked down as far as the bottom of the spade and the relief of seeing Grace's trouser leg moving backwards was completely overwhelmed by the effort of keeping the bookcase raised against arms that were starting to shake. "Nearly there. Quick."

"Almost got it."

The spade started to push back against Mina and the bookcase started to slowly lower back down. Grace had to twist with another anguished cry to get her foot free. As soon as there was a gap between foot and book case, Mina hurriedly dropped the spade down to the ground clutching at the biceps and shoulders on each of her arms.

A moment later, she looked down at Grace's leg. It was bad. She thought quickly and covered it with her own jacket.

"Grace, I somehow need to get you back to my house so you can get painkillers, water and food in that order. Can you think enough to tell me where there might be a cart or a wheel barrow or anything that I might be able to take you on." Grace lay on her side clutching at her thigh through the jacket. She was taking heavy breaths and barely looked awake in her eyes. "Grace," Mina prompted.

"I'm thinking."

"Forgive me."

"Three doors down, Mr Jennings has a small box trailer for his car. He keeps it in his garden."

"Thank you, let us both hope that we are lucky enough for it to still be standing."

Chapter 25

"You know, this isn't anywhere near as bad as I thought it would be," Shannon said.

Leighton regarded the comment. "The camping experience?"

"The lack of people."

Leighton dwelled on the words a moment before sniggering. "-And you kept trying to convince me that you were an extrovert!"

"Okay, I concede," Shannon started. "Having just you and Zeke and no-one else to drop their bullshit on you is pretty nice."

"I've been trying to tell you for ages that this is the case. You don't believe me until you decide that a post-apocalyptic wasteland is kind of your bag."

"Don't say that!"

"Don't say what?" Leighton asked, hands spread out wide.

"Post-apocalyptic wasteland. It reminds me of those awful 80's movies you like to watch. Makes it sound like we are the only ones and that we will always be struggling just to get by. The word 'wasteland' makes it sound so endless, so desolate, so – I don't know – miserable."

"I think that's what it is supposed to be like, though. Don't you think that is the exciting bit?"

"It's not exciting. Not for me. I grew up with struggle and wastelands. It's not fun, it's tiring."

"In that case, I'm sorry. Right," Leighton clapped his hands. "We are going to make this fun! We got everything to survive right now, so let's play a game. Are you ready?"

Shannon looked across at Leighton a smile slowly crossing her lips. "Okay," she said.

"The game is…" Leighton drummed his hands on his thighs. "-we all go…" The tapping continued as Shannon urged him on with movements of her head. "-get some water!"

"That's not a game," Shannon said crossly.

"Well, if you come with it me, it will be more fun for me!" Leighton gave Shannon a thumb up on both hands.

"No."

"Fun."

"Fine. We'll all go and watch you carry water back."

"Yes," Leighton said triumphantly, jumping to his feet and offering his hand for Shannon to take. She took and pulled herself to her feet.

"Shouldn't we put the fire out?"

"No. That's why we build a fire pit."

They walked for a few steps and the dry pine needles crunched loudly under their feet. After a few paces Leighton turned around to go and douse the fire. Shannon stood still and watched on with pleasure.

Mina returned to Grace after leaving a wheel barrow that she had found in the garden four doors down. Their luck had returned her something, if not what they had hoped, it would still do the job. The fence between the gardens had been completely flattened which had allowed her to see it sat in plain sight and she had also managed to find a bundle of thick nylon garden rope to secure Grace's leg for the journey back.

It felt like it had taken somewhere near an hour to get Grace to the wheelbarrow just outside the door. Grace seemed to have been close to passing out and took a few moments to rouse, saying things about needing to sleep deeply. Then after a single attempt to stand that ended badly and Mina seeing her friend's leg wobble as if completely void of bone or structure, she had moved as much debris as possible from the path and shuffled Grace inch by inch backwards. Grace roared as Mina had lifted her in to the barrow with some support from Grace's good leg and arms on the side. The wheelbarrow had almost tipped several times, but they had managed it.

Once in place, Mina used the rope to tie Grace's right leg to one of the wheelbarrow's arms that were long enough that mina could still grip the handle competently without her hand being displaced by the limp foot that seemed to hang lifelessly in the air. Mina was proud of herself for thinking of it, perhaps she had seen it in a movie or perhaps some deep awareness, thick with common sense that so often alluded her, had brought the obviousness of keeping it elevated and unable to move.

Grace settled down significantly once she was strapped in place by her leg and gripping tightly to the metal sides. Her head hung awkwardly just over the top of the far end, but at least she had to just keep her head raised a little and let Mina do the hard work for the way back.

Tariq thought again about the ringleader of Anton's town, another almost certainly dead. If it wasn't for his ill actions, he would have surely died with him and Anton in the violent display. Buildings being torn apart from above, fires raging through any building left standing; spreading into the woods around. He looked up for the tell of smoke throughout the treeline, suddenly panicked by that thought, but he saw nothing but a smouldering, thin line of grey coming up from behind the treeline. Nothing to warrant fear, though he did turn to look at the garage petrol pumps with a wary glance. He could barely control his thoughts as they raced between different scenarios, most induced by panic or attached to his feelings of confusion. Anton wasn't a saint, though. He had taken Tariq in when ill, but that was convenient enough for him. When push came to shove, it was he who had sold him out to the lion's den. A pit of fury swelled in Tariq's stomach, but it subdued quickly with the thought that the anger was being expressed towards something no longer living. Some*one* no longer living. This idea didn't stop Tariq for cursing himself for a trust mislaid. He damned himself. If there was anyone left on this earth, he wouldn't trust them. This was survival and there was no room for trust.

He contemplated another bottle of whatever he could find behind the counter, but he subdued it. He needed a clear-headed plan right now, rather than his preferred option of another drink. Nothing would beat a way out of this poor outlook than a well-executed strategy. Tariq stepped back into the dark, grabbed a pen and paper and an 'A – Z' street map and went back out onto the step of his fire escape to see what he – alone – could come up with.

Chapter 26 - Day 5

It was raining, so Leighton spent the time prone with his head at the tent opening, desperately trying to calibrate the air rifle's sights. He was shooting at a knot on the trunk of a tree around thirty meters away. He deemed that would probably be the range at which he could hit a stationary rabbit – and at the very least – stop it from running away and with a little luck kill it outright. It was a simple, break-barrel, spring-loaded air rifle given to him by his dad. It was a simple enough design that he felt it would last a suitable amount of time and didn't need refills of carbon dioxide cartridges or constant maintenance. Its simplicity was its grace and in this instance reliability was far more important than range or power.

The day passed slowly with a knot of frustration growing in his stomach and an annoyed wife, concerned that he didn't seem to be getting it right first time. Shannon was tending to their son who was getting increasingly restless without the usual music and toys that he could interact with. It was well into the afternoon when he was finally happy with both the iron sights and optic sights. He decided, however, that it was too wet to take it out and try it out for real.

Mina sat under the porch, watching the rain pour down in great sheets that spat up sporadically off the edge of the decking onto her cold feet. Her mind ran dully with exhaustion. It was hard to know what was going on in her own head. Memories of yesterday's trip to the village broke through the haze intermittently. Her muscles ached and with the lack of food and sleep in twenty-eight hours she had to regularly stretch and move to stop her calves from cramping up. The sound of heavy raindrops bouncing off the roof above her was suddenly broken by a wild scream. It took Mina a few seconds to realise that it wasn't an echo in her mind and got up quickly, but shakily from her seat.

She moved quickly through the kitchen picking up a glass of water as she went. As she walked into the living room, she flinched. She still wasn't used to the site of her friend in such a mess. Grace lay on a wide and deep sofa, her head at the far end from the door lifted with a few pillows. She was pushing herself up on her elbows and a grimace clung unwaveringly to her face. Mina spotted the problem instantly as she looked back and by placing a hand under Grace's calf and the other under her foot, she smoothly and swiftly lowered it onto a more stable part of the arm rest. Grace exhaled deeply and let herself back down against the pillows. She gasped as if she had just stopped running before whispering gratitude while taking the proffered glass of water roughly from Mina's hands.

While Grace sipped awkwardly from the glass with her chin against her chest, Mina checked her friend's leg. It was currently tied tightly by bandage in between two pieces of wood that extended past the end of Grace's foot. It was not perfect, it allowed a little bit of movement – mainly in the limp foot – so it hurt to move it. Mina, restacked the pillows and cushions that lay underneath the angle between Grace's hip and where the foot was placed on the armrest. She still hadn't managed to arrange them in a way that would stop Grace's leg from shifting little by little towards the end of the arm and after a few hours cause her to strain and try to move it to a more stable place, inevitably requiring Mina's help to do so.

So far, Mina's only continual level of care was to dose Grace up with as many painkillers and sleeping tablets of various types that she felt would be reasonable enough to not destroy her liver. Every time Grace was woken – usually because of her leg shifting uncomfortably – Mina would give her something, which worked out to around every two hours. She switched between two sets of three different types which seemed in her head, to complement each other suitably. She had tried a few times to see where the problem was and work out if she could do a better job of helping it heal. It was so swollen around the area and black and thick from bruising, she couldn't tell for sure. Even when she had put ice on the wound, the skin never loosened enough to give an indication of how bad it was on the inside.

Mina shivered, she was so exhausted that she felt a wave of cold run through her. She lay down with her arm under a left-over pillow which she placed her head on. She stared at Grace adjusting her arms and torso uncomfortably as the tablets started to dissolve in her stomach. Another shiver came over just the moment before sleep caught her.

The weather front slowly pushed over their location, bringing with it unceasing torrential rain and thick clouds that barely let the day appear. The couple were both disappointed that Leighton could not use his freshly calibrated gun to catch some worthwhile food.

Shannon gently sloshed the small remains of water in the bottle they had through the air. "Looks like we will need to leave the tent at some point." She took half a sip and passed the rest to Leighton.

He made a face as he drank the last of it. "Backwashed and all. I suppose complaining is not required here. Well neither you nor Zeke are going out, right?"

"No way," Shannon replied. "You know rain will mess up my hair, it has shrunk enough as it is. Better sooner than later for you though, right?" She jabbed Leighton's ribs with her fingers. Leighton returned the gesture, but Shannon quickly defended herself. "No fighting, now. You'll hit Zeke."

Leighton looked down to see Zeke sat on his bum, intently picking at his toes and sporadically making a lunge to try and see what they tasted like. "Alright then, I'll play nice. You look after him."

"What else am I going to do? Can't exactly go to the shops or visit a cafe," Shannon said.

"What I wouldn't give for a coffee." Leighton sighed loudly as he rolled back the tent flap that opened into the middle of the tent and tied them back. It was raining hard enough that droplets were bouncing and dispersing off the leaves and roof of the tent. Most of their camp site was surrounded by broad-leaved deciduous trees that stuck out in a clearing of tall evergreens foresting most of the hill that they were temporarily calling home. The presence of these trees to shelter their tent made sense after seeing how thick with pine needles the rest of the forest floor was.

"This is going to suck. Can't I just leave the bottle outside?" Leighton asked, wiping his wet hand down on the coat lying beside him.

"Oh, come on, it's not that far! Zeke is thirsty." Shannon smiled to herself.

"He still breastfeeds! You can't use that on me." Leighton sighed. "I could do with the exercise," he said in an unenthused, monotone voice.

Mina startled as she woke up. Grace was somehow sat up on the sofa opposite, calling her name over and over. "Grace, what are you doing?" she asked.

"Oh my, I am so glad you are awake. You had me scared," Grace replied.

Mina tried to expel her panic with a long-accentuated breath. "Are you OK? How did you get upright? Do you need anything? How long have I been asleep?" Mina saw that the pillows that once supported Grace's leg were now strewn across the room in her direction. She must have slept deeply for once to have not been roused. Grace perched on the edge of the sofa, with locked arms taking most of her weight as if she had started to push herself up and then froze at that point.

Grace replied, "It took me around an hour to get from lying to seated, you were very deeply asleep. I tried throwing all the pillows at you, but to no avail. What I need is a hug, painkillers and to use your bathroom. Perhaps best in reverse order. I feel vibrant right now, at least from the knees up. I think I am all slept-out."

Mina perched herself on Grace's sofa and put her arm around her and Grace reciprocated firmly. "Ok," Mina started, "Let us get you to the bathroom. Wait here just a moment."

Mina wrestled an office chair from the upstairs study down the narrow staircase of the house. Grace seemed to be full of a strength that Mina wasn't expecting and so managed to move herself from the sofa to the wheeled chair with ease. It took a few minutes to get Grace through the kitchen to the downstairs bathroom on the other side. While Grace rolled herself slowly forward with her good leg, Mina held the bad leg aloft with one hand grasped firmly underneath the wooden splint and the other left free to open doors and move objects out of their way. Mina could see the pain on Grace's face as they went, but she didn't let out any noise to match. She was a hardy woman in the moment. Mina supposed you didn't see how strong someone is until they absolutely needed to be.

Once positioned onto the heavy porcelain, Mina placed her bad leg onto the office chair and left with the door slightly ajar. "Just shout if you need help. I may as well put on some food for us. Do you feel up for eating?"

"I know I should," Grace replied. "Not sure if I can, though. I feel very sick."

Mina started putting together something simple and varied, hoping to accommodate whatever taste her friend would have. Bread with optional jam, some potatoes onto boil and a mixed green salad from the basement store. She placed the bread and the salad on the table along with some salad dressings. She could have the potatoes if and when she felt up for it. The toilet flushed and Mina trotted to the door. Tapping the door lightly she called through, "Are you ready, honey?"

The reply came and Mina worked with Grace to return her to the office chair. The tight space made it difficult, but Grace looked fresher and more limber than she had before. "Those painkillers do a number on you, right?" Grace said.

Mina laughed as she released the weight of her friend back to the chair. "So are you ready for breakfast. Or whatever meal we are supposed to eat now. I have no idea what the time is."

"Most definitely," replied Grace.

Chapter 27

By Leighton's return, he was soaked through. The waterproof overcoat only held back so much and the water had seeped through to his t-shirt in places. "I'm not going out again. Not a chance." He took his shoes off as he came through the front flap of the tent, leaving them neatly by the entrance. The rain jacket, jeans and the t-shirt were all laid out over the bags, spread as much as possible to dry.

Shannon watched and laughed to herself. "Look, Zeke, your daddy is grumpy. Watch out!" She let the compartment flaps off their ties and they closed together loosely.

"Oi! Not fair at all," Leighton said. He pulled his socks off and threw them into the other compartment and pushing the flaps aside he pulled himself onto Shannon, nestling his wet hair into her neck and face. Shannon tried to fight him off and fell back away onto the sleeping bag.

"No touching. Prison rules apply here," she called out, trying not to laugh and feebly attempting to push him back.

Zeke rolled backwards too in replication of his mum and laughed. "Don't side with him, I'm the one that tends to you twenty-four hours a day, all he does is carry you places," Shannon joked.

Leighton finally resided and pulled himself onto his knees, still pinning Shannon's legs together. "Just think how I feel. I had to spend twenty minutes in this tropical storm." Zeke crawled forward and pulled himself onto Shannon's chest. "Look at his smile. At least he finds me funny."

"Someone has to," Shannon said. Zeke made a timely short laugh and Leighton looked at him sceptically.

"You're training him to laugh at me, right?"

"Maybe," Shannon said playfully.

"I'm going to get those cooking pots out and leave them to collect rainwater. I abstain from any more outings until this rain subsides. At least for as long as I can."

Grace sat at the kitchen table with her leg up on the opposite chair. Mina sat to one side, splitting concerned looks between Grace and her friend's plate. It wasn't emptying as quickly as Mina had hoped.

"Okay, Mina. Do you know what actually happened, then?" Grace asked.

Mina chewed her mouthful, shaking her head. "No, not really. There isn't any communication. The phone line and all the electricity is currently out. I wouldn't have picked up much anyway given that I don't own a TV nor anything that can connect to the internet, even if we did have any of that. The last thing I heard was on the radio before communications cut out. They mentioned a dirty bomb somewhere, perhaps Russia. There was an emergency conference of some kind with the Prime Minister, it sounded like it was one of ours, traced right back to the British."

Grace interrupted, "I heard that part too. That was the day before the village-, the village became the way it is now. Do you know any more now?"

"Well, I suppose. If your village got hit the day after that, you may know more than me. I had a conversation with Drew later in the day."

"Your Drew, why?" Grace asked.

"He wanted to express his love and sorrows to me," Mina said. "That wasn't really the crux of the call. He kept blabbering on about these planes he could see and the city burning to the south of him. At first, I thought he was high, I was about to hang up and call his doctor to go check on him. At one point, it sounded like he was about to commit suicide."

"Ouch, that's bad," Grace interrupted.

Mina continued on in rhythm, "It sounded like it, but kept on adamantly about these planes coming in, he even made me go look outside. My house faces west so I just saw the overcast sky." Mina puffed her cheeks out. "When I got back, the line was dead. It wouldn't even get a dial tone. After that I passed out with shock. In my mind, then, he died, either by his own hand or his apparitions were real." She paused for a moment. "I then just tried to carry on like normal as much as possible. Ignore the thoughts. I guess it took a little while to realise how disconnected I was. I just couldn't build myself up to go into town, scared of what I might find. Though I am glad I eventually did, to find you."

"Aw, I literally owe you my life, you are a legend!" Grace said.

Mina averted her eyes coyly. "I wish I could have made it down sooner, how long had you been there like that?"

"I can't say for sure," Grace started. "It was very hazy. It happened at night, it must have been near the morning as I had gotten up for a glass of water. I think I remember seeing two more nights after I was trapped, but I was in and out of consciousness for most of the time."

"After all the phone lines went out, did you have a day before the attack on the village?" Mina asked.

"Yes, there was one I think. I shut the shop mid-morning because the delivery never happened and no-one had internet or phone lines. There was a point where a load of us met on the green, probably just before lunch when everyone had gone to try to work out if it was just them affected and we talked about how we could get help. While we were there a few people had heard on the news that something had happened in London and the south-east. They spoke of an attack on British soil, but we had no evidence to support what we had heard until that night when we heard the planes coming nearby and then later some people from the south came through in their cars. Maybe about twenty cars or so in all. One stopped and spoke with Jaq who had walked outside to greet the commotion, saying that everyone should leave and head north as quickly as possible." Mina nodded her head, intent on every word.

Grace continued, "Most of the people laughed it off as if a prank the next day. I didn't open the shop and a lot of us went to the pub in the day and joked about putting up the black-out curtains. It was early enough when I got back home, but I was drunk and so ate some toast and took myself to bed."

"-And that was the night you got up for water?" Mina asked.

"Yes. As I walked back through with the water, the floor just rocked violently with enough noise to deafen me. I fell and shortly after saw the back of my house just cave in behind me and a piece of debris knocked me out." Mina took a sharp breath in as if feeling every word. "I awoke as you found me, but I couldn't get out. I passed out regularly, but every time I would wake up again, I would still be trapped."

"I tried to come down the day before I did, I could have found you sooner." Mina screwed her eyes up and then breathed out heavily. "If only I had not been such a loser about it."

Grace placed a hand on Mina's shoulder. "Don't worry about the 'when', the fact is you got me out of there."

Mina looked up. "Fine. You need to finish your breakfast then. For me."

Grace agreed and picked up the piece of bread and took a bite. Mina sighed with frustration, though couldn't work out what difference it would have made by a day. She was more worried about what would have happened if she had stalled for another day after. She shook off the thought and took her plate into the kitchen.

"I get the impression that we are probably not even meant to be alive. We are certainly not meant to *know* anything."

"That's dark. We *are* alive. What are we going to do? Where do you think we can go?"

Mina thought deeply for a moment, giving Grace a chance to take another bite of food. "I need to get to Leeds. Somehow. I need to find out what has happened to Rebecca." Grace's face dropped and she shied her head away from meeting Mina's eyes. "It would be nice if you would come. But first, you need to heal. We won't get anywhere with you scooting around on an office chair."

"Oh, Mina. You need to go."

"I have not seen her in over seven months already, Grace. I see you every day and you have carried me through some tough times. I can see you through yours. I want to see you well. Rebecca is with family who love her almost as much as I do. She will be safe. If I leave you, you won't have anyone. I am dragging you across the country for as long as I can. I don't want to hear any more of it until you can walk straight."

"Then let me promise to heal as quickly as I can, and cover my pain as well as I can to get on the road sooner," Grace said.

Mina scowled at her. "I will allow that, but only because if you can cover it, it can't hurt that much. I still get to control your pain killers. Deal?"

"You could be very cruel, but I trust you."

Chapter 28

Shannon and Leighton kept themselves inside the tent, laid out on the bed. Zeke seemed to love having both his parents giving him attention and he crawled around and babbled to himself, filling the inside of the tent with joy. Leighton lay him on his own chest, faces together and blew exciting new sounds to his son. Zeke tried to replicate the mouthing but ended up just repeating the same syllable with more and more intensity each time.

As they subsided – laughing – Leighton pulled Zeke in close for a hug and rolled over to plant the young boy back onto the sleeping bag in between them. Shannon spoke, "Just my two favourite men, lazing about in bed. When I kept asking you to take days off from everything, I had this in mind. Well, not exactly *this* of course, but this feeling. In the bed, this way. You get it?"

"Yea, I definitely get it. I suppose our current situation brings us perspective. Shows us what is really important," Leighton replied.

"I suppose that for now, the degrees are useless, the savings are probably lost. You're unemployed. Again!" Shannon taunted. "Technically I am still on maternity leave. You've not been to work in four- is it five days now? Anyway, you would have been fired by now, gross misconduct. That makes me the main breadwinner, right?"

"No, I'm in charge. I convinced you to pack these bags, I picked the campsite and I carry the baby!"

Shannon looked at him incredulously. "You carried him for a day or so. Try nine months, you cheeky bastard." Leighton nodded down at Zeke. "No judging, he doesn't understand. Do you Zeke?"

"Oaba," replied Zeke.

Shannon and Leighton looked at each other for a moment. "No," Shannon said. "I am marking down a coincidence, not a reply." Zeke continued to babble to himself. His parents listened and watched.

Tariq had pulled up the corrugated metal shutters to two of the three windows in the shop part of the garage. It would have let in much more light if it hadn't been for the thick dark clouds that filled the entire sky. He had wanted light so he could go through the tools that the garage had and replace his now useless bike-tool. He had found a key to the cabinet they were in on the bunch of keys that he had found on his first day at the garage and picked through all of them. The fake Swiss Army knives looked sturdy enough for a while and he took two with slightly different arrays of parts attached. He then went through the more standard tools and decided that a stubby screwdriver with a variety of heads in the handle could also come in useful at some point.

Tariq stared out through the window. Rain poured down in thick sheets of water, distorting the dark grey image of outside. He resided that today was not going to be the day to start enacting his plan. He figured he wouldn't be trapped this way for too long, but his plan would be far too damaged by sleeping in sodden clothes for the first night. If he was to walk out west and find some survivors he would need to travel as fast and as light as he could and being bogged down in waterproofs or heavy, wet clothes simply wouldn't do. If he had to deal with a downpour later, he would rather do it many miles down the road and would likely take shelter in somewhere like this again then too. Presently, he had a choice. he seemed safe enough right now and the day stuck inside and a day behind his schedule was payment enough to avoid a cold night with wet skin and no shelter should it come to that. The breather had at least offered him a chance to make a thorough plan, an opportunity which may not have been taken if the conditions had been favourable to leave that morning. Tariq thought to himself that it was perhaps an omen that he should give suitable attention to something that he expected to get him across the country.

Leant back against a freezer full of melted ice cream, Tariq allowed the sight of the grey, rain-soaked landscape to fill his vision. He had prepared his bag already and now all he had to do was wait. Wait for the rain to pass and the summer skies to return light and heat to his onward journey towards the sunset. His first thought about food had been to pack his bag full of chocolate. It seemed like the best ratio of calories to space. After a few moments of joy, the idea of a hot body and hot sun on the bag would very quickly turn the entire contents into plastic wrapped fondue. He had cursed himself shortly after that when he stumbled across an aisle of nuts and dried fruit and decided that it would be equally good on the calories while also providing a more sustainable diet, devoid of regular sugar crashes. He tried to fit in enough of a mix that he wouldn't get too bored, but every time he put in some lighter dried mango slices, the urge for longevity of his food stores overtook him and in replacement went in another bag of peanuts. His small cycling bag held a hefty weight. At one point, he considered allowing a little air out of each packet to gain more space, but after lifting the bag with one arm he realised that he would be best off managing on what he already had. He was still going to have to carry a milk bottle of water in each of his hands too.

It was still raining and the skies were darkened enough to feel like dusk, though it was likely too early. Tariq decided he was best off with as long a rest as he could manage. Hoping for a dreamless sleep, he sluggishly dragged himself up and into the encapsulating darkness of the back room.

With the rain relentlessly crashing down on the tent roof, Zeke received the most amount of attention as he had at any point since they had left home. He clearly enjoyed it and interacted with beaming smiles and squeals of joy at his dad's tickling hands.

Shannon thoroughly enjoyed seeing her two boys reconnect. The amount of time that Leighton worked to support them both into the future meant that she had her worries as to how much Zeke would understand his father. She valued his days off.

"This is nice," She said almost dreamily. "-But you struggle to stay still. You enjoy it though, I can tell. When there are no distractions, mobile phones or laptops, you and him are so cute together. I didn't quite think it would take for this-", she gestured her arm around the tent, "-for you to just sit down and spend a day with us playing."

"I know. I am seeing what I was missing out on. I guess I still get caught up in my own world sometimes."

"If things ever return to normal, we are going to have this at least once a week. No excuses!"

"Deal," Leighton agreed. He reached his hand out and Shannon shook it, "I am starting to get the feeling that normal, like we knew it, may never come around again."

"Let's call it 'stable' then. Is that okay?"

"Yes, stable is more suitable. I love you both, you know that," Leighton said.

"We know. You know, Zeke?"

Zeke didn't respond, being as he was too fascinated by his own feet.

Chapter 29 - Day 6

Wet leaves glistened and continued to drop rain to the ground. The skies were clearing, with the thick clouds just draping their foreboding shadow over the horizon. At least for now it had passed and the trees could continue to feast on the leftovers seeping deep into the ground.

To Leighton's bare feet, the ground was cold, but the new sun hit his chest with warmth, making up for its time spent hidden. After leaving Shannon and Zeke with the necessary containers of water, he walked out, axe and air rifle only. He headed deeper into the woods parallel to the main road some miles over to try and test his newly adjusted weapon. He crept with soft feet, the rifle pulled in close to his shoulder so he could quickly aim and shoot at anything he saw that could constitute being a meal for his family.

He saw a grey squirrel at the base of a tree and pulled the sight to his eye, but even with only minimal magnification, the narrowed line of sight removed the creature from his vision. When he lifted the sight from his eye, the squirrel had already scarpered high into the branches above. He looked around the canopy, but the relative weight of the gun aimed at the sky meant he gave up quickly.

Continuing onwards, he saw another. This time he stopped dead in his tracks a little further away, at the edge of his perceived range. Standing, he tracked the crosshair from the ground to the creature, which had started moving in its unpredictable, bounding way. Leighton managed to track it through the sight, moving diagonally away from him. It bounced in and out of the crosshairs. Leighton pulled the trigger. The squirrel continued its run with a little more pace, the hit of the pellet into the ground was indeterminable. He sighed, not even knowing if he was close or not.

He carried on regardless, firing the odd shot at a bird or squirrel, occasionally stopping to check the calibration against a tree. It was always true when he checked, but any pellet fired towards a living creature was going massively wide or high. He doubted himself and was starting to think that he didn't want to be able to hit anything, perhaps it was his own mind pulling his hand away on each shot.

He tried to conjure a killer instinct, picturing himself carrying the spoils of meat back to Shannon and the passion it would re-instil in his wife. He lined up a target and imagined that bird's fall to the ground after his pellet went through its head. He convinced himself it wasn't his imagination. He was the bird and the pellet, the gun and his hand, but before he could take the shot the bird leapt into flight. He had wasted too much time.

The sound of his stomach and a waiver of his hands from hunger caused him to return to the tent. A disenchanted conversation with Shannon ensued and after a morning of walking stealthily through the woods, his parched throat's requirement for hydration quickly broke it.

The afternoon, after having ditched the optic sight for the iron sights, proved equally as futile, not only finding less creatures to attempt to kill, but still not having an indication of getting any closer with his pellets. Before the sun had even started to wane, he returned to sit in grim silence with his wife and child, the unavoidable disappointment emanating outwardly from her. She couldn't help the way she felt about it and Leighton could empathise with her for that.

Mina had to perform a long list of motions for Grace as they tried to get her upstairs. The stairs were narrow and walled on either side and Grace appeared to have suffered serious wastage of her muscles and was left unable to lift her injured leg, hanging as a dead weight to her. They had to move Grace's leg onto the step underneath her before Mina pulled Grace from under the shoulders, lifting her just one step at a time. It involved Mina starting off on the lower side and then climbing around using the bannisters to above Grace on the stairs as they performed the elaborate process.

Eventually they got to the top of the stairs, where Grace waited patiently for Mina's bath to fill. Grace heard the tap being turned off and started trying to shuffle herself backwards towards the bathroom along the hall. After a few slides, Mina came back to her and helped by supporting her injured leg, stopping it from dragging along the floor. They reached the bath and Mina lifted from underneath Grace's armpits while Grace herself used the side of the bath and the heavy sink basin to pick herself up to standing.

Lowering herself into the bath, Grace had to do alone. Mina placed a small wooden board in front of the bath's faucets and guided the wrapped-up leg towards it as Grace slowly slid herself into the water, tight muscled arms gripping firmly to the edges of the bath as she did so. With Grace mostly submerged and settled, Mina placed her friends injured leg on the board to keep it dry for the time being. Mina sweated from the heat of the bath and the exertion of getting Grace into it and settled herself on the lowered toilet seat to get a quick rest while the other woman soaked. She looked concerned at Grace's chin hovering just above the water level and tried to judge her friend's weight distribution to determine the chance of her slipping under. After a few moments of stillness, she rested her mind on the matter.

The room was dim. With only a small frosted window to the outside and no electricity to use the lights, it provided a comforting and safe atmosphere. The pair enjoyed the silence, the heavy breathing left in both sets of lungs by the ordeal gradually faded away and the most was made of the relaxing environment. Both women sat silently, deep in thought.

Grace was the first to fill the silence. "What do you reckon it is going to be like? We've all seen the refugees and migrating people in Syria, Iran and Iraq. Is that now us? I mean – like – the news in other countries is going to look at this as a humanitarian crisis. Well." She paused. "I mean if there are enough of us left to be deemed a crisis. How many other survivors do you think there actually are?"

Mina shrugged her shoulders, as much to hold back a sudden surge of tears than to display her incomprehension. "I think there must be a fair few. Some will be loners. Some in groups. Maybe there will be whole towns or cities that will be left untouched. I for one certainly hope it is the case further north."

"Oh, I know. I'm sorry." Grace glanced over at Mina who continued to sit on the toilet lid with her head down and elbows firmly planted on her thighs. "Your girl is smart, though. I think she has an instinct that will keep her out of trouble."

"Yea," Mina resided. "She's alright. She is currently with someone who doesn't have common sense. It's *that* I am probably more worried about. My sister is an idiot."

"She's probably not the only one there. If they have survived, the chances are that others around them have too. There will be a little society building up that will look to source food, get power on, get those without, sheltered-"

"She's a dick," Mina muttered over the top of Grace's words.

"Anyway," Grace said with a childish giggle. "You're right with that. She is. You should just remember, Mina, that just because you haven't seen many of them, it doesn't mean there aren't kind and caring people in the world. Of course, there's me for one." She looked over at the top of Mina's head with a grin, but without response. "You and me, mate. We will get your daughter, ditch the ones you don't like and build our own society.

"Think about this, what if *all* of the arseholes have been wiped out and all that are left in Britain are the cultured, the sophisticated and the delightfully spiritual kind. We all realise that we are together with a fresh start. We rebuild society from the ground up to be loving and kind and forgiving. Our buildings are even better than before, built with statues telling the story of our glorious future. People write poems that are spray painted into murals and shrines to those that had to pass to give the rest of us a clear future. It will be a dreamlike place devoid of delinquents, defilers and – erm – the dastardly. What a world that would be to raise Rebecca in. You never know, but Leeds could be intact and become the centre of a new transcended breed of human that rises from the ashes of destruction and despair. What do you reckon? You want in? You'll have to be nice to me though, for I will be the one-legged queen of the north."

Grace looked over to see a smile touching Mina's mouth, the rest of her face covered with her wild hair hanging down. Grace grinned as she continued. "You can be my prince if you'd like."

"Alright," Mina said, raising her head with a deeper smile that touched her eyes. "Though, I want the title of princess. I am not the kind of girl to be wearing baggy pantaloons. It will help with the spread of tolerance if the queen looks like a lesbian, right?"

"Right!"

"Rebecca will be our heir, too. We will need someone to continue the society on in the right direction."

"Absolutely! Now your queen could *really* do with her back scrubbed."

"Oh, my word, Grace," Mina yelled up the stairs. Grace lay in clean sheets on the bed, revelling in the feeling of comfort and cleanliness that had evaded her for the past week. She heard the rapid thuds of Mina sprinting up the stairs. "Check this out."

"Oh, no," Grace said. "Not the death book."

"Oh, no 'oh-no'. It tells us in here how to make a proper cast for your leg. It'll be equal to the ones they put on at the hospital!" Mina jumped onto the bed excitedly, rocking Grace who had to clutch at the structure currently enveloping her broken leg. Mina leant the book over in front of her and pointed a rigid forefinger at a set of bullet points within a grey box in the margin. "I have all the shit we need right in this house. Well, apart from the plaster, but that's only as far away as the shed down there." Mina gesticulated towards the window that overlooked the garden.

Grace looked quizzically at Mina and then down at the book to read the text. When she finished, she looked back up at Mina. "You think you will be able to make that?"

"Yea, sure. Why not?"

"You?"

"Yes." Mina mocked a slap towards Grace's cheek, slammed the book shut and bounced up to face Grace with her feet tucked underneath her. "Let me tell you. First, we take off that weird contraption that I put on your leg. It turns out that it sucks. Then, we get a long sports sock that will go up to your knee. Happy so far?"

Grace nodded, maintaining her original puzzled look.

"Good. So, then we take some soft bandage – which I have – and wrap it around your leg, from foot to about halfway up your calf muscle. Okay? Then the key bit is we do a light mix of plaster, dip more bandage into it for a few seconds and then wrap it around the leg so it is over the top of the rest. We keep doing that a while 'til its thick and set hard. Hey presto, you will have yourself a fine leg cast." Mina puffed out a long breath. "-And I could have thought of that before building some bizarre frame around your leg."

"Okay," Grace said tentatively. "I will let you try, you better magic up some proper crutches while you're at it too. Are you ready to become *Doctor* Mina?"

Mina nodded excitedly.

"You want to do it now, don't you?"

"I will go get it all together."

"No, wait. Get it together, but I would rather do it in the morning. I'm shattered."

"Alright then. Do you want me to bring you a book?"

"What'd you recommend, nothing gory though, obviously." Grace nodded down at her leg.

Mina thought for a moment. "Carrie's Waffle House."

Grace looked quizzically at Mina.

"It's like sex, drugs and revolutionaries."

"Alright then. Sounds strange. I guess that's why you own it."

Mina rushed off to get everything she needed, firstly, dropping the book off with Grace so she could read and sleep. Mina laid out everything on the kitchen table which was swept clear. She proceeded to read the small entry in the medical book, visualising every part of the process until she had it memorised and clear in her head. The she went through reading all the packaging on the plaster mix until that was also memorised and adjusted mentally for the slightly thinner mix that she would need. When she was confident she could do it without the instructions, Mina took herself up to her bed. The light was still on, but Grace had fallen asleep on page three. She slipped under the covers next to her, placed the pillow lightly over her own eyes and dreamt heavily of loneliness and failure throughout the night.

Chapter 30 - Day 7

As morning broke and the bird song celebrated a new day of calm, the couple stretched their bare toes on the ferns at their feet. Shannon's heart was heavy, but she held it, lifting Zeke into the sky with ease and coaxing a cute attempt at a laugh from his small lips.

"We need to catch something to eat soon," she spoke, her gaze carefully avoiding eye contact.

"I know. The air rifle is calibrated, I know that it works. I suggest we move closer to the stream today. If we move to the edge of the trees nearest it, we can spend more time fishing and hunting and we can hopefully get some organic protein. I am well and truly sick of these bars."

Shannon blew out her cheeks. "Let's get packing. If we don't get something, then we must try going towards one of the towns to scrape some tinned food together. There must be something that has survived."

Leighton felt a heavy weight of realisation. Thriving wasn't an option for them until they were at least self-sufficient. They had eaten a few berries that bloomed on bushes near their campsite, however a few blackberries and currents were not going to sustain them long term and so far, had only managed to keep their bowels regular against the synthetic food that was making up the rest of their diet.

"A fish would do nicely," he said. "Let's get things together, it's only about quarter of an hour to move to a better spot. It will take longer to pack than to move, but it will save us an hour or two each day and allow us to set up fishing during the day. I don't think we are at so much risk from the skies above now anyway."

They packed up as quickly as they could. Zeke cried the whole time on a blanket to one side as they did so. Shannon kept a wary eye on him and in all directions, dreading that a person or creature would sprout from the woods and take him the moment she pulled together the tent or averted her eyes for more than a second or two at a time.

It didn't take long to reach the edge of the wooded area and running further down the slope the river flowed east. Leighton suggested they move further uphill so that in a short walk they could get a three-hundred-and-sixty-degree view from the top, still reach the river much quicker and maintain cover from the skies. Shannon agreed with the suggestion and quickly fixed the tent while Leighton held Zeke on his lap and unpacked the tools needed to try and fish. Once things were carefully packed into the various pockets of his jacket, he gave Zeke back to his mother and carefully dropped down the slope towards the river with his air rifle in one hand and fishing pole in the other. He heard Shannon sniggering at him as he walked away, cumbersome as his walk was.

Once they were set up again, Shannon temporarily left the camp to pick some berries from nearby bushes and discern the driest branches and twigs from the floor. Having Zeke strapped to her chest in the carrier made for slow work and she only got together enough branches to have one fire and enough berries to give them a boost for two days. As the sun started to lower, she followed the path downhill to catch up with Leighton at the riverside. He was sat cross-legged on the river's bank, his fishing line taut in the current downstream and his air rifle nearby, cocked and ready.

Leighton swung around as she approached, smiled then groaned as he saw his line had caught yet again in reeds at the other side of the river. He carefully put the pole down on the ground, cut the line and stood up to give it sharp tugs until the hook freed from the plants and finally pulled towards him.

Grace gradually came to from a muggy and broken night's sleep to find Mina in the bed next to her. She was on top of the covers with an arm flung loosely over Grace's stomach.

Her leg felt as though it was on fire. Having only had the option of sleeping lying on her back had proved difficult and she couldn't move to satisfy her urges for comfort. Her eyes stung dully with tiredness. Sleeping in the bed with Mina didn't make it any easier as her anxieties kept her body restless. She thought to herself that now was probably the only time Mina had been truly asleep.

"Mina. Mina." Grace gently rolled her friend back and forth, continuing to call her name. Mina stirred a little and turned her back on her. "Mina, it's morning," Grace said with more vigour.

Mina groaned, opening her eyes on the white ceiling. "Stop it. I'm awake," she said finally. Mina stretched her eyelids to take in the light, fighting against their will to close again almost instantly.

"You remember it's arts and crafts day today, right?" Grace said.

"Arts and… Oh! I see what you did there."

"Yay. I had a thought while I was trying to sleep, you know. I have never had a cast before so there will be absolutely no way that I will be able to judge your handiwork, whether it is actually good or not. I am imagining that it will be vastly superior to this clunk of junk."

"Aw, I am glad you have so much faith in me," Mina said.

"You know what I mean, groucho. This has stopped me doing any more – visible – damage to it, so count that as a success." Mina, lifted herself up to sitting, with two large pillows that had been thrown to the ground during the restless night sleep behind her back. "Are you getting up?" Grace asked when Mina stirred.

"No, why?" Mina asked abruptly.

"No, don't worry. It's all good for now." Grace waved a hand to dismiss her unasked question. "So-" Grace paused. "Where are we going to make this cast then?"

"I don't know yet. I have everything together downstairs, but I think it would be easier to bring it all up here than you down there. What were you *going* to ask?"

"I was just going to inquire as to whether such a fine lady as yourself would be venturing to the kitchen for coffee and painkillers." Grace pulled a wide grin with teeth showing and clutched her hands together pleadingly.

"You kill me."

"That's why I said to never mind. I'll go make it if you like."

"Are you taking the piss?"

"Yes." Grace kept holding her exaggerated smile in place and fluttered her eye lids. Mina turned a stern face towards her friend, saw the smile and couldn't help, but to let out a chirp of a laugh that she tried to subdue as quickly as she could.

"Fine. Only because you look cute and I've never seen you *need* help before this week."

"Thank you, thank you." Grace leant over and pecked Mina on the cheek.

Mina said, "That's gross," and dragged herself to the edge of the bed, partly to cover a reddening of her cheeks.

"I'll make it up to you when I am better. I will do all the driving or something. Thank you."

Mina dragged out her words to accentuate her tiredness, "You're welcome."

She stood up, stretching her arms high above her head and twisting her back to the left and then right. As she took her first steps she tensed her thighs and calves, lifting herself onto tip toes before slinging her arms into a night robe hung beside the door.

Once she arrived in the kitchen, she switched the tap on and to her surprise, nothing came out. She tried the hot tap and the same result occurred. "Damn," she said aloud. She had already supposed that other amenities would be lost at some point, but it still came as somewhat of a shock. She buried her head in her hands while she thought of another solution. "Any water," she said to herself. "The stream. Oh, that can wait."

She opened the cool – but not cold – fridge to find an unopened carton of orange juice. Pondering it for a moment, she decided it would have to do and took that and two glasses back upstairs to the bedroom.

"Coffee is off," Mina said sadly.

Grace let out an exaggerated "NO!" with arms outstretched in mock agony and outrage.

"I brought orange juice and your painkillers."

"Well that shall do then, I guess." Grace held a sullen look on her face with her bottom lip pushed out.

"Do you want to know why there is no coffee?" Mina asked as Grace chased down her tablets with a gulp of juice.

"Oh yeah. I guess that might be some useful information. Why is there no coffee, Mina?"

"Well, Grace. We no longer have running water. I guess we used it all up last night."

"Oh, I'm sorry."

"It's not your fault. It was inevitable. Luckily, we live near a pretty clear stream. I am not sure if we can drink it safely, but we will certainly be able to wash in, and most importantly use it for the cast."

"Frustrating?" Shannon asked.

"Slightly. We'll get there."

"Looks like you'd be better off shooting at birds." She had Zeke clutching each of her thumbs, facing outwards from the harness on her front.

"Tried that already today. I haven't hit a thing yet." He paused. "-With either approach. I do know I am getting closer. With the iron sights and me knelt, I saw my pellet chip the branch the bird was on. I only get one shot at any single target. No creatures have trusted my bad shot enough yet to let me try twice at it."

"Well, take a break. I brought us lunch."

"That's the first good news so far!" Leighton said.

Shannon pulled two of their standard army surplus protein bars from her pocket and opened a broad leaf full of berries on the ground.

"It's like those picnics we had when we started dating, right?" Leighton said.

Shannon blushed as she thought about how some of those picnics turned out. "Perhaps. We were doing alright weren't we?"

"Don't say 'were', we *are* doing alright," Leighton reassured her. "I'll have something sorted for dinner tonight. The law of averages indicates that at least one creature will die near me eventually."

"I got some wood together in the tent that looks dry enough to light. I am ready when you are."

Leighton continued, "Good. If I don't catch something today, I'll go down in to the town on the other side of the hill in the morning. I'll see what I can find for us."

"Thank you. I always worry that if we don't eat right, I won't produce enough milk for the little man."

"Shannon, don't think like that. Regardless of anything else I will get something sorted. I'll get proper food, if not today or tonight, tomorrow."

Shannon leant over their picnic and kissed her husband on the lips.

"Thank you," Shannon said again. She knew it would be a knock to his pride to have to go into town to scavenge for food rather than bring her something fresh. *'At least he has enough pride to make the trip for us,'* she thought.

Chapter 31

Tariq had a day of slow walking behind him. He had set off at dawn, walked until noon and after eating, continued onwards until late afternoon when finally, his legs got too tired to continue. He had not slept well. He had lacked proper shelter when he had stopped so he merely rested up in a children's play park. He had found a climbing frame in there with old wooden boards on the side that acted as a windbreaker and kept him sheltered from a cold wind that would have made his night of shivering worse without. It wasn't until he woke up and ventured out that he noticed the 'Keep Out' signs by its gate and play equipment. He supposed that whoever would enforce that sign would no longer be bothered anyway.

Today had started out along a similar thread, however, yesterday had all been down narrow country roads and today he caught himself on a slip road to a dual carriageway. He hadn't intended to take major roads, lest he find people or the wreckage of them. This one was empty as he walked up to a wide road. The lanes felt majestically wide with no cars on them and down the slight incline as it went, his tired legs seemed to carry him effortlessly.

He continued along the clear road, though as he did so, the concrete grew more and more potholed. Further along he started to see sharp scraps of heavy metal and he had to direct his eyes more towards his feet than the horizon ahead. It dawned on him that he would be getting closer to a town. He noticed the position of the sun at its highest point and realised that he had been turned from his targeted route and was heading directly south.

After traversing a large roundabout, the skeleton of tall industrial buildings came into view. The sight of the concrete structure, devoid of windows and walls all the way up the two sides he could see reminded Tariq of the drone pictures from Mosul and Tabriz from the British and American bombs on those cities after Muharid took control of them. It was shocking to see it in front of him in real life and he found himself rooted to the spot between two crater-like potholes in the road. With the trees no longer blocking his view from here, he could see out over most of the industrial estate. A multi-story carpark was collapsed on one corner, the two bottom platforms compressed onto each other. To the far right of the area, a low, two or three-story building with a huge footprint had its roof caved in at the middle. It also looked to have been struck on one end of the building with the outer wall, roof and the second floor splayed into the car park that surrounded it with the gleaming metal of cars underneath that showed in between some of the debris.

Tariq remained planted for five or ten minutes, maybe more. He lost track of time taking in the view. He remembered his recorder and started to describe the sights, the intricacy of the skeletal buildings that once stood as complete sheets of glass and concrete. He could have stood there for an hour or more, he felt like it would make a wonderful painting, with the contrast of light and dark around the deep shadowed pockets displaying the building's innards. He felt something inside of his mind urging him on, though. Tariq looked all around him, the feeling of being watched crept up on him as he scanned the tree-line alongside the road behind him in detail. Eventually he lifted his foot, feeling the swell of blisters pull away from his sock and started on his way a little quicker than he had done before, ignoring the dull ache in the balls of his feet.

Leighton showed Shannon how to pull the fly and hook against the current, letting it out little by little and once she got the hang of it, he took his air rifle towards the woods. He looked out with his telescope, hoping to see an oblivious, stationary animal somewhere. A few times he saw squirrels and he desperately attempted to get close without being seen. He continued for some short time, but each lost opportunity and missed shot brought him closer to despair.

Shannon, meanwhile, let Zeke play on the grass a few feet away from the river and worked the line. He lay down on his back, tired, and played with his feet. Each time Shannon let the line out, the hook got caught in reeds and she had to walk down the river to alleviate the tangles. She made attempts short distances up and down river, each time having to pack and unpack the pole and tackle and carry that and her son to each new spot. As she moved down the river she got more paranoid about Zeke and set him down further and further from the water. Like Leighton, the lack of success quickly ran down her patience and after one last tangle, a show of frustration ended up with a snapped line and another hook lost to the riverbed.

Leighton gave up with his hunting after spending several pellets to no reward and returned to Shannon, who had resided herself to feeding Zeke, her feet swishing around in the river. She lied that she couldn't do much as Zeke had been needy and Leighton accepted the lie gracefully, sitting next to her and splashing his face with the cool water. They gathered everything together and returned to their campsite. The meal in a tube was even more disappointing than normal after their hours of effort ended fruitlessly.

Mina picked up a large bucket and went down to the side of the house where the small stream ran down alongside the path to town. This close to the source in the hills behind her house, the water seemed crystal clear. Mina dipped the bowl in until it was full and inspected it closely through the transparent plastic. It was a little murky with a white precipitate, assumedly from chalk in the hills, but Mina was happy enough with it for the purpose for which it was intended. She walked straight through the kitchen, and eventually placed the bowl down on the floor next to the bed.

After a few more trips, she had everything she needed upstairs. She laid out a few beach towels on the floor with the rest of the equipment to one side.

"Do you want me down there now?" Grace asked.

Mina thought a while looking around at everything. "I think so. We will take the frame off before I make the mix so that it stays good as we put it on."

Grace groaned, puffed her cheeks out and started to take her weight on her arms. Mina stopped her with a hand up and got up quickly to help. Mina held Grace's bad leg firmly, allowing Grace to do most of the work in moving herself along using her three remaining limbs. At the edge of the bed, Mina guided the bad leg out forwards and Grace gradually dipped herself until her bum reached the carpet.

Grace exhaled as if she had been holding her breath the whole time she was edging across. Mina wasn't quite sure whether she had or not, though it must have taken more than two minutes to get Grace comfortably where she needed to be, leant against the side of the bed with her injured leg outstretched along the towels.

Mina and Grace both worked to remove the convoluted wooden frame and once off and the leg bare, Mina started to mix in the plaster to the water. She sat for a few minutes stirring and adding powder bit by bit while Grace sat awkwardly, clasping her hands under her calf to keep her lower leg from bending around the break.

It wasn't long until Mina was happy with the thin paste and she started wrapping Grace's leg with the dry bandage. She wrapped it twice over from knee to toe before she started submerging the rolls of bandage into the plaster mix first. After the third roll, it was starting to look a lot like plaster and Mina smoothed down the thickening mixture after each roll and after the fifth, Mina was proud of the results as she continued to rub her gloved hands up and down the leg to create a smooth finish as it gradually hardened.

"So, apparently, you must be really careful for a whole day for it dry," Mina told Grace. "So as your doctor, I am telling you to stay in bed today. I will bring you painkillers and juice as appropriate and you can just read your book in between meals and naps. Sound manageable?"

"Yea, I think I can just about do that."

"I used to be good with this damn thing," Leighton started. "During the last couple of summers at school I had this friend, I've probably mentioned him before, Henry. He lived down on this massive commune, just outside the nearby village to where I went to school. He had an air rifle as well, so one day, during the summer holidays, we went out into the surrounding woods. In one clearing, we took a load of random items, our air rifles and lunches from the canteen and spent an entire day shooting.

"So, we lay prone for about eight hours shooting at anything we could find. We had printed targets, positioned small plastic toys that had been left nearby, basically anything that we could stand up and would fall off a log when hit. I was better than him by some way, we did some scoring rounds and apart from shooting from stood, I tended to win the competitions. I think most of his advantage standing was that he was stronger than me. He played rugby and, as you can tell by my physique now, that mean he was much bigger than I was at that age too.

"We did this for most of two summers. At the end of the second summer, we had gotten good enough that the targets were getting smaller and smaller and our targets were not that much wider than the pellets were. He took it a bit further and started to leave the clearing to shoot rabbits that were a bit of a problem to the commune's crops. The rest of the inhabitants didn't mind too much. He was eighteen then and anything that was going to stop their crops getting ravaged was supported by enough and had the fact hidden from those that would be too averse to the idea.

"Henry kept saying that I should go with him, that because I was better on the targets they would be able to kill loads if we hunted together. I always found excuses not to go out with

195

him. I fantasised about doing it, but I never had the bottle to go out and kill a living creature, even though I desperately tried to convince myself it was more than just sport. There was a human benefit to it."

"That makes sense though," Shannon said. "I don't think you have that killer instinct. I can believe that you are good with that gun, I did see you calibrating it and not many shots missed the tree knots you were aiming for."

"You think it's killer instinct? I don't know." Leighton sighed. "I would have thought given the need that we have for me to get us some food that I would have gotten over that subconscious desire not to kill by now."

"Have you killed anything before? In a car, a mouse, insects, anything at all?" Shannon asked with concern.

"I've killed insects. I normally trap spiders under a glass, we had mice once when I was younger, but we had 'humane' traps and then a cat," Leighton said.

Shannon looked despondent. "You've been in fights thought, yea?"

"Yes, I have been in a few. I have succumbed to a fit of rage once or twice. Pounded on guys that have messed with my mates. Once, at a pub in Dorset, a load of lads came around messing with one of the girls in our group. That resulted in a chair leg to a man's head and a very swift exit."

"You!?" Shannon said, wide eyed.

"Yes, me," Leighton said sheepishly. "As hard as that may be to believe."

"You need to use the rage and emotion from that, or worse. Imagine that squirrel is ten feet tall and about to scratch my face up, like that guy on your girlfriend or whatever." Leighton opened his mouth to interject with the fact that it was a female friend, not a girlfriend, but she continued. "Embrace the rage and feast on the beast, we need it. Zeke needs it as much as us."

"OK, you are kind of messed up."

"You need to be more messed up."

"First, I will try town, we need carbs for energy, regardless of how much I can hunt. At first light, I will go down and scout for anything that may prove useful. After that, I hunt and I will kill something for you."

Chapter 32

Tariq reached what appeared to be a busy roundabout near the edge of town. Cars were backed up for around a mile before he reached the blank traffic lights at the front. On his way in between the vehicles, he saw some that were sunken into the soft shoulder of the road where part had collapsed. The cars were all empty and only two pockets along the way showed damage. In those pockets, there were wide spaces with cratered concrete where the metal of vans and cars alike had been twisted apart and Tariq was thankful that all the cars had been empty before that had happened. A footbridge above the roundabout had collapsed and the only way that Tariq could get around it was to walk off to the left along the middle of the road and in between the stopped cars.

Before Tariq reached the next roundabout, he worked on protecting his mind. He focused on the menial task of stepping over potholes and debris amongst the stationary traffic and whenever his mind bolted towards deeper thoughts, he consciously refocused on the simple task. He knew that before he could get back on the road heading west, it would be likely that he would see some real sights of death that this level of destruction must have caused. He dreaded it to his core.

He took the third exit off the next roundabout and the dual carriageway gave him hope of finding a route back out of town. It didn't. Instead of taking him away it seemed to lead towards the centre of the town. Ahead of him, a building that had once stood tall, spilled out across the next roundabout. A massive red beam looked as if it had been peeled back and he saw from one of the remaining beams that it formally stood as one edge of a large pyramid. It was so mesmerising, he didn't notice the shopping complex that stood to his right until he was about half the distance along the straight road. In the direction he was now travelling the traffic was much lighter. A few abandoned cars lined the left side of the road and he had to force his mind from imagining people leaving them as the first bombs dropped in front of them, tearing a landmark apart in front of their eyes. If he had let his mind think on it more, he perhaps would have realised that they must have made some distance as he had seen no-one.

Tariq noticed the low sun disappear behind one of the buildings to his right as he went. The feeling of needing escape started to wane as he evaluated his tired body. Deciding on finding somewhere nearby to sleep, he came to a stop and reviewed all the buildings around him. He wanted something that stood complete. Something he could rely on not falling in the middle of the night. He saw a potential target over to his left. It was positioned about ten feet below his current road level. It looked whole from his angle which was better than anything else he could see. He continued towards the torn, formally-pyramidal building looking for a way down to that building.

Tariq's heartbeat grew loud in his chest, each note beating heavy with reverb as it seemed to fill his whole being. He darted his eyes around the streets looking for any movement. He felt a presence up ahead. His eyes were tricking him, darting around to follow floaters in his vision that he mistook for people walking at the edges of his sight. He suddenly felt something under his foot and Tariq looked down. He instinctively pulled himself away when he saw legs that had caused it. Then he followed the legs up to the hips, torso and eventually a greyed-out face leant up against a fence that protected the drop to the lower level of road. Tariq twitched and moved back around six feet in one sudden jerk. He went to speak an apology, but his stomach took the opportunity of an open mouth to empty itself onto the path between Tariq and the dead woman.

Once Tariq could lift himself up from being doubled over, the smell of death and sick wrenching at his gut, he took a last glance at the woman's face. Images of injured women lining Cairo's streets flurried through his mind and he wretched loudly once more. The red steel splayed out into the air in front of him and he walked uneasily towards it. He fought the urge to look back again, but managed to keep his eyes straight ahead as he aimed towards a road that went down a hill and to the left of the building, bending its way behind it after a short walk. It seemed to head in the right direction for his continued journey. His desire to rest his limbs was counteracted by the desire to not see any more of the dead bodies that must be lining the roads and the debris in the town. He wanted out. He would rather sleep in the cold, uncovered, than seek shelter in this cemetery.

As he moved around the building, he saw that the other side had been hit harder. The glass was smashed completely and the steel and concrete that made its construction poured out onto the street. The red support that originally ended at the apex of the building was split back and now ended deep into the middle of the road, breaking apart a traffic island and making a deep pit with curbs stones thrown up and arranged like many broken teeth that restricted Tariq's view of the impact. His route would have led him to pass underneath the arc, but a bout of superstition took him around, close instead to the old traffic island in the road. As he passed it he saw a shoe, then jeans and finally realised that the body of a teenager had been impaled and stapled to the concrete. Tariq's stomach rolled, his head went light and he averted his gaze quickly. As if seeing his second dead body close-up was a catalyst, now Tariq noticed other piles of shaped clothes around the edges of the street, limbs twisting out of rubble and corpses lying directly in the road. He retched, but only a spit of green and vile contents came forth and as soon as he was done with it, he started to run.

Leighton separated some items into an emptied large rucksack to take with him into the town. He wanted to be able to bring back as much food as possible. He knew he had no choice, but to attempt the trip and hope that there were supplies left that he could get hold of. He wanted to go as close to first light as possible to give him the maximum amount of time to find his way and get back while light remained.

Tariq kept running for twenty minutes. At first it was flat out, running from death, but he gradually slowed as he moved onto tree-lined roads clear of the problems brought by a high population density in a time of war. If something this one-sided could even be considered such. He was then just running to give himself something else to focus on. He focused on deep breaths, the sound of his pounding heart, the feel of the ground reaching every rhythmical step. The road became dark as the sun was blocked out by the trees and then the rises in the land and he slowed to a walk. He let his feet land heavily as he took big gasps of air to rid his muscles of lactic acid. His head was light and felt about to drop. He diverted his path into the treeline and came across a large fallen branch that could provide a little shelter from the cold of night. He unrolled his sleeping bag and pulled a bag of mix nuts and dried fruit from his bag. He nestled himself against the tree trunk. He ate until the exhaustion took him.

Chapter 33 - Day 8

As soon as light came, Leighton dressed and collected his prepared necessities. He was on his way within half an hour of waking, leaving Shannon in half-sleep after he kissed her goodbye.

Leighton kept his head low and followed his left shoulder along a hedgerow running straight in towards the town. A corner shop towards the centre of town became his target. It was the most obvious food store discernible to him through his telescope. He gauged the roads into and through the town, rubble lay thick in places like snowdrifts and dust coated what else was visible so that even the curbs alongside the road were no longer apparent. He was wary that anyone else that was here would not be of a friendly disposition. The bombs had stopped falling and those left would be out for themselves or their own families. Survivors would have an instinct right now that he didn't want to come across. For this reason, he stopped often and checked by eye and by telescope in all directions. If there was anyone out here, Leighton wanted to know where they were first.

Entering the boundary of the town, Leighton stayed low, still constantly stopping to check all directions at each junction in the roads. He often had to divert his path around great mounds of debris that sprawled in front of his path. His knuckles were white with the strength of his grip on the axe in his hand. In the places where rubble was clear, bins had spread their contents into the dust. Bird call rang at the edge of his hearing, interrupting the otherwise silent air, but no more than a solitary pigeon showed itself.

Across his path lay a three-story building collapsed and laid out all the way to the buildings on the other side of the street. His target lay the other side of the wreckage. He stopped with his back against the fallen structure and used his telescope to check in all other directions, including up into the sky near the horizon. No movement. The windows on the next building were all out, but the walls stood. He pulled himself through, treading carefully over plaster and splintered wood. He followed the path through to the back door which was now merely an opening in the wall and joined the open street via a wide gap in the fence.

The corner shop stood alone on all sides, though was previously terraced. It was three stories with dormer windows and the heavy metal shutters were down. Leighton walked to view the edge that once joined the adjacent building. A door in the far corner caught his attention, easily the most passable entrance as the other side of the building was piled up to the first floor with remnants of its neighbour. He reluctantly fixed the axe to his bag and clambered on all fours over the rubble. He found the door unlocked and pushed it open, but doing so caused the rubble on which he was precariously perched to slide down into the opening. Leighton grasped the edges of the door frame to reduce the weight on his feet and he pulled against the tide of debris pulling his ankles down. His feet worked quickly against the shifting support beneath him, but a wooden joint pulled his foot down and into the sliding mass of debris. As his foot stopped digging its way deeper, he felt a sharp pain just above his ankle.

He looked down and carefully replaced all his weight onto his free leg. He found that even small movements in his trapped foot was causing a pain to shoot up his leg. He leant down slowly, wincing against the pain. He could only just see through the pieces of wood and concrete that was currently enclosing his calf, but he could just make out a large nail piercing his trouser leg. He could feel the tip of it and it was certainly breaking his skin, but he couldn't tell how deeply that might be yet. His heel was being supported from underneath, at least that was good, but his toe was underneath a breeze block. The weight wasn't down, but its position meant that he would need to move his leg back whilst twisting in order to free it.

Leighton looked out around him. He heard a scratching sound and quickly refocused on his leg. He felt an urge to hurry. The mound of rubble blocked most of his line of sight except for the street that he had come from. He took a deep breath, he had to get his leg free, but he already knew it was going to hurt as he tried to twist around the immovable s of his trap while ignoring the nails path through his skin. His trapped leg tensed as he imagined the movement he would have to make to free it and as it did so it reminded him with a sharp jolt as why he would need to move quickly.

He breathed deeply again and shuffled his free leg to ensure it was stable enough. He reached his hands down and grasped his calf as close to the ankle as he could reach. A deep filling of his lungs. Slow breath out, eyes focused. A pull and a twist. Leighton groaned heavily and pulled his leg from the hole. His ankle throbbed, with each pump of blood to the area. The pain caused him to shudder. He sat with his arm over his eyes, at one with the warm pain in his ankle.

The throbbing subsided quickly though, as Leighton realised again where he was. He decided it would be best to check the injury with Shannon there. His focus returned to his wife and son and the food that they desperately needed. He pulled himself back up to standing using the doorframe, placing as much weight as possible on just the one leg.

He dropped himself inside the shop, feeling blood trickle down over his ankle as he returned his full weight to his feet. It was dark and he let his eyes adjust with the door as closed as far as it would do behind him before moving further inside. Gradually, shapes formed in the darkness and he saw that the shop was still well stocked.

He placed his bag down and checked the stiletto dagger in his pocket. The first thing he went for was antiseptic which he found alongside some paracetamol and aspirin. Hurriedly lifting his trouser leg up, he poured some antiseptic straight onto his cut and winced, doing everything not to let out a yell.

He went around grabbing any tins of meat and vegetables he could find and shoved them hastily into his bag. He was smiling on the verge of laughing. Salivating at the thought of his next meal as he packed each item. He ripped open a chocolate bar and exhaled deeply as the sugar hit his tongue and he let the wrapper fall straight to the floor, devouring the rest in just a few quick bites. It felt good. He noticed a rack of papers and rolled up one of the freshest looking papers and shoved it deep inside the rucksack with barely a glance as he was then distracted by a five-kilogram bag of rice. He was eager to get back to Shannon and get a full meal on the go now. His stomach reverberated with a sound of agreement.

A slowly flashing red light caught his attention on the counter and Leighton moved towards it. It was small and Leighton couldn't work out what it was attached to. As his hand moved forward it stopped. The distance was deceiving him against the contrast of darkness around it. He re-focused, reached again and finally found a mobile phone in his hand. Turning the screen on dazzled his eyes, he clenched them shut quickly and then opened them slowly – bit by bit – to pick out the images on the screen. A photo of a young man took up the screen, the battery was on six percent. He focused again. It seemed that the phone had signal and he swiped across the bottom of the screen to unlock it. His parents at the farm had limited signal at the best of times and calls to a mobile would never work, but a text could get through eventually, at the very least a message would be shared, even if they wouldn't be able to reply.

He remained sceptical that the signal message was true, even as he typed,

Hi mum it's Leighton. Shan and Zeke ok. TB if well, we are coming to the farm soon.

It vibrated in his hand *{message sent}* appeared to Leighton's wonderment. The phone clicked over to four percent and flashed a warning to plug it in. He pocketed it in his breast pocket where he would be able to feel a reply come in if it were to. He hoped that something would come back before the battery died.

Tariq had slept straight through for around four hours before he woke up needing to relieve himself. He climbed out of the sleeping bag to find that it wasn't anywhere near as cold as he had thought it would be. He thought he could easily sleep out without the bag at all. He urinated a little way away from where he had slept, ensuring it was both downhill and downwind. Once back in his covers he struggled to sleep well and tossed and turned with dreams of being visited by the corpses, of having to kill for himself and of being terminally injured and unable to find help.

After the fourth time waking up from one of his nightmares, he decided that he had rested enough and needed to move on regardless of the ill-slept tiredness that ached his bones. He was not recovered enough, but he felt as though he may never be again. As he was packing up his sleeping bag, he noticed a lot of individual hairs in the hood of it. He flicked them out and rolled the bag into its pack. He thought about the hair again and ran a hand over his head. Glancing down at his palm he saw a load more and when he ran fingers through his hair, it caught a larger clump and he shuddered as he felt it come out easily. He felt around his head for any bald patches or injury, but it felt normal except for a touch dry and he saw dandruff flick into the air. It was just another thing that would have to go to the back of his mind as he continued.

He walked on a little way, occasionally having to stop himself from checking his head every few minutes for more hair loss. It would only make it worse if he didn't leave it alone. Eventually, he noticed a car park open up in between the trees to his left. He scanned around it suspiciously as he went past. It looked as though it was an activity centre of some kind and the thought of finding a bike in such a place occurred to him. He guessed by the sight of just a single car residing, that it was unlikely to have been open at the time of the nearby town's destruction. After a short walk around the buildings of the complex he found one that judging by a quick glance through the window contained a row of mountain bikes. He leant away from the side and clenched a fist in joy. He much preferred cycling to walking, especially as he didn't know how far he may yet have to travel. He just needed to get in and procure one.

He walked around the building twice in order to judge the sides for any easy access points and realised one of the side doors was screwed in to the outside. He thought of the tools in his bag, he could try and – rust permitting – unscrew the entire door and walk in. It was a Yale lock on the door which he would stand no chance of picking or forcing open too easily otherwise. Then it dawned on him that it would open easily from the inside and eyed up the single glazed window. It was not long before Tariq started rooting around for a brick or tool by which he could smash the glass in. He came up trumps with a shovel that lay not far from a dirt jump on a track and he flung with all his waning strength at the glass which shattered much easier than Tariq expected, nearly resulting in the shovel going straight in. Tariq needed a little more use from it before he was done. He smashed a remaining piece of glass and then went about chipping all the small but deadly shards along the bottom of the window frame. The whole window was more than large enough to fit through, but instead he poked his head all the way in and realised that the inside of the lock was within reach and the door opened heavily outwards on its hinges.

The individual bikes were not locked down inside the building and he went along trying to find the one that looked best and had wheels that spun as smoothly as possible. He ended up finding one without a saddle on it at first, but it was a fast job with the quick releases to put one in as high as Tariq could secure it. He was also grateful for finding a row of identically coloured helmets, causing him to express out loud his thanks as he fitted it on his head. He felt as though a touch of completeness had returned to him. He was going to make much faster progress this way and it would make him feel much safer being able to make a quick move if it became necessary.

Chapter 34

A creak of beams sounded above him. A thought dawned on Leighton that the building might not be stable. The flash blindness from looking at the phone left plenty of rectangular red and purple marks in the centre of vision and he stumbled to reach his rucksack and rice. Another creak sounded and Leighton froze, hunkered down over his bags. Again, it came, then a pause. Leighton remained still, he lifted his bag onto one shoulder and the other hand grasped the large bag of rice. Leighton was blinking rapidly trying to clear the spots on his vision. A door opened and torch light poured out, he dropped his head lower, hoping stillness would stop him from being noticed so readily. The torch light moved methodically around the edges of the room. It was too late to hide any better and the beam of light dazzled Leighton, pausing on him for a moment without further reaction.

"Thief," spoke a man's voice confidently. "What are you doing in here? Where the bleeders did you come from?" Aggression came through with the smell of stale tobacco smoke.

Leighton refused to speak. He was shocked at seeing an adult that wasn't Shannon. He remained still.

"Hey! Can you hear me? I can see you, put that stuff down." The man's voice, coming from behind the torch homed in on him, seeming worn and old. The man clanged something against a metal shelf, a noise that reverberated through the small shop with vigour. "Are you mute? Talk!" He practically barked the last word.

Leighton lifted his head and tried to see past the light while he searched for something useful to say. "Look, I've got a wife and a young baby. We are camping in the woods away from town. I'm not taking much. We are struggling and need just a bit to get by." He spoke softly to induce calmness in the man, but his words came out ineloquently and rushed.

"Too much. I worked all my life for this shop, now put them down."

"You have plenty here." Leighton forced a laugh. "If we come and join you we can work out what to do once the surplus runs out."

The man paused, the torch light wavered. Leighton let go of the rice and reached his right hand into his jacket pocket slowly. He remained hunkered down.

The man spoke again, "That doesn't fit my plan. I am sorry. Just put the stuff back and you can leave. I don't want this either. When the troops come in, I can speak German well enough that they won't react too badly to my surrender."

A bin fell outside and the torch light flashed towards the shuttered window for a moment before blinding Leighton once more. Leighton caught a glimpse at the man in the interim. He had the beer belly of an older man than himself and he wielded a baseball bat uneasily in his right hand. The cause of the loud clang earlier.

Leighton felt his heartbeat rise again suddenly and his chest felt instantly tight. Images flickered in his mind of his possible ways out, so rapidly that he could barely grasp a single solitary idea of what could – or should – come next. His hands were starting to shake. The man in front of him was clearly as edgy. A cornered animal was unpredictable. Both men were cornered and they both knew so. The pain in his ankle throbbed, the intensity of the distraction rising and falling rhythmically.

The man took a few slow paces towards Leighton before he spoke again. "This is your last chance, put the rice down and get out." He leant forward with the baseball bat to push the bag of rice away from Leighton's hand. Leighton reacted to the sudden encroachment into his space, remnants of fear still blocking his mind from clarity. He threw the rucksack off his shoulder, grabbed the hot torch bulb and ran his thin blade straight under the rib cage of the man, who yelled out loudly in pain. He pulled the blade out. The man gasped heavily, struggling to react. Leighton pushed the blade back in again nearly in the same spot, the force of the thrust taking both men to the ground. The heavy landing forced a sharp exhale from the man's lungs. His whole body tensed underneath Leighton as he tried to throw himself back, his breathing sounded forced and raspy.

The baseball bat struck down feebly against Leighton's back, which did nothing, but to remind Leighton that he needed to make sure the man who would now have a great deal of vengeance against him did not get up off the floor and be able to enact that vengeance on his attacker. He drew the blade out and stabbed again, this time feeling much more resistance and a slide of the blade as it went in between two of the man's lower ribs.

Leighton continued to hold himself close to the man to be near enough that any retaliation would not strike with full force. None came. He stabbed a final time for certainty. The man convulsed, but nothing more. Leighton simply ignored the tepid liquid that had poured over his hand. He pushed himself back and turned the discarded flashlight onto the man's face. Blank eyes met his. Clearly no longer a threat, he spun the light away quickly and lit around the edges of the room and fought to get his breath back. A constant pounding seemed to fill his chest cavity, threatening to tear his ribcage apart and for a moment he felt his vision wavering. Not a time to pass out. He let his legs give way and dropped to the floor, leaning up against a cabinet. The body left only just out of hands reach.

"Fuck," he said aloud. "What just happened to me?" His breath was ragged and deep as he wiped the dagger off on a rag left on one of the counters. He got back to his feet, picked up the bag of rice and stepped out through a fire exit into the hazy morning light. Looking down at his jacket he nearly fainted again. More expletives left his mouth and he tried to pat the blood away with his sleeve. He felt his eyes start to haze over and he filled his mind with an image of Shannon.

213

He breathed in as deeply as he could and consciously pushed down on his diaphragm to steady his breathing.

Feeling a vibration in his pocket, he pulled the phone out, catching the first few words of the return message before the phone screen blanked out for good,

Hello Leighton. Not quite sure what is happening atm. We are very much looking forward to seeing you though. Is Zeke alr-

Chapter 35

Grace and Mina were both in the kitchen enjoying the security and additional range of motion that a plaster cast offered Grace's leg. It made a hollow sound when tapped, just like a real one and as far as either of them could tell it was as good and as strong. Grace was weak from the wastage of her muscles that days of immobility had induced. Even if she couldn't focus on the cast wrapped leg, she wanted to get herself moving and be able to support herself better. Grace spotted the high stool in the corner and asked Mina to pass it over. Grace planted it in front of her and found she was easily able to use it like a walking frame, such that would normally be shuffled around behind by the old and frail.

Mina watched on anxiously and after one slight slip on the hard floor, she decided on finding some rubber for the feet. She wandered around the house for a few minutes before noticing the door mat at her back porch and took to cutting the corners off the rubber backing and superglued them to the bottom of the chair legs. This helped with her stability significantly and Grace was quickly confident in hopping around the kitchen and living room across the ground floor.

Once Grace was tired out and throbbing under the cast with the blood building up near her injury, they both sat in the living room. Grace lay back in the sofa that she had previously been confined to and read her book. Mina was curled up opposite flicking through the medical book for anything else she could find on healing broken bones.

"You'll be alright, you know, love," Mina said, breaking the silence.

"What do you mean?" Grace replied.

"I reckon by this that it is just a part fracture."

"*Just* a fracture. It bloody hurts, you know. Fracture makes it sound like I am over exaggerating."

"No, a *part* fracture. It's still broken, but instead of being clean through the bone it is just part way through. I think your leg would be far more deformed than we can fix ourselves if it was a clean cut. It would never heal."

"That's a gross and horrifying thought." Grace squirmed. "Stop it. Actually, how long is it going to take to heal then?"

"It's hard to say," Mina said, pondering and flicking back between two different pages held accessible by fingertips shoved between them.

"Well, roughly?"

"Well, it kind of implies that potentially it could take maybe around or up to about four months or so. Hard to say." Mina looked up to gauge Grace's reaction.

"Four actual months. Shit, dude."

"Okay, it's quite shit. On the sunny side of the street, you are alive. -And you're wearing a cast so that will help dramatically; especially at protecting from further injury."

"I see your point, Mina, but it is still four fucking months!"

Mina shied away a little from the anger in her friend. "I know, I know," she said. "Look, we'll be alright, we are together. We are in this together and we will do what we need to do."

"I'm sorry for snapping," Grace said sullenly, shaking herself back into control.

"It's fine, you are in a lot of pain, it is to be expected." Mina spoke her words with dismissive finality as though an apology would not be necessary next time.

Deep breaths, muscles ravaged and clothes gripping his body with sweat, Leighton arrived back at the tent.

"Honey," Shannon called from inside the tent. "Are you ok?"

Leighton dropped his bags and started ripping off his clothes to resist the onset of heat exhaustion. The midday sun was beating down. Shannon saw him and passed a bottle of clean water and Leighton gulped the lukewarm water in abundance, stripping completely down to his boxers. Shannon saw the bag of rice lying on the ground and her jaw dropped. She draped her arms around his neck, his sweat tacking their skin together. Leighton restrained from putting his arms on her back, continuing to drink over her shoulder.

"Well done, I'm so proud of you. Zeke has been feeding non-stop this morning, breast milk doesn't seem enough for him." Shannon straightened her arms to consider Leighton's eyes.

"I need a wash," he said.

"Aren't you pleased?"

"It's fucked up. I'm going down to wash. Come or don't come."

"What's up? This haul is great. Did you get anything else?"

"Yes, but I need to wash myself," he repeated.

Shannon looked over his full rucksack and clothes sprawled over the ground. "Let me get these together and Zeke. I'll wash them for you now. You deserve clean clothes for this. And maybe a little more," she said, lowering where her hand was positioned on his back.

"Now is not the time, Shannon, seriously. I need a minute to get myself together."

A murmur of a cry came from inside the tent. "Wow, how are you still hungry, Mr Whingey?" Shannon turned and picked Zeke up. Leighton turned and leant his head against a tree trunk, arm over his eyes.

"What's that on your hand, Leighton?" Shannon's voice wracked with concern. "Leighton. Talk to me. Something happened down there. I can see it in you."

Leighton stopped still, his shoulders threw themselves up briefly, but he staved off the sobbing. He gestured down at the jacket and Shannon noticed the hard, darkened brown stains on the side pockets.

"What the fuck?" She asked, her face settling from the exuberance of knowing they had food. This was no feast, no party. "Who?"

"A guy was left there." Leighton struggled to speak, his body shivered, yet no breeze passed.

"Was he injured? Why the blood?"

"Fuck."

"Did he die while you were there?"

Leighton breathed in deeply, but raggedly and held an index finger aloft.

"Ok, ok. I'll leave it." She exhaled loudly. "Tell me after we eat. I bet you're starving." Shannon retired from the questions, the distress of her husband was too much for her to continue the inquisition and she forced herself to withdraw into herself and distract herself with the new options for lunch.

It was a long time before sunset that Tariq had to stop for the day. He eventually felt his legs turn to jelly and once he had started slowing he couldn't find the strength to regain the speed. He turned into the soft verge, dismounted and pushed his new bike into the tree line. He found a cut tree stump and dropped the bike as he squatted to sit on it. He pushed his legs out in front of him to stretch them out. He knew he would not get going again until tomorrow and that he was going to sleep right there. He was happy with himself with how far he had come on a heavy, low-seated mountain bike, but he didn't know how far exactly. He had at least moved quickly at first and the land around him seemed higher and hillier than where he had left from.

Tariq forced himself to eat, which didn't make him feel any less wretched. He was starting to get bored of dry nuts. He may have been tired, but he didn't feel restful. His body felt as though it was shaking him to death. He lay inside his sleeping bag, in between his bike and the tree stump. Against the light sky and the feeling of perpetual motion, he remained awake for some time. He told himself over and over that rest was as good as sleep. He would be okay if he didn't move and eventually he would find sleep.

Shannon talked incessantly to Zeke while they washed at the river. Leighton, his clothes, Zeke and his clothes all got washed. Leighton remained silent, enduring the cold of the river as it diverted around his submerged, goose pimpled skin. On their return to their resting place, he was finally convinced to carry Zeke and he held his son tightly. His sleeping son's head rested on his shoulder and he drew from the boy's presence what strength he could. His mind was numbed. His vision seemed as though through a thick fog. He had no time to collapse and fall apart. He was a ship carrying his family in the deepest of waters. What good was an incomplete boat? Zeke's hair tickled his cheek, but he refused to let go of his embrace to scratch it.

They sat down, clothes were hung and Leighton ritualistically started the fire. He placed dried leaves methodically at the base and built up a covering of small twigs to grow the fire. He took great care in the construction, scraping a vast space around the base to ensure nothing but the meticulously placed wood would catch light. He was autonomous in his motions.

Meanwhile, Shannon picked through the rucksack, spreading everything Leighton had brought back across the ground to view in front of her. Her mind raced as she connected items together for future meals. She put some of it to the side, a tin of tomatoes, canned ham and a cup from the bag of rice. She thought for the first meal after a week on food from a tube, they should eat one full meal. She stopped her preparations as she realised the newspaper in her hand.

She unrolled it carefully, the cover had no photography, but just simple text filling the front cover: 'Devastated London leaves uncountable death toll.'

"Have you read this?" Shannon asked.

Leighton, still deep in concentration, replied after an extended moment of silence. "Not yet, I haven't had a chance. I just picked it up quickly. What does it say?"

"Ok," Shannon cleared her throat. "'Last night, German bombers lay waste to the UK capital. So far, the death toll can only be assumed to be in the tens of millions. Major landmarks including the 'gherkin', the arena and the houses of parliament are all flattened in a daylight attack.'" Shannon's voice quivered as she spoke and she stopped to take a sip of water. Leighton remained seated next to his construction, eyes still fixated on the sticks. "With communications including television, radio and internet all remaining down since the bombardment, it is impossible to tell exactly the reasons. Most suspect it is due to Germany forming a new alliance with the Russian president and acting out against Britain after Downing Street steadfastly held the Russian sanctions. No news has yet to reach us as to whether the government provoked the attack, or even if any members of parliament have managed to survive."

Leighton took a wind-proof lighter to the kindling and blew out carefully to encourage the flames.

"We have to get to my parent's farm," Leighton said.

"Do you- do you think they are OK?" Shannon sniffed loudly.

"I found a phone. It was on low battery, my text got through and it then shut down shortly after Mum replied. They are confused, but alive."

"Why didn't you say sooner? How long do you think it will take to get there?"

"I am not sure. We do know they will have a food store there with provisions for up to a year. I should have said right away that I had heard from then. My head isn't in the game."

"I- It's alright," Shannon stammered, carefully trying to ease Leighton without much grace. "We'll eat first and then work out how we'll go. Did you learn anything else while you were there?"

"Only that it is possible that troops may have landed too. To what ends, we can only guess."

"What really hap-" Shannon cut herself short. "Just... hmm... tell me when you can."

"Thank you," Leighton murmured, still not turning to look at her.

They ate Shannon's meal and it was delightful, even without her usual way of spicing foods. They continued till the pots were empty and their stomachs heaved with fullness, which didn't require too much. Shannon had kept some rice aside, watered it down and re-boiled it until it became close to a thick paste. Zeke ate it as eagerly, grabbing at Shannon's hand to pull the spoon into his mouth quicker.

Leighton declared that he needed some time and that he would try to get something fresh to eat for their next meal. Shannon mildly protested, but knew herself that they would need some energy to walk with all they needed to carry across the country. He took his air rifle and tin of pellets and walked in the woods. He drifted deep in his mind as he walked and he desperately tried to subdue his inner voice. He lay in the soil, part covered by a collection of ferns and aimed out with little haste. The stillness and the active patience washed away the terrible meanderings of his mind. He decided grimly, that the country must be done in its entirety already. Perhaps less than a week was all that was needed. He would need to catch up on some news, when and if that ever became possible.

Leighton recalled his summer shooting sessions with his friend. Laid down prone supporting the rifle on one hand, he got used to the weight of the gun as if shooting for the first time. He consciously practised his breathing.

Chapter 36 - Day 9

The village stood desolate, and had done for over five days. Across it's footprint on the earth, houses that once stood tall and would have sold for far above their market value, lay strewn into roads. Gardens were coated in rubble and debris from the fall of roofs and their tiles. The streets were covered in dust from the brick and mortar roughly torn apart and pits and potholes marked the surface. One corner of the village held some complete buildings, but they were still devoid of people. Most of the inhabitants had left, but not all. Of the three thousand people that would have called it home, now just a few miles up a long path that joined near the edge of the village remained the last two survivors.

The east side of the village held only a handful of houses with any of their original height left. From the sign for the village's name next to the road, to the green at its centre that hosted a grassed space in between the two pubs and a large church, barely anything in a single piece. The church itself had caved in from above and the bell tower now lay over two of the adjacent houses. One pub remained standing in all but a few of the outhouses that formally held rooms to rent, the Blue Boar. The green held the culmination of three roads. The one leading west simply paved the way towards more of the same complete destruction of its estates as it wound up the edges of the valley and onwards towards similar towns and farms beyond the changing name of the road. That heading north lead to areas lower than the centre that, although still standing in a mostly completed state, had been abandoned just the same.

It would not be long before Aldbourne would become somewhat of a hive of activity again. In comparison to the current populations of the other towns and villages in the area, it could end up being described as bustling. It was still early in the day and the two inhabitants, Grace Vogel and Mina Bird, resided just at the very edge of the official village borders high up in the valley that ran east and slightly north of that first village name sign at its entrance. Now, though unaware, they were joined by a young Egyptian man cutting a solitary figure with the sun at his back.

Tariq Al-Noor rode slowly into the village taking in the sights of collapsed buildings. He passed a splintered red plastic doorway to his left that opened into a roofless space that was formally a hallway or a dining room. Most of the house had collapsed and only a large bookshelf lying face down was determinable in the mess. Tariq felt as though he was looking for something, rather than just passing through and he took in every detail. He supposed that he was looking for signs of survivors, listening for gasping breaths or calls for help from deep within the piles of bricks and mortar

The street he followed, walking and pushing his bike in between the rubble, took him past the remnants of grocers, tea shops and post offices now only determinable by shards of signage lying in the road and matching colours in paint upon parts of the nearby buildings. Some of the buildings were clearly houses and some others simply crushed their way into the road and could not have been returned to their former uses by any of the best guesses of expert architects. The road bent around to the right and the green came into view. A solitary building stood to one side amongst the rubble, a bold-coloured picture displaying an angry blue pig indicated the likelihood of a pub. However, it was the view of the church tower split at its base, now lying across plots of terraced housing, only lifting as high as a single story from the ground, that inspired awe. Tariq placed his bike down in the middle of the grassy area and dropped his helmet – with wisps of hair – alongside it.

Grace and Mina sat in the kitchen, a few miles away. The mood was grim and silence lay between them as they delicately sipped at a waning supply of slightly warm orange juice. A heavy heartbeat raged inside Mina's chest, and although her hands shook whenever she reached out, she tried with conviction to not let it show to Grace. It wasn't as if Grace had never seen Mina in one of her moments, but she felt that with everything Grace had going on, a little touch of anxiety would not help their situation if shared openly. Today it would be her battle alone. Mina's thoughts darted quickly between the state of the village, whether there were more that had needed help still lying in wait, trapped with the worry that they may not have escaped all the bombs. She wondered if whoever was doing it would scan the country from top to bottom again and make sure that every house was flattened.

A short distance away, a couple with their baby walked up the slow incline of a hill that at the top would open a view of the village and its position within a natural bowl. They climbed slowly, carrying all their equipment with them.

"I think there is going to be a village to the other side of the ridge here," Leighton said as they came within a few hundred meters from where the ground appeared to level off. "I should go ahead. Wait here." Leighton dropped off a few of his bags and ducked his head down before he reached the top. The land descended much more steeply on this other edge and he crawled prone for the last few metres. He looked down and saw that the steepness lessened quickly and then edged a village at a much lower angle. It gave him a fantastic view, encompassing the other hills and ridges that went around. Some valleys lead the roads away up to the hills, looking like the arms of a star shaped impression. On the side nearest his vantage point, Leighton saw a river winding along within the largest valley with a steep opposite wall. The rest of the village lay north-west of him, a smudge of brick, plaster and tiles spilling into the roads on both sides. The streets to the right of the village defined their roads more clearly with most of them still standing.

Leighton looked through his telescope for a long while, tracing the roads that he could see clearly, tracing every point and turn that he could for signs of life down there. He was happy for now and turned to pick up Shannon and their packs to keep walking. She had sat down on one of the packs, changing Zeke's nappy. It took her the same length of time as it did for Leighton to walk the distance back. Leighton told her of his decision to go through the village to get on a good road.

When they had lugged everything to the top, Leighton stopped again to get the bearings for where they had to go and get to. He traced the roads that they would have to take back to where they would reach he village. As he looked on the nearside of the damaged buildings on the nearest side of the village, he noticed movement. He tried to look with the naked eye and pinpointed the source of the movement and then brought the telescope back to his eye. He could see half a dozen people moving through the gardens of the houses, a number splitting off to wind around on to the road side before they all ran together to join with eight more people alongside a green. He could see a mix of women moving quickly alongside men who seemed to be carrying hunting guns, but before he could focus in on any individual, they all piled into the only standing building by the green.

Chapter 37

Tariq heard a distinct noise like a crowd's footfall and turned his head back the way he had come to hear it become clearer. It sounded like a large crowd, though with empty streets devoid of the white noise of cars on concrete and their engines, the sound was echoing off the buildings around him, making it hard to tell how many could be there. He wondered whether to run towards it to see what was happening. It could be a chance to join with some other survivors. It could be another group, like the people he was briefly with nearly a week ago. He was not as ill as he was then, but with his hair gradually falling out, he could easily stand out as a target again. The sound of an engine getting closer ahead of him picked up, but was still a few miles away. Its noise easily cut through the sounds of the wind and the wildlife.

The sound of footsteps stopped and only the engine noise remained. It grew louder before cutting out abruptly and Tariq tried to look through the buildings to pinpoint where the sound had cut out, but couldn't see anything. He glanced a couple of times back towards the town, in case the noise there picked back up. He needed to get out of the road. If someone came, he would rather it be on his terms and see them first. Looking around, he saw a door left ajar and headed straight for it. He didn't think of luck and just took the opportunity.

As soon as he got through the door, he jumped two steps at a time to a front facing bedroom above. He kept his bag on and looked out towards the centre of town, the direction that he had heard the footsteps, and from time to time pushed his head against the glass to look back down the road in the direction of the engine noise. It felt like hours, but only minutes had passed when Tariq finally caught sight of movement. It was a man in an army uniform patterned in dark grey and green camouflage. He pulled his head back from the window and hunkered low. He looked around the room and saw a walk-in wardrobe along one wall. He stooped over to it and pulled the door open, finding it mostly empty. Whoever had lived here had left prepared in at some way. He picked himself up to standing, looking out the window from deep inside the room and angled his head until he caught sight of one of the men. They were currently walking up the driveway of one of the houses almost opposite. Two of them used a hand-held battering ram and left the door swinging inwards, an audible bang to Tariq's vantage point. They were checking the buildings.

Tariq crawled into the wardrobe, sliding the door shut behind him. He had to push at it with his fingernails to get it all the way shut, but to cut out the outside light it was worth a set of aching finger tips that throbbed hotly for a few moments. He stretched out his fingers and pressed the backs of his nails into his palm.

He scrambled around in the dark and took his bag off, placing it in his lap as he pulled himself far into the back end of the wardrobe. In a part – he thought – that would not be noticeable until the entire door was slid back. He hoped that if they opened it at all it would only be a tiny crack to peer in and they could still miss him. He hoped that they would skip this house completely.

Leighton tensed. His eyes struggled to focus. It appeared that a group of around ten soldiers, guns raised were entering the town from the north. The sight suddenly clicked in his mind and he quickly got down onto his stomach and crept further back from the hill edge. By the time he got the lens to his eye again, he could only see a stationary vehicle, just away from the border of the town and glimpses of the soldiers darting between the cover of buildings. He ushered Shannon down just behind him, but she came up alongside him to see what the fuss was about.

"What?" she whispered. "You can't look panicked and drop to the floor without telling me what is happening."

Leighton shushed her and passed her the scope. With his finger, he pointed down to the side of the village that the soldiers occupied.

"Are they ours? It might be an opportunity to be rescued," she said with difficulty. Her excitement blended with the necessity for quiet and caution.

"I don't know. There is some more movement in the centre." Leighton pointed at the spot from earlier. "I thought little of it before, but now I am worried." He kept his voice hushed in case it carried.

The solitary standing building by the green bustled with movement as people came in and out of various doors. They were wearing heavy woollen shirts and boots from what the couple could make out from the scope. Every one out of three appeared to have a gun, appearing to be shotguns or long hunting rifles.

Leighton took back the telescope and turned to tracking the soldiers intently as they moved through each empty building and drew closer to the assembly of farmers. They seemed to be taking a ram to the doors and two or three would spend a few moments in the house before they moved off to the next. The curve of the road blocked his vision of them for a few moments before they moved over to a house on the left side of the street that required no battering ram to enter.

Chapter 38

"Right," Grace said, rolling her tongue for emphasis. "We need to get ourselves out of this rut."

Mina made an acknowledging noise and eventually looked up, wrapping the book around a finger marking her place. "What do you want to do?"

Grace, lifted her leg off the chair in front of her and leant forward. "I don't know, what do you want to do?"

"Distract myself from our woes by reading this book. It's good. I could read it out loud for you if you want?" Mina asked.

Grace gave her a flat look.

"…across my face, glugging down water from the large bottle," Mina read. "I couldn't hear her, but she was animated. Her skinny figure giving her the appearance of a string puppet. She was clearly giving whomever-"

"Ok, bored," Grace interrupted. "That's the book I finished yesterday. There must be something fun to do around here." She started looking at the shelves towards the hallway for something to pique her interest.

Mina held the page open with her finger again as she thought, following Grace's glances for a hint as to where this was going. "Okay, let's work out how to make soup."

"I like it. We get to play with fire, right?" Grace looked excited.

"Yes. That would be a good start." Mina sighed. "Well, at least you seem to be feeling better. It's a shame we can't just burn your energy to heat the water. Do you want to pop down into the basement and get some good veg?" Grace looked sullenly at her leg and Mina let a smirk cross her mouth. "I'll let you off this time. Let's try getting a fire going first."

The pair shuffled slowly towards the porch and Grace lowered herself with a grunt into one of the chairs there. Mina went off towards the shed and came back with an armful of untreated off-cuts of wood. She placed them down on the edge of the porch a metre from Grace's feet and trundled back to the shed. This time she returned with a green crate filled with bricks and placed it alongside the wood. She moved one of the loose paving slabs from the step of the house and heavily dropped it down on the grass and then started to build a small square structure from the bricks.

"You need to put an air-hole in at the bottom," Grace ordered, pointing at the three-brick high construction.

"Oh, so I guess seeing as you can't do any work that makes you manager, huh?"

"Of course! -And you can tell it isn't a council job because the managers on site don't outnumber the workers."

"Well, I don't react well to management, so I would stay out of it, if I were you," Mina joked. "You can be useful by finishing this while I get some newspaper and a grill rack. Do you reckon you can manage?"

"Yea, that sounds fun."

Grace worked her way to the porch edge, sat down on it and then shuffled herself over to the paving slab and took one of the bricks out from the completed bottom row, before placing new ones to the top row. She had only managed to complete one row before Mina returned from the house and shortly after completing the structure, they were taking lighters to the newspaper and flicking them in to the pit once they were suitably alight.

The first thing Tariq knew of the troops entering his building was the footsteps on the stairs. He wished he had thought to close the door, but when he had entered a desire to make no noise determined his actions. Either way, right then in the almost pitch-dark wardrobe, there was nothing that he could have done by knowing anyway. There was no action he could take other than sit and wait and hope to be passed and pray he could tell when they were gone at the end of their investigation.

He listened intently to the multiple sets of footsteps as they moved around the top floor of the building. The sound seemed to reverberate around his head as the noise filled his little space. Heavy boots on floorboards didn't make for an inconspicuous sound. A few times he thought they must both be in his room and he braced himself for whatever would happen. He sat praying for them not to think about checking the wardrobe at all.

After a few minutes of listening, he heard a new set of footsteps growing in intensity up the stairs. This set halted the noise of the others and sounded more determined in its purpose. It moved at first in clear defined thuds towards the back of the house and he heard the shuffling of the other two pairs as they moved out of its way. It stopped a moment then loudly rang out for three crashing stamps at the floorboards. Tariq wondered if others had been hiding here that he had missed. The footsteps moved into the next room along and the same happened again. Tariq tried to work out what they were doing as fear took hold of his body. He noticed he was sweating profusely as a drop of sweat stung his eyes.

The steps came into the room. Tariq held a hand over his mouth and tensed, waiting for the three loud footsteps. Maybe they were trying to scare a noise out of anyone hiding. He had to fight off the urge to let out a noise as the sound of the three deafening thuds filled the cavity in which he hid. He waited some more, picturing his reaction as they opened the door and saw him huddling there, hugging his rucksack and sitting in a pool of his own sweat which seemed to be pooling at the back of his trousers.

Instead, a loud shout rang out in a staccato yell which preceded the vacation of the room and eventual descending footsteps. It sounded like all three sets were leaving and Tariq held his breath for about thirty seconds before the loud double bang of them opening next door brought on a wave of relief. He slid his back down until his legs were bent, but his back was flat against the ground and celebrated internally, breathing out raging deep breaths that were filled with the fear that was then leaving his body.

Shannon took Zeke and sat a few metres behind Leighton, cradling her little boy. Leighton watched the troops moving from north to south along the main road as they stopped to spend a few minutes in each building along the way. It was a fair few minutes before they reached the last complete house in the village and once that was checked, they all came together and fell into a single line. All of them seemed to be pointing themselves in a different direction as the man at the front, moved his arms in short rigid positions, silently giving orders for the next part of the investigation.

They moved off and split into a group of four walking down the centre of the road and two groups of three that followed each pavement. Where they met roads branching off from the one they travelled, the main group would stop, dropping to their knees while the opposite group of three guarded the way that they had come from. The group of three on the side of the road would walk down until the buildings ended and then returned to the main party and on they moved again. Leighton thought that if the village had been bigger or more complex in its road's design then this strategy for complete coverage would never have worked.

The green and the inhabited pub eventually came into view at the edges of the telescopes lens and Leighton could see at the nearside of the building there was movement. It was an ambush. The people inside had a plan and were only a few short seconds from executing it. The troops moved with a relaxed gait, they were following a well-rehearsed script and it looked unlikely that they would have found any resistance if they had checked any other towns. Leighton braced himself as they took each step closer to the trap that was clearly about to be set off.

Chapter 39

Tariq, exhausted now the adrenaline was wearing off, had almost found some unwanted sleep when gunfire suddenly perked his ears up. "Shit. What the fuck's happening?" he said aloud before clapping a hand to his mouth. He could hear the louder blasts of shotguns cutting through over the rhythmical triplets of assault rifles. A scream hung in the air and the rhythm broke into the sound of chaos.

He picked himself up and against his better judgement he left his hiding place to see what was going on. He had been told by his dad once that if he heard gunfire, he was better to run than to hide, as much as his instinct told him otherwise. You did not want to get found by someone who had just fired a gun freely and their reduction in adrenaline shortly after a firefight meant they were unlikely to be up for a chase. He couldn't take that advice until he knew exactly where it was happening. He could assume that it was the centre of town at the green, but his mum had told him that to assume was to make an ass of yourself and he certainly didn't want to be an ass running into a fight like the one he could hear.

The window opened easily and Tariq angled his head until the noise was loudest, confirming his assumption and making it worth acting on. The houses opposite had a thick treeline that extended from the back gates on for around a hundred metres or so before it went into a steep farmed field. Past that, where the hilltop reached the sky, was another line of trees that seemed to descend the other side, the way he had come into the village. He ran through to the back bedroom, the view of clean, open farmland put him off. He wanted some cover for as much of his run as possible. "East it is," he sighed.

The firefight was now just a lot of shouts and the occasional triple burst of rifle fire. He had hoped it would have lasted longer. The troops had a car up this road. He had to be quick. He threw his bag over both shoulders and sprinted down the stairs. He edged around the front door, he could see their open-topped Land Rover parked with no-one in attendance and a brief thought to steal it crossed his mind and carried on going. He looked right towards the green, but the curve of the road meant that houses blocked his sight of anyone or anything happening. He sprinted across the road towards the messiest front garden and straight through the open front door. He stopped his hand from closing it as he went through and darted quickly through the rest of the house until he came to the kitchen and back door. He fumbled around with the handle and the key for a moment until the door swung in towards him. He didn't look back, urged on by the possibility of a gun aiming straight at his back at any moment and he thought if he looked around it could slow him just enough for a clear shot to be taken.

The back garden was equally as messy as the front. A low wall bordered the right-hand edge and he saw it as an opportunity for a quick way to launch over the rickety back fence. He climbed onto it and stood up straight. Then, grabbing the top of the fence, he vaulted over. The ground was lower on the other side and he landed heavily, sliding down a slight embankment and turning himself over until he came to a halt in a ditch in between the fence and the wooded area. He was winded and gasped for breath. He looked both ways along the back of the fences and up where he had come from, a good ten feet above his head, and fixed his eyes there. Imagining repeatedly the sight of an unfamiliar face, there to hunt him down, peering over. When it didn't come for at least a minute he rested his head against the dirt and evaluated his pains for anything that should be worrying to him.

The first blasts of shotgun fire caused Leighton to jump and drop his telescope which then proceeded to roll a few metres away from him. He could only just hear the noise and a he crawled forward and fumbled around until his hand finally met the metal, warm from the intensity he had been gripping it with. By the time he had got it back to his eye, smoke seemed to be piling out of the windows, perhaps from a grenade thrown in or perhaps from the number of shotguns all firing at once. The cloud spread quickly with all the fire in such a small space and it made it difficult for Leighton to see what was happening.

The fighting died down to more sporadic shots, all controlled bursts. He could only assume that in the clouds of white smoke, the ambush had failed. It had lasted less than a minute, all told.

As the smoke dissipated, he could see the clothed mounds of the dead. Four of the mounds seemed to be cloaked in the camouflage of the troops and about half a dozen – mostly close to the door and nearside of the pub – wearing a variety of typically rural outfits. A sudden flashback of a dark shop interior and a heavy, lifeless body lying underneath him entertained his thoughts and Leighton shuddered and pulled himself back from the vision. He took another fascinated look at the aftermath and saw a small crowd of three men and five women being ushered from the front door with arms held aloft. Once they were clear of the large barrels that stood along the front, two of the troops moved in to handcuff the three men and roughly push the women north while the rest of the rifles were kept aimed at them.

Leighton shuffled backwards out of sight of the village and saw Shannon rocking erratically with her hands over Zeke's ears, cuddling him tightly to her chest. He moved over to the pair and lay on the ground to focus on them so intently that it fought off further flashbacks from reaching him.

Mina was stooped over a very lightly boiling pot of water when a faint sound of distant pops reached her ears and she lifted her head, gazing down the valley towards the village.

"Grace," she said with urgency. "Did you hear that?" Grace was staring past Mina with a deeply furrowed brow.

"Yeah." She paused with a finger over her lips trying to make out the sound. It carried on gusts of wind and died down in between. "I have no idea."

"No, me neither. It doesn't sound natural."

"I don't know. It sounds like distant firecrackers. Maybe it's proper gunfire."

"It must mean there are survivors though, right?" Mina questioned.

"If it does, I am not sure they are the sort we want to bump into."

"What do we do?"

"I don't know. Hope?" Grace said uncertainly.

"I don't like this. We should get inside."

"If they come here and see a thriving, standing house, they will check it. You're right, let's go. I'd rather not greet them in the open where they can sneak up on us. I don't think this is good. Help me up," Grace said.

Mina picked up the pot and emptied it onto the flames to douse them, helped Grace to her feet and followed her in. She locked the door and pulled the blinds down in the kitchen, before the two of them took the slow journey up the stairs with Mina gripping Grace's waist to keep her friend steady as she hopped step by step.

Leighton retold the events he had witnessed to Shannon, whose mouth gaped open in shock. "What are we going to do now?" She asked.

"I just don't know," Leighton answered.

"Well, I need you to make a call on it. You saw it happen so will be the best judge. Take another look at what is going on. I trust whatever decision you make. I am really scared for us, Leighton."

"It's okay. It will be okay, my love. Let me have a few minutes to think. I will get us out of this. You've got me. I got us this far and it hasn't been too shit so far, right?"

"Well…" Shannon said. "Not as shit as it could be, anyway."

"Let me take a few minutes to have a think, I will have another look out over there and work out how we continue to the farm. Are you okay?" he asked sincerely and seriously.

"I don't know. I am shaking. It's a shock."

"I know, I know. Just wait here. I will only be there," he said, pointing to where he had looked out across the valleys.

Leighton walked stooping to half the distance and then hunkered down with a hand gripping his chin, while he tried to clear he thoughts. His brain was a jumble of images all layering on each other and blocking him from being able to think clearly. He needed to see what was happening, then just make an instinctual decision. Any chance of a clear-cut plan was well out the window now. He must take in all the facts and be sure to react to anything new to keep them safe.

At the hilltop, he saw a canvas covered army truck had turned up at the village and had driven all the way to the green to collect the troops and their – he supposed – prisoners of war. Way over to the right of the village he saw a small grey plume of smoke lifting and twisting in the wind over in one of the valleys and leaving the green in that direction, the Land Rover that the troops had arrived in carrying two of the soldiers.

Chapter 40

Tariq heard a loud diesel engine going past him leaving the village and he realised he had been dreaming of something. He had fallen asleep there on the ground. He cursed himself and got up. All his muscles ached, particularly those in his lower back. He had fallen hard and unprepared from a fair height and remembered a phrase that he had heard for the first time not too long ago, 'look before you leap', and almost laughed. He moved away from the noise as it faded into the distance, trying to head perpendicular to the fence behind him in order to get to the edge of the wooded area in a straight line.

He managed well enough, by the time the fence was out of sight behind him, it was clear where the ground opened up in front and he quickly covered it until reaching a barbed wire fence that crossed his path. It was low enough that he could have pushed it down and straddled his way over and on the other side it looked out over the acres of open farmland to the next treeline. He thought for a moment that he could see smoke, but he dismissed it as being a part of the loose wisps of cloud that raced high in the atmosphere.

It looked to be just short of a kilometre away and he would be an obvious figure in the middle of acres of flat farmland on the side of a hill. The only way around would take him close to the town again and require at least twice the distance to travel. He was meant to be running and so run he would. He gathered his breath and stretched out his aching legs and then run he did. Starting off at somewhere close to a sprint and, seeing the treeline barely move towards him, he gradually slowed to a steady jog. As the land got steeper, he slowed down until he was barely moving faster than he would have done walking, but the treeline was close and drew him in.

He slowed to a walk once he reached the tree roots that caused the land beneath his feet to undulate and once he felt suitably hidden, he let his legs drop him to the ground and held his side against the stitch that had developed in his left ribs. He was truly sticky under his clothes with the exertion induced sweat covering the dried, fear induced sweat from less than half an hour ago.

Mina checked outside the window of the bedroom to see a plume of smoke drifting into the air, giving away the presence of at least a single living human. She sighed loudly and drew the blind closed. "Wait here," she told Grace as she headed downstairs. Once she reached the porch, she went hunting for her shovel, found it and dug into the edge of the vegetable plot, picking up an onion with the mound of earth. She poured it down the brick chimney they had made earlier and the smoke halted right away. She watched it for a moment longer and saw a few tendrils of smoke working their way out of the earth and decided on another shovel load to finish the job.

As she thrust the shovel into the earth, she heard an engine erratically revving as it worked the way up the overgrown driveway to her house. She entered the house and sprinted up the stairs. "Find somewhere to hide. Right now!" She shouted through her deep breaths. "They're coming."

Grace reacted with a start. "Where?" she asked.

"Somewhere you can lie down. Under the bed?" Mina questioned. "Yea, go down on that side, I will pull the duvet down so it hangs down a bit. Like when you were a kid, try and stay as close to the wall side as possible."

"Right, okay. Let me give it a go." Grace worked herself down onto the floor and awkwardly pushed her casted leg underneath the bed in front of her. Mina started off quickly, happy enough that Grace would be safe.

Mina reached to the top of the stairs. "Grace," she called back.

"Yea?"

"If it is safe for you to come out, I will lift the corner of the duvet, otherwise don't come out for anyone. That includes me. Got it?"

"Yea, Okay."

Mina ran down the rest of the stairs to see through the glass in the door a grey-green Land Rover on its way towards her. It had no roof or doors other than similarly coloured roll bars behind both rows of seats.

Shannon, carrying Zeke, followed around a hundred feet behind Leighton as he led the way down the hill into the town, now cleared of the army presence. The going was slow as he paused to look out with his scope every dozen paces or so. It was certainly a time to display caution, but it didn't stop Shannon from feeling frustrated and conspicuous.

Shannon didn't stop as Leighton did and he didn't make a fuss this time. When she caught up, she whispered to him, "I want to stay close. We are too open where we are."

"Okay, let's get down into the town, but you stay away from the green. I don't want you to see the carnage on the streets too closely, I'll deal with that and get what we need," Leighton returned in equally low whisper.

Leighton ushered Shannon and Zeke against the edge of the collapsed houses as they moved towards the green. He halted Shannon and Zeke behind the last building before it, placed his bags down and went on alone carrying one of the axes in his hand. She remained with the bags and took a seat on a low portion of the wall, bringing Zeke to her breast.

The strewn bodies came into view as he rounded the corner and the sight froze him for a moment. He threw a glance back at Shannon, who was engrossed in Zeke's company. He looked back at the bodies and fought the urge to retch.

The male bodies in front of him still wore the terror of their final moments sharply on their faces. The whole scene was laid out like a photograph. A snapshot of time played out by these dishevelled, mannequin-like beings. Not that they were beings any longer. Some held hands over their chests as though still trying to stem the blood flow long after the blood stopped flowing. Others were simply splayed out, limbs in all directions and clearly well distanced from consciousness before the concrete pounded up against their backs.

Leighton turned away and rubbed at his eyes vigorously with his fingers. He leant against one of the large barrels and tried to spot the closest soldier. He just needed the gun. A proper gun. He cleared his mind and slowly turned around scanning his eyes blankly, trying not to truly see the farmers' bodies until his eyes fell upon the army camouflage covering another body.

Grace could hear the car pull up outside from her position under the bed. She heard the engine cut out and tried to work out where Mina would have hidden. Her biggest worry was that she hadn't, either in time not to be found or because of a choice not to. Then she heard the front door open. It opened calmly and that meant the Mina had probably been the one to open it. '*You fool,*' she thought to herself.

Mina stepped out the door with her palms open, hands held wide out to her sides. She knew she could protect Grace and leave her with plenty to eat if she met the troops head on. They wouldn't assume that a second person was living with her, so she could talk her way around any questions they might have.

She complied willingly with everything they needed as they asked where she kept the food and she showed them down to the basement. They handcuffed her to the oven door handle and never even asked whether anyone else was there as the two of them went back and forth between the basement and their vehicle, clearing it of as much of the vegetables –

particularly potatoes – as they could be bothered to carry. Each time they passed her they gave an angry glare to ensure that her compliance remained true, though it was not as if she had much choice now. She just continued to sit on the cold kitchen floor with an arm hanging loosely next to her head.

Grace just listened on as heavy footsteps moved below her. There were a few laughs between male voices and fewer words spoken. She never heard Mina's voice, she had either been left outside, hurt or even killed. She hoped for the best. She hoped she was hidden, but she knew in her heart that it wasn't the case.

A while later, Grace heard light footsteps creeping up the stairs. *'Mina,'* she thought. the footsteps continued into the room. At the foot of the bed, Grace finally saw Mina's ankles come into view and her heart jumped with excitement.

Mina opened the wardrobe on the other side of the bed and knelt to pick up a pair of Dr Marten's black boots. As she was knelt, in her finest whisper she said, "They're here," and pointed to the floor. "I need to go with them, it'll keep you safe. I hope not to be long. Maybe a few days until I work an escape of some kind. They seem a bit – erm – thick."

Grace went to retort, but was shushed with some intensity.

Mina kept on her long flowing skirt, but pulled some thick black tights on underneath and slipped on the Dr Marten's, doing the laces up tightly. She changed out of her shirt and swapped it for a thicker cotton shirt which had a pattern in reds and blues which clashed a little with the lighter pastels and yellows of the skirt. She put an equally colourful, warm woollen jumper that was oversized and covered the body of the shirt, but displayed the collar. Finally, she picked up a warm wool poncho in black and grey that draped over her shoulders and came down to around her knees, covering the array of colours that she had underneath. She adjusted herself in the mirror and then quickly scrubbed off her make-up.

A yell came from downstairs, "Hurry up! You have sixty seconds before I come up there and drag you down." It made her jump and she left the wipe on the table. She quickly rooted through one of the drawers and took a sheet of sixteen Tramadol tablets and thrust them down the neck of her clothes into her bra.

She took the last few seconds of her countdown to lean down next to the bed. "Stay safe, Grace." Then after a small pause she said, "I love you."

She stepped out the bedroom door onto the landing as a first heavy boot landed on the bottom step. The sight of her at the top, stopped any more. "Get your arse down here!" the voice bellowed, loud in the confined space of the stairwell.

Chapter 41

Tariq had spent the best part of an hour leant with his back against a thick pine tree. The bark was rough and uncomfortable, but far more comfortable than standing or sitting straight would have been given how his body ached. He dozed for a few minutes at a time – the sense of danger and vulnerability kept him from sleeping fully – and he felt significantly better.

Suddenly, he heard an engine start and he rose quickly, hunkered on his heels and ready to move. The engine idled, not far away. He would never have heard it in the old world that was full of bustle and traffic noise that generally faded away into the background of white noise, but in this new environment where the sound of nature ruled the airwaves, it stood out clearly.

There were trained killers on the loose in this area and he knew that some innocent – if either of the sides in the firefight earlier could be considered so – had died already today. *'What if someone needs help?'* he thought. This thought drove him to action.

He moved east through the treeline until he caught sight of a lone house with that Land Rover parked outside. He was peering through the canopy of the wood as the treeline descended steeply towards the scene. Two men in the recognisable camouflage stepped out of the main door of the house, pushing a young woman out ahead of them in a grey poncho. She walked gracefully towards the vehicle and got into the back of her own accord. The two men looked at each other and one of them leant over from outside to fiddle around with something near her before they got into the front two seats and started to manoeuvre the vehicle around and drive back down a rough road.

Tariq continued towards the house to source himself a good place to recover fully and a clean bed to sleep in. The side of the valley was very steep and he had to hold on and switch his grip from branch to branch as he struggled to keep himself upright. Just before the land levelled off, he came across a long tyre swing hanging from far above and could see the house under the canopy of the trees.

Ahead of him, he saw a woman step out of the door. She was leaning heavily on a kitchen stool and as he took her in from head to toe, he noticed a thick cast around her leg. His heart felt heavy and he moved quickly to see if she needed help. As he burst through the edge of the trees, she turned and looked at him in fear and shock and he pulled up quickly, holding his arms out and ducking his head to show submission. She looked as though she was about to turn and run – not that she would get far – and Tariq took a few steps forward. He looked around him before speaking in a projected voice, "Are you okay? I promise I will not hurt you, but you look injured. Are you okay?" he asked.

Grace inspected him, an image of disgust painting her face. "Who the fuck are you?"

"I am Tariq," he started. "-Al-Noor. I live in London. I work as an intern at a paper studying to be a journalist. I am twenty-three." He thought for moment. "I suppose you can stick that all into past tense now," he joked. "Except for the age. I have ID on me if you want proof."

"That would be good. Walk slowly so I can see you."

"Absolutely. Absolutely," he said convincingly, taking slow steps forward and holding his upper body still and free of any rapid movements. When he was close, he motioned to his bag, "It's in there. I honestly want to help you, that's all."

"Okay, I believe you. Where are you from? You don't sound British."

"I am Egyptian. Can I ask your name?" Tariq tried his best to sound friendly, but felt almost as scared as the injured woman appeared.

"Alright, I am Grace. This doesn't get you out of showing me your ID."

"No problems, one moment, Grace." He slid his hand easily into one of the inner pockets of the bag and pulled out his passport. "It's nice to meet you, Grace. Do you know who the woman was that just left with two of the soldiers?" He asked, handing over the document.

"All right, Tariq," she said, inspecting the passport. "That was my good friend, Mina. It's good to meet you." She held out her hand and Tariq shock it, bowing his head slightly as he did so. Up close, the reddened eyes and gaunt face didn't detract much from her underlying handsomeness.

"Why did she go? Does she know them?" Tariq asked.

"No, I don't think so. You need to come in, Tariq. I'm a bit shaken up right now. I need to get my head together."

Moving out onto the green, Leighton quickly found his way to the soldier's corpse. The gun was lying less than a foot from him and Leighton picked that up first as to delay looking at the man in detail for as long as possible. He was the most likely person to have anything of worth on him. He would need extra supplies and so planned to pick ammo off his body.

The man's face had blood splattered up it from the shot that he had taken straight in the chest. The front of the shirt was crisp to the touch, dried under the blood that had oozed over most of it. The first breast pocket snapped open and Leighton carefully slid his fingers inside. It contained only a metal lighter, a small dent in it not penetrating too deeply. Leighton flicked it on, it still worked and he put it to one side. The second pocket opened with the same effect as the first, but the contents was already visible. He pulled out a small binder, with laminated cards attached. A distinct hole went all the way through every page in the lower right-hand corner of what Leighton now saw was a detailed map. He flicked through them hastily. There were some places of interest and each edge held the numbers of the map pages that would line up with them. He would be able to lay them together later to get a full picture of the area.

The trouser pockets were free of blood, though he had to straighten out the corpse's left leg to get into the main pocket on that side. He found two full magazines to fit the rifle, the bullets seemed huge in comparison to the pellets that he had grown accustomed to firing. The other pocket contained an all-purpose blade and multi-tool which Leighton also took and a laminated photograph of a blonde woman which Leighton quickly turned over and placed down on the open palm of the corpse. Leighton felt a distinct tension pick up in his chest.

Shannon took a step around the edge of the building to see her husband lifting his own body up to standing. His stayed hung for a moment, a hand visibly covering his eyes from her view of the back of his head. Zeke tried to look behind him at his father, but Shannon placed a firm hand on the back of his head and pushed it towards her breast. A rifle was hanging from a strap clasped in Leighton's other hand and his pockets bulged awkwardly on both sides of his jacket. Leighton seemed a statue as he was stood. Shannon felt as if viewing a grim painting. Her husband, rifle in hand, stood over a corpse with many others splayed across the street and pavements in front of the pub.

A glimpse of movement caught her eye and she snapped her head to the left. Her eyes darted between points. Decimated buildings, abandoned cars and fallen lampposts in the distance, limp limbs lining the road in the foreground. She saw it again and managed to focus in. An Alsatian dog prowled towards her. Even from distance and front on to the animal she could see its hunger. Gaunt shoulders rose and fell like pistons either side of a large, bony head. Its eyes seemed sunken into its skull and its dry and greying tongue lolled over the side of its sharp yellow teeth. It looked straight at Shannon. Leighton still hadn't moved an inch from where he was stood, she wasn't even sure if he was aware of her being just behind him. He certainly wasn't aware of the dog.

It kept a steady walking pace towards her, eyes unmoving. She edged away from the open doorway at her back, panic filled her from the soles of her feet. She edged slowly towards Leighton issuing a light cough to attract his attention, her eyes never wavering from the lock of fear they had with the dog's own. The lightest touch of her fingers on Leighton's back caused him to flinch wildly. He dropped the rifle to the floor, spun and taking an awkward step back away from her, tripped over the soldier's corpse and landed flat on his back.

In neither of the couple's line of vision the dog started to speed up. It saw the larger human fall and decided to try its luck.

Shannon gasped and leant over to give Leighton a hand back to his feet. As she did, Zeke came away from her breast and said, "'Oof," pointing a middle finger directly at the hungry beast.

"Leighton, get up. Look," Shannon said pointing across the green at the incoming animal.

"Shit," he replied. He leant over the body to pick the rifle off the ground, getting to one knee as he did so. He let the magazine fall out into his hand to see the glint of a bullet lying on top and with a quick, sharp motion shoved it back into place. The dog was trotting now straight towards him, teeth bared. He stared down the barrel and slowly pressed the trigger, but it resisted him. He turned the gun on its side and flicked the safety off and on again. He stared down at the dog a second time and more rapidly pulled the trigger down. Rather than a loud crack and powerful recoil, the gun did nothing but eke out a sombre click. Something was wrong with it. He looked back up at the dog, pushed Shannon back towards the building and inspected the seemingly useless gun in his hand.

About thirty metres measured the space between him and the jaw full of saliva covered teeth. The dog skipped its feet as it picked up to a full run, still not deviating from its direction. Leighton judged the space between himself and the house. Twenty metres now. Too late to run. He scanned the ground in the opposite direction. Ten metres. "Shit," he exhaled and rolled to one side getting both hands onto an abandoned shotgun as he did.

The blast felt deafening and his ears instantly started to ring. The animal's front legs buckled and it slid to a halt a few feet from where Leighton lay. Its back legs kicked, throwing the torso into the air. A raspy sound bellowed and heaved and Leighton scrambled himself away. The thrashing continued far longer than Leighton was comfortable with. When the creature stopped, he could see the chest still rising and falling erratically. He stood himself up and with two hands tightly wrapped around the grip of the shotgun he bought it down hard on the dog's neck. He had aimed for what remained of the head, but the sporadic movements of the animal made it difficult. The breathing became hoarser and now held a faint whistle deep within the sound. Leighton raised the weapon directly over his head and with a woodchopper's motion he finally struck true. Stillness remained.

Leighton let go of the gun where it was and checked in all directions from the green before picking up the rifle again and scarpering into the open doorway. Shannon was not there and Leighton slumped on the bottom stair. Guilt burned at his chest and he let a sweep of images flood his brain. A tsunami of horrid things he couldn't undo. With no time to steady himself before the flashbacks hit, he was engulfed. Engulfed in flames and water with nothing that would douse the flames and no light guiding him to the surface. He wept. Shannon, leant with her back up against one of the large barrels and surrounded by death, wept too.

Half an hour passed Shannon and Leighton by, while they sat where they were with bodies strewed around them. It was Leighton that managed to recover first and before rousing his wife from her trance, he picked up a different rifle and another two magazines of ammo which now hung out of his jacket pockets.

After picking Shannon up off the ground, he loaded them both with the bags from around the corner and ushered her in the direction of the western road that he had confirmed on his new map was the best way to get towards his parents' farm. Shannon didn't speak a word the whole time. As much as Leighton was worried, he understood and he needed to get them safe as soon as possible.

They walked past the church and past more buildings that now barely resembled the original plans designed for them. When they were about to leave sight of the green, Leighton told Shannon to keep moving while he turned around, released the safety and fired a successful test shot into the closest barrel. He checked through his lens and saw that it was dead centre.

"I've still got it," he said to himself with a smile. He turned on his heels and saw that Shannon had stopped to watch him. A smile crossed her face and she put her hand into his as they walked on.

Chapter 42

Grace and Tariq sat at the kitchen table across from each other with a bottle half-full of clear stream water and a glass each. Grace sat with her back against the wall so she could see the door just behind Tariq's shoulder. Her hand shook visibly as she lifted the glass for each sip of water and Tariq wore empathy on his face. He didn't know what to say or do to help her feel comfortable. At the moment, she needed silence and so he let it ring out.

She eventually broke the peace. "I need to know I can trust you. How did you get here and what do you know?"

Tariq started near the beginning of his cycle ride out of the city, the information he had that led to his decision and seeing the bomb. He went on to talk about the witch hunt he had been victim of at Anton's house and his short time at the garage and then spoke in far too much depth of the various ailments he had suffered from over the last ten days. He demonstrated, by removing a handful of hair and proffering it across the table. He described the town with the red pyramid and carefully avoided going into too much detail about the dead bodies that he had seen. While he talked, he regularly coughed away a dry throat and took sips of water, filling his glass three times in all.

Meanwhile, Grace stared across the table at him, intent on every word he spoke. Tariq had encompassing and expressive eyes that she found hard to not get lost in. He seemed genuine and open and she decided that she had no option right now than to let him into her life.

"Well, if it is any consolation, I think you have the bone structure to pull off being bald," she said to break her hour-long silence.

Tariq laughed. "Well I haven't looked in a mirror since my hair started to come out so I am just imagining it is currently as patchy as anything. I have a question for you."

"Go ahead."

"Do you have the facilities to have a wash and a shave? I can tell by the wrinkling of your nose that I must stink like someone who hasn't showered in a week and slept outside almost that entire time."

"We don't have running water, but we certainly have soap, shampoo and razor blades that you are more than welcome to take down to the stream just outside."

"Thank you, Grace. I must say I very much appreciate your hospitality. Is there anything I can do for you first?" You can tell me how you came here once I am smelling bearable again. Is that okay?"

"You go ahead. While you are there, take these two bottles and fill them up before you wash. Oh, and you can find what you need in the bathroom. It's upstairs and to the left."

Tariq thanked her sincerely and went upstairs to return with a towel and lavender shower gel. As he walked past, Grace stopped him. "I want to thank you for finding me, Tariq. When you get back I will tell you my story and we will make a plan."

"That's good. I like a plan. Also, I am glad I found you. No offence, but it looks like you could do with a bit of assistance." He glanced at her leg

Tariq returned with the large towel wrapped around his waist. He had only been planning on a day or two away from home and a change of clothes was not on his priority list. "Hi, Grace," he said. "Sorry about…" he pointed himself up and down. "I have laid my clothes out on one of the chairs out on the porch to dry. Is that okay?"

"Yea, that's fine. Come and take a seat and I will fill you in."

Tariq pulled up a chair and sat cross-legged under the towel while grace started talking. She took a little while to get her story started and Tariq had to ask probing questions to get a good account of everything. She went through the events of being trapped in the house and finally getting rescued by Mina.

"So, you and Mina are quite close, then?" Tariq asked.

"Yea, we are really close. She is like a sister to me. -Or something like that anyway," she answered.

"We need to go get her back then, right?"

"I don't know, she told me before she left that she was going to escape, because they were stupid as shit."

Tariq pondered for a minute. "We don't know really where she is though, do we? Except for that they must be somewhere north or so from here. It isn't exactly going to be easy. Did they let on anything, or would Mina have left a note about something they could have discussed while here?"

"I don't think so. The only clue I have seen is the handcuff hanging from the oven door. I guess if they undid the cuffs that way around, she is probably right about their intelligence."

"Let's see," Tariq said.

"See for yourself. You aren't going to get a guided tour from a cripple," she said with a laugh.

Tariq sniggered compassionately and got up to look. He pulled on the handcuff and the oven opened, revealing an out of date flyer for an amateur dramatics production and a pen. "It looks as though your girl is a smart one." He picked up the flyer. "Do you know where 'Draycot, west' is?"

"There is Draycot Foliat a little to the west of here. Let's take look," Grace said reaching her arm out towards Tariq who placed the note into her hand, while with his other he kept his towel up. "She means west of that Draycot. That's my clever little bestie."

"How far exactly?"

"I would say about five miles. I have only ever driven. Maybe… Definitely no more than ten."

"That's manageable." He eyed Grace's leg. "-For me certainly. How does that thing feel?"

"It's manageable. I haven't left this house since we put the cast on, but I can't put weight on it yet, I am not sure I trust the cast to handle it. We made it ourselves."

Tariq was shocked. "Really!? That's ace. Can I have a look at it?"

"Yea sure," she said, lifting the baggy pyjama bottoms so that he could see the whole thing. Tariq knelt next to her and inspected it.

"Looks fantastic. Well done, Mina."

Tariq felt awash with exhaustion suddenly. "Is there anywhere I can sleep here?"

"Yea, well," she started. "I was thinking about this while you were outside."

"Uh-huh," prompted Tariq.

"Would you mind helping me upstairs... And I would quite like it if you were to sleep in the same room as me. Would you be comfortable with that? I mean I don't make a habit of asking naked men to stay in the same bed with me, but I trust you and it would help me feel safe. I'll find you some bedclothes of course. None of *that* thing. You know what I mean?"

Tariq laughed and his cheeks reddened a little. "No problem. If you will feel safer, it is the least I can do for your offer of accommodation. I can sleep on the floor if you want?"

"No, you sound like you need a proper bed after your ordeal."

"Then I promise to keep my hands to myself, then. None of *that* stuff."

Shannon awoke in the night to suppress her restless son. The sound of his suckling seemed to fill the tent with noise and she wondered how it was not loud enough to wake Leighton from sleeping. Below that sound, she could only make out the softened rustling noises that usually filled the woods that had offered them home for the past few weeks.

They had discussed staying in the houses in the town, having a fresh bed and possibly some clean running water. Leighton had taken the experience hard and Shannon fought her desire for warmth and comfort to take them back out into the forest and towards their target destination.

A rustling outside the tent seemed to become rhythmical and Shannon checked the edges to see if some creature was leaning against the sides or even trying to burrow in, but the sound seemed to be coming from multiple directions around it. She nudged Leighton to rouse him.

Before he was even awake, two blades appeared above them and the tent was torn into two halves that pulled away like a magic trick. Leighton picked up the taken rifle beside him and stared wide and bleary eyed into four torch lights directed down and dazzling him.

A few seconds passed as Leighton weighed up his situation. Shannon was stunned to silence holding Zeke to her chest tightly. Her husband deliberately released his right hand from the grip and held out the gun by the barrel. It was swiftly grasped from him. Zeke started to wail and two of the voices behind the torch light spoke a few indeterminable words.

"Get up," said a voice that was quickly followed by an arm under Shannon's armpit lifting her. She barely needed to use her legs, such was the force that dragged her up and instead she focussed on rocking Zeke, with much more anxious vigour than would be able to calm him.

Another voice spoke, motioning with a torch close to Leighton's face, "You too. Get up."

Leighton took the hint and neglecting his nudity, stood up with his hands still, palms outwards in line with his face.

"Ah, wear some clothes," the voice spoke again with disgust. The torch lights surrounding him moving slightly back.

"My jeans are here, no funny business." Leighton asked slowly pointing to the pair that lay on the ground sheet of the tent. "Just don't hurt her or my boy. I am coming quietly."

"Hurry up and you won't have a problem."

Deprive

Chapter 43 - Day 10

Grace lay awake in the early morning light. Tariq had slept restlessly all night and had managed to get himself on top of the duvet. Mina's light pink pyjama bottoms contrasted against his tanned skin, his body was all clearly defined muscle and protruding bones. He looked fit, but certainly not healthy. She inspected his patchy hair and decided she would help shave his head when he was up. She eventually got bored and nudged him awake gently.

Tariq roused slowly, adjusting himself before realising his company and quickly pulling the cover up to his stomach. Grace looked at the confused and disorientated expression on his face as he erratically picked his watch up off the bedside table and checked the time.

"It's still early," he murmured.

"I don't think there is any rush. You can go back to sleep if you want," Grace told him.

"Nah, I need to get up to pee anyway. I think I've slept better outside this week than I did last night."

"You were restless. You woke me up a couple of times."

"I'm sorry. Do you want me to let you sleep?" He asked.

"No, don't worry. The only work we have today is to organise a rescue, so it should be light going." Tariq looked over to determine where the sarcasm was in her comment. Grace laughed at Tariq's further confusion. "You're good. Go pee, then we'll get you neatened up and shave that head of yours. We'll have to sleep in a bed full of hair if we don't."

Tariq laughed and ran a hand over his head. It felt lighter. "Alright. That'd be good."

He got up, carefully twisting himself to the side as he did so. After he peed in the toilet without thinking and tried the

263

handle he heard Grace call through, "I should have reminded you that we have no running water."

"All right. I'll sort it soon. You may as well go too and I'll flush it before I go get more water."

"That's a good idea. You know, I don't want to come across too needy or anything so soon, but could you give me a bit of a lift?"

"Yea. No problem," Tariq called back, stepping across the landing.

"Mina looked after me pretty well, I hadn't even thought about what it would be like without her being around."

"Well while we sort everything out, if you need anything, let me know."

Mina sat near the locked door of a large barn. She had pulled herself as far into the corner as she possibly could with her knees tucked against her breasts and her poncho pulled down until it covered her feet. The poncho's hood was wide and lopped over most of her face leaving her as a small grey bundle in the corner, almost unnoticeable, the way she wanted to be.

Along the left side of barn lay five sleeping bodies – three men and two women – slightly tucked under long-abandoned church pews pushed up against the outer wall. The five of them had been here before her and she had yet to attempt communication with them. She wasn't even sure if they knew she was there. On the opposite wall hung shelves and a work bench hosting some decrepit and rusted tools. Mina could tell by the empty hooks that those considered the more dangerous had been removed. The rest of the far side was bare. There was plenty of straw in the barn adding to the smell, which was stacked neatly in large cuboid bricks against the entire edge of the farthest wall, shaped as four long steps leading up to an abrupt stop.

At some point during the night, a couple had been let in. It had been too dark at the time, but she could see where they were lay now, nestled on the lower level of the straw stack, with the morning light that streamed in from the old and cracked wooden walls. The woman was clutching a bag that they were allowed in with and the man faced outward in front of her. They were as asleep as the others.

A rattle to the right of Mina's head indicated that the doors were about to open and she adjusted her hood a little lower. The opening of the door let light flood in, the air moving visibly from the dust swishing around in small circles. After a few moments and a few footsteps, the door slammed shut and an addition of a tray remained. Mina freed her legs and moved quickly over to it. She pulled an end off one of the loaves of bread and filled one of the small plastic cups with water from a large jug. It was barely a blink of an eye until she had retreated to her corner, only she held a glass of water between her feet and a chunk of bread in her hands. She took a small nibble of the bread and glanced carefully under the hood. The man was sat up now, revealing his partner's colourful head wrap behind him and their eyes met. He had noticed her.

A slam roused Leighton and he fought his urge to roll over and shut his eyes when he noticed the unfamiliar surroundings. The first thing to catch his eye was a small grey clad figure move from the corner of the barn to a point a little way in front of the barn doors at the far end. At first, he was concerned that it was a farm animal they had been shacked up with all night without him realising, but as he strained his eyes to focus, he saw a pair of pale hands reach out from the stooped figure and take something. It moved back quickly and covered itself with its cloak, almost disappearing in the dim light and shadowed corner. He stretched his arms, staring quizzically at the figure until a pair of fierce eyes peered directly at him from under the hood. It was a woman.

He made a useless, but concerted effort to divert his gaze which led him to look directly away into the corner behind him where the walls should have met the high-pointed roof. He looked straight through a large hole and he moved his head around to see that blue was peering through some of the light cloud that covered most of the small amount of sky he could see.

Leighton looked down at his wife and child, who remained deep in sleep and decided to explore for himself first and introduce himself to the huddled woman. As he stood, the space she had briefly visited glinted. He walked over to it slowly, occasionally glancing over to the corner to look for an opportunity to smile or wave, but the woman was stock-still. He knelt with the tray of bread and water in between him and her and poured a glass of water. The woman still hadn't moved, but he decided to go closer and say hello.

A few meters away he hunkered down and took a sip of the water. "Hi – er – I wasn't expecting room service here," he said and chuckled to himself. The hood moved and he could see her left eye peering anxiously at him. A finger slid over her mouth, shushing him and then she pointed ahead of her. Leighton followed her finger until his eyes found five sleeping bodies, their clothes familiar. His jaw dropped. "Oh," he said, unable to find any more syllables as his brain – still warming up – struggled to fit together all the pieces of the puzzle he had found himself in.

The pair were silent for a few moments as Leighton took in the view of the barn from the woman's angle. "Sorry," he said eventually in a whisper. "I'm Leighton." He reached out a hand that wasn't taken. The woman cleared her throat before residing to further silence. "Over there are my wife, Shannon, and my son, Zeke-"

"Son?" the woman asked. "How old?"

"He's nearly seven months."

"Oh. I'm sorry," she said. Before Leighton could say any more she dropped her head at the sound of movement from one of the rurally-dressed figures. "You should take him food. There's bread." A finger closed her mouth once more before the hood came down fully over her face and closed the conversation.

Chapter 44

Grace and Tariq sat on the edge of the bed and ate dry granola bars that Tariq had sourced from one of the kitchen cupboards. The water – fresh from the stream – was refreshingly cool and they drank heartily. Tariq eyed his pillow from the night before, seeing the loose black hairs that covered it. Grace noticed his glance.

"Don't worry," she said, placing a hand on Tariq's shoulder. "We will sort that now. The scissors and razors are in the bathroom."

Tariq blew his cheeks out. "It's not really the hair exactly that I'm worried about," He sighed. "It's what else might be wrong."

Grace shushed him. "You can't think about that now. There are far more pressing things to deal with. You may not live long enough to find out what the damage is anyway, right? Silver lining."

"You're dark," he replied, his eyes widening with the thought.

"I guess."

Tariq picked Grace up with ease and walked through to the bathroom. He placed her down so she could sit on the edge of the bath and reach the sink. After moving the shaving equipment next to her and filling the sink with some water from a bucket he knelt in between her legs and bowed his head.

"Ready?" Grace asked, her hand poised with open scissors somewhere above his head.

Tariq released a breath and nodded.

Grace started cutting into the longer hair until it got close enough to the scalp that she could start the wet shave. Before she started she could see where it had thinned in patches and some areas left the scalp bare. She took care and time, applying a small patch with shaving foam and rinsing the blade in the water after every few millimetres of her stokes. The concentration on the task was allowing her to relax and for the first half an hour they spent like that, no thoughts of injuries or illnesses crossed either of their minds. They talked naturally and Tariq told her about the things that seemed weird in England after growing up in Egypt.

That conversation moved on to him explaining what it was like when he was growing up and particularly about being a teenager during the Arab Spring uprising. Grace found it hard to grasp the concept of such a large revolution happening and was disbelieving when Tariq talked through in detail the mirror in events to the KoYΔ riots he had witnessed in this country.

"That was here?" She asked incredulously.

"Damn straight it was. Me and-" Tariq cut off for a moment. "Me and Anton were reporting on it, right amid it all happening. We fled when we saw the soldiers coming in to meet the group as we would have been right behind the path of the bullets. The shocking thing was the lack of coverage. During the Arab Spring, we had Al-Jazeera and BBC News keeping a mediating eye on proceedings. The riots – and the deaths – in London recently never got mentioned in detail. The subjugation of that news after the event was more terrifying. Here was me thinking that Britain was a freer country than my own. Perhaps I was wrong."

All Grace could manage was a murmur and an erratic nod, taking in the information that opposed her belief. As she finished Tariq's head she figured she should be less surprised after everything that had happened in the last fortnight.

Mina spent the morning huddled in her corner slowly picking at the bread she picked up from breakfast, ignoring the sounds of people talking mutedly and moving around the rest of the barn aimlessly. She had found a gap in the wall near her that allowed her to see the rest of the farm complex.

In what she assumed was the centre, was a circular raised flower bed within which a large oak tree flourished, leaves spreading out in the sun. The other side of that hosted a large metal structure to house animals, though it was devoid of them now. It looked to be made of several stalls made up of metal bars. In two places, the back wall had a break that showed behind it the rising ground densely covered with trees. The roof was flat and not steeply angled, meeting the rear wall at its lowest point and the canopy of the woods could be seen easily rising over the horizon line at the top of the hill.

To Mina's right, she could see the main two-storey farmhouse, which stood grandly with dormer windows in the steep roof that had a white trim that matched that of the roof peak on the near end.

She could see a few soldiers milling around throughout the morning. The first was a while after breakfast, when a lone man, young and blond cleared a bunch of bags out of the Land Rover that she had been transported in the day before and threw them into a shed that stood some way to the left of the animal stalls. She watched the front of the house for some time before she noticed a silo that reared up behind it. Later, a pair of men, one greying at his temples and the other in a dark blue beret, walked down the driveway that stretched out of her line of sight to the left and two others returned, both with dark hair.

She spent her time that way, pressed up against the hole, trying to gauge how many may be around. Since her capture yesterday, she had picked up that the young blond man was always one of two that came to open the door to leave food and empty the bucket of water that had been left as a toilet in the corner on the other side of the door. He was always accompanied by a fatter brown-haired man, but she had convinced herself that there were two of a similar build and hair colour, but she couldn't see enough detail in any of the men's faces to be able to know for certain whether to count two or just one. She had seen the two men that had taken her the previous day on one of the patrols, but most of the other six she thought she could account for had been on two.

Her train of thought was broken by the in-swinging door. They must have come from the other direction as she hadn't seen them, but a presence must indicate lunch. She was sucked deep into thought. Why was she in that barn? It seemed clear to her that there was no risk of a court marshalling for not following the rules of war, not that she felt that rules of war were even adhered to or relevant. War was war. Mindless killing of children by other brainwashed children for money or power or both. They could – should – have just killed her in her own home and taken what they wished. They must have a purpose that involves her being alive for at least a while longer yet. She contemplated the packet of tablets in her bra and subdued her thoughts. Grace still needed her.

Tariq sat next to Grace at the kitchen table. In front of them lay an array of reference books, pens and half-used pads of paper, with an unfolded ordinance survey map spread out underneath it all covering most of the table. Tariq had taken a pencil to the map which traced a route from Mina's house to the western edge of Draycot Foliat. Off from the thickly blackened path, various faint lines branched off still coated in rubbings where his ideal route had changed repeatedly. While he had been focussed on a route that would take them west of the destination town without going through any villages, Grace had been jotting down a list for things they would need. She had scanned through several books on self-sustained and off-grid living and had come to a list that in two columns filled an A4 page of the notebook.

Tariq looked over the list and asked, "How are we going to shift all this stuff? -And you?"

"Well, I saw Mina come down to the shop once with a little bike trailer to carry groceries. We could look at that."

Tariq mulled it over. "That will certainly do. So, on the list how much of it do we need?"

"That depends on how long we are staying. This is the long list of potential equipment and supplies. How long does your part of the plan take?"

"Let me see." Tariq unravelled a ball of string and held it carefully along his proposed route. "I reckon a day and a half should be comfortable. That allows for the awkwardness and energy sapping process of carting you about, regular stops and getting lost on at least two occasions."

"I can take the stool 'a.k.a. Zimmer-frame'. Would that be easier?"

"Two days." Tariq said firmly, "No. I can take you."

Grace was taken aback by his tone. "I can stay here and you can go. You could be there and back in a day without me."

"No chance." Tariq realised what he was doing and softened his face deliberately. "It's all good, Grace. I don't want to get Mina back here and see you having had an accident. The day and a half is only there, so we would still need that again to get back and we don't know a single thing about where they are set up, nor the intelligence of the other members of the squad. I want to have you close over there so I can look after you. Plus, once we get Mina it would be easier to plan for whatever else we need to do if we're mobile already."

Grace pondered the man's already fierce loyalty to her wellbeing and why he would be like that so quickly. She stopped as she noticed herself staring quizzically at him. "Will you have a look at this list and see if we can narrow it down."

Tariq leaned over her shoulder while she read off the list. He took it all in before questioning her on the availability and feasibility of each item and as he did so they put pen marks through those that answered 'no'.

Leighton had spent the day almost silently as he huddled his family back into the straw. The dominant noise in the barn was the sniffs and sobs coming from the five people over to their right. It was some time into the afternoon when he had figured out they must have been involved in the failed ambush the day before. His mind had been numb and very little attention could be channelled into the situation they found themselves in. Lunch had been very much like breakfast except for the addition of some slabs of cheese. He had gotten to it second – after Mina – and picked the softest bits of bread and cheese for Shannon and Zeke. Mina, having simply ripped the end of the bread off must have endured the stale crust. The group inside the barn had a glass of water each from the jug provided with each meal.

There was a bucket in the corner by the door which was for use as a toilet. It was not often used such was the parched throats they all endured in between the meals. It did seem to Leighton that it was thankfully changed each time the door was opened.

The rest of the day drifted lazily past. Shannon rarely spoke except for high-pitched whispers with Zeke. Leighton thought that it was being rudely awakened in the middle of night that the boy felt more docile than normal, Leighton felt the same. Zeke seemed more than content to live on his mother's lap for the day's duration. Eventually, dinner came. It must have come late as the sky outside the barn door was starting to dim. This meal was certainly better than the previous two. It consisted of a baked potato and a pot of something resembling a pasta sauce. It tasted bad in comparison to Shannon's last carefully prepared meal. Compared to the seven meals before that, it was a veritable feast.

The crying from the other group seemed to get louder as the dark of night washed over them. It was reaching pitch darkness inside before the artificial lights in the complex came on. It was a while after that one of the soldiers came and banged on the outside of the wooden wall near them to encourage them to quieten down and it was only then that Leighton noticed behind him the rhythmical sounds of his family in deep sleep. He spent a while attempting to join them, before getting lost in the sight of the stars through the opening in the roof. He told himself to talk to the farmers tomorrow, before it would be considered weird not to have done so before, even allowing for their grieving state.

The sky grew darker and the stars grew brighter. Leighton had no idea how long he had been awake for, shutting his eyes together only for the briefest instants. He was disturbed each time by the feeling in his mind of pushing himself off that warm, but dead body.

Chapter 45 - Day 11

Tariq loaded the panniers and another rucksack along with his own onto the bike. They were all loaded with as many dry foods as they had been able to conjure up from Mina's cupboards. Grace sat herself forward in the cart with her cast leg leant up quite comfortably on the pannier in front of her. Her head would have overhung the back if hadn't been raised up on a stack of water bottles that Tariq had found in the basement and had filled with water from the stream.

The first part of the route took them back through the town so they could leave it again heading south-west. Tariq tried to take a good pace from the outset, but had found it hard going over the rough path and when he turned to glance at Grace over his shoulder he could see her bumping around, just about holding her leg on the pannier. He slowed down quickly after that, which made it harder to push through the potholes without the momentum behind the front tyre.

They went through the town quicker once on the smoother road with enough space to weave around the more damaged parts of the concrete. Grace saw the building that was previously her shop and kept her eyes on it sadly and silently for as long as she comfortably could as they went past. As she straightened her neck forward again, the green appeared to her right in between buildings where the road led up to it. She noticed Tariq sneer awkwardly and look away from it quickly. She took a moment to work out what had caused him to do so, until it dawned on her what those dark mounds indicated. She thought back about the pops and cracks she had heard alongside Mina two days prior. She was grateful when it became obvious that that was the closest they would go to it, but it lingered in her mind longer than she was comfortable with, wishing she could at least be doing something that could distract her. Walking, hobbling along using the bike for support, anything, but be pulled along helplessly.

They were out of the town and out along a long straight road that had a bend that would take them north-west for a number more miles. It was on the outside of that bend, able to see over a mile in each direction, that they stopped properly for the first time. Tariq had worked up a sweat under his t-shirt and stared down the road ahead of them as he gulped from one of the bottles. He looked tired. He passed the bottle roughly to Grace who took more controlled sips and he flung himself onto his back atop the soft verge.

Breakfast seemed to come later the next day. Late enough that the farmers were already awake by the time the door swung open. The baby at the other end of the barn was what woke Mina up. She had stayed awake for as long as she could, staring out into the floodlit complex looking for clues to the patrols and routines of the soldiers. She figured that it may be pointless without a watch and paper to make notes on, but still wanted to try in case it became useful information when time for her escape came around.

When the door opened to deliver breakfast, the three male farmers stood up quickly to ensure they reached the plates first. As the door swung closed they tore into the bread before the chain and padlock were even locked and in place. As they walked back to the two women with them, Mina noticed from under her hood, a disgusted look thrown in her direction. Anxiety flared up in the depths of her stomach and she lost all appetite. She saw that they had taken a larger share than would go around the nine of them fairly. She noticed Leighton walking towards the tray and she went over to intercept him. She needed a distraction.

"Hi," she said. "I think they took more than they should have." She had aimed for a conversational tone, but couldn't keep bitterness from her tongue.

Leighton looked over at them sat in a closed circle eating and talking, but he couldn't work out what they were saying. "Oh well. Never mind." Leighton shrugged it off.

"I'm not hungry. You take the rest and make sure you keep that boy fed."

Leighton chuckled and waved her offer away. "Why don't you come meet him? Might be more comfortable for you to sit in a group. You don't look like you can afford too many missed meals."

Mina blushed and with another glance over his shoulder, Leighton picked up the whole tray and walked with Mina in tow back to Shannon and Zeke. Leighton's son was sat upright with a bale of straw as a back-rest and seemed unfazed by the stranger. She waved enthusiastically enough to get a smile back in return.

"This is my son, Zeke, and wife, Shannon. This is-." He cut off. "Sorry I don't think I remember your name."

"It's Mina," she filled in. "Nice to meet you." She reached out her shaking hand and Shannon took it and then did the same for Zeke to grab which he took, directing her little finger straight towards his mouth. She pulled away before he could take a bite.

Leighton put out his hand, "Nice to meet you, Mina. Come, sit down." Over Mina's shoulder he could see glances in their direction from the others and he dropped his look to Shannon, who was giving him a quizzical expression. "She was on her own over in the corner, I figured she might want some company. You'll never guess what *they* did, Shannon." Leighton was suddenly enraged, snarling around his words. "They took too much bread!"

"Settle down, honey. We'll do fine. Sit down," Shannon said with a nervous smile to both Leighton and Mina. Leighton obliged, thrusting a fist into the straw as he did so. Shannon turned to Mina, "So how long have you been in here?"

Mina cast a wary glance at Leighton before answering. "Only the afternoon before you came in during the night,"

Mina replied. "Where are you two from and how did you wind up in here."

Shannon started and eventually Leighton and she took turns explaining parts of the journey, starting with leaving the house and their slow walk across the country. They didn't mention the town with the convenience store as he led that part of the story. They explained what they saw at the village, to occasional gasps from Mina, especially when it became clear who the other people in the barn were. After that, she explained her own part at the village, hearing the distant bangs like fireworks and the eventual arrival of the soldiers that had brought her to that farm. She left out the fact that she left her injured friend at that house to fend for herself and that she intended to escape in the not-too-distant future.

The conversation ended when the door opened and flooded the barn with midday light. The barn otherwise had a reasonable ambient light given the cracks and holes in the wooden walls and roof. The silhouettes of the three men close in front of the door, broke the light. "Look, Shannon, they're going to do it again, this isn't right. It's not fair." He gesticulated wildly towards the men. After a short rant, Shannon was able to calm him down.

Shannon told Mina, privately, "I'm sorry about him, Mina. He's taken things pretty hard. I'm not sure I even know the full story behind it."

Grace switched her eyes between the road behind, the road ahead and Tariq, who was now sat up on the verge flicking his eyes in the same manner down the road. There was no sound of vehicles. Grace felt as though they were truly in the middle of nowhere, although only a few miles separated them from named towns and villages, even if those settlements had no body to settle in them.

"You look tired already, Tariq," she said. "Do you want a snack before we get going?" He looked pale.

"Yes, please," he replied. "What has the most sugar?" Grace lifted her leg from the pannier and pulled herself forward to rummage through it. She came up with a flapjack bar with honey and threw it gently to Tariq who caught it easily in one hand. "Thanks, I just need sugar to lift my energy levels. It's a hard walk with the bike, I can feel it in my back and shoulders from leaning across it."

"I can imagine," Grace said empathetically. "You need to switch sides as we go. It looks as though it will be easier going for the next part along this road." Tariq nodded, eyes focussing on his next bite while he continued to chew the last one. Grace watched him eat. Once he was swallowing the last mouthful she spoke up again. "Why do you even care about me, Tariq? Why are you looking after me? -And why are you helping me rescue Mina? Surely it would be the sensible option for you to just pack up and leave me here or better yet, never come to me at the house. You could easily survive much more efficiently on your own than with some poor injured woman."

Tariq mulled over the questions deeply before answering. "There would be no point surviving if surviving was all it would be. For any of us to truly survive we need to live and create a healthy society and that doesn't stem from leaving the weak behind, from only looking out for yourself.

"It was predominantly a selfish act by me to approach the house. I needed food and shelter and figured it would be empty after seeing your friend carted off. I assumed they would have taken everyone, but wouldn't have been able to take everything. When you appeared in the doorway, I was surprised and even more so to see that you had a broken leg. It was the influence of seeing how my dad acted back in Egypt that came through in me when I realised that you needed help. When I was about sixteen or seventeen, my dad joined a group of people that were looking to overthrow the government. They were all men of the people and wanted a better world for their children. He originally started out in the political wing of the organisation, which was run in small cells at that time, but as things started to build in momentum and things got more violent he was moved over to a military cell. He ran things differently to a lot of the others, which from the reports we would see on the news, were running a much more aggressive campaign. My dad was kind and fair and our house ended up being somewhat a sanctuary for people passing through. If he came across people injured or in need he would put himself out to make sure they were safe. My mother studied as a nurse for some time when she was young and still living in England and the downstairs became a makeshift hospital for children and elderly people, whether they believed in the uprising or supported the government. He didn't care. To him, if someone needed something he could give, he would give it. It was that care for others that was the most resounding trait he had. I want to continue that. That's why I can't leave you behind. He wouldn't have." Tariq lowered is head a little and muttered something to himself.

Grace was leant forward over her leg, which had started to throb wildly as the blood flowed into it. "Well he certainly taught you well. I don't know what I would do without you coming to my need."

Tariq waved the gesture away. "I could have done more," he said only just audibly above the wind. He looked up and met Grace's eyes. "I could have done more. I knew that-, *this* was happening."

"What?" Grace asked.

"The bombs. The killing. I knew it was going to happen. I tried to get an article in The Vigilante, but no one would listen. They wouldn't publish it out of a duty to peace. I only survived because I knew, but I couldn't save anyone else. Nobody would take it seriously. The editor seemed to, but even taken seriously, he didn't act on it. I could have been more influential, I should have rattled every door, taken to the streets or something. If I could have gotten more out of the city or got some backing somehow, maybe the death toll would be that much lower." Tariq slammed his fist suddenly and violently into the dirt beneath him and the motion made Grace flinch. He seemed otherwise so calm and controlled.

She felt a tear in her eye, seeing his emotion at helping a society that wasn't even his.

"Remember that you tried, Tariq. It's okay," she told him. "You want a hug?" She smiled compassionately at him and he glanced up to see it, bringing a slight hint at a smile to his face.

"No. I am fine. We have a mission. Let's go get your girlfriend and we can do hugs then." Tariq sniggered to himself as he pushed himself to his feet.

Grace opened her mouth to retort, but decided to set herself up for the ride ahead instead.

Chapter 46

Mina sat alongside Shannon, with Leighton lying at her feet a bale below. Zeke had made his way onto her lap and was playing with the edge of her broad hood, hiding his face behind it and peeking out periodically. Mina was enamoured with Zeke and talked to him quietly and continuously, almost completely ignoring the adults in her company. Sat there with her whole attention on the little human reminded her of the best of times of bringing Rebecca up and she revelled in it. She copied his babbles until the volume rose alternately between them, only stopping when it garnered the attention of the other group. She quickly averted her eyes from them and slowed Zeke down by holding his arms and rocking him back and forth to her hums of a nursery rhyme. However, she could still hear their loud huffing over her tune.

Leighton tapped Shannon's shin with his elbow and she leant forward. "Zeke seems to trust her," he whispered.

"He does. Although I'd be keeping an eye on her too. We really don't know her. You are too trusting too easily."

"She seems alright. Aren't kids meant to be good judges of character?"

"Yes. Don't take this as me *not* trusting her. Okay? I'll give her a shot."

Mina could hear the whispering between the couple and raised the intensity of her humming to give them privacy.

Leighton turned to look at Mina and found her to be sobbing to herself. "Are you okay?" he asked louder than he expected.

Shannon reached and took a bemused Zeke onto her lap whilst she put her hand lightly on Mina's shoulder. "What's up, Hun?" Mina had her hands over her face now, her shoulders bobbing up and down.

Mina shook herself, almost brushing Shannon's hand from her shoulder unwittingly. She sighed loudly. "Sorry," she said, giving her head another shake.

"What's the matter?" Shannon asked.

"I was remembering my little girl. She was up north with my sister when the things started happening. I don't know if she was still there- or is now, I mean."

"It's okay," Shannon said calmly. "Do you want to talk to me alone?"

Mina nodded. "Thank you."

Shannon passed Zeke to Leighton and then moved to the corner under the section of open roof. Leighton lay back on the highest level of straw and placed Zeke front down on his chest. Zeke played with his father's lips, giggling while Leighton stared up into the blue sky. A thought played out across his mind, a thought where he had super powers and flew straight through that gap – he thought he would fit – and blast away all the soldiers and the lock on the barn door before flying his family over to his parents' farm. He chuckled, bouncing Zeke lightly and receiving a laughing smile. The pleasant idea didn't last long. His thoughts moved to the farmers. He pictured himself confronting them and ran through line after line of his confronting speech that would put them in their place. He mulled over the ensuing fist fight where he beat all three of the men down easily, ducking and leaning around their punches as easily as a professional boxer in a bar fight whilst landing damaging punches to their jaws and chests that knocked them out standing or winded them so hard that they struggled to breath. Variations of these thoughts played repeatedly in his mind.

As the sun settled onto the edge of the horizon, Tariq and Grace reached the point in their route closest to Draycot Foliat. Tariq was sweating profusely, the hot day still not cooling into the evening by much. A few turns along the country road later and with a steep rise then to their left, Tariq spotted something to cause him to stop.

"Looks like a good place to stop. Look." Tariq pointed a third of the way up the rise where rocks protruded from the long grass.

"What is it?" Grace asked. "I can't bloody see from down here!"

Tariq stooped his head a little to see closer to her level. "Ah, sorry," he said. "It looks like there is a bit of natural cover up there. I'm going to run up and have a look."

"Good idea. I think we will be stranded without any light soon, anyway." Grace calmly watched as Tariq ran far enough up the grassy bank for his head to be level with the rocks. It didn't take long for him to come back.

"Right, it will take a bit of effort to get up there, but will be worth it. It seems to go back into the hill a little bit so we will have good cover above and on three sides. What I don't know is what we are going to do with the bike and cart." Tariq stood anticipating the clever response from Grace.

"Wherever we are looking from here, we must be close. I reckon if it's good enough cover in your opinion, then we should take it up with us out of sight of the road, hopefully."

Tariq thought for a moment. "Sounds good. I will need something to eat before we start getting everything up there. It'll take a good few trips." He grabbed a bag of raisins from the pannier and stuffed a few handfuls into his mouth. "Let's go. We start with you."

Grace offered to take herself up, shuffling on her bum. It took quite a bit of persuading and she was a quarter of the way up before Tariq was confident enough to go back down for the first of the bags and by the time she was halfway to the rocks, he was already shoving water bottles under his arms for his third trip. Every time he went past her he would ask if she was going okay or give a thumb-up or questioning smile. She reached the top at the same time Tariq had managed to haul the trailer up alongside the opening.

"Let me help you up," he said, taking her under her arms and lifting her easily to standing. He walked her over to the small cave. It had just enough space at the back to shuffle under in a sleeping bag, maybe just about the two of them at a squeeze. In front, it opened enough that you could sit up and still just be under cover and if they turned the cart over to cover the rest of their gear they could keep most of that dry if it did happen to rain. Grace was helped down to sitting just under the cover. The ground was cold and the top of the sun was only just visible over to her left. "One more run," Tariq said. Grace watched his bald head disappear down the hill.

"I'm going to speak to them," Leighton said. "They can't get away with taking food from Zeke."

"Don't," Shannon replied. "You'll only make things worse. If they get pissed off, they could withhold it all. There's three of them and one of you."

"They'll understand if I talk to them. Calmly," he iterated. "They've taken more than their share at every meal today. They need to understand."

Shannon looked away, frustrated. "If you were calm, I would let you go over and make peace. You're not. -And I don't want you going over there. I don't know what's the matter with you. You've got a look in your eye like talking is the last thing you want to do."

Mina looked over at the pair concernedly.

Leighton looked fiercely at Shannon and she held his gaze. "Right," Leighton said firmly. "You're right. I'm sorry. I'm on edge. We all are."

"Zeke. Give Daddy a hug." Shannon passed their son to him and he held him close, Zeke's chin resting on his dad's shoulder. Shannon looked at Leighton's now softened eyes earnestly. "Get your shit together."

Tariq helped Grace under the cover of the cave, snuggly inside the thick sleeping bag taken from Mina's home. Tariq laid his out next to hers ready to get into later. He knelt at the mouth of the opening, neatening up their stores of food and other supplies and again covering them with the upside-down cart. He leant in close to Grace and spoke her name. She didn't stir. He got up quietly, taking a torch and the rear reflective panel from the bike in his hand and climbed up the hill above where Grace slept. He dug the reflective panel partway into the dirt and turned the torch on and off quickly to check it would reflect his torchlight adequately. He quickly glanced around for any other signs of light and noticed that the only lights he could see were that of the moon and stars above him. He would have been awestruck by the clarity with which he could see the Milky Way, if it had not been a reminder of the night view he had from atop the garage forecourt roof.

Tariq moved away from the cave slowly and carefully up the hill. He wanted to get sight of the land at night. If Mina was hidden away somewhere by soldiers there was a likelihood that they would have been able to get a fire going or otherwise get a generator fired up for some electricity. He figured they wouldn't be too scared of being seen either, seeing as they were comfortably rounding up anyone left in the area and easily subduing any resistance.

He reached the top of the hill and instantly saw what he was looking for. At the foot of the hill was a large complex, lit by floodlights. A tall silo blocked half the light coming from the windows of a large farmhouse and he could see a few larger structures dotted around a large, eerily under-lit tree in the centre of a driveway. Farmed fields ran out to the left and far sides and along the side closest to him a patch of dark trees grew up the incline that must have been too steep to farm effectively. The treeline met the complex near the back of a large, rectangular roof. '*This* must *be it*,' he thought to himself, moving his lips soundlessly to the words.

He started moving back down the hill and ensured he was well below the top before turning on the torch to scan for the sign of the cave. His light went back and forth several times before it returned a flash of red light. He aimed towards it and continued to work his way back down, one arm touching the grass behind him as he did so. He used the torch to navigate his way around the top of the cave and get himself into his sleeping bag. It was a long night of thinking and planning, lying still next to Grace, before a short amount of sleep found him.

Chapter 47 - Day 12

Leighton rolled over from where he lay to see Zeke already awake, facing him with open eyes. Zeke smiled and babbled something indecipherable at him and Leighton picked up the boy and sat him against the straw while he pulled one of the bales free to give himself a back rest that faced the two sleeping members of their party. He watched them both sleep for a few minutes expecting them to wake up only shortly after he had, but his gaze drifted up to the hole in the roof. Another clear day was dawning. He felt as if he hadn't slept, but knew he must have to be able to recall such long stress-dreams. It involved either running without the pace to outrun his pursuer or fist fights in which he had inadequate strength to land a proper punch on his target and they left him feeling drained and frustrated in the waking world.

Zeke started to moan and Leighton checked the door to see that he must be too early for breakfast. He nudged Shannon with his foot until she roused.

"He's probably hungry," he said to her quietly, trying not to wake Mina in the process.

"Oh, really?" Shannon asked. She looked around her, she was disoriented. "Yeah. Pass him here then, let's see what I can offer. I've got a headache. Is there water yet?"

"Not yet. Sorry. Can't be too long, though. It's getting quite light outside."

"You've barely stopped staring up at that gap."

"It's tantalising," Leighton said.

"You're obsessed."

"No, I've been thinking."

Shannon stared up at the gap, Zeke suckling at her breast and covered slightly with her jacket. "No, love."

"No, what?" Leighton asked with a smirk.

"You want to get through that gap, don't you?" Shannon spoke a little louder than intended and Leighton took a glance round at the group on the barn floor and turned back to shush her.

"No, no, no." Leighton shook his head. "Well, actually…" His eyes darted left and right. "-Yes. Great idea. We aren't going to just walk out, we need to get outside, unlock the door and get somewhere out of sight before they notice anything is wrong. That is currently *a* potential route to making that happen. Perhaps the only one!"

Shannon groaned. "-And how do *you* expect to get up *there*?"

"It's a plan in progress. When we were up on that hill a couple of days back you said you trusted me to get us out of our predicament. I think I recall you saying you trusted me to make a decision."

Mina interjected, surprising both Shannon and Leighton. "Don't act yet. We need to think about this properly. Do either of you really know how it looks out there? How many soldiers? Whereabouts of all the cover, tools, weapons?" Mina urged them for an answer.

"No," Leighton responded. "Not yet, but now we have a plan we can do some investigation."

"Well, I can already help with a lot of that," Mina said. She smiled.

The door opened and all three of them looked over. "Everyone is getting a shower," yelled an older voice. The usual young, blond soldier placed the tray in the middle of the floor and swapped over the bucket in the corner for a fresh one. "One at a time. Come on!" One of the farmers stood up suddenly. It looked like the older of the men.

He walked towards the door with his chest pushed out. "Go on, then," he said aggressively. "Where're we going?". The barn door slammed shut and something was shouted from the other side, covered by the noise of the chain rattling.

Mina grabbed Leighton's arm. "We don't have much time then to give you your bearings. If I fill you in before we go, you can get a better look on the way to the showers. By the way the one that left, that's Glen."

"Yes, after you. You ok, Shannon?" She nodded. "I'm sorry about getting angry last night. We won't be long."

"It's fine. You just make sure you think this through *thoroughly*." Shannon's eyes shone fire at Leighton who held his hands open to her.

"You trust me?" he asked. Shannon nodded reluctantly.

"Where did you go last night?" Grace asked Tariq. They both sat in the mouth of the cave looking to the right where the sun was resting above the horizon. The sky to the east was faint with a morning haze and it darkened on their left to a royal blue where the sun was yet to touch.

"I thought you were asleep. I'm sorry for leaving you without saying anything. I wanted to catch a good look around while artificial lights and fires were going to be obvious and I wasn't going to be."

"So," she prompted. "Find anything?"

"Yeah. It looks like there is a farm down the other side of this hill. There is power, probably from generators or something. It is the only source of light I could find, so I would make a guess that it is probably where Mina is being held." Tariq pulled out the map and unfurled it between them. His dark pencil line marking their route was clear towards one edge of the map. "We should be somewhere near here." He marked a circle with his finger. "Draycot Foliat is over here which we passed by yesterday. There are a few farms that it could be, here, here and here." He had three fingers of one hand pointed at the separate points. "Now, I can't be sure but it looked like there was a treeline at…" He thought for a moment. "I guess it is the northern and western edge of it. So, that one." He removed two of the fingers. "-And we must be here by this road." He rummaged his free hand into his bag until he had hold of a pen and marked a cross at their location and a circle around the probable farm.

"-But we don't know *for sure* she's there though."

"No, but I intend to take our binoculars and camp out up there for as long as possible to get some confirmation that we are right."

"That's a plan, I guess. If you can see them – and they are trained soldiers – couldn't they see you? I mean Mina said they were dumbasses, but can we believe that they *all* are?"

"I'm not a man fond of taking risks, but I think in the situation…" Tariq paused and said tentatively "Insha'Allah," shrugging his shoulders.

Grace laughed heartedly. "No offence, Tariq, but I never thought *my* country would get bombed and I would be getting bailed out by a Muslim man."

Tariq joined her continued laugh. "Maybe that's only because you guys here never see what Islam is really about. I consider myself an atheist, but some circumstances seem only feasible with help beyond man. A bit of luck or a god."

"Well you seem to have the air of luck around you. If that's God – or Allah – then so be it. I won't be going anywhere, as you may have already guessed. You eat before you go and head east as far as possible so the binoculars won't reflect light towards the town."

"Good shout," Tariq said, with the information processing displaying on his face.

"I watched a sniper movie once." Grace winked.

"-and a good job you did. Maybe help beyond man is woman."

"Don't forget it."

Chapter 48

Mina managed to press her eye against one of the wall's cracks in time to see the man enter the large house to the right. "He's gone into the house. Look through here to the right," Mina said moving away from the wall. Leighton saw the house straight away. Two men stood guard outside. "Behind is a large silo." She waited until Leighton gave her an affirmative grunt. "-And then look left, slowly. You will see a tree in front of the house and then the other side of the driveway bit is an animal shed."

"Mostly open," Leighton said.

"Behind that, is what I think is the most important part. The trees start quite close to the back of that building. It is quite steep, but the trees from ground level cover to the top of the horizon line."

"I like that. I need to see how much cover there is on the ground. I want to know if I can hide in the short term or whether running is the only option."

"I don't know the answer to that yet. Let's go look from the front. You can see the rest."

"What about out those ways?" Leighton pointed to the two walls next to the roof hole.

"You'll be pleased to know that there are no other buildings that way. Straight out onto farmland. I don't think they have any lights on that side. You still want to climb out of that, don't you?"

Leighton nodded and shrugged. "I don't have any other ideas yet." Everyone else in the barn watched as they crossed the long length of the barn to the wall by the door.

The cracks near where Mina had huddled were longer and allowed both to peer out, Mina sat down and Leighton stood leaning above her. She talked him through the rest of the buildings in the complex, mostly small outhouses and sheds.

They saw Glen, in the clothes he had left in, shadowed by three soldiers. They passed out of sight shortly before the chain rattled and the door swung open, hiding Leighton and Mina from their view. "The next one," the same voice as before bellowed out.

Glen walked in with a grin as the next man stood up and started for the door. The older man clapped him on the shoulder as he passed and said, "Give him some grief, yea?" The younger man grinned as a walked forward and made a jerked motion as if he was about to sprint towards the door, before dropping his head and laughing as he disappeared out the door.

"Find something funny, kid?" The younger man asked bitterly. A dull thud and a moan followed shortly after, cutting the laughs short.

"That kid is Warren," Mina mentioned as he walked past the corner of the building. "The other guy is Mark."

Leighton and Mina returned to Shannon and Zeke. Zeke threw his arms out to be picked up and held by his dad. Mina continued to talk through every scrap of information she had about the complex, the soldiers – somewhere around eight of them – and the routines and routes they walked around. She couldn't put times to any of it. While she was talking, each of the other group went to take their shower.

"Why are we even here, Mina?" Leighton asked after a few minutes of silence passed between them. "It makes no sense."

"I've been mulling that very question over in my head, but – alas – I'm at a loss."

"It caught me so much by surprise at first, I never questioned it. The more I think about the situation it seems unnecessary. I mean, technically we're all prisoners of war, but is it a civil war now? I've heard the soldiers' accents. They're just west-country squaddies. Nevertheless, they were still attacked too, by above."

"You'll have to ask one, if you get a chance." Mina shrugged.

The morning observations had already showed Tariq that this farm did contain soldiers in the same camouflage as those he had seen the village. He thought about it and concluded that it probably didn't mean too much. He watched them move around, he was too far away to differentiate anyone, except that there appeared to be one wearing a blue beret, who was at that time near the main passing road. They seemed to have a few periodic patrols set up to maintain a perimeter around the buildings of the complex. No-one had yet taken up a look out position from the top of the silo, which in Tariq's mind would have removed the need for walking. Perhaps they didn't do it through fear of heights or – more accurately – a fear of falling from a great one, perhaps it was that they hadn't thought of it. The sun was high in line with his left shoulder when he noticed someone being walked from the barn. The door of it was on the other side of the building from where he was, but they had walked around it, coming towards him. The man in the middle of the three was not wearing camouflage, instead a dirty flannel shirt and jeans. Tariq saw him get pushed and the man nearly fell. He supposed that if Mina was taken, others would have been too. As the morning progressed, more people came out of the barn, went into the building, only to return about quarter of an hour later.

The rest of the farmers took their turns and it was left with just them to make the walk to the main house. Shannon went first, taking Zeke with her and Leighton recapped the main things he wanted to look at out in the open. When Shannon returned having taken longer than any of the others, Leighton proffered Mina to go first and she stood up reluctantly.

She reached the door without a word. The youngest soldier with the blond hair that she had been watching through the cracks grabbed the hood of her poncho and pushed her roughly around the corner of the building. "Eyes forward. Straight to the house," he said using a fake growling voice.

Mina looked around conspicuously and saw the man in the blue beret walking alongside one of the fatter soldiers down the path from where the driveway eventually met with the main road. She caught him looking straight at her and proffer a hard-lined smile and she turned away, just catching a glimpse of his hand raising in her direction. She continued with her head down and started raising her hood instinctively, but the man behind pulled it out of her hands before she could cover her head.

Within the large two-story building, she was pushed firmly by a calloused hand on her right shoulder. Most of the furniture in the house looked like it was from the 1960's with a few more modern items squeezed in with them. In the downstairs rooms that she was pushed through, most of the inhabiting items had been stacked up against the rear wall. In the dining room, she could just see the top of French windows at the back. She only caught a glimpse at each room the most important of which was a utility room at the other end of the living room, stocked with guns and ammunition.

The sun was warm, beating down on Tariq's back and making him sweat within the only top he now owned, a tight cycling jersey. A few men came first followed by women wearing similar rural dress then – he was surprised to see – a black woman carrying something bundled tightly to her chest. Just before she disappeared behind the cover of the house he noticed it wriggle and a small hand reached up to the woman's shoulder.

"A baby?" he whispered "How many people are in there? Still no Mina. Damn."

Tariq pulled his eyes away from the binoculars to look around him and shuffle until the course patch of long dry grass was irritating a different part of his stomach. When he returned to viewing the complex, a blond woman in a grey poncho walked into sight, cowering her head.

"There you are, Mina," he said to himself, excitement filling him.

Leighton paced from one end of the barn to the other recalling as much of Mina's insight as he could. As he did so he became more and more furious. It crept up on him slowly and unprecedented until his fists were balled up and his shoulders so tight they were almost cramping his undernourished muscles. He made yet another turn just before reaching the bucket by the door and as he turned, he noticed that the five farmers were staring straight at him. He lowered his head, keeping an eye on them as they watched him walk back towards where Shannon and Zeke were napping.

He drew level with them and pulled up abruptly and sighed. "What's up?" he asked, fighting to keep the welling anger out of his tone.

"-With us?" Glen answered. "You're the one looking like your gonna punch your way through the door."

"We're just sitting here. All chilled out. You're making me real nervous, though," Warren added, pulling his feet round as if he was about to stand.

"Well, you don't have to sit there watching me." Leighton pushed his head forward.

"Why don't you just go sit down with your immigrant wife and wait for that weird-ass woman you adopted to come back." Warren looked at the other two guys for a laugh and got only a chiding slap on the back of his head from the woman to his left. Mark was smirking, but Glen seemed impervious.

Fire rose in Leighton's stomach that pulled the corners of his mouth down fiercely. He breathed deeply as if that could put the anger out, but it only fuelled the flames.

"Looks like you got to him, Warren," Mark suggested.

"You alright there?" Warren asked Leighton. "You don't look too good." The other two men seemed to enjoy watching Leighton's internal battle. He could see them both free their legs from how they were sitting.

"You wanna fight or something? Let it out."

Leighton blew his cheeks out. "Why," he sneered. "Why on earth would I want to fight in front of my family? Are you guys fucking serious? What in God's name are you doing by taking an unfair share of the food. I got a baby and breast-feeding wife. You lot are pitiful." Mark looked up to where Shannon was only just stirring.

"Oh, here we go," Warren goaded.

Before Warren could get to his feet, Leighton has covered the distance between them and lifted him the rest of the way to his feet by the front of his shirt, catching the young man off balance. Warren had no time for feet to get purchase on the ground, Leighton had pulled him into the middle of the barn and flung him onto the ground. The other two were still scrambling to their feet as Leighton pulled his arm back and swung down open-handed landing hard just above Warren's Adam's apple. He clenched his fist tight around the man's neck who lay against the dusty ground trying to get all his limbs between himself and Leighton, but he was already at a loss.

"This what you want?" Leighton spat. "Do you wanna say shit about my wife again, huh? You wanna die here in the middle of this God-forsaken barn? Do ya? Do ya?" Warren's eyes started to roll before the large force of Mark's body charged him, rolled Leighton off the cloudy-eyed man.

Mark moved slowly enough towards him that Leighton was up on one knee as the hulking mass of man got within reach with large hands stretching towards him. Leighton twisted quickly hurling a right hook that connected with the man's lower ribs, causing enough pain that the main retreated a step with a grunt. Leighton got to his feet and lunged forward to swing for the man's open jaw, whose left arm clutched his side.

As his arm pulled back to launch the assault, he stopped. Shannon's voice cut through the cacophony of noise. He realised he had been watching as if a third party while his body enacted his rage, but now he was back in the driving seat. It didn't stop Glen and Mark from moving on him. He raised his hands to show the end of his fighting. Either of the two men, could have reached out and grabbed him easily, but he still refused to take a step backwards, knowing that doing so would put his back against the wall.

"Wait a minute," he said, exhaling deeply.

Shannon chis name incessantly, increasing in intensity, as Leighton worked out what he could possibly say to alleviate the tension. Glen's face was still impervious to emotion, eyes locked on Leighton's. Mark still clutched his side with one hand, holding out the other as if about to lock into a wrestling move on him. Between the two men, the women farmers tended to Warren, who was still on the ground, but had at least rolled onto his side.

"Okay," Leighton started. "I think it's clear that we don't get on." He chuckled to try and lighten the mood. Neither man said anything. "What we need to do is look at the bigger picture and realise that none of us have any clue why we are in here and that we can't *stay* in here indefinitely. As much as that might not be your guys strong point we need to think of a way out. If I do it, I will make sure you're out too. I have a plan. I keep telling my wife this, but trust me. Okay? It doesn't need to be so fighty nor stealy in here. It's bad enough already. What do you say? Peace?" He put his hand out for either man to take.

A long moment passed before Glen finally took it. "Peace," he replied. "-For now."

"You only get this one do-over," Mark put in before finally taking Leighton's hand.

It seemed to take ages before Mina left the farmhouse. Much longer than the others had taken. Suddenly, one of the pairs of men started running towards the house, rounding the tree with one either side. Then it became obvious why. Mina was now in view to Tariq, running towards the large rectangular building to the right of the complex. She appeared to be naked, but was pumping her arms to run. The man that had passed the tree closest to her managed to grab her and was only just able to keep the two of them upright and suppress her pace, wrapping his arms tightly around her middle. A soldier in a blue beret walked gingerly up towards her and grabbed her by the hair, pulling her roughly towards him.

The image went black as the edges of the binoculars blocked his sight. He realised he had been wincing. He couldn't quite grasp what he was seeing. "What are they doing to you?" he murmured. The man who had caught her slapped her on the bum as she was pulled away and the man immediately got slapped back-handed by the soldier in the blue beret. The man doubled over clutching his face. Mina somehow escaped the man's grasp in that moment and took off for a second time, this time heading back towards the barn. She disappeared around the corner then into Tariq's line of sight came two soldiers with rifles raised to their shoulders. The man in the blue beret clutched his crotch with one hand and held a pistol aimed at the grey-haired of the two men with his other.

Mina dropped to the floor as she got out of sight of the men. Two new men were walking towards her with guns raised, but they weren't aimed at her.

"Stand down!" The older man shouted.

"That bitch attacked me in there," the man in the blue beret said. The second man turned his rifle on Mina instead.

"I don't care. Lower your weapon!" It seemed that the last words reverberated around the complex for an age before the older man loosened his body and relaxed his hand on his trigger. "Get rid of that fucking beret while you are at. I know it isn't yours, private. I think you are forgetting your station here." The man held his distaste apparent on his face. "-and you two wazzacks. Go get this woman her clothes. -And I bloody *hope* you had nothing to do with this."

Mina heard hurried footsteps moving away. She was pleased a few moments later when it was the older man who passed her the bundle of clothes. "Get dressed. God damn," he said with clenched teeth as she took the clothes. "I can't trust that man for a second. It would have been easier just to kill you all. I am a fool to think the same rules applied in this cursed land." He seemed to be speaking to himself more than her, his tone filled with aggression. She focussed on getting dressed as quickly as possible. The other man kept his gun trained on her until she was safely back inside the barn and the chain closed behind her.

Chapter 49

Mina moved swiftly to the back of the barn and without talking to anyone curled up against the corner, as far back among the straw bales as she could. Leighton and Shannon moved over quickly to check on her. Warren had been moved over to sitting on one of the pews and Glen was giving him a check over.

"Are you okay?" Shannon asked.

Mina sniffed loudly and looked up at her. "I'm fine. I just got scared."

"Sure of that? You look really shaken up."

"I had some really strong painkillers. I just need some rest. I'll be all right. We really need to get out of here."

Mina sniffed loudly again and Shannon pushed Leighton a little way back to give her space. "I'll have words with you in a minute," she said sternly, pointing a finger in his face. She stroked Mina's hair from her face and spoke softly. "What happened, darling? We're here for you." Mina breathed in deeply as if about to speak and then shut her mouth again. "You're shaking."

"I don't know." Mina shook her head. "The man with the blue beret. With the squiffy face." She stopped. "He wouldn't leave the bathroom. He really scared me. I somehow got past him, but was outside. I was grabbed. I lashed out. I don't know." She took a stuttering breath. "The soldier with grey hair. He stopped it."

"Oh, oh, oh." Shannon tried to soothe her. "Let's give Mina a hug, Zeke." She leant over Mina's foetal body with Zeke. "I'm sorry, honey. It'll be all right. We've got Leighton. He'll get us both out. Not before I scold him for fighting, though."

"Fighting?" Mina asked.

"He's been really erratic the last few days. I was napping and when I woke up, he had put that young boy to the floor and I think cracked one of the big man's ribs." She chuckled and Mina joined her for a fleeting moment.

"Leighton? He seems so nice."

"He is. He's just out of sorts. Something happened to him on the way here. I – er." Shannon's throat caught and she coughed. "I think he may have killed someone."

"Leighton!?" Mina asked incredulously.

"I don't know. He's been periodically weird since and won't talk about it."

"The world that's been left for us here is messed up. Maybe I'll wake up soon."

Shannon hummed, pulled a frown and then leant her head upon Mina's side. "We'll get there." Mina's light sobs bounced Shannon's head, and she rubbed the woman's back softly.

Tariq wanted to run straight back to Grace and tell her what he had seen. Instead he continued to watch on. He couldn't work out exactly what he had witnessed, but Mina had looked flustered and was clearly naked. He thought that the man that had grabbed her by her hair must have either intended to, or did abuse her, but perhaps she had just tried to run while she could shower. Although, to Tariq, that didn't make much sense.

He saw one of the soldiers jogging around the complex for some time, but apart from that, very little happened. The patrols and movements of those people he could see seemed sporadic and he couldn't put a routine on them at all. Eventually, hunger pangs got the better of Tariq and he returned to the cave.

"Grace," he started. "I think I have seen her, but something happened."

"Tariq, what?" Grace said urgently, hearing the tentativeness in his voice.

Tariq explained what he had seen and Grace listened intently with a look of distaste masking her face. He took sporadic bites of dry food as he explained and Grace waited patiently between mouthfuls. As he was explaining, he felt himself getting more and more wound up.

"I need to go in there soon. I think she has compromised her ability to escape with whatever has happened. Although she is probably safe now as those guys came in with guns raised to scare the others off her. -At least, that's what I reckon."

"Don't be too rash, Tariq. It's hard to comprehend and you still don't know enough about them apart from the obvious. They have guns. You don't."

Tariq sighed and shook his head at the ground. "We have to do something. If I get an opportunity, I will take it now. Otherwise, tomorrow night I will go in."

Grace said, "Rest now, then. Go back to see what it is like at night from dusk tonight. Try and work out an opening for yourself. You need to be a ninja."

"I'll need darker clothes. What do we have that's black?"

Grace looked Tariq up and down taking in his light-coloured cycling jersey. "Well, you could try dirtying that up. Stain the colour out somehow. The other option is the black vest top that I am wearing. It won't give you much warmth late at night, though."

"I think I can forgo warmth for inconspicuousness."

"Damn you journalists and your long words."

Mina lay back, entranced by her slowly undulating visual disturbance caused by the Tramadol she had taken earlier. She patted her bra, contemplating taking more and stopped herself. Behind that veil-like disruption was the hole around a patch of blue sky. For a moment, the neurons in her brain aligned and formed an idea and she picked herself up to sitting. She caught eyes with Leighton and waved him over.

"Leighton, I have a plan." His face picked up eagerly. He opened his mouth to speak. "Listen first. Before I lose the thoughts." Leighton nodded. "I know where they keep the guns. In the farmhouse, downstairs, the room furthest from here. It looks like it used to be the utility room and I would assume that you can get in there from a rear door, though I don't know for sure."

"Well, that's a great find-" Mina cut him off abruptly with a raised hand.

"I think that the hole up there you are slightly obsessed with-"

"Not *obsessed*."

"Obsessed. If we stack these bails – they seem to move easily – you will be able to pull yourself through it. The corners of the building are concrete and stick out from the walls so you should be able to climb yourself down safely enough." Leighton opened his mouth to explain why that might not work, but Mina continued anyway. "We can't stop those guys from noticing, but if we do it a small build at a time we can at least hope that the soldiers won't notice when they drop off our food and water."

"You think they won't notice?" Leighton asked.

"The ones that drop off the food are the ones that picked me up at my place. They are as thick as pig-shit."

"You better be confident of that. How do we deal with the others? We have a peace treaty of sorts, but they are highly strung."

"I heard. Well, I figure that if we escape, they escape. That fact should keep them on board and maybe even get them to help."

"Should I talk to them about it?"

"No. Wait until they sleep tonight and we will start, get a few bales moved. I don't trust them not to sell us out. They might have their own plan-"

Leighton interrupted, "Which might be damaged by ours. Telling the guards about us might give them privilege."

"Leighton," Mina said. "Try to spare the old man out there. If you can."

"What do you expect me to do?" Mina gave him a concerned look. This plan of Mina's involved a strong likelihood of more death. He moved away morosely and sat back down next to Shannon. Mina watched him. He gave her a thumb up before raising his hand to Shannon's inquisitive look. "I need a few minutes to think, first. Then I'll explain the plan."

Chapter 50 – Day 13

Night had fallen along with the other inhabitants of the barn. All except for Leighton, the last one awake as usual. He lay waiting for the deep breathing and snores of those around him to reach a regular rhythm that would signal the start of his working time. He had made sure that Mina and Shannon had slept close together near the middle of the back wall to allow him access to either corner. He counted his pulse to sixty, fifteen times after he felt sure that everyone was asleep.

Quietly, he picked himself up and stretched out, staring up out through the hole to see a thin sliver of a waning crescent moon. The only light in the barn was coming in through the cracks and breaks in the barn wall from the fluorescent lights surrounding the main house and tree that centred the complex. He trod carefully to the far side from the hole and felt around for the ties keeping the straw together on the first bale and eventually got both hands dug underneath.

The bales were cumbersome, but not too heavy for him. He carried it past his sleeping wife and placed it down carefully in the corner, starting off what would eventually become a steep set of stairs to freedom. He repeated the journey a dozen times leaving a rectangle of six bales packed two high on top of what was already underneath. He left the job for the night and curled up next to Shannon. It took time to fall asleep as his mind worked on imagining the final steps, though he would have to be flexible with it as they progressed.

Mina felt as though she had been waiting for Leighton to wake up for over an hour when the other group in the barn stared to rouse. She had specifically been waiting to chide him for starting work on the plan without her, but after that long wait the emotion had worn down to an arduous boredom and then into a state of anxiety as she thought about the soldiers both seeing what they had done and working out what it might mean, when they opened the far door to deliver breakfast.

"Morning, Mina," came Shannon's voice.

"Oh, hey," Mina replied, pulling her gnawed fingers from her mouth and wiping them dry on her skirt. "Sleep well?"

"As well as can be hoped for on this itchy bed. He started without us," she stated in an angry, but hushed voice.

"It looks that way."

"I'm waking him. What if they see it at breakfast? Leighton," Shannon called, rocking her husband to the waking world.

Leighton groaned and rolled over to face them. "What's the matter?"

"That." She pointed towards the corner.

"Don't make it too bloody obvious." He looked up to check on the other group. "We want to be as close as possible before *they* notice."

Mina put a hand on Shannon's back. "Leave it. If they notice at breakfast or not, they may well notice at lunch. Or dinner."

"Alright, alright. Is it late or early?" Shannon asked. Leighton folded his arm under his head and rested onto it.

"I think it's still early. I was awake just after the sun. I would guess it's not far past six-thirty," Mina replied. The door's chain rattled. "Hold your breath."

The door swung open and the light caused both women to squint into it. Mina recommenced chewing the ends of her fingers, watching for a sign in either of the men that something was wrong.

The door closed after what felt like an age to Mina and she let out an audible sigh, her shoulders dropping. Leighton presently picked himself up. "Let's go. We have until lunch. If we build up another block of eight bales out this way and another eight on top, I think we'll be good. If we go to high too quickly it'll be more obvious."

"Don't you want breakfast first?" Shannon asked.

"Save me some, I want to get going."

Mina said, "I'll get the remaining breakfast. You wait here, Shannon."

"Thanks, honey," Shannon told her. By the time she looked around, Leighton was in the corner, pulling out another straw bale.

Mina turned around after picking up the remaining bread and water from the tray. She noticed that the three men from the group of farmers had stopped eating and turned around to watch Leighton. She drew level with them and one of them waved a hand as if to flag her down.

"What's he doing?" Glen asked.

Mina shied her head away, but noticed him taking a step towards her. She thought quickly but couldn't hold her voice from wavering as she lied. "He's building a better bed for his son."

The man regarded her and grunted thoughtfully.

Mina gave him a quizzical look.

Warren spoke up. "You just go back to playing maid. We don't trust that one," he said pointing at Leighton. "Things could get a lot worse for all of us in here if they think somethings up. We can make it much worse for you lot too if *we* think somethings up." The man waved her on.

Mina hurried back to Shannon and placed the plate of bread and jug of water down in front of her. "They're suspicious. Keep an eye out," Mina told her. "Though it looks as though Leighton earned us our rightful share of breakfast."

Tariq crept up to the brow of the hill to look over the farm complex. He had promised himself early on that he wouldn't stay long. He just wanted to stay long enough to absorb the layout while it was daylight so when he went in after dark he would be able to find his way around.

He would go without a torch and stay until well after sunset so his eyes could adjust to the darkness. He would start his descent at the western most point that he could still see the farm from and that would take him down well into the treeline and protect him from showing up in the lights until he was almost at the outermost building, the one from his view that appeared as a silvery rectangle standing less than fifty meters or so from the last tree.

As he looked out he tried to picture how the lights would overlap, where he might find the darkest of paths over to the barn that would be on the other side of the complex. He had contemplated for a while approaching from the east, across the large, flat and open fields, but even under the cover of midnight and only a waning moon, he scared himself away from that idea with the thought of night vision goggles. They were soldiers after all.

After the commotion he had seen yesterday, when he had managed to catch sight of Mina, there seemed to be fewer of them wandering the complex. He supposed that they could have split into factions of some kind and the three he saw grabbing at his future rescuee might be refusing their duties. That thought was one that Tariq was happy to dwell on. Anything that would potentially make his attempt to free her easier was worth its weight in gold, balanced against his fragile confidence in his plan.

Back under the protection of the cave, Grace rationed out some of their food and talked at a silent Tariq who was as nestled back in the depths of his mind as he was at the back of the cave.

"I changed my top while you were up there," Grace said, "When you get up, you can put it over your jersey." She stopped as she took another bite of her carrot, crunching loudly. "I was thinking about the rest too. There was a small stream on the other side of the road that we left. You could get some mud from there and smear it across your arms and legs. I figure it will help you blend in. If you can get some leaves and twigs too and get them to stick while the mud dries, you'll be almost as inconspicuous as one of the guys in the hairy sniper suits!" She waited for an acknowledgement and eventually received a grunt. Tariq had his arm across his eyes and sleeping bag pulled up to his nose. Grace continued crunching on the carrot. "I am sorry. I am a bit of a talker. Let's let you get some sleep."

"Sorry," Tariq murmured almost unintelligibly. "The mud is a great idea. The ghillie suit sounds like a pain in the arse."

"Ghillie suit?"

"The leaves and shit. It's what snipers wear."

"Oh."

"I'm kind of stressing out. Not worth anyone's time right now. Let me sleep, yeah?" Tariq raised a hand to try and flap away his agitated tone.

"Sorry," Grace said, searching for something quieter to eat.

Chapter 51

Warren and Mark stood in close to the door in time for it opening at lunch. They stood near enough that Warren helped to swing the door wide. Leighton watched on. He was taking a break over the lunch time window and took the opportunity to give Zeke some attention and bounced him on his leg, though kept one eye on the farmers to try and work out what they might be doing.

Without warning, the younger soldier lunged forward and put the butt of his rifle swiftly into Warren's stomach, dropping him to the ground with a retching sound. Mark picked him up easily and hurriedly moved backwards, clearly stunned by the unforgiving suddenness of the motion.

"You. At the back. These guys here just lost you lunch," the chubby soldier bellowed out. "-And fuck it. Dinner too."

The younger picked up his head. "You should let 'em know how you feel about that."

At that, the door swung shut and was locked in place.

The three men, returned to their usual positions and Leighton called out, "Thank you." He added a nod and a thumb up as they looked over.

A recovering Warren called over, "You, what?"

"I said, thank you."

"That's what I thought." He started walking towards Leighton and Zeke was taken by his mother as he stood up in return, confidently. "You can keep the sarcasm to yourself, arsehole." He stopped.

"I am not being sarcastic," Leighton said across the distance.

Shannon whispered to him, "You're not? Just settle down. Don't lose your head again."

Leighton looked down at her, shaking his head. "No. I won't"

"Sorry," Shannon said loudly "My husband always sounds sarcastic. *I* can never tell when he is serious."

"Then if he's serious, why is thanking us?"

"Leighton?"

"-Because that was hilarious." Leighton bowed his head and raised his palms in front of him. "Sorry. That was me trying to be funny. I am not."

"Stop playing stupid games before I come over there," Mark said, standing just off Warren's shoulder.

Leighton stepped down to reach a distance that wouldn't require raising his voice. The two of them puffed their chests out. "I am saying thank you," he said conspiratorially. "-Because you just won me the time I need to complete the first stage of my plan. Genuinely, thank you," he said sincerely. He pushed his right hand out in front of him and neither man took it. "Like I said before, you guys go free too. Perhaps our two plans were divinely intended to intertwine and lead all of us in here to freedom. Assuming – that is – that whatever you did there was a plan."

The two men stood still, maintaining a stone-like eye contact with Leighton. "Whatever you just said, I still think you're going to get us all killed. I haven't yet decided whether to dob you in to the guards. Think really hard about what you're doing." Mark gave him a stern nod.

"I will." Leighton smiled and turned his back on the men whom he could still feel at his back, unmoved.

Leighton, knowing the guards would not be disturbing him until the next morning, boldly ignored the farmer's warning and worked as hard as he could throughout the day. Shannon and Mina took shifts helping, but Leighton was fervorous and even between the two of them, they couldn't equal his rate of movement. Sweat covered him from head to toe by the time dinner would have been due and he finally took a break, just in case they were to suddenly turn back on their plan or simply swing the door open for a look.

All three of them were parched from the lack of water. Leighton kept them going, telling them that it was only for a few more hours until death or freedom – he focussed on the freedom – would present itself to them all. While they all rested, Leighton sat half way up the quarter pyramid of straw that now pushed into the walls. Only a dozen or so bales not part of the pyramid steps remained and Leighton's thighs ached at the mere thought of hauling them up the considerable structure.

Luckily, the farmers were still debating their warning. They hadn't shouted out to the soldiers as they heard footsteps. Perhaps they had decided that even if Leighton died – assumedly quite quickly – to the rifles, they would not be impacted. Leighton occasionally nodded politely to them as they looked in his direction, but still held an anxious distrust. He dropped down to the ground and walked as if to use the bucket. He stood above it. but had sweated out most of the moisture he had and feigned going, whistling loudly as he pretended to wee with his back turned to the farmers. He checked the other group again as he walked back along the opposite edge of the barn. Without looking he flung his right arm up and managed to grasp hold of two rusty tools from the rack that was screwed to the wall. Looking from under a bowed head, he could see that they had either not seen or not cared what he was doing. '*Perfect*,' he thought. He shoved the two implements in his right pocket and continued back to the straw.

Tariq had slept fitfully through the day. Most of the time had been spent repeating a mantra of '*rest is as good as sleep*' in his inner voice. Whilst awake, he ignored Grace – who never seemed to have moved – and simply focussed on himself and getting back to sleep again. It eventually became apparent that the sun was nearly finished traversing the sky, indicated by the deep orange glow on faint haze that hung in the air.

He donned Grace's vest top, covering most of the brightest parts of his jersey and wandered down the slope to the main road. After smearing copious amounts of mud all over his body he walked back up. Only the top half of the sun was visible at the horizon and the unnatural orange light deepened, fading into dark blue in the eastern portion of the sky where the waning crescent moon was haloed through the haze.

"How do I look?" Tariq asked.

"Who said that?" Grace joked. "Positively invisible. You should definitely wear more tank tops and fake tan. You should have done more on your head, though. They'll see the moonlight reflecting off your bonce from miles away."

"At least you're in good spirits," Tariq grumbled. "The way I see it now, it's to a flip of a coin. Given how many of them are down there, perhaps I need it to come down on its edge to end up on top."

"Come here." Grace picked up a handful of soil and with her other hand pulled Tariq's head down to her level. "This should matte you up a little more," she said, vigorously applying the soil to his bald head. "That's better. Takes the shine right off." She laughed.

Tariq let out a deep breath and loosened shoulders that had been held taught for around two weeks. "Okay," he said. Then in his cheeriest attempt at a British accent, "Shan't be long, dear."

Grace copied the accent, "I will have a pot of freshly boiled tea ready upon your return."

Tariq walked off parallel to the road, watching the sun slowly disappear. He was always one to be early. It would be a while before it would be dark enough to make his move, but as with meetings of any kind in his previous way of life, he would rather be in position and then wait than feel like he was losing time sitting around at home. He normally had his phone and plenty of media to keep him entertained. This time he would simply be waiting with his own thoughts for the next few hours on the unseen side of the ridge. With that thought, he dragged his steps. He had no need to rush. The darker the better.

He took up in his first position with his binoculars. The complex looked different from this new angle and it took him a little while to get all the buildings in the right place in the map of it he kept in his mind. He worried for a moment that when he got *into* the complex it would look so different again that all his planning would be wasted. If that was the case, it would be too late to do anything about it. He recalled a phrase from his English lessons back in Egypt. It was inside the cover of one of his mum's favourite books. '*The best laid schemes o' mice an' men, gang aft awry*'. He figured it was probably from something else originally, but it was the book by John Steinbeck that stuck it in his mind.

He climbed away from the edge and laid on his back, watching the sky turn darker blue. Stars started to become visible and the moon crept further into his vision. It was there that he waited for complete darkness to envelop the land.

The finished structure within the barn still left Leighton with quite a stretch to the lip of the hole, but it was secure and certainly the most stable part of the plan that they had. Leighton ushered the two women and Zeke to a point about a third of the way up and against the furthest wall from the farmer's group.

"Before we pretend to sleep, I have a temporary parting gift for you both," Leighton whispered. Shannon gave him a confused look. "Shannon, to you-" he started.

"Damn, do you have to make it so formal?" Shannon interjected.

The three of them laughed.

"Okay, okay, shush," Leighton said. "Hold out a hand each." Shannon and Mina did so tentatively. "Now, shut your eyes." Mina obliged.

Shannon didn't, "Come on, Leighton. It's not a surprise birthday gift, hand it over."

"Shut your eyes and we'll get this part over with." Shannon rolled her eyes and then shut them.

"Ready?" Leighton asked.

"Yes," they said in unison. Mina softly excited, Shannon more apathetic.

Leighton placed an item in each of their hands. "Open your eyes, then," he urged.

"What the hell's this?" Shannon asked.

"Not so loud."

Mina made a perceptive noise.

"Yea, right?" Leighton asked excitedly.

"Yea, what?"

"Leighton?" Mina asked. "Are you really worried about them?" She waved the screwdriver across the expanse of the barn. Shannon looked stunned at the short, thin wood saw in her hand.

"Really?" Shannon asked.

Leighton took a submissive posture. "It's just as a precaution. Once they see me gone-" he stopped and lowered his head along with his voice. "Once they see me gone, they might react-. Like, over react. I want you two to have the upper hand. Now, no more questions. Keep those close, we sleep. Well, you sleep. I pretend to sleep. Mina, can I wake you first when I leave. If I wake her," he said pointing his thumb at his wife. "All she will do is worry until I open the door."

"I don't mind. I'll keep watch." She lowered her head. "You just make sure you come back."

"Promise?" Shannon added.

"I promise. You know I'll avoid making a promise about anything. This, I promise. Now, get some sleep, it'll be a long night."

Chapter 52 – Day 14

Leighton had caught himself almost falling asleep. Both the inside of the barn and the sky were almost pitch black, only the artificial lights offered any visibility. He pulled himself upright. Everyone else in the barn was asleep, told by the sounds of contrasting heavy breathing. He nudged Mina and she woke easily and silently as if she had also been faking it herself too. He pointed to his left wrist and mouthed the words '*the time is now*'.

Mina merely nodded and lay back down, her eyes focussed solely on the group of five sleeping on the other side of the barn. Leighton smiled to her grimly and started climbing as quietly as possible up the straw structure. He was parched. If he could find some water lying around on his travels he would succumb to it easily. At the top, he reached up and found he could just get his fingertips onto the exposed wooden support beam, the entrance to the outside world. He lifted weight off his feet until he was sure it would take his weight and then used his feet against the wall to scramble up until his head emerged through the gap.

His dehydrated forearms pumped quickly and gave him a sense of urgency to get himself clear. Using his feet on the corner support and reaching across to part of the roof, he eventually got himself out and he flattened himself to spread his weight against the decrepit asbestos. His left arm hung over the edge and he shook blood into it, suppressing the lactic acid. He tried to do the same to his right arm, but as it was above him on the sloping roof, it had little effect.

Leighton slid his legs towards the edge as he turned, taking hold of the grip of the beam and shuffled his hands until he could grasp the corner of the building – slightly jutting out from the rest of the wall – with the soles of his feet. The corner was in almost complete darkness, but he could see the light from the main centre of the complex spilling a path of light between him and the house. His hands started to cramp and he was spurred on in his descent. He shuffled his way down, hand over hand and feet together, lowering himself quickly. He put effort into not releasing a massive sigh of relief as his feet touched solid earth. He shook his hands out and pressed them together, it felt as though minutes had passed by the time the pain dulled. He was surprised at his calmness and supposed it was for the best.

Tariq walked down the decline towards the trees, he avoided looking at the lights so he could maintain his night vision, holding a hand in front of his eyes to block it. As he thought about it, he felt well rested. The chances of him being shot dead brought him a sense of impending death that was – in fact – quite comforting. The feeling as pre-operation morphine triggered, where one feels as though they will most probably not wake up and it most probably won't matter. He felt as though it should worry him, but it seemed more likely that it would be necessary to making the risks he needed to complete his mission. Maybe that is how his father felt each time he had gone out. A feeling as though he wouldn't return, but the rewards to everyone else would be worth it. Up until the time he didn't return to his own family.

He took care not to trip as the hard ground undulated under foot. It would certainly do no good to fall and break a leg before he even got them free. He thought of them as being like the radicals he had known from Egypt. Fighting the army and the system in as much as a teenager could. Except that when he pondered it, those soldiers ahead of him no longer represented any existing system bar through the clothes they wore. The clothes and insignia of an archaic system.

Tariq realised that his hand was no longer blocking any light and he dropped his arm. The trees started in a clear-cut line dividing the inclined field with the woods. He paused and braced himself for a moment, knowing his footing would become worse from here on in. He stepped over roots, barely seen in the low light. He stooped low with his eyes locked no more than a few inches in front of his feet and pushed through with hardly a look up until his shoulders and neck became sore with the strain.

By the time he straightened up to save a tight knot from forming in his neck, the lights from the complex were visible between the trunks and branches ahead of him. The ground sloped down in front of him and he could see the shadows that the irregular ground caused. Each rise and fall creating crisp areas of shadow on the ground. He moved close to one, keeping thick trunks between him and the lights whenever possible, and tested it out. Lying down in one of them, he stretched his neck down to see the rest of his body. He was covered by the shadow. He mouthed to himself '*let's see how it looks from here, then*' and held his binoculars up to his eyes for one last time before he was to leave them behind.

The utility room on the other side of the house was Leighton's next destination. He had crossed the path of light between the barn and main house and found another dark place. He was nestled down prone under one of the house's dimly lit windows and looked out into the main part of the complex. He could see two of the soldiers patrolling at the far end where the path led up to the main road. The only real moving beings he had seen since being on the outside, though many a paranoid twitching turned his head in the time since reaching the ground.

He turned around and army-crawled to the rear corner of the house, his left shoulder grazing the wall the whole time. He inched his head out around the corner. The back of the house was mostly dark. At the ground floor, only a few small tendrils of light crept out, mottling the floor up to the opposite side of the building where a rectangle of light spread onto the unkempt grass. The upper floor looked to have no lights on at all. He figured they probably had people looking out from up there.

Leighton crawled his way to the other end, stopping only briefly to consider the interior of the house at a set of French doors, but finding that the furniture piled against it allowed for limited sight into the room. He reached the door to the utility room and hunkered next to the door. A small window next to the door sat ajar and neither that nor the glass in the door had a blind or curtain of any kind. He decided he would trust the darkness that shrouded him and stood up, pulling a couple of meters away from the wall and slowly shuffled to his side until more and more of the room became visible.

Mina was correct. It was full of guns. The soldiers had clearly brought much more than they needed, otherwise there were many more of them than the eight or so that manned the complex. Mina said she had seen the same people day in day out since her arrival, although a few seemed similar enough at a distance that she couldn't be sure. Either way, there were a lot of guns. Apart from the guns, however, the room was thankfully empty, but was unlikely to be for an extended time. Leighton crouched back down under the door's window and pressed his ear against the thin wood, listening intently. From there, the house seemed to creak and moan, but no obvious footsteps were sounding near enough to the utility room for him to make them out. The sound of his own heartbeat eventually drowned out all other noises and he pulled back.

He breathed out deeply to settle himself and stood back up. He needed a bold and quick movement and fighting his inhibition, tried the door handle, expecting either a loud creak or some resistance, but was received by neither. It opened easily. He furrowed his brow. *'They hadn't locked the door to their own fucking armoury,'* he thought, holding back a laugh. Stepping in, he quickly saw a rifle that looked the same as the one he had lifted from one of their dead and slung it over his shoulder swiftly and silently. As he turned to pick up a few magazines from the opposite shelf he noticed a dozen grenades in a small box in the corner and placed one into each of his trouser pockets. He took a quick glance for anything else of use – a sense of urgency building in his chest – and noticed a half full bottle of water on the window sill next to a handgun.

Picking both up gently enough not to make the warped plastic crack noisily, he left, pulling the door closed behind him. It was dark all the way to the treeline, he could get himself sorted when he was in cover. The magazines were still haphazardly clutched in his arms and the rifle swung into the backs of his knees with each step. He couldn't bring himself to look back around. If one of them saw him, he would be dead, whether he saw it coming or not.

At this distance through the binoculars, the farm complex was so much more detailed it was strange. Over to his right, he could see two soldiers moving their way back down the path from the road, guns sitting in relaxed hands. He scanned as far as he could before the large grey animal shed blocked his view point and saw another two soldiers on the near side, walking away from the main buildings. Closer to the building, he saw a man sat lazily picking his teeth in the driver's seat of a Land Rover with a rifle perched next to him on the passenger side. The main house itself had light spilling out the windows on the ground floor, but nothing except darkness from the upper.

His attention turned to the back of the house. He saw a rectangle of light distort against the grass. One of the soldiers must have entered from there. He couldn't see anyone now, unless they had turned and gone behind the house itself. He swung the binoculars to the front of the house again and tried to judge the distance between it and the barn on the far side. The middle of the complex was well lit and he supposed that around the back of the house and the opposite side of the barn would be the best route to take. He scanned until he found the two men walking back in to the complex. He needed to know which side of the barn they would take on their way back.

Rustling to Tariq's left disturbed him and he pulled the binoculars away from his eyes. Had he been seen so quickly? Lying covered in mud in a trough of mud, surely not. Purple spots from the light sources in the main complex seemed to completely cover his vision and he – disoriented – tried to pinpoint the movement by sound alone. It was coming closer, but was slowing in pace. Eventually it stopped somewhere ahead of Tariq. He heard a metallic click and clenched his eyes shut, willing the spots away. None of the soldiers had come out anywhere near this far while he had watched from the hilltop. This was throwing him off. He placed the binoculars under an exposed root and pulled himself flat in the lowest part of the natural gully. Next, he heard loud gulping. Whatever was creating the noise, it probably had a gun and was thirsty. The crack of plastic reached his ears along with a gasp.

Leighton downed the bottle and sorted his various weapons into his pockets so that he could move more freely. He hadn't been shot yet, that meant a major portion of his plan was listed as a success so far. From within the trees he could move unseen until he could get a good few shots lined up. He needed to start away from the house as far as possible and see if he could kill – he shuddered at that thought – as many soldiers as possible without any more finding out about it. Neither the rifle nor the handgun had any silencing on them and he had heard neither type fire while he was here to know how loud they would be until that first shot.

He walked away from the complex until he found a dip in the ground that ran parallel to the complex towards the road and stooping low and focusing ahead of him he carefully stepped forward, blindly testing the ground with each foot as he went.

The man appeared in Tariq's gully, moving straight towards him. Tariq kept himself as perfectly still as he could manage, his hands under his shoulder ready to spring up in an instant. The man was looking past and above him. As each step brought the man closer, Tariq realised with more certainty that he was going to be either tripped over or stepped on. -And that man had a rifle.

A foot landed lightly within a few inches of Tariq's ear. Tariq decided to move.

Leighton felt his foot snag and his body lurched forward. Letting go of the rifle to brace against the fall, he hit the ground. Before he could turn to look back at what had tripped him, a large weight came down on his shoulders. He grappled for the rifle, eventually grabbing it by the barrel, but it was stuck fast, pressed down into the dirt. He felt two hands push his face further into the ground.

"Shh," came a voice. "You're not a soldier. Are you?"

Leighton tried again futilely to move his head. He resided and spoke back. "Most certainly not. Does that mean you're not?"

"I am not."

Silence hung in the air, Leighton tried desperately to process all the information.

"Does that mean you might let me up? Why are you-? I don't know anything. Please explain," Leighton said, lifting open hands out in front of him. He was caught so unaware that rage had not been able to kick in. Given his recent bouts, he was impressed with himself.

Tariq rolled the prone man over, keeping his foot placed firmly on the rifle.

"First, you explain. Why and how are you here?" he asked.

"I was born without knowing why and then continued to never find out why. They call me Leighton. In the context you want, I was in the barn-"

Tariq interrupted. "I don't recognise you."

"Why would you? Wait. Please tell me what's going on," Leighton whispered earnestly.

"Fine. I am here to rescue a girl named Mina. I met her friend in a town a few miles over. I've been nearby for two days working on a plan," Tariq explained.

"Oh. That's good. I know her."

"You were in the barn with her, then?"

"Yes." Leighton afforded a smile and Tariq dropped his shoulders.

"You didn't leave yesterday. I figured I would have seen everyone."

"If you lean in close enough you can probably smell my lack of basic hygiene. I was due to be last to go, but before I got a chance, something happened with your Mina while she went to shower and they cancelled mine. More importantly, we basically have the same mission. I am looking to save my wife and child. You may have seen a woman with a baby."

"I did, she must be the black woman, right?" Leighton furrowed his brow. "Get that look off your face, it means nothing bar a way of identifying her once we get in."

"All right, all right. The last time someone mentioned her skin colour, it was with much more derision. What's your plan then?"

"I was going to sneak in, somehow find a way to open up the doors of the barn and then free everyone inside and run off into the night." Tariq paused. "It- er- sounds a bit crap said out loud. Especially said to a guy that apparently has real weaponry and assumedly some kind of better plan for freeing his captive wife. I'm sorry."

"Well, if it makes you feel any better, my plan is to get really fucking angry and kill somewhere between eight and ten trained soldiers."

They both sniggered quietly and Tariq removed his foot from the gun and sat down next to Leighton, offering a hand to help him up to sitting. "Tariq," he said as they clasped hands.

Chapter 53

Mina fought her eyes from closing, it had surely been an hour or more since Leighton had jumped out. The barn remained filled with an oppressive silence that seemed to overwhelm the sounds of deep sleep breathing. Shannon remained asleep next to her, clutching Zeke tightly. The knot of anxiety in her stomach increased its pressure minute after minute as she willed the sight of Leighton entering the building again. This time he would swing the doors open wide, letting the light flood in, in juxtaposition to slinking out of it under the cover of darkness. She wanted to wake Shannon for the company, but it would do no good for them both to sit here worrying. She was glad that Leighton had asked her to wake first. If she was as nervous as she was, surely Shannon would find it unbearable.

After another frustrating and undeterminable period, Mina heard movement from the other side of the barn and leant her head up against the wall to get a better look. One of the younger two men had gotten up and was stretching his arms and legs in the dim light. He looked over, Mina felt as though he was looking straight at her, but he didn't react. As he turned his back, Mina gave a nudge to Shannon, who woke easily.

"What's up?" she whispered before Mina could motion a finger to her lips. Mina pointed delicately across the room to where another of the men was sat up at the feet of the first.

"They are awake," Mina whispered as lightly as she could.

"You're up too? That's strange," said the indeterminable man directed to Mina and Shannon. "The little one keeping you three awake?"

Mina and Shannon lifted themselves to sitting. "Something like that, did he wake you?"

"No, he's not made a noise all night."

"Shit," Shannon said to Mina. Then to the farmers, "So why are you up at this time?"

"We supposed that your man has already made a dash out into the night and we are going to do the same before he brings the whole army out there tearing this barn apart."

"Eight men is not an army," Mina interjected derisively.

"Well they are more armed than us now and you may be aware that they did a number on us even when we were armed too." Warren thumped him on the arm. "Get off." He continued. "We're going. I'm guessing you'll be waiting for the door. Unless he is just hiding in the straw." The farmer bobbed his head around as if considering the stack.

"Give us a moment please," Mina said, raising a finger. Covertly to Shannon, "I'm not sure what to do. If they get out they could distract the soldiers from what Leighton is doing. If they get seen too early, then it could either lead to the lot of them being killed – including us – or them ending up back in here, but leaving all the soldiers on higher alert for when Leighton makes his move."

Shannon thought for a few moments before answering. "We stall them. The soldiers are lazy and unorganised. Leighton doesn't need them turning their backs on that lifestyle."

"Okay, how are we going to do that?"

"In any way we can."

Tariq and Leighton had talked for a while, bringing both of their plans together and working on one that if unchanged by the laws of Murphy and Sod, would be successful. They knew it would never be that easy, but would act as their foundation plan on top of which all the numerous possible permutations and reactions could be piled on top. They had contemplated not having any sort of plan, but that would make it too difficult to start. What they had was enough to go ahead with.

After the conversation, they shook hands again and Leighton led the way towards the far end of the complex away from the main house, rifle loaded and poised ready in his hands. They stuck to the gully, their heads low and eyes switching between their feet and the soldiers wandering the complex. Tariq felt strange with the two grenades lining his pockets and knowing that in a few short minutes he would be firing a rifle for the first time in his life.

Leighton slowed to a stop, raising a closed fist. Tariq stopped and immediately lay prone, shuffling each of the grenades so that they didn't dig into his protruding hip bones. He was slim before, but certain things like that reminded him how much weight he had lost in the last few weeks. Every bone he had seemed to stretch the skin around it.

Tariq watched Leighton move forward, getting closer and closer to the ground until he was dragging himself forward to the lip of the gully about twenty meters in front of him. Leighton pressed the rifle's barrel length into the dirt for support and after a few little shuffles to his position, brought his eye to the sight.

Leighton watched the outgoing pair of soldiers for some time as they walked on towards the road, getting closer to his gun with each step. He held steady taking deep even breaths, keeping the closest man in the crosshair. As the men passed him, he held a long breath and blew it out steadily through his mouth. He waited for a clear shot of their backs. A few more steps. He took his breath in. -And squeezed the trigger gently.

Tariq flinched as the first shots fired. Five shots rang clearly defined in the otherwise still air. It was loud to him, being so close, but he couldn't be sure how far it would travel. Tariq anxiously anticipated a barrage of return fire. It never came. He looked up at Leighton, who held deathly still and willed him to move. Tariq was just at the point where he was going to get up and check the man for a pulse when Leighton pulled himself back into the gully.

Leighton returned to Tariq and placed the rifle carefully down in front of his hands. Leighton leant in close, clapping a firm hand on Tariq's back. "You're tagged in. Remember, five minutes or until the need arises."

"Did anyone see?"

"No idea. We'll know soon enough. You just keep to the plan and it will all be okay." Leighton left immediately with the metallic sound of a round entering the chamber of the handgun. Tariq started the slow count to three hundred, while he attempted to replicate Leighton's firing posture.

"Insha'Allah," Tariq replied.

"Huh?"

"I fucking hope so."

Everyone's eyes suddenly turned towards the door as five evenly spaced pops reverberated in the air. Each inhabitant of the barn was frozen for a whole minute. Staring as if they could see through the walls and see the sound. It may have been faint, but they all knew what had caused it. Shannon was the first to move. First, a shake. Then it was as if she was vibrating to a low frequency of fear. Mina moved next to rub her back, vigorously from the manifestation of her own fear for the woman.

Mina kept her eyes on the door until one by one, the heads of the farmers turned towards the two of them. She felt instantly fragile under their serious and cutting gaze. They moved towards them with the three men standing side by side and the two women clutching each other's hands behind. Mina stayed her course, patting Shannon's back firmly to bring her attention up while she clutched the handle of the screwdriver in her other hand.

"Which end of the gun do you think your husband ended up at?" Warren asked. "Up against trained soldiers."

"Shannon, stay here," Mina said privately. She stood – high in the straw – and faced the incomers "What is your point? Are you fancying yourselves against them out there? If you think you stood a chance, would you be in here now. I heard that there were more of you before. -And didn't you say you were all armed too? You are here. What were you even trying to do? Nothing you have done so far has got you any closer to being free. You're just waiting for death. Leighton is out there. Still! Looking to save the life of his wife and child. You should count yourself damn lucky to be getting freed at the same time. He's got a strategy that you lot could only dream of. If I were you, I would sit down and wait to be let on your way." Mina's hands shook violently and her knuckles were white with the strength of her grip on the screwdriver. "-And Warren, you're a fucking dick."

"You little bitch. What are you doing about it?" He opened his mouth to speak more, but Mina cut him off.

"I've been watching, I've seen how they work out there." She pointed violently at the door of the barn. "I may not be strong or be able to fire a gun, but Leighton is enacting the plan that the three of us made. You're getting a free ride." Spit flew with her words.

"We are very grateful for your hand-me-down," Glen said.

"Give it up. Get out of the way. Wait for your hero to come save you," Mark added. The three men were now stood at the base of the pyramid.

Mina leered over them. "No."

"Do you want him to come back and find you with black eyes?" Warren goaded.

Everyone simultaneously ducked their heads as louder pops of gunfire rung in the air.

Chapter 54

Tariq started firing wildly in the direction of the two soldiers nearing the bodies that Leighton had left for them to find. They returned bullets equally erratically into the trees around Tariq as they retreated towards cover behind the animal sheds. Once they took cover, Tariq let time fill the gap between bullets. He wanted to drag this out for as long as possible, keep them pinned down to let Leighton do his part of the plan. His partner was clearly a much better shot and Tariq figured that even if he was aiming at either of the men, the chances of injuring them in the slightest was low. Even so, he aimed high, wide, low, any direction he could keep them from firing back without doing any damage.

The soldiers fired in bursts of bullets from around the edges of the building and judging from the distribution of the bullets, they didn't yet know exactly where Tariq was. He squeezed the trigger once more. Out of ammo. Time to move. Tariq dragged himself away from his firing spot, the rifle dragging along by the strap over his shoulder. Once he was out of the general spread of bullets heading his way, he pulled a magazine out of one of his pockets, fumbled around with the rifle's various switches until the other popped out and took three attempts to fit the new one into the slot. The situation seemed crazy to Tariq, his heart rate and mind were both racing. He could barely recall what he had discussed with Leighton. Time to just faff and pray.

Leighton was once again stooped under the glass part of the utility room door. He heard the gunfire die down at the other end of the complex and heavy footsteps and shouting were filling the building at his back. He told himself to wait. He nodded his head in time with his rapid breathing. The thudding was dying down. He burst through the door. Time no longer on his side. He had to get his part done before they locked down Tariq's position in the gully. He hoped that he was remembering to move closer to the house after every reload. He cared much less for his noise and crouched while he grabbed another rifle and slammed a magazine in. He cocked it and released the safety, aiming straight at the door into the rest of the house. Nobody came.

He pocketed a grenade and slowly inched around, the next room was clear but he saw a dark figure through some frosted glass at the far end. A stair case stood to his left next to a window with cardboard duct taped over it. He moved back into the utility room and took cover behind the door frame as he targeted the shadowed outline. Squeezing the trigger, Leighton was surprised to find three bullets burst from the end of his gun, the recoil sending the barrel towards the ceiling. Only one of the bullets was anywhere near where he aimed, shattering the glass from the top of the door. "Shit," he murmured to himself. He pulled the barrel back down, once he knew what to expect he braced himself against the burst fire's recoil and sprayed into the room. In tandem with his second squeeze of the trigger, a triplet of gunfire was returned. He pulled back and blind fired. A pained shout rose and he fired again, lower.

"You bastard," came an agonised cry. "Oh shit. Medic!" The man yelled before a hacking cough. A flurry of rapid footsteps sounded down the stairs.

"Oh man," Leighton said out loud. "This is fucked up. What next?" Leighton shook his head back and forth as he racked his brains. "Think computer game. Grenade!"

"What the-?" a gruff voiced man said in surprise as a heavy ball of metal bounced loudly on the floorboards at his feet, "Cover!" he yelled.

Leighton was fairly sure his eardrums had just burst, the only sound, a piercing tinnitus. He was covered in plaster from the wall by which he had huddled next to for protection from the blast. "That was much louder in real life," he said to himself. He clenched his eyes shut. "Real life. Shit." He let out a growl. "Don't think about it. Don't think about it. Where's my mind-drowning rage when I actually need it." He moaned. "Tariq," he suddenly remembered audibly.

Shannon tied Zeke to her back using a head wrap and stood near the top of the straw bale structure. Mina took up a position a step lower. Suddenly, an explosion reverberated as if it had originated inside the barn. Shannon and Mina steadied themselves as if the shock wave would knock them off their respective perches. The women down below grabbed at the arms of the oldest two men and struggled to pull them back.

"Guys. We are going," said Warren as he placed his first foot onto the crunching steps.

The darker haired women called at him and tried to get past the thick arms of Mark. "No, Warren. Come on. Just leave it. Sit it out. Please, Warren." Tears were glistening in the low light on her cheeks. "What will you even-" She shrieked as Mark pulled her back and flung her down to the cold ground.

"Seriously!" He yelled. "Get a grip. The lot of you."

Mina edged towards the wall to her right. "Settle down," she screamed. "-And you," she said firmly. "Get. Down." The boy looked up at her and almost obliged, seeing the stern set of her eyes locked on his.

"Right," he said, looking back at the men and women he fought for survival with. "Fuck the lot of you. I'm outta here. Seems like no-one here gives a shit about living any longer. You've all lost your complete set of fucking marbles."

He turned to proceed up to the roof's gap to find Mina inches away from his face. "No," she breathed. She swung her arm around in a wide arc and thrust the screwdriver deep into the back of his thigh. A high-pitched shriek left his throat and he fell backwards, clutching his pierced muscle. He landed heavily on his shoulder and writhed back.

"Glen, do something," urged the lighter haired woman, who went from pulling his arm back to pushing him forward.

Glen moved forward calmly, removing his shirt and rolled Warren on to his side without a word. "Okay," he said, "On three. One. Two." On two, he pulled the screwdriver from Warren's leg and immediately wrapped it twice around with the shirt, tying it tightly just above the wound. He looked up square at Mina. "I think we can come to an agreement. This boy's getting a thrashing."

"I ain't no boy. Fuck you, Glen!" Warren managed before sprouting a further flurry of swear words.

Glen picked up Warren and seemed to wrestle him over to one of the old church pews yet again. The others followed him with nothing, but a concerned glance at the two women.

Shannon watched Mina clamber up to her. "You certainly calmed that situation." Shannon opened her mouth, found no further words and shrugged.

Tariq found that his control of where the bullets were ending up was getting a little better. He continued to fire single bullets at a time, periodically as to not use them all up too quickly. He pinged them noisily off the roof and walls of the animal sheds successfully – so far – keeping the two soldiers in its cover. At the house, he could see the smoke billowing thickly out the window into the path of one of the floodlights, gradually darkening the area just outside. A figure ran across the complex, stopping behind the tree in the centre. Tariq saw the muzzle flash at the top of his sights and immediately ducked down. The man had seen him.

Instead of returning to firing the rifle, he grabbed it in both hands and rolled into the gully. He didn't know how many bullets remained in the magazine so he swapped it while behind the cover and then started dragging himself further towards the building. Bullets whistled over his head by only a short distance, he dared not stand for fear of one passing directly through his skull. The man must have emptied his magazine as the firing stopped, but it was quickly taken up again by the erratic fire of the two soldiers from the animal shelter.

When he was far enough away from where his location was last known, he bobbed his head up to regard the situation below him. A fourth soldier was rounding the corner of the animal sheds from the other side, but halfway between that and the treeline which provided Tariq his shelter, another point of gunfire flared up and cut the man down as he ran. "My brother," Tariq said. "He probably just saved my life." The loose cover fire into the treeline paused for a moment before intense fire focussed on an unseen target near the house. Tariq scrubbed his face with his palms. He knelt face down in the dirt, covering his head for a few moments before rising to a stooped run back in the direction he had come. He could see the backs of the two soldiers closest to him. "I had better return that favour."

He found what he was looking for, a clear path between the trees and before he found time to stop and think, he pulled the pin out of the first grenade. He gripped it tightly and locked his eyes at those soldiers' feet. He threw it hard and it went soaring out into the complex, just touching the underside of the canopy leaves as it reached its highest point. Tariq dropped to the ground and had just enough time to start wondering how long the fuse was before the explosion ravaged his ears.

Stopping the man from finding Tariq in the woods had given away his position and part of Leighton regretted it a lot. That same part also wished especially that he hadn't had to leave the cover of the house to do it. The smoke from the interior of the house that had initially gifted him some cover dissipated quickly in the cold air and he had only just enough time to dive behind the Land Rover before three rifles homed in on him. Bullets came in a steady stream either side of the vehicle including some that moved the air around his trousers. One of the soldiers was clearly shooting from prone towards his feet.

He had to move and the only thing he could think to do was to drop the rifle and pull his feet up with his hands gripping the back edge of the vehicle. It was not a posture he could keep up for long and had to drop his feet periodically. Just as he was lowering his leg, he heard the faint sound of a grenade blast. The same instant, he moved back from the vehicle that was then rocking on its suspension from the closeness of the blast. He took a step back towards the Land Rover and collapsed, his left leg no longer able to support his weight. It wasn't until he saw the wound – just above the inside ankle bone – that the searing pain started. Blood drained from his head leaving him dull and woozy. His stomach turned and tears ran down his cheeks. He wanted to scream, but couldn't find the breath to.

Tariq didn't want to see the carnage. Silence filled the complex and tinnitus roared in his ears. He knew he had hit the target. After years of lobbing rocks and returning canisters of tear gas at police officers across Tahrir Square, he had become adept at judging these kinds of distances. The lack of gunfire returning in his direction corroborated what he knew. -But he also knew there was one soldier left out there. Last seen somewhere near the tree in the middle of the complex.

He started his consideration of the landscape below him by trying to spot Leighton near the house. The air was already clear by the time he brought himself to look up, but he couldn't see his partner anywhere. He used the rifle's sight to get a slightly magnified view and scanned around the house searching for any signs of movement. He lowered the gun and roamed his eyes back and forth between the buildings. He simply wanted to see either of the men out there. Tariq felt surprisingly lonely as thoughts of Leighton's state rubbed at his mind. The fact that a man with an obvious motive for a vendetta against him was also nowhere to be found felt as though it was grinding apart his stomach lining.

Tariq considered the two options to him. Stay still; if the man knew where he was already, he dies. Move in; if the man doesn't, he would then and he dies. Tariq then also considered that the man was probably hiding somewhere in the complex with the same dilemma. -And somewhere else – he hoped – Leighton was having the same thoughts.

After minutes of thorough thought, he settled on his answer. Move. He edged slowly from tree trunk to tree trunk through the wood towards the house. He dared not go towards where his grenade landed. At least the only body between him and the house was not one that he had created. He followed the outer wall of the animal shed around until the house came back into view along with the Land Rover. Still he saw neither of the men he was looking for.

Movement caught his eye and he swung the rifle to his shoulder. Through the scope, he saw – what he assumed in that instant – would be his final image. A grey-haired, well-built man aiming a similar rifle straight at him. One of the floodlights cast a grim shadow across the angular features of his face. What should have been only a fleeting moment dragged on. Tariq wasn't sure if he was not already dead. Maybe the soldier's gun had already fired and instead of heaven or hell, all he would be left with for the rest of eternity would be the single image of his last sight. While contemplating his eternal fate, Tariq noticed a sound float over the continuous rise and fall of ringing in his ears. It was neither him, nor the man ahead. It varied in pitch and intensity. Time still passed.

"Hey, hey, hey," Tariq said pulling the gun away from his body. "We're done here. Okay?" He placed his rifle on the ground and held his hands palms outwards. "You're the last man standing. Neither of us need to pass on, yet." The man's hard eyes softened an infinitesimal amount as Tariq darted his to the source of the moaning. "We have someone left alive, but injured. The rest of this is senseless. We've done enough. If I need to die for it to end, so be it, but there are some innocent people being held captive in that barn. A

341

mother, her child, an innocent young woman. This is too much. I've already put my gun down. I just need you to make your decision quickly with regards to me, but let those guys in there go. Let a child be reunited with its father. Please. Come on." Tariq held his hands together palm to palm, physically pleading with the man.

The barrel of the man's rifle lowered slowly.

"Thank you, thank you. Are you okay?" Tariq asked sincerely.

"I am fine." The man frowned heavily in disgust as he regarded all around him. "Are you?"

"Shaken up. For sure. Now, one of us has an injured, but living friend close by."

"Tariq?" came Leighton's voice weakly. "Tariq?"

"Leighton? Where are you, man?"

"Land Rover. Shit, I got hit by something."

"I'll get the medical kit," the soldier told Tariq, before darting into the house.

"It's okay, Leighton." Tariq moved over to the Land Rover, checking the front seats as he rounded it. He found Leighton lying in the flatbed part, clasping his ankle. Blood ran into the grooves of the floor in glistening black streaks. Tariq reeled away from the sight.

The soldier returned and instantly started to work on Leighton's wound with pungent antiseptic wipes. Leighton gasped and flinched his body, but Tariq's weight on his calf stopped him from being able to escape the agonising sting as it worked its way into the hole in his leg.

"You've taken shrapnel. There isn't much I can do except to wrap it up right now, though you'll have to get it out at some point. That point isn't now," the soldier told him.

Leighton regarded the man for the first time properly. "You," he said. "You're the one that Mina asked me to spare. I can see why. Thank you. I'm sure Mina would say the same too."

The man remained stone-faced. "Don't." He shook his head. "You don't have long until the rest of our survivors return. So, you'd better go let *them* out." He placed a set of keys in Tariq's hand. "The large bronze key." The man let the pressure off Leighton's leg – now tightly bandaged – and turned on his heels. Tariq jogged to the barn and out of Leighton's view. The grey-haired man, however, turned and took a step forward.

"Before you go," Leighton called after the man. "Why weren't we just killed?"

The man stopped, his back still to Leighton. He turned his head half way around. "Because we're all still the same. Whether the rest of these pricks thought so or not." Then he continued onwards towards the horizon.

Mina had taken to sitting for what felt like an age after the shooting and explosions had finally stopped and it already felt like another age since she had sat. Apart from the continuous swearing spouting from Warren's mouth, the cohabitants of the barn had remained silent. There had been some crying, mainly from Shannon who was worried – quite literally – sick, but no words formed themselves in the dark, heavy air.

The chain rattled and Shannon eagerly turned her head before jumping down to the ground with Zeke clutched tightly to her shoulder. She had crossed half the barn by the time light flooded in with the opening of the doors. A solitary figure stood silhouetted.

"Shannon, I assume?" the figure said.

"Where's Leighton?" Shannon quizzed. "Where is he?"

"He's out here. He's-" he paused. "He will be just fine. Where's – er – Mina? You in there, Mina? Damn, it's dark in here."

Mina jumped down, confused, and walked into the light. "I'm here. Who are you and how do you know my name?" As she drew closer the effect of the light silhouetting him dissipated and she saw the man was wearing a mud-covered vest-top over otherwise skin-tight clothing. His bald head and face were also covered in dirt with sweat streaks digging trenches that tracked from the top of his skull to his pointed chin. She looked at him with perplexed distress.

"I'm a friend of your Grace."

She was about to ask what made her a Catholic priest when it dawned on her. "You know Grace, where is she?"

"Not far, but we don't have much time. Come on, the two-, three of you. Hello, little one," Tariq said. Zeke turned to the voice and started crying, burying his head into his mother. Tariq looked down at his bony mud-covered form and shrugged. "Don't worry, little one, I'd cry too."

"What about us?" The voice of Glen called out of the darkness. "You just leaving us here?"

Mina turned to regard them. "The door is open." She ran to catch up with Shannon with Tariq already jogging across to the Land Rover. The outside felt oppressively bright under the floodlights and Mina squinted as she ran.

Chapter 55

Tariq jostled with the set of keys until his fingers finally got hold of the black, plastic-topped key for the Land Rover. Shannon leant over the back of the vehicle, draping herself over Leighton, whose arm pulled her in tightly.

"Mate," Tariq said, coming to life again with the project of getting everyone away on his hands. "You've got to get yourself into one of the seats. I take a corner too fast and you are in the ditch. Come on." He shoved the key in the ignition and turned the engine on and went to the back to pry Shannon off her husband. "Come on, guys. We can't hang around here 'til sunrise. Shannon, get strapped in, I got him. Mina, stop staring. We are going to get Grace now. Sit passenger side." Tariq was getting frustrated at his itch to leave and everyone else's seeming reluctance. "Come on. Come on. Come on." He clapped his hands loudly for emphasis. Shannon finally got out the way. "Go. Strap in. I got him," he urged, placing a hand on her back. "Come on. Your weight on me. Let's hop you over here."

Leighton moved easily and let Tariq almost throw him into the rear passenger seat.

"I've got Tramadol, if you want it." Mina proffered the packet across and Shannon took it, thanking her.

"Strap in guys. You may notice there are no doors, so keep your hands and feet inside the vehicle at all times." Shannon started popping the tablets into her hand. "Give him that. You, sit in the middle cross both seatbelts across you and Zeke." Tariq revved the engine and put it in drive. "Leighton, Mina. Are you both strapped in? Shannon, you holding on tight?"

Everyone murmured their affirmation.

"Right then. We're going."

At the main road, Tariq took a right and drove steadily straddled across both lanes of the country road. After batting various levers, the high beams came on and lit the land eerily in front of them. The only noise any of them could hear was that of the loud diesel engine chugging comfortably at low revs. They took another right after Tariq had to slam the brakes on to slow in time and thereafter the road eventually twisted and turned until Tariq recognised the steep banks on the right of the road. He slowed gradually to a crawl until the small rocky outcrop came into view.

"Mina, give me a hand." Tariq pulled the handbrake up sharply before jumping down. "Grace!" He called. "I bring a visitor."

Mina cried out into the darkness. "Oh, Grace. It's me!"

A moment of silence passed as they started hastily scrambling up the thick grass.

"Mina?" Grace's voice came, drifting on the wind.

"Yea, honey?"

"You made it." The excitement in Grace's voice was rampant. "Yes. Come here."

Mina skidded on her knees as she lowered herself to hug her friend. They embraced while Tariq started rolling a few of the water bottles down the hill.

"All right. You two. I hate to be the buzzkill here, but we really got to get out of this area as soon as possible. There's – like – seven dead bodies in a well-lit area less than a mile away and that old man suggested a very strong possibility of his friends turning up back there sometime soon."

Mina asked Grace, "Is he always like this?" Loud enough for Tariq to hear.

"I for one, will let him off for bringing you back to me," Grace replied.

"Aw, thanks. Now. Come on!" Tariq said with urgency.

Grace was held up by Tariq on one side and Mina on the other down the slope and Tariq lifted her himself into the remaining seat in the back while Mina grabbed up the bottles. Once Grace was strapped in next to Shannon and a bottle of water doled out to each of them, Tariq drove off. Grace made acquaintance loudly with Shannon and Leighton in the back.

They continued for over an hour and a half with Tariq aiming as close to south west as he could manage in the dark landscape. He battled a tsunami of tiredness and the other passengers drifted into silence. He could tell Mina was still watching his eyes intently for any sign he might pass out and drift them all off the road. Eventually Tariq pulled over and chugged noisily on his bottle of water.

"Tariq," Leighton said behind him. "You all right?"

"I don't know. I mean yea. I'm exhausted."

"I don't blame you, man. You've pulled through for all of us right now."

"It's all good." Tariq barely had energy to reply at all.

"Are you still good to drive?"

"No, not good to, but I can."

"It shouldn't be long from here. Shit, this Tramdol is good," he said, suddenly distracted. "I recognised some of the road signs. We can get to my parents' farm with just – maybe – twenty minutes more driving. Can you do that? I promise you a bed, a bath, a-, whatever we have to offer you. It'll be worth it."

"Let me have five minutes to gather myself. Then, yes."

"I'll direct you. I feel great. It's like my leg is someone else's. Are these even legal, Mina?"

Mina laughed, "Yes, prescription only though. Class A otherwise."

"Mina," Grace chided. "You can't be giving drugs out to strangers. I thought I taught you better." Mina reached over her seat and swatted at her friend. "Have you given some to this little guy too? He's out for the count," she said, regarding Zeke. "He's so cute, though. Looks like you, Shannon."

"Thanks. I'm glad you said that. See, Leighton. He's cute because of me too!"

347

Tariq rested his head back against the seat and let his eyes shut. He pictured a slowly ebbing flame in the centre of his mind's eye and watched it flicker ever smaller until he was left in the darkness of his own eyelids. The rest of the vehicle sat watching him, simply waiting for them to get back moving again.

The engine started back up suddenly, causing everyone to shuffle in their seats. Leighton called directions from behind Tariq as they moved through the seemingly endless, indiscriminate roads. Leighton occasionally slowed Tariq down to catch a glance at the road signs, often calling one direction first and then correcting himself with another.

Tariq couldn't tell whether the time was passing fast or slow. They could have been driving for five minutes or five hours as far as his wearied brain could determine. He could feel Leighton moving restlessly in the seat behind him. His knees knocking into the seat in front. Tariq fought his irritation and desire to collapse.

Ahead of them, a shimmer of orange lined the horizon. They were heading back east, but Tariq had barely noticed the sky paling, his focus solely on the asphalt in front of them. His eyes held at a position closer and closer to the car as his cognisance declined further and further.

"Slow, Tariq," Leighton said. "It's on the left in just a moment."

The three women in the car cheered.

"Oh, thank fuck!" Tariq screamed.

"Language!" Shannon scolded.

"Oh, we can change the word to one of celebration when we write the history book detailing this particular fu-, day," he said, remembering slightly too late to censor himself.

"Left here. Take it slow. It's bumpy," Leighton indicated.

Tariq drove the car slowly and carefully down the narrow lane. The pale wash of early morning light casting shadows from the silos and outbuildings. Reminiscent, but different enough to subdue the memories of the last farm he had the misfortune to visit.

Tariq pulled up the handbrake and all remnants of energy drained from him. He flopped across the vehicle, his head landing in Mina's lap. He faintly heard Leighton calling for his parents to come down.

Mina rested her hand on Tariq's dirty, sweat-streaked head. She spoke softly. "Thank you."

Leighton threw his arms up exuberantly and yelled, "Thank FUCK!"
"Language, Leighton!" His mother chided.

About James M Hopkins

It is an important thing as an adult to continually have something that you can always get better at. For me I have always had a creative outlet I have allowed to absorb me; an activity that I can focus on and improve at little by little, taking from it small regular senses of success or achievement. Writing itself - with music and bass guitar before that - is for me a perfect method of escape from the world. The other thing it gives me is a way to legitimise my aloof and fantastical nature; and a way that I can share that with the world.

My first forays into reading completely obsessed me with developed worlds and engaging characters. The earliest I can remember being the Chronicles of Narnia (I read the whole series cover to cover around the age of six or seven, I couldn't even eat without one of the books in my hand) and the second being The Hobbit and Lord of the Rings (I remember reading this for a second time instantly after reading the last word from the first and probably has been read by me around seven times in total). My more recent excursions have taken me through all fifteen Wheel of Time books (rereading early ones in the gaps between releases) taking a total of twelve years between reading the first word of book one to the last of book fourteen (a late prequel accounting for the fifteenth).

In real life, have an intelligent wife, who gives me amazing support and I fully realise her belief in what I do; my biggest fan and harshest critique. She gave me a wonderful son, whom we are enjoying fully. Watching him learn about the world is distinctly fascinating. He is massively into space and has an almost encyclopaedic knowledge of the solar system.

Prior to writing, my creativity was expressed through the bass guitar. Learning from DVDs of Victor Wooten, Stanley Clark and the almighty Geddy Lee, I played studiously from the age of fifteen and, although time does not permit very often, I still get to enjoy it from time to time. I have been lucky enough to gig with a few bands, the most notable being Pistola Kicks and Dirty Thrills.

I was once told that the only thing that no-one can take from you is your knowledge. I try to make the most of that fact and I indulge myself in the world of science, particularly chemistry and physics; subjects that I find fascinating. I am also keenly interested in languages, whether that is English or foreign (to me) languages. I decided to learn Arabic on the basis that I love a challenge and a challenge it certainly it is for me, but it is very rewarding to speak with people from other cultures and learn new insights from them.

I would love to connect with my readers, so please join me via one of the channels below

JamesMHopkins.com

connect@jamesmhopkins.com

facebook.com/jamesmhopkinscreative

instagram.com/jamesmhopkins

Future Release: Carrie's Waffle House

Lost in Florida without a visa, a family or a purpose, Paul is ready to tread down any new paths that open up before him. An infatuation with an intriguing and beautiful waitress at Carrie's Waffle House provides such an avenue.

Paul tells us his story of how his entanglement in her family's revenge against the government takes him on a wild adventure of sex, drugs and terrorism. His powerful and passionate relationship with the woman provide him the lust for life he lacked before she stumbled - stoned - into his world, but fails to tear them both from the violence and destruction that burns at her heart.

"The heat of her soul reignited mine. My soul, a soul long cold, bored and unforgiving, realised the light of the world in hers. I couldn't pull myself away for her gravity was too strong. I felt that forever I would be chasing her like a moth to the kaleidoscopic light of her radiance. The beats of my wings pushing me up and pulling me down and no matter how hot it got, I would always want to be hotter, be closer. I wanted our souls to collide, like two atoms being smashed together in fusion, like two galaxies drawn in towards each other ever so slowly amalgamating; I wanted it to take fractions of a fraction of a second and I wanted it to take until the end of time."

Coming soon.

Join the mailing list at JamesMHopkins.com